KILLER DEAL

A TECHNOLOGY TRANSFER THRILLER
TAILCREST UNIVERSITY SERIES, BOOK ONE

By Edison Daly

KILLER DEAL: A TECHNOLOGY TRANSFER THRILLER
TAILCREST UNIVERSITY SERIES, BOOK ONE

ISBN-13:978-1475161557
ISBN-10:1475161557

TAILCREST UNIVERSITY SERIES TM
TAILCREST UNIVERSITY TM
TAILCREST U TM
TAILCREST TM
Tail-U TM

Tailcrest University TM authorized merchandize available at www.ZAZZLE.COM/TAILCRESTUNIVERSITY

For Edie

Chapter 1

(Monday: Dawn)

Kaitlin Clark woke early in the resort cottage she and her husband, Aaron Konrad, had rented for their much needed vacation. The morning sun was just brightening the window shades and the birds outside were welcoming the dawn loudly. Kaitlin slipped out of bed, trying not to disturb her husband. She padded over to the window and stretched before gently pushing back the window shade to gauge the morning weather. "No rain, clear sky, perfect for a morning ride," she thought. Turning back toward Aaron, she saw that he was fully awake with his hands folded behind his head, watching her.

"Was it me or the birds?" she asked softly. "I tried not to wake you."

"Birds, mostly," he replied, smiling, but otherwise remaining perfectly still. "Why do they do that every morning here? I thought only roosters woke up and made noise this early."

"It's a bird thing. They do that at home too. There are just fewer birds there, and you normally sleep through it."

Laying there watching her, he noticed how good she looked and thought that she could not possibly be the age he knew she was. He then watched her pull her night shirt over her head, toss it on the bed and walk topless over to the dresser. "Waking up early has its benefits," he said to her, while openly staring at her breasts.

Arching her back for added visual effect, she leaned slowly down and opened the bottom drawer of the dresser. She took her time reaching in and taking hold of something in the drawer before looking over at him seductively, pausing and then pulling out her bike riding cloths. Thoroughly enjoying the effect she was having on him, and the look on his face when he saw her riding outfit, she wondered whether she had pushed her teasing a little too far.

"You're going out riding again this morning?" he asked, watching her pull on her riding shorts, a sports bra and a t-shirt. It was less of a question than a statement of incredulity in light of the little show she had just put on for him.

Seeing him there, she thought about climbing back into bed, but instead opted for the best of both options. "The morning air and empty bike trails should be just right for a morning ride," she offered apologetically. "I will definitely make it up to you later."

"Promise?" he asked, raising an eyebrow. He then pictured himself working with his laptop out on the porch with some hot coffee for an hour or so and then seeing her come back all sweaty. Imagining this, he thought that waiting didn't seem like too bad of an option.

"I did say 'definitely'," she responded playfully. "I shouldn't be too long, Aaron."

Leering at his wife, Aaron said, "That's what you said yesterday morning and the morning before that. Both times you were out riding for almost two hours. Your credibility in this area has taken some serious hits."

"I know. I'm sorry," she said.

"Seriously though, I'm kidding. We're on vacation. You don't have to apologize for your morning rides. I actually feel bad that I am too lazy to join you, not that I could keep up."

She then walked over and climbed on top of him, her tiny five foot one frame not touching the bed at all. Looking into his eyes from just a few inches away, she smirked at him and said, "Sure you can. You would just rather sleep in."

"Got me," he joked. "I am a sloth among men; prone to lethargic hedonism fueled by a need for beauty rest and freedom from the pressures of the outside world."

Enjoying the sarcasm from her Type-A husband, Kaitlin climbed off of him and wheeled her bike out onto the cottage porch, leaving the door open. Staying in front of the open door, she checked her bike quickly out of habit, making sure the components were functioning and her cell phone was still in the small zipped bag attached to the handle bars. She loved her ancient bike; a Lotus twelve speed from the late nineteen eighties with chromed forks and over eighteen thousand miles under its wheels. Seeing the cloudless sky from and feeling the cool breeze, Kaitlin thought that the two week delay in the start of their vacation had been a blessing, even though she had been frustrated that her work as General Counsel for Tailcrest University had forced the delay.

"I won't be more than an hour. Promise," she said, smiling seductively to Aaron before closing the door, walking the bike off the porch and straddling it. Before pushing off on her ride she took a deep breath and looked around, partly wondering why she could not see the birds that were even now starting to quiet down, and partly taking in the wonderful morning air and surroundings.

Travelling the same route that she had the previous two mornings, Kaitlin passed several other remote cottages similar to hers and Aaron's. There were no signs of activity at any of the other cottages, just expensive cars parked alongside each. Kaitlin enjoyed the morning air moving past her face and the feel of the tires on the paved trails as she slowed down to pass by the main building of the resort. Like every other hotel she recalled staying at, this one had a semicircle entrance for passenger drop off. It also had several restaurants and lots of glass for an open feel. Thinking to herself that she was glad that she and Aaron had chosen the cottage over a room in the main building, she glided past the front entrance and could see that there were already people in the restaurant. Early risers like herself she mused, recalling several college roommates who gave her grief about her lifelong early riser habits. Passing through the parking lot, she reached the section of trails running through and past the golf course. This was her favorite part of the rides she had taken the past two mornings. The trails were designed primarily for walking so they rose and fell and curved more abruptly than true bike trails, so riding on them was actually challenging for her. Kaitlin picked up her speed and cruised over these particular trails a little faster than she knew she probably should. The curves and dips gave her a roller coaster like feeling that was very different than the more normal roads she usually cycled on.

Leaving the golf course portion of her route, she coasted down a long hill on a section of trail leading to a sharp curve just before an ornate stone bridge over a stream. The long coast through the heavily treed section was a welcome break after having pushed herself pretty hard during the previous portion of her ride. Coming close to the curve, she leaned down and into the turn. Just as she rounded the curve and the bridge came suddenly into view, she felt a hard impact from something hitting her on the side. In that same instant she saw an image as she felt her bike bending as it hit the stone edge of the bridge. She then felt the hard stone impacting the side of her face and body. Then there was intense pain and a sensation of falling; then another hard impact, and then nothing at all.

Chapter 2

(Monday: 6:40 a.m.)

Trying to open her eyes, Kaitlin realized that only one of them would open. Her vision was at first blurry, but became clearer as she recognized the side of the ornate stone bridge and the blue sky above it. She felt tremendous pain, everywhere, and her ears were ringing. She recalled amid the dull haze and throbbing in her head that she had hit the stone bridge. Seeing the bridge above her, she concluded that she must have gone over the edge and been knocked unconscious, and that she had probably sustained a concussion. She felt fortunate to still be alive and breathing. The word "splinting" came into her mind as she realized the pain in her chest was causing her to take tiny breaths because inhaling deeply was too painful. She recalled the medical people using the term to describe her breathing many years earlier when she had clipped a curb, fallen and broken three of her ribs. The pain all over and the throbbing in her head made her think that this time was much, much worse than her earlier crash.

As the haze in her mind cleared she tried to take stock of herself and her injuries. She could feel considerable pressure around her eye that wouldn't open. 'Probably swollen shut," she thought. No big deal. Tasting blood in her mouth, she moved her tongue thickly around her lips and felt a scab that had already formed on one side of her mouth. Repulsed somewhat by the feel of the scab, she concluded that for it to have already formed she must have been unconscious for at least a few minutes and that she probably did have a concussion. Focusing on just breathing for a moment to calm her growing anxiety, she thought about how remote this section of the trail was from the main building of the resort and even from the cottages, and how it was really not the best location to be injured in a bike crash.

Trying to move her legs, Kaitlin felt a pain more sharp and intense than anything she had ever experienced before. Once again taking a moment to focus on just breathing, this time trying to push the pain out of her mind, she imagined that this must be what it feels like to be electrocuted. Then, taking as deep a breath as she could, she tried to move her hands and arms. She found that her left arm would not respond at all. She took comfort in knowing that she could feel it throbbing when she tried to move it. Focusing on her right hand and arm, she was relieved to learn that they responded some and that she could move her fingers.

"This is good," she whispered to herself. "Look for the positives."

The ringing in her ears was subsiding, and she could hear a stream, very close. "Too close," she thought as she turned her head slightly to see more of where she was. She did not like what she saw. She was partly in the stream from about her knees down. One of her legs was broken on the side of a large flat rock at the edge of the stream badly enough that it made a sharp forty five degree angle with part of the bone sticking out. She also realized that she could not feel her feet in the water. Seeing her positioning and realizing that her bicycle and cell phone where nowhere in sight she realized that her situation was much worse than she had thought. She felt an overflow of emotion and gave in to the pull of tears, allowing herself to wonder whether her future was suddenly different than what she had hoped and expected it would be. Having no choice, she waited.

Counting her short breaths to calm herself, her tears stopped quickly and she focused on hoping that someone would find her soon. Aaron would not be expecting her back at the cottage for at least another half hour. She saw from her ground level view that there was a lightly worn footpath along the edge of the stream. Not being able to do anything else, Kaitlin resigned herself to counting her breaths and watching for someone who could help her.

Before reaching seven hundred breaths she saw a man walking toward her along the footpath at the edge of the stream while talking on his cell phone.

"A little help?" she whispered, smiling slightly, knowing that the man was too far away to hear her.

As the man walked toward her she could see that he was looking right at her. He looked handsome and kind and she knew he would help her. She closed her eye for a moment and pictured Aaron staying with her in the hospital and teasing her about how she should have stayed in bed with him.

Kaitlin's moment of relief ended abruptly and turned to horror when she saw the man's face more clearly. The image she had seen before she crashed her bike came back to her with intense clarity; a man, this man, shouldering into her as she went by on her bike, and him watching her hit the stone bridge. She realized with instant certainty that he was not there to help her at all, and that she was now in greater danger and utterly vulnerable.

She thought to herself, "He tried to hurt me. Why? What can I do?"

The pace of her short breaths quickened and she felt the throbbing in her head get stronger. The smell of the grass and stream came intensely into her awareness as the man walked purposefully toward her.

"Plan, plan, plan, plan," she thought over and over to herself as he walked toward her. Then a realization came to her and she managed to calm herself down. She knew there was only one thing she actually could do. She could leave clues for the Medical Examiner to show that she survived the fall and maybe, maybe get a DNA sample to link this man to her death. "A message," she whispered to herself as the man stepped up close enough that she was looking almost straight up at him.

"What was that little dear one? I could not make that out," the man asked, looking concerned and speaking with a noticeable Russian accent. The man then gave Kaitlin a warm, supportive smile, just as one would expect from someone who was genuinely there to help.

"Call for help," Kaitlin whispered, playing along as though she did not realize who he was. At the same time, using her right hand, she pinched grass between her thumb and middle finger and scraped the grass under her middle finger's nail.

"I already have. That is what I was doing as I walked up the path." The man's warmth seemed absolutely genuine as he spoke. If she had not recalled the image of him, she would have believed him completely.

Scraping some of the hard soil under the finger nail of her little finger, she tried to buy time by making conversation. "Miracle I survived the fall," she said through her short breaths. "Glad you showed up. No telling how long it would have been."

"Yes, no telling," he replied, crouching on one knee to look at her more closely. He then extended his hand as though he were going to push aside the hair that had fallen partly over her face.

Scraping the nail of her ring finger on the mossy edge of a rock to collect some of the moss under that fingernail, she felt quite desperate inside and tried for more time. "Please don't touch me. Everything hurts, and my leg is really bad. The medical people will know what to do when they get here."

"I am afraid I must, Miss Kaitlin. I have no choice," he said, putting one hand under her jaw and the other behind her head.

In the next moment she looked deeply into the man's eyes, knowing both that she was about to die and that she was going to seize the moment before that happened. Putting all her strength into moving her right hand she grabbed the man's ankle and scratched his skin lightly near his calf with her fingernail. Willing the words "Find this Aaron," they did not pass her lips as the man twisted with all his strength, snapping her neck in a way that he hoped would look like it occurred during her fall from the bridge.

Standing and walking quickly away from Kaitlin's lifeless body, Lenko Egorov made another call from his cell phone. "Things are looking up," he said curtly into the phone before ending the call and continuing to walk along the path toward the copse of trees he had come out of earlier.

Thinking that the Kaitlin Clark problem was taken care of and now in the past, Egorov put it out of his mind. He then decided to take his time walking a roundabout path back to his cottage before heading to the main building so he could enjoy breakfast and check out with the other guests.

Chapter 3
(Monday: 10:45 a.m.)

Lenko Egorov had enjoyed a big breakfast at the restaurant in the front of the main building of the resort. He spent the better part of his morning drinking coffee and people watching; one person in particular. The restaurant's large windows and open arrangement gave him a clear view of the main lobby and the front entrance of the building. Egorov knew that the hotel's cameras would show him relaxed and enjoying his morning meal if ever there was a question of where he was and how he was acting. It was from this vantage point that he saw Aaron Konrad park his Mercedes and walk anxiously into the front lobby and up to the desk for the third time that morning. Egorov could not hear the conversation Aaron was having with the clerk and the manager who had come out upon seeing him, but he could see from their gestures that they had not yet found Miss Kaitlin and that Aaron was very anxious. From his observations of Aaron's comings and goings that morning Egorov surmised that he had waited for his wife to return, then went looking for her there at the main building and by driving around, and then by enlisting the help of the resort's management and security. Egorov imagined Aaron checking back at their cottage after each trip out, hoping to find her there.

Having finished his breakfast and coffee, Egorov pulled his wheeled luggage bag along as he walked casually up to the hotel desk and waited for one of the clerks to turn around. While he waited, he could see more clearly the obvious distress Aaron was in while speaking with the hotel staff.

Egorov became absorbed in observing Aaron and did not notice the clerk looking at him and waiting to offer assistance. "May I help you?" the clerk asked Egorov, smiling as though she was pleased to see him.

Holding out a credit card he replied, "I am here to check out. I will also need a taxi to the airport."

As she took the card and typed quickly on the computer keyboard behind the counter, he continued, "I also noticed that the staff name tags each have a country written on them. I am wondering why that is. Yours says, 'South Africa.' Is that where you are from?"

"Yes," she replied, while continuing to process his room charges and print his receipt. "Hotel management hires people from other places to provide an international flavor for our guests. Was your stay here enjoyable?"

Egorov enjoyed listening to the lovely blonde's accent. "Yes. Very relaxing, I plan to return when the opportunity presents itself," he said, while glancing over at Aaron. "Hopefully on my next trip here I will be able to learn more about you and what it is like growing up and living in South Africa."

Leaning in as though to whisper, Egorov asked the clerk, "Why is that man so upset?"

"I am not sure," she replied. "I think he is looking for someone. He has been in several times this morning."

"It is difficult seeing someone in such distress," he lied. "I hope things work out for him."

The clerk smiled warmly at Egorov's concern for the other guest. Handing Egorov his card and a copy of his receipt, she continued, "You are all set. A taxi will pull up out front in a few minutes. Have a pleasant trip home, and I hope you do return for another visit. I would like to spend some time telling you about where I am from."

Egorov smiled and nodded graciously to the clerk, pleased by what she had said. He then walked over toward where the taxi's pull in.

Aaron was deep in thought walking across the lobby when Egorov walked up alongside him. "You look concerned about something. Is everything okay?" Egorov asked, looking concerned about Aaron's obvious anxiety.

Not knowing exactly how to respond to this total stranger who was asking how he was, and thinking that he must really look a mess, Aaron responded, "My wife went out for a bike ride and has been out for several hours. I am worried about her because she is never out that long. Hotel security is looking for her along the bike trails."

Egorov offered a supportive smile. "I am sure everything is fine. She probably got a flat tire and is enjoying a long walk back. Within an hour you will probably be having lunch with her while she complains of having sore feet from the walk."

Aaron smiled at the image, grateful for the words of encouragement.

A taxi pulled up just as Aaron's cell phone rang. Stepping away, Egorov said, "See. That is probably her now. Have a better rest of your day."

Aaron nodded politely to the stranger and answered his cell phone, "Anything?"

"There has been an accident," the voice on the phone said. Aaron realized that it did not sound like the hotel security officer he had spoken with earlier, even though the call was from the same number the security officer had used. This person sounded older and more official, like a police officer.

"Where are you now?" the voice asked.

"In the lobby of the main building of the hotel," Aaron replied, suddenly becoming nauseated and feeling his adrenaline level surge.

"We will have an officer there to pick you up right away," the voice continued. "Please wait by the front door."

"Is she okay?" Aaron asked, wanting to hear something positive.

"We will have an officer there in just a few minutes. We will talk more when you get here. Please stay right there and meet the officer."

"Okay," was all Aaron could manage to reply.

The officer ended the call and Aaron stood there stunned; watching but not really seeing Egorov's taxi pull away.

Chapter 4
(Monday: 11:00 a.m.)

In what seemed a mere instant to Aaron, although dozens of guests had walked by him in the hotel lobby, an unmarked police car pulled into the main building's roundabout. A plain clothed police offer stepped out of the car and entered the lobby. The man's manner and dress made it obvious to Aaron that he was a police officer, even though he was not in uniform.

Taking a deep breath Aaron walked right up to the officer. "I am Aaron Konrad. Are you here to bring me to Kaitlin?" The authority and aggressiveness in Aaron's voice was surprising to both himself and the officer. Aaron realized he was in the aggressive business mode he sometimes used in difficult negotiations and that he should tone it down with this man who was here to help him.

Aaron momentarily flashed back to his teenage years in a wealthy suburb where policemen repeatedly harassed him and his friends for smoking pot. To Aaron all street cops where like the ones he had encountered back then. This officer looked to Aaron like the street cops he remembered, having all the attributes Aaron found distasteful, right down to his neatly trimmed mustache. Aaron expected the policeman to respond with an assert-control tactic that would have been typical of the cops he encountered in the past.

What the officer did next was surprising to Aaron and almost unnerving. The officer's expression softened and he showed genuine compassion as he replied, "Thank you for waiting. I am here to bring you to Detective Baskin. He will explain what happened and bring you to your

KILLER DEAL: A TECHNOLOGY TRANSFER THRILLER

wife. I have been instructed not to answer any of your questions until he speaks with you. Please come with me Mr. Konrad."

"Very well," Aaron said more evenly. He then walked with the officer to the unmarked car and got in.

After the officer drove out of the resort and made several turns, Aaron asked, "Where exactly is she, in the hospital?"

"Detective Baskin will explain," the officer answered. "There is a road along the back of the resort that is just a few hundred yards from where Detective Baskin will speak with you. We will park there and walk in." Aaron presumed, or at least hoped that this meant that Kaitlin had been in a serious bike accident and was being treated for her injuries where the accident occurred.

A few minutes later the officer pulled off the road and parked next to an additional unmarked car already parked there. Aaron got out of the car and followed the officer. The trail the officer was leading Aaron along wound through thick woods before coming out onto a sloping paved path not far uphill from a stone bridge that Aaron thought seemed like one Kaitlin had described from her rides. A man came up from around the stone edge of the bridge and looked closely at the stones of the bridge. The officer and Aaron were only a few yards from the man when he looked over at Aaron.

"This is Detective Baskin," the officer offered, gesturing toward the heavy set man who Aaron thought looked more like a kindly grandfather than a cop.

Walking up to Baskin, Aaron extended a hand and said, "I am Aaron Konrad. Where is my wife?"

Baskin shook Aaron's hand and held his gaze. "There has been an accident. A very serious accident," Baskin said. "When did she leave your cottage?"

"Just after dawn," Aaron replied. "This was the third day in a row she went for a morning ride. She loved bike riding and has been an avid rider for at least the last nineteen years."

"Has she had any health problems lately, anything at all?"

"No. She has been in perfect health. We've both been very lucky that way." Aaron's expression showed that he was curious why the detective was asking these questions.

"You said she was an avid rider," Baskin said. "Has she been in bike accidents before?"

"Not for a long time," Aaron replied. "She had a bad one about fifteen years ago, broke several ribs and was out of commission for a while. Nothing since then. Are you telling me she was in a bike accident? Where is she?"

Baskin did not answer his question, but continued, saying, "So you would say that bike riding was something she loved to do, that it brought her joy?"

"Yes, of course," Aaron replied, getting frustrated. "She loved to ride. It brought her joy for many years. What are you getting at? Where is she?"

"And she had an accident years ago, so she knew that accidents can happen, but she chose to ride because it brought her joy?" Baskin said, more as a statement than a question.

"OH GOD!" Aaron cried, leaning forward and trying not to vomit as he realized what Baskin was getting at. "Are you telling me she's dead?"

Putting his hands on his knees to steady himself, Aaron saw the scrape marks on the stones of the bridge and what looked like dried blood.

"There was an accident. Our investigation is far from complete but it appears she came down the hill too fast and misjudged the turn onto the bridge right here." Baskin pointed to scrape marks on the bridge. "I'll take you to her now. She is on the bank of the stream below. It appears that it was quick, and probably painless. She was doing something she loved. Try to keep that in mind."

Aaron's adrenaline was instantly at its maximum. He felt strangely weightless as the three of them walked around the small edge of the bridge and down the embankment to the stream where Kaitlin's body was lying motionless. Aaron did not speak. He just walked right up to Kaitlin, kneeled beside her and put his hand on the uninjured portion of her face. "My wife is dead," he said very softly to himself, and he began to shake as tears formed and rolled down his face.

The policemen observed Aaron and said nothing. They intended to give him as much time as he needed to absorb the news of the tragedy.

A few seconds later something happened that Aaron would not have thought possible. He willed the emotional pain away and it stopped, not just lessened but was just gone. He actually felt numb, but with great clarity in his thinking. Aaron thought that there were arrangements to be coordinated, calls to be made. He consciously knew that Kaitlin was gone, and his logic told him that some sort of psychological defense mechanism had kicked in, maybe some sort of denial. He felt a tremendous need to observe everything about what happened to Kaitlin there at the bridge. Standing abruptly, Aaron turned to Baskin and the other officer, who were both looking at him with puzzled expressions, having observed the sudden change in his response to seeing his wife. Aaron then said, "Show me everything."

The tears had not yet dried on Aaron's face when he asked in a firm businesslike manner, "Has everything been photographed?"

"Yes," Baskin answered. "Everything here and up on the bridge for the accident report"

Aaron then looked fully around the scene, mentally noting everything he observed. He took in the positioning of Kaitlin's body, her injuries, where her bike was positioned in the stream, the dry hard footpath along the edge of the stream, and the copse of trees not far away. He then walked back up the embankment, followed by the officers, and looked at the trail where she would have come from. He imagined the route she would have taken to negotiate the turn he knew she had taken twice before. He then looked closely at the scrape marks in the rock where the bike had impacted the stones wall. Then, looking back up at the trail and the scrapes on the bridge, and then over the wall at Kaitlin's body and the bicycle in the water, he mentally processed what he saw and stood very still. Addressing the officers, Aaron said, "This was not a one person accident, if it was an accident at all."

The two officers looked at Aaron and said nothing for a long moment, waiting for the grieving widower who was acting oddly to explain his conclusion. Baskin broke the silence, asking, "Why do you think that? It looks like an accident. There is no indication that anyone else was here. There are no foot prints, no tire tracks. It looks like she simply misjudged the turn."

Aaron leveled a fierce, cold gaze at Baskin. "Kaitlin was a very experience rider who had negotiated this same curve twice before. She described the hill and the bridge to me the first day and mentioned it yesterday. The chances of her misjudging it on the third time are nil. Also, look at the angle. For her to hit the bridge here and land there, she would have to have hit the bridge from this angle," Aaron said while using his hand to make a line in the air showing a line that was at a harsh angle from the sloping trail. "She would not have impacted the bridge from that angle unless she was swerving wildly, in which case she would have ditched the bike, or she was hit by a vehicle or a person and knocked that way really hard."

Baskin looked closely at the angle Aaron was describing. "Maybe," Baskin said, partly because the angle was in fact curious. He knew that her positioning could just as easily have been the result of how she impacted the bridge. He did not contradict Aaron though, partly because he wanted to draw as much information from Aaron as he could in light of the oddness of his reaction to seeing his wife's body and his suggestion that someone had possibly harmed her.

"Do you see anything else?" Baskin asked Aaron.

"Look at the bike," Aaron said, pointing to it in the shallow stream. "The front wheel is crumpled. So is the front fork, like it was a front on collision. She would not have come down that hill and then hit that section of the bridge front on without help."

Then Aaron saw something small and odd, a fleck of paint matching the bike's color on a rock further along the bridge and near the base of the wall. "And, if the bike hit here, it could not have ended up there without help," Aaron offered, pointing to the small speck of paint on the rock.

Baskin looked at Aaron and held his gaze for a long moment before saying to the other officer, "I would like to continue processing the scene. Take Mr. Konrad back to the main building and buy him lunch. I would like to ask him some follow-up questions later."

Then Baskin said to Aaron, "You may be on to something. I will take additional photographs and scrapings and walk a larger perimeter. The Medical Examiner has already been called and should be here shortly."

"I want an autopsy," Aaron said seriously to the detective. "I want to know everything."

"There will be an autopsy," Baskin responded. "Was there any reason why anyone would want to harm her?"

"She was General Counsel to Tailcrest University. She told a lot of people 'no' and dealt with lawsuits brought by disgruntled employees. She also played a key role in negotiations with several unions," Aaron responded before looking around at their remote surroundings. "And she was an attractive woman who rode through this remote, secluded section at about the same time three days in a row. Someone may have noticed her and tried to attack her."

Baskin listened intently to what Aaron said while watching his expressions very closely. The Detective continued to observe Aaron after he stopped speaking. There was another long silence.

"Thank you," Aaron said, breaking the silence, before walking to the edge of the bridge for another look at Kaitlin. Fixing the image in his mind, he then walked with the second officer back toward the unmarked car.

Chapter 5
(Monday: 1:30 p.m.)

Tailcrest University's Center for the Future, as it was officially named, was a standalone, single story building that served as the reception hall for most events held by the University's Administration. It was nicely appointed inside and out and was well suited for its intended purpose. Located within a section of the University campus mostly reserved for future construction, when Tailcrest secured funding to expand, it was as far away from the administrative offices, dormitories and lecture halls and as was physically possible while still being on campus. Because of this it always had plenty of available parking.

Keith Mastin pulled his car into the Center for the Future's front parking lot and chose a parking space close to the building and near the only two other cars there. Keith's boss and co-worker had arrived earlier while he was picking up the office's intern, Ginny, from her dormitory. As Keith and Ginny climbed out of his car and walked toward the front entrance, Ginny looked at the building and asked, "Why do people call it 'Future Land'?"

"Because its real name is The Center for the Future and people have an odd sense of humor," he replied, while holding the door for her and trying not to notice the way the nineteen year old intern seemed to be holding his gaze admiringly. He was also trying not to notice how the few extra pounds on her five foot three frame did not detract at all from her attractiveness. In the several months since Ginny joined Tailcrest's Technology Transfer Office as an intern, she had shown herself to be very competent, bright, enthusiastic, and prone to subtly noticing Keith in a way that he found both flattering and awkward because he was ten years older than her and had a wife and two young children.

Walking together through the arched entranceway to the main room, Keith noticed that the room was set up exactly as it had been during the last three Annual Inventor's Receptions arranged by the Tech Transfer Office's Director, Dennis Gearin. Keith recalled an inventor's comment, after the previous year's similar inventor acknowledgment event, that Dennis had invented a time machine and brought everyone through the same event once again. His expectation was that the event this year would be exactly the same as each of the previous ones he had attended, boring.

Keith looked around as they walked. He saw that, once again, the podium was set up on an elevated section toward the back of the room, just a normal step's height higher than the floor. In front of the podium and elevated section he saw the numerous round tables covered with white linen, each large enough to seat ten people. Off to one side he saw a long buffet table set up with an assortment of foods representing a standard selection off of Tailcrest's catering services catalogue. He also noticed a movable bar, currently without a bartender, but which he knew would become quite busy in a few minutes when the guests started to arrive.

The only other people in the main room where Dennis and the office's Office Manager, Carol Jamison, whom both looked over when Keith and Ginny walked in. Each waved briefly, then went back to their task of arranging plaques with inventor's names on them on a table off to the side of the podium. "Setting the plaques up in the order the inventor's names will be called helps the event flowed smoothly," Keith said to Ginny as they walked up to the table where Dennis and Carol were working.

Focusing intently on the last minute preparations, Dennis and Carol didn't look up as Keith and Ginny walked up beside them.

"Anything we can do?" Keith asked, just as guests started entering the main room.

"I have it under control," Dennis responded, feeling the nervousness he always experienced during the lead up to events where he had to speak publicly. "You and Ginny can mingle, get something to eat if you want and take a seat toward the back so you can get a good head count of the attendees."

Looking over at Ginny and gesturing toward the long table at the side of the room Keith said, "Shall we explore the buffet? I hear it is delightful." He knew that she had not been to one of these events before and sensed that she might feel a bit out of place among research professors who were mostly two or three times her age.

"Sounds good to me," she replied, as they headed toward the buffet table. Walking with Keith, Ginny was quite pleased that she would be able to stay by him and observe the event, probably having to do little more than smile and nod.

Over the next several minutes the guests poured in and, as Keith expected, talked among themselves and formed natural lines at the buffet table and bar. Keith and Ginny mingled with the guests, all of whom Keith knew from their interactions with the Technology Transfer Office. Keith introduced Ginny to numerous accomplished scientists, some world class researchers, several Department Chairmen and several patent attorneys with local law firms that the Technology Transfer Office relied on to write patent applications for the inventions developed at Tailcrest U. Ginny was enjoying herself and liked being introduced to these ordinary looking men and women who were brilliant and accomplished in their respective fields. She also liked that several of them showed interest in her and her educational track and prospective career. She explained repeatedly that she was a science major taking some business school courses and that she sought out an internship with the Technology Transfer Office because they commercialize the University's inventions and she wanted to learn more about how that worked. She also mentioned a few times that she hadn't yet made up her mind whether to go to business school for an MBA or to Law School to be a patent attorney.

Noticing the time, and that the actual ceremony would start shortly, Keith saw several people glance toward the entrance to the main room. He looked over and saw that Dr. Steven Walker, Tailcrest University President, and Dr. Christopher Campanaro, the Vice President for Research, had walked in. "Watch what happens," Keith whispered to Ginny as Dennis made a beeline over to greet the two men. The obviousness of Dennis' effort to ingratiate himself with the men was not lost on Ginny or on the two men themselves. The part that Keith found more interesting and amusing though was how the researchers, and particularly the Department Chairmen seemed to shift their positioning so they could keep an eye on where Walker and Campanaro were, eager to possibly talk with them to pitch whatever it was they wanted from the University. Keith could not help but think that if the two men had not been moving targets engaging in conversations with various people that the guests would form a line like they had at the buffet table so they could each take a turn speaking with them.

"Why are people so focused on President Walker and the man with him?" Ginny asked, noting the obvious effect the two men had when they entered the room.

"Discretionary authority and money," Keith responded quietly. "The other man is the Vice President for Research, Dr. Campanaro. They have tremendous authority over Tailcrest's resources and the researchers' efforts. Most of the researchers here have federal government grants to fund their research efforts, but things like lab space and money for projects that are not grant funded are all influenced by those two men. If you are a researcher or Department Chairman, or, frankly, if you work for Tailcrest at all, it is very good if they like you and very bad if they don't."

With the two key people in attendance Dennis felt it was time to start the ceremony. He stepped up to the podium and politely waited a moment for people to quiet down before saying into the microphone, "I would like to get started. If everyone could please take their seats."

With that cue people continued their conversations while walking among the tables and seating themselves, mostly in the chairs facing the podium so they would not have to twist around. Keith and Ginny waited near the back tables until the others were seated. Keith gestured for them to sit at the two seats right in front of them at the last table in the back. The chairs at all of the tables where positioned close together in order to fit ten of them around each table. While Ginny slid her chair out, she accidentally brushed the back of her hand against Keith's hip. She was pleased to see that her somewhat innocent slip did not trigger any negative reaction from Keith, or even a comment. She also thought she saw a hint of a smile as Keith looked forward toward the podium.

Chapter 6
(Monday: 2:30 p.m.)

Standing at the podium in the front of the room, Dennis waited while the guests took their seats and quieted down. Dennis looked over at Carol one more time to make sure everything was set regarding the inventor's plaques, and then opened the Ceremony. "Thank you for joining us for this year's Inventor Awards Reception. Each year we hold this event to acknowledge the efforts of our University inventors who have made discoveries and brought them to our Technology Transfer Office for patenting and commercialization. As you likely know it is a requirement of the Bayh-Dole act that universities receiving federal research funding must attempt to commercialize inventions resulting from the use of those funds. But, more than that, part of our mission as a University is to help society at large by disseminating information and technology and ensuring that inventions developed at our institution are brought forward in a way that will help society and individuals. The primary way that our office achieves this is by patenting Tailcrest's inventions and then licensing them to established companies or start-up companies so the companies can invest additional money in developing the inventions. This additional investment, usually in the form of capital and managerial talent, brings the technology forward into the marketplace so that people may ultimately benefit from the fruits of our inventors' creativity and hard work. These technology licenses, as many of you know from past interactions with our office or other institutions' Technology Transfer Offices, are contracts that give the company permission to use the inventions in exchange for money. This remuneration usually includes some up-front payments for entering into the contract and a share of the money the company makes from using or selling the invention. Money received under these licenses is shared among the inventors themselves and the University. Tailcrest uses its portion to fund additional research. The inventors, well, they can use their share for whatever they like. Everyone involved wins. It is a good system and we want to thank all of you for participating and being a part of it. Without further delay, I would like to acknowledge each inventor who this year has received an issued patent, brought a new technology to our office or had a technology licensed to a company. When your name is called please come up the podium. You will receive an engraved plaque, and we would like you to have your picture taken with President Walker and Vice President Campanaro, who have graciously agreed to join us here this afternoon. Our first inventor is Dr. Sean Shen."

Keith clapped politely with the announcement of each name. He also watched each named inventor or group of inventors stand, walk forward and accept the plaque handed over by Dennis, and then stand between Walker and Campanaro for a picture before heading back to their seats. Keith could see that the inventors seemed pleased to be acknowledged and photographed with Walker and Campanaro. He also saw that Walker made several of them laugh by whispering something to them just before their pictures were taken.

As Keith clapped once again with the announcement of yet another of the many inventor names, he noticed that Ginny was absorbed in the event and taking it all in. He also noticed the contrast between her current appearance, wearing a dress with her hair pulled back, and her more normal look, which included jeans and a Tailcrest University T-shirt or sweatshirt. He was happy that she was not as bored as he was. Looking at Carol, while she was dutifully handing Dennis the plaques for the inventors, Keith wondered how many of these event she had attended since she started working at the office, years before either he or Dennis had come onboard. Just then Ginny leaned in toward Keith so her shoulder touched his arm and whispered, "Ladies room," before sliding her chair back and walking toward the building's lobby.

"Too much information," Keith thought silently to himself while leaning back in his chair and watching yet another inventor walk up to the podium.

A few minutes later Ginny returned and sat back down, this time being more careful with her hand but doing something uncharacteristically bold for her. While positioning herself in her seat she quite deliberately positioned her leg from the knee down up against Keith's and then looked at him for his reaction. He noticed her action immediately and found it forward, intimate and welcome; and of the sort that would probably make his wife fly into a rage and possibly harm them both. In that instant of deciding how to react he simply looked slightly down for a moment, smiled and looked back at the podium. He did not make any effort to move away. He also found that the event was no longer boring, and he noticed that Ginny seemed pleased with herself and with his reaction.

Without speaking they simply watched the event and remained as they were while several inventors walked up to receive their plaques and be photographed. He noticed that she seemed a little self-conscious; glancing over a few times like she was trying to make sure that her being close to him like this was okay. "I am glad that you are enjoying the event," he said to her quietly, giving her forearm a gentle squeeze and hoping to reassure her that he did not mind her assertiveness.

Feeling relieved by his gesture, she relaxed some and whispered, "The President seems to be having a good time, but Vice President Campanaro looks like he wants to be somewhere else. What does he actually do here at Tail-U and why would he not want to be here?"

Continuing to look forward, but leaning toward her, he whispered in response, "The VPR's role spans the University's research operations. He allocates lab space, recruits researchers and is ultimately responsible for maximizing the research funding awarded to the University. Tailcrest gets over two hundred and fifty million dollars a year in research funding. That money is 'taxed' by Tailcrest at about fifty percent to fund its operations as 'indirects'. Tailcrest needs that money, so the VPR's time is valuable to everyone. My guess is that he has other things he would rather be doing. He is also Dennis' boss, and indirectly our boss too. I don't think he likes Dennis much, but I'm not sure."

While Keith was talking, Ginny listened intently and watched his expression. She liked that he was comfortable with her forwardness, but thought she had taken things far enough for the moment. She wasn't sure exactly where her relationship with Keith would go in light of his being married, but she wanted to explore it more fully.

After another ten minutes of inventors' names being called, Dennis said, "I would like to thank you all for attending this year's event. We look forward to seeing all of you bringing new inventions into our office this year. I would particularly like to thank President Walker and Vice President Campanaro for joining us this afternoon in honoring Tailcrest's inventors. Enjoy the rest of your day."

As the guests applauded and got up to leave, Ginny leaned in close to Keith and whispered, "My boyfriend's supposed to be waiting for me outside." With that she smiled at him, gave his forearm a gentle squeeze and got up from her chair to walk toward the lobby.

Chapter 7
(Monday: 3:45 p.m.)

With the successful completion of this year's Inventor's Awards Reception, Dennis felt that he had done a pretty good job. He collected his notes off the podium and handed them to Carol before walking over thank Walker and Campanaro for taking the time to participate in event. "I appreciate your taking the time to be here. It means a lot to us and the researchers," Dennis said.

"It is always a pleasure," Walker replied, stepping down off the raised platform and making his way toward the exit.

Dennis and Campanaro followed behind Walker. Campanaro said nothing to Dennis; instead checking the e-mails on his phone while they walked toward the lobby.

While Dennis was attending to the dignitaries, Keith moved toward the side of the room and caught Carol's eye while she moved the boxes that had contained the inventor plaques. He then used a simple hand gesture to ask if she needed help by pointing to the boxes, then making a thumbs-up sign. She understood and responded with a subtle palm forward hand gesture while shaking her head "no". From their wordless exchange it was clear that she was all set and did not need any help.

Keith also saw that most of the guests had already stood and begun walking toward the main exit, except for a few people who lingered to talk or compare plaques. Keith thought that this event, however similar to previous ones, would be remembered as successful and as having gone off without a hitch. He also knew that Dennis would take full credit for the whole office's efforts, as he consistently did, without any attribution to Carol or himself.

As Keith turned to head for the exit he found himself face to face with Kevin Taft, Director of Tailcrest's Technology Incubator. Kevin had walked up behind Keith without him noticing and had been waiting for him to turn around. Standing there with his usual mischievous grin and dressed in jeans and a sport coat, Kevin extended his hand to Keith saying, "Déjà vu anyone?"

Keith shook hands with the somewhat eccentric man who was twenty years his senior and whom he admired a great deal. He also thought the handshake was a show for someone because that was not their usual practice. "Is it still déjà vu when you have experienced it four times?" Keith asked in response. "I didn't know you were here."

"I wasn't, but I bet I can tell you what happened in my absence," Kevin offered, not too subtly cutting down Dennis' predictable annual event. It was no secret that there was no love lost between Dennis and Kevin, partly because Kevin thought Dennis lacked creativity and intellect and partly because Dennis was envious of Kevin's considerable wealth.

"I actually came in a few minutes ago and waited in the back," Kevin continued. "I'm here to talk to a good friend of thirty years. He's walking up behind you now. I'll make the introductions if you would like."

At that moment President Walker walked up next to Keith and greeted Kevin warmly. "Kevin, I heard you wanted to talk with me. I have a few minutes before my next event. I'm curious what mischief you're up to now."

"Oh, you'll like it," Kevin replied. "How about we talk about it on the way to your next event? I can catch a ride back from wherever it is."

"That would be perfect. My car is outside."

"Before we go I was wondering if you have met Keith Mastin?" Kevin asked, gesturing toward Keith. "He's the licensing guru in Tech Transfer. Several of the companies in our Incubator are operating under technology licenses Keith negotiated."

Walker looked toward Keith. "It is good to put a face with a name. I've heard good things about you from several people. I recall General Counsel mentioned that you are an attorney."

"Yes, I am, and thank you. It is good to meet you," Keith managed to reply, feeling a bit nervous from the attention and noticing that Dennis, Campanaro and several others were observing their interactions.

"Let's be off," Kevin said, walking with Walker toward the exit and Walker's car to discuss the matter to which Kevin had alluded.

Keith stood there for a moment appreciating the introduction and hearing that he was well regarded while the people around him moved toward the exit. He also found it interesting that, while he had known Kevin for four years, Kevin had never before mentioned that he and Walker had been friends at all, let alone for so long. Keith then recalled that when he had first gotten to know him as the Director of Tailcrest's Technology Incubator he had come across as a regular guy who happened to be really bright with a taste for the kind of political intrigue all universities have; what Kevin called "mischief." He also recalled that it had been almost a year before Keith learned from Dennis that Kevin was a multi-millionaire many times over from his starting technology companies, building them and then selling them, and that he had donated huge sums of money to the University. Keith then thought of his and his wife's friend, Heather, who had often spoken of her "Uncle Kevin," who was not really her uncle but had been like a second father to her, and how it had been another year after learning of his wealth that Kevin had mentioned something that allowed Keith to make the connection that Kevin was the same "Uncle Kevin" Heather had talked about. It amazed Keith that his having mentioned Heather's full name several times had not triggered a reaction or inspired a single question or comment from Kevin, until the comment that allowed Keith to make the connection himself. Lost in thought for a moment as he left the building, Keith wondered what other interesting things Kevin had not yet mentioned to him.

Making his way out of the building and toward the parking lot, Keith observed Dennis talking with someone out in front of the building. Keith at first did not recognize the tall handsome man he had not seen since High School, back when they were both handsome teenagers focused on the girls in their classes, but then he heard the man call out to him.

"Keith Mastin? What are you doing here?" Dale Wade called out to Keith, smiling broadly.

"I work here, with Dennis," Keith replied, walking over to his old friend and shaking his hand. "What brings you to Tailcrest?"

"I have some business with the University. I had no idea you worked here. I've been meeting with Dennis and one of your researchers trying to fit one of your technologies into a new company I started. It's called HematoChem. We're focused on blood chemistry."

"Good to know your back," Keith said. "I haven't seen you since your family moved away back in, what, eleventh grade?"

"Yes, it was the summer before twelfth," Dale confirmed.

"You free this evening around seven to stop by my house?" Keith asked, taking out a business card and writing his home address on it.

"Sure," Dale said, taking the card and putting it in his pocket. "I'll be there. We can catch up."

"I may have a friend stop by too. Would you mind?" Keith asked, knowing there would be no objection.

"I am open to anything," Dale answered.

With that Keith nodded politely to both men and walked to his car thinking that this déjà vu Inventor's Awards Reception had turned out to be pretty interesting after all.

Chapter 8
(Monday: 4:40 p.m.)

President Walker rode the elevator toward his office on the fifth floor of the administrative building feeling thankful that the alumni fundraising planning meeting he had just participated in was short and well run. Walking from the elevators past the open mid-section of the lobby, which allowed a clear view of the fourth floor lobby below, he entered his office suite and greeted his personal assistant and very close personal friend, Bobbi, at her desk. "Anything shocking or outrageous while I was out?" he asked her, winking as he spoke.

"Normal flow of e-mails and a few phone messages," she replied. "They are all urgent of course, and require your immediate attention."

"Good to know I'm needed," he replied before starting off toward his private office.

"There was one phone message I took from Aaron Konrad. He said it was very important that you call him on his cell phone. He wouldn't say what it was about, and he seemed really off. I put his number on your desk."

"Thanks, Bobbi," Walker said, turning to face her. "I wonder what's up with Aaron and Kaitlin. They're on vacation."

With that he entered his private office and set about preparing for the second half of his normal day. Tapping his computer to bring his screen up, he saw that he had an alumni dinner off campus and then an event to mingle and have cocktails with local political leaders. He also saw that he had almost sixty e-mails that had come in just during that afternoon.

Picking up the message pad note with Aaron's cell number, he dialed the number and waited.

Aaron answered his cell phone with a simple, "Yes."

"This is Steven Walker. I got a message you called. I hope everything is okay and that you and Kaitlin are enjoying your vacation."

There was a long pause on Aaron's end of the line while Aaron tried to pull together the words to describe the situation.

"Aaron, is everything okay?" Walker asked in a more level tone.

"No. No it's not. Kaitlin was out riding her bike through the trails this morning and..." He could not finish the sentence.

"Is she hurt?" Walker asked, genuinely concerned. "What hospital is she in?"

"She crashed her bike and did not survive. It happened this morning. I thought you should know."

Walker sat back heavily in his chair and felt as though gravity had somehow increased in strength. "Oh no, I am so sorry. I can't imagine...what can I do?"

"Nothing really," Aaron replied. "Actually, there's one thing. Services will be in a few days, once I work out the details. You could let the people she works with at the University know what happened. I would appreciate that."

"I will. How about you? I can't imagine what you are going through. Is there anything at all I can do for you?"

"Thank you, but no. I'm okay," Aaron replied sincerely. "Maybe it's too big and I haven't fully absorbed it, but I am functioning okay for now."

"Call if there is anything, anything I can do."

"I will," Aaron said. "Thanks Steven."

"Okay."

With that Walker put down the phone receiver and saw Bobbi standing in the doorway of his office looking grave. "What happened to Kaitlin?" she asked, having overheard his portion of the conversation.

"She was in a bike accident...and didn't...," Walker said, looking sadly over at her.

They looked at each other for a long moment absorbing the news.

"Aaron would like us to let her co-workers know. The services will be this week but it's not clear when. I'll write an e-mail. If you could find a list-serve that will ensure the e-mail gets to all administrative staff. She worked with most everyone."

"Okay," she replied. "Forward it to me when you're done. I'll send it out."

Walker found it difficult to find the words for the e-mail. It was as though the words wouldn't come, or he would get them down and they didn't seem good enough or respectful enough or warm enough to convey the right message. After multiple tries, and Bobbi stopping back in to ask if he was okay, he felt he had a simple message that would have to be good enough. It read, "There was a tragic accident today that took the life of one of our own. Kaitlin Clark, Esq., General Counsel to Tailcrest University and a friend to so many of us passed away after a cycling accident this morning. Information about services will be available on my office's website as it becomes available."

After forwarding the draft message to Bobbi, he walked over to her desk. "What do you think?" he asked, putting his hand on her shoulder.

"I think it is good," she replied warmly, touched by the way he struggled with it. "I'll take care of sending it out. You're going to be late for your dinner. Should I call them?"

"No," he replied, understanding her meaning. "I am still going. Call me on my cell phone if Aaron calls again while you're still here."

"Okay. I will," she said.

Stepping back into his office to verify the location of his dinner event and noticing that he was in fact already late, Walker left his office and touched Bobbi's shoulder again as he went by heading toward the elevators.

Bobbi took Walker's message and put it into the standard format for list-serve e-mails from the President's Office and then just looked at the screen for a few moments thinking about the petite, tough woman she admired. Then she hit "send," letting people know the news about what had happened to Kaitlin Clark.

Chapter 9
(Monday: 6:30 p.m.)

Early that evening Keith spent some time in his two and a half car, "man cave," garage working on his latest project with his two young sons, Eddy and Thomas. The garage was more of a woodworking shop blended with an office that Keith had outfitted with a series of shelves for the many tools that he had accumulated, ample overhead florescent lighting and a seven by five foot whiteboard that Keith often used to draw design ideas for his various projects. The whiteboard also helped to occupy Eddy and Thomas when they were out there with him.

Keith's latest project was a nearly completed sailing canoe that was twelve feet long and three and a half feet wide at its mid-section. Keith had "glued and screwed" all the seems of the wood boat and finished it with honey maple wood stain and three coats of clear polyurethane sealer. The result was a watertight, old fashioned look that Keith liked. What Keith liked best were the functional sailing elements he had designed and built, including the mast, rudder and side-mounted leeboards, which were all detachable and designed to be stored inside the boat for easy storage and transport.

At that particular moment though the only things in the boat were Eddy and Thomas, who were actively sitting, laying and standing in different places trying to find the ideal place for them to be when the boat was launched for the first time the following weekend. Thus far the little craft had not seen water. While keeping an eye on Eddy and Thomas and letting them get covered in the ever present sawdust, Keith was sanding of one of the two keel-like leeboards he had cut and shaped earlier that evening.

Keith finished sanding the leeboard and, after looking at his watch, estimated that he had enough time to stain it before Dale's visit. Just as he dipped a brush into a newly opened can of wood stain, Keith heard the door to the main part of the house open behind him. Turning around he saw Sharon standing in the doorway with her best friend, Heather, standing partly behind her. "Keith?" Sharon said in a tone suggesting she was about to interrupt his efforts on the project. "Chrissy wants to sit in the boat while her Mommy and I look for something on the computer."

The obvious meaning was that they wanted him to watch Heather's little girl because she was interrupting their on-line shopping. He offered no resistance. "I bet she is going to like it. Where is she?" he asked, intending for the little girl to hear.

Sharon stepped back from the door to let Heather by. Keith saw that Heather had actually been carrying Chrissy, but she had just not been visible behind his wife. Stepping carefully down the two steps into the garage, Heather, who was very petite, handed her little girl to Keith. "Thank you, Keith," she said before disappearing back into the house.

Keith adored Chrissy and never minded watching her. She seemed almost weightless to him in contrast to how heavy his boys had been at her age. Keith often marveled at how different she was from his boys and how his helping to care for her sometimes felt like he was learning how to parent all over again. He also had always hoped for a daughter. Chrissy could talk pretty well for her age, but usually remained silent when she was with Keith, Eddy and Thomas.

He gently placed Chrissy in the boat with Eddy and Thomas. She promptly looked around at the saw dust on the gunnels and deck of the boat, walked back and forth in it once, and then lifted her arms for Keith to pick her back up again. Keith found this amusing, picked her up and carried her over to the white board figuring he could put her down in front of it so she could draw like she had done many times before. Not this time. The breeze from the open garage door had blown saw dust over most of the garage, and she apparently was not interested in getting down. Gravity did not help. Neither did trying to place her down. She had a grip on his shirt that was disproportional to her tiny size. "You want to stay where you are?" Keith asked the little girl softly, already knowing the obvious answer.

Chrissy looked up at him and nodded.

Keith then looked over at his foam brush and open can of wood stain and then back down at Chrissy and said, "Okay." He walked back over to the leeboard and picked up the brush. With Chrissy clinging to his shirt while he used one arm to hold her in place, he stained the entire leeboard. Other than wrinkling her nose at the smell of the paint stain, which was pretty strong even with the garage door open, Chrissy was content to stay where she was, silently watching her surroundings as Keith stained the board.

As Keith placed the lid back on his can of wood stain and tapped it down one handed with the back of a screw driver, Sharon and Heather came out to check on him and the children.

Heather saw Keith carrying Chrissy and the saw dust on the floor of the garage and on the boat and realized what had probably happened. "I hope she wasn't too much trouble?" she asked Keith apologetically, while walking over and taking Chrissy back from him.

"None at all," Keith replied.

In the moment when Keith was handing Chrissy back to Heather both mother and daughter looked at him with the same expression and he noticed just how much the lovely little girl looked like her mother.

Not long after Heather and Sharon brought Chrissy back into the main part of the house, Keith saw Dale pull up and park along the curb in a beautiful old Camaro. Keith stepped into the main part of the house and said, "Our first guest is here. Heather, if I can get in touch with Kevin Taft I am going to ask him to come over in a few minutes."

"Are you sure he is coming over?" Heather asked, hoping to see the very busy man who had known her since birth and been at times more of a father to her than her actual father had been.

"No," Keith replied, stepping back out into the garage. "I don't even know if he's available. I am trying to get him together with our guest to get his input without my boss around."

"Make sure he knows I'm here if he shows up," she said, starting to close the door.

"Okay," he replied, taking out his cell phone and quickly dialing Kevin's number.

Kevin had just left his high-end home in the most sought after residential area in the region on his way to an informal social engagement when his cell phone rang. He recognized Keith's number and answered on the first ring while making his way through traffic. "What is it Keith?" he asked.

"Sorry to bother you," Keith replied, "I have an old friend coming over to our house. He just started a technology company that may tie into Tailcrest. We both may become involved in the interactions, and I thought you might like to meet him without Dennis around."

"When is he supposed to show up?" Kevin asked.

"He actually just did," Keith replied.

"I'll be right over. Thanks," Kevin said, pleased to be included early and in a way that did not involve Dennis.

When the call ended Dale had already gotten out of his car and made his way up the driveway to the open garage. Keith saw his tall friend standing at the entrance to his garage dressed in business casual, carrying a leather briefcase and smiling at him, and Keith momentarily thought of a similar image from years before when Dale had come over to Keith's parents' house dressed very differently.

Chapter 10
(Monday: 7:00 p.m.)

"Hi Dale. Awesome car," Keith said, while walking over and shaking Dale's hand and inviting him in. Dale's expression and manner suggested to Keith that he might not have changed much since High School.

"Thanks. Are these your boys?" Dale asked, stepping over to the little boat and shaking each boy's hand.

"Yes," Keith replied. "This is Eddy and this is Thomas."

"It is very nice to meet you gentlemen," Dale continued, offering an exaggerated bow that made the boys laugh.

"So how have you been?" Dale asked Keith.

"Good, real good," Keith said, thinking about how to condense a decade or so into a few words. "Finished High School. Then Tailcrest University for my Bachelor's degree. Then Law School to become a patent attorney. Big firm legal work for a while. Banked some money and learned licensing law in addition to patent law and then switched over to University technology transfer at Tailcrest about four years ago. In amidst all that I married a great girl, had two boys, and, other than my wife having some chronic health problems, we're pretty much living the suburban dream. How about you? What have you been up to?"

"Wow, not bad," Dale replied. "My parents moved us to San Diego that summer before senior year, so I finished High School there. It was amazing. The weather was perfect every day all year long. The girls were almost all beautiful. If you haven't been there, you have got to go. Then college at a small private school. Marketing degree. Lots of student loans. MBA in a nights and weekends program while I worked sales positions making decent money, spending lots of money. I have never married, and I plan to keep it that way. For the last few years I was Director of Marketing for a technology start-up company that focused on medical software. That company eventually went under, but the CEO took me under his wing and I learned a lot from him. I like the start-up company environment, and there is lots of money to be made, so I formed a new start-up, secured an initial investor and now I am licensing in promising technology to develop and bring to market. I am apparently persuasive enough to get people to invest, well, one investor so far. Starting a company is a great way to get really, really rich. I could make you a part owner of HematoChem if you would like, so we can both get really rich. We work well together. What do you think?"

"No conflict of interest issues there," Keith replied, chuckling, while declining Dale's invitation. "Actually, I think the University and the State Bar ethics panel might not be okay with that, given my working in Tailcrest's Technology Transfer Office while you are looking to license technology from Tailcrest. But thanks for offering."

"Suite yourself," Dale said.

"My wife, Sharon, is inside with her friend. I'm sure they'll both stop out soon. Would you like something to drink, beer, soda, coffee? I also called Kevin Taft from our Technology Incubator. He is the friend I mentioned might stop over. He is great with start-ups and if you're thinking about cheap space with access to wet lab facilities on campus, he's the guy."

"Nothing for me, thanks," Dale said, declining the drink offer. "I am looking forward to meeting this Kevin Taft. Your boss mentioned him, but the nonverbal between-the-lines message was not positive, so naturally I am curious."

"Kevin is an okay guy. He and Dennis just don't get along well," Keith replied.

"So, tell me about this boat your kids are playing in," Dale said, turning back around and looking inside the sailing canoe and at the mast and sail stored up against a wall of the garage. It looks home built. What is this thing on the side?"

Keith picked up the newly stained leeboard using a rag and walked over to the leeboard holder Dale was pointing to. "There is one on each side," Keith said, sliding the leeboard down into its holder like a knife into its sheath and then taking it back out again. "Each is like a removable keel or a dagger board and keeps the boat from being blown sideways. Having two of them and having them be adjustable for depth should make it sail effectively in really shallow water. We'll see next weekend when we take it out for the first time. The rudder is over there by the wall and clips onto the back. I kept it as simple as possible."

"You sure it won't leak?" Dale teased.

"I know you're kidding," Keith replied. "It's as water tight as can possibly be."

"You always were a cautious and detail oriented," Dale offered, smiling, "and of course I was kidding. You're going to stuff the inside with extra flotation just as a precaution, aren't you though?"

"Thought about it," Keith responded half-joking, and they both enjoyed the banter that had always been part of their interactions.

While they were talking, Keith and Dale had not seen Kevin pull up in one of his favorite cars; one of the several he never drove to Tailcrest. Kevin had walked right up into the garage and was just a few feet from Kevin and Dale when they noticed him. Turning, both men saw Kevin standing there smiling pleasantly, wearing faded jeans and a polo shirt with a wrinkled collar. "Kevin Taft," Kevin said to Dale, extending his hand to shake.

"Dale Wade," Dale responded, not looking too impressed by the additional guest's appearance, "pleasure to meet you. I heard that you have experience with start-ups, and that you would be the person to talk to if I need space in Tailcrest's Incubator."

Kevin noticed Dale's initial reaction to him. "I have started, built and sold a few companies over the years, held onto a few others. Some failed, but that is to be expected. Tailcrest's Incubator is currently full, but space will be opening up soon. I am definitely the person to speak with about it. I also serve as an informal entrepreneur in residence so I can help guide the young entrepreneurs, or at least whisper questions to them that they can find the answers to on their own. Keith mentioned that you have a start-up in mind. What sort of business model are you looking to move forward with, and what type of opportunity are you pursuing?"

"Actually, I was just about to describe it to Keith," Dale responded. "I have been meeting with Dennis Gearin and Dr. Shen over at Tailcrest. We have a few other technology licenses in place related to gas exchange in the blood, but they are very early in development and far less interesting than one that was developed at Tailcrest. Dr. Shen developed a small molecule that interacts with nitrogen in the blood in a way that prevents it from forming bubbles on depressurization. If we can show that it lacks negative side effects and can secure FDA approval, we can offer a pill that divers can take to prevent them from getting The Bends when they come up from a long dive."

"Interesting market," Kevin commented. "Are you sure it is large enough to justify the investment in FDA clinical studies? Given the cost of bringing drugs through clinical trials toward FDA approval for sale to the public, the market would have to be pretty substantial."

"That is one of the things we are sorting through," Dale answered. "We believe the market is large enough. Recreational and commercial divers would pay top dollar for the safety the pills would provide. I am still refining the market data, but the worldwide market, including recreational divers and industries that require underwater commercial efforts such as maintaining underwater cables, is larger than one might think. I am really excited about it."

"Interesting," Kevin added encouragingly. "How are you situated regarding fund raising, if you don't mind my asking?"

"Don't mind at all." Dale replied, his enthusiasm evident in his speech and manner. "I have raised some initial money from one private investor who asked the same questions you just did, and I have provided some of my own money as well as my commitment of time. I am also meeting with a potential large investor this week. As you know, fundraising is a very big hurdle for tech start-ups, particularly nowadays, and especially with this being my first company as President and CEO. It is kind of intimidating and exciting all at the same time. Things will hopefully move quickly, particularly with this investor, so we may need to work out a license on the quick. I am already talking up the Tail-U technology as our lead project, and funding from these investors may actually depend on our closing on a licensing deal quickly with Tailcrest. Dennis knows about this and he was absolutely clear that he would clear the deck if necessary and get the deal done. He seems to think the technology does not have much potential value in the absence of a start-up company like this being formed around it."

"He may be right," Kevin agreed, "especially in light of clinical trial costs and the unusualness of the market opportunity relative to the large diseases that more established drug development companies tend to focus on. But, that said, the approach you are taking could work effectively. I would be very interested to learn how things progress."

Keith knew that when Dennis said that he would clear the deck, it meant that he would insist that Keith clear his desk to take care of it. "Given what I do at the Tech Transfer Office," Keith said, "I will probably become involved in the discussion and drafting the License Agreement. We can move quickly when we have to. It shouldn't be a problem."

"What sort of corporate structure have you put in place, C-corporation, LLC?" Kevin asked.

"Limited Liability Company," Dale responded. "This provides beneficial tax treatment for now, and they are very flexible. If we need to switch it to a C-corporation later, we will, but I have heard that investors have become comfortable with LLC's in recent years."

"Most have," Kevin agreed. "Are you at liberty to mention your current investor and investment leads? I may be able to help."

"I would rather keep the investor information close for the time being," Dale said diplomatically, while thinking that it was presumptive of Kevin to ask for that information and recalling Dennis' having cautioned him against giving much information to Kevin. "Of course we will disclose existing investors to Tailcrest Tech Transfer as part of the license."

"Fair enough," Kevin agreed.

Dale then used the smell of the wood stain that pervaded the garage to shift gears. "Mind giving me a tour, Keith?" Dale asked. "The fumes from whatever you put on that board are making my eyes water."

Keith looked at his boys quickly and processed how best to work out a tour, but before he got any words out, Kevin offered a solution. "I'll keep an eye on these little men, if you don't mind, Keith."

"That would be great. Thanks," Keith said, surprised at Kevin's offer. "Oh, I almost forgot. Heather and Chrissy are inside with Sharon. Heather insisted I mention it."

Kevin's face lit up at the mention of Heather and Chrissy, both because he liked seeing them and because of the mischief Heather's presence brought to mind.

Chapter 11
(Monday: 7:30 p.m.)

Kevin thought the smell of the wood stain in the garage wasn't really too bad at all, just noticeable, while he remained there to keep an eye on Eddie and Thomas. Kevin guessed accurately, as Keith and Dale walked out of the garage door for the "tour," that Dale had used the smell as a pretext to continue the discussion with Keith in Kevin's absence. Kevin also guessed that Dale might have drawn incorrect presumptions about Kevin's experience, wealth and level of previous success because of his faded jeans and polo shirt, and because he had probably not seen the eighty thousand dollar car parked outside by the street.

As soon as Keith and Dale stepped out of view on their way toward Keith's backyard, Kevin grinned and initiated his mischief. Eddy and Thomas remained in the boat and had switched from trying to play a card game to bouncing a small ball inside the boat with each trying to grab it before the other did. Neither boy noticed as Kevin stepped over, unsnapped Dale's briefcase and pulled out a small stack of papers. Thumbing through them Kevin didn't notice anything noteworthy. He then went over to the door to the main part of the house carrying the papers and knocked quietly. Heather opened the door and came out when she saw Kevin.

"It's good to see you," she said, giving him a warm hug. "You've been so busy lately."

"I know and I'm sorry. I get caught up in so many things. It's great to see you too," Kevin said, "but I need a quick favor."

"Anything," she replied.

"Remember 'protocol?'" Kevin asked, referring to the unscrupulous practice he had taught Heather years before at his house, where he made it her informal job to photocopy or photograph anything in any unattended briefcases or purses of business people who visited his home as a form of competitive intelligence.

Heather saw the briefcase in the garage and the papers in Kevin's hand and gasped lightly, a smile broadening on her face. "You didn't."

"Yes, I did," he replied, matching her smile and handing her the papers. "Hurry!"

As Heather closed the door and hurried to copy them, Kevin walked back over by the boys and recalled Heather and his own now grown sons when they were that age and how he had included Heather in their family activities as much as he could. It had always bothered Kevin that Heather's father, who served as Chief Financial Officer for all of the companies Kevin started back the, did not make time for his delightful little girl. She had quickly become part of their family, just one who was only around sometimes. He had always kept closer tabs on her than she knew, and when her best friend's husband's name came up for a position in Tailcrest's Technology Transfer Office Kevin had used his position on the search committee to actively push for him to be hired. Neither Heather nor Keith knew that a big part of the tension between Kevin and Dennis stemmed from Kevin's outmaneuvering Dennis in getting the committee to choose Keith over another candidate who was less qualified but who had a personal connection to Dennis.

Stepping out of the garage momentarily to look into the backyard; Kevin saw that Keith and Dale were still on the back deck and had not yet entered the house. "It might be close. Make it quick Heather," he said quietly out loud to no one in particular as he stepped back into the garage to keep an eye on the boys.

A short while later Keith led Dale through the sliding glass doors from the deck into a spacious living room with a stone inset fireplace and an open dining area. Dale admired the open layout of the first floor of the house with the living room extending across the house to the front door, near which Keith and Sharon had used a roll top desk and free standing bookcases to create a partially enclosed space they called a "computer nook." As Keith and Dale walked in they saw two female faces turn their way. Sharon had looked over from the Kitchen and Heather had looked over from the computer nook where she was feeding papers into a copier.

"You must be Dale," Sharon said, walking toward them. "Keith mentioned you went to High School together."

"Yes we did, but we actually met in a karate class," Dale elaborated, shaking Sharon's hand. "It was an unlikely paring between a geek, him, and a jock, me, as sparing partners. No offense."

"None taken," Keith said. "Geeks get things done. I am proud to be a geek."

Sharon smiled at the exchange. "How did that go?" she asked.

"Well," Dale continued, "after I landed flat on my back half a dozen times and came out bruised, without being able to land a solid hit for the first several classes, I started to think that there might be something to what the instructor was saying about size and strength being less important than balance, timing and speed."

"I appreciate the complement, Dale," Keith added, "but, it was not like I was all that good at karate. You were just sort of big and when you went to throw a punch you telegraphed it and were so slow that I could go out for a cup of coffee and come back before it would hit me. I also recall you getting really good at karate, really fast."

"It was a jock pride thing. I wish I had stayed with it after my family moved away; new school, new activities."

"I'd like you to meet our friend Heather," Sharon offered, feeling curious about why Heather remained focused on photocopying something. "Heather, are you still with us?"

"I am. Sorry," Heather apologized. "I am just finishing up; okay, done."

Holding the originals and the copies so the print sides were not visible, she walked over to the group. "I am so sorry. My husband is a CPA but he is so busy that I end up copying his business documents and filling out our quarterly tax forms. I got totally absorbed. You're Dale. I heard that much. It is very nice to meet you."

Dale smiled at the lovely petite girl and wished she had not used the word husband. Shaking her hand, he said, "No worries. It is a pleasure to meet you."

She then winked at him. "If you'll excuse me I have to ask Kevin a question about these. He is an amazing resource."

"Sure, that's fine," Sharon said, wondering why her friend was acting so strangely.

As Heather scooped Chrissy up and walked toward the garage through the kitchen, Dale mentioned that he had to leave as well, saying, "Unfortunately, I have to get going now. I am supposed to meet someone."

"Girlfriend, I bet," Keith offered.

"Yes, actually," Dale responded, taking no offense. "She's a great girl."

"Good for you. Let me walk you out."

"It was nice to meet you," Sharon added. "We'll have to have you over for dinner."

"I would like that," Dale replied sincerely.

Walking with Dale through the kitchen, Keith opened the door to the garage and saw Heather holding the stack of papers and talking with Kevin, who was holding Chrissy. Neither Keith nor Dale noticed that the stack of papers in Heather's hand was only half as large as it had been.

"I am heading out. It was nice meeting you Kevin. I'll call you if I need space at the Incubator," Dale said as he shook his hand and then stepped around him to retrieve his briefcase. "And, it was delightful meeting you, Heather."

"Likewise," Heather replied.

Kevin remained very protective of Heather and was put off by Dale's obvious flirting with her. "Nice to meet you too Dale. I wish you luck," Kevin said in a formal tone.

Dale and Keith then walked out toward his car. "This is really a beautiful car," Keith said. "How long have you had it?"

"I bought with a loan from my parents my senior year of High School. It has been my ride ever since. Someday I will be able to afford one like that over there," Dale replied pointing to Kevin's car. "Whose is that?"

"Probably one of Kevin's," Keith said. "He is wealthy and has a collection."

Keith noticed Dale's stunned look and said, "I'm glad you came by. It's good to see you. Sharon wasn't kidding about dinner either."

"I would like that," Dale said, climbing into his car. "Next week is wide open."

"Great. I am sure we will be interacting on the licensing deal too," Keith added.

As Dale pulled away, Keith walked back toward the house and saw that Kevin had handed Chrissy back to Heather and was walking toward him carrying the small stack of papers. "Thanks for inviting me over to meet him. I think he's a lightweight, probably a salesman, but it was worth talking to him," Kevin said, patting Keith on the shoulder as he headed out to his car. "I have to run."

"Thanks for coming by," Keith replied.

Walking over to Heather and the three children, Keith felt pleased and relieved that Eddy and Thomas were still playing in the boat and had remained well behaved the whole time.

"Kevin really likes you," Heather said warmly as she carried Chrissy back into the house, gently touching Keith's arm as she walked by him.

Chapter 12
(Tuesday: 10:30 a.m.)

Keith noticed that the overcast sky made the night look particularly dark while he was putting Eddy and Thomas to bed. The nightly ritual of getting the boys ready and tucking them in felt routine to him and had been his responsibility since Sharon had first become ill several years earlier. After saying "Goodnight" to each of his boys, he joined Sharon in the living room and sat close to her on the couch. "How are you feeling?" he asked while putting his arm around her.

"Like crap, actually," she responded, "but not as bad as some days."

Changing the subject, she continued, "Having Dale over was fun. He wasn't here very long, and I didn't actually get to talk with him much, but it was nice having a guest over. Heather sort of doesn't count as a guest."

"I agree," Keith replied, stretching out sideways and laying on his back with his head on Sharon's lap.

"Do you think he would actually come to dinner like we said?" she asked him.

"Sure, if we let him bring his girlfriend du jure. Handsome Dale was always a ladies' man. His priorities were always aligned in one particular direction, and I would guess they still are. I'll try to talk to him during the week to set something up."

"I don't know about the girlfriend part," she responded. "Did you see the way he looked at Heather? He might not want his girlfriend around if he knows she'll be here."

"That would be like Dale," he replied, pleased that she was trying to be positive even though she obviously was not feeling well.

Sharon then stood slowly, stretched her shoulders and gave Keith her I-really-feel-like-crap look. "I am going to bed," she said, walking toward the stairs.

"I will be up in a little bit," Keith replied, watching her make her way up the stairs.

Laying alone on the couch and listening to the quietness of the house, Keith recalled how they used to entertain often before Sharon developed her still undiagnosed illness. He recalled clearly the way she used to be; an energetic classroom teacher who was mildly obsessed with her work, before she had to go out on disability. Then he thought about the progression of her symptoms; how her persistent nausea showed up first, then migraines, fatigue, digestive issues, rashes, too much hair coming out when she brushed it, and then the sudden fevers so high they caused seizures that terrified her and made her afraid to drive, especially with the children in the car. He wondered whether her most recent symptom, periodic bouts of extreme irritability, was actually a sign of depression. Keith recalled the word each of the doctors they had visited had used; "idiopathic," and how it meant that they did not know what it was or how they could help her. Hearing or even thinking about the word invariably made him feel helpless, because the illness impacted Sharon and his family so fully, but the doctors, and he himself, could not design a solution to a problem they could not identify. He then thought about Heather and felt grateful that she liked to spend time with Sharon and the boys and that she had stepped up to help out as much as Sharon wanted. He knew that heather's husband was a very busy accountant who didn't seem to mind at all, and Keith guessed that she was filling a void in her life.

Trying to shift his focus, Keith took out his cell phone and checked his work e-mail, even though he knew that it was generally not a good thing to do just before going to bed. The first and only e-mail he read before going up to bed was the one from President Walker indicating that their

General Counsel, Kaitlin Clark, had passed away suddenly. He knew Kaitlin and the news saddened him.

Sliding into bed and pulling Sharon close, Keith thought for a moment about Ginny's flirty contact earlier that day and his having allowed it to continue before turning his thoughts back to the e-mail. "Remember my mentioning our General Counsel, Kaitlin Clark?" he asked softly.

"Yes," Sharon replied, "the one who ticks people off by standing her ground and not taking any crap."

"Yes. That one," Keith said, amused that Sharon recalled the way he had once described Kaitlin. "An e-mail went out tonight saying that she was killed in a bicycling accident earlier today."

"How sad," she said. "When are the services? We should go."

"It didn't say, but I agree, we definitely should."

At that moment Kevin Taft was in his car port, standing alone and finishing off his third scotch. He had read the e-mail from Walker about an hour earlier and had tried to call his friend Aaron Konrad, only to find that his calls were sent directly into Aaron's phone's messaging function. Having left a message for Aaron to call him when he could, Kevin had spent the intervening time walking, scotch in hand, around the grounds of his home recalling the countless interactions he had had with Aaron and Kaitlin over the years. He had also stood for a long time in front of the old car he had used the evening, many years before, when he had first introduced Aaron to Kaitlin. While standing in front of that particular car, he couldn't turn his mind off, even with the help of the alcohol, and he knew he was having trouble absorbing the news.

Chapter 13
(Wednesday: 7:30 a.m.)

Dale was a picture of contrast, wearing a suit while sitting in his 1967 Camaro in the parking lot of the hotel near Tailcrest University where he had reserved a meeting room for his presentation to new potential investors. Focused intently on his laptop, Dale went through his Power Point slide deck for the third time that morning. He recalled watching his former boss do several similar presentations and the way the man had always stressed the importance of keeping the presentations short and concise. Dale liked the fifteen slides in the presentation, although he had not prepared most of them. The initial investor in the company had prepared the presentation, but had then allowed Dale to tailor it to the way he liked. This same investor had made the initial contact with the potential investors he would be presenting to this morning and was supposed to have already shown up to join him. Dale was nervous about the presentation, but not as much as he thought he would be. He was mostly concerned that he had told the potential investors that HematoChem would be represented by two people at the presentation, and that the arrival of only one would make the management team look less solid. He knew that investors value and put their money behind the management team as much as the opportunity the company is pursuing.

Taking the flash drive containing the presentation out of his computer and putting it in his pocket, Dale decided to give the initial investor a call to see when he would be arriving. "Lenko, I thought you would be here by now. Where are you?" Dale asked Lenko Egorov as soon as he heard the phone connect. "I'm already here and it may be best if we are both in the room when they arrive."

"I see you are nervous," Egorov responded, "but this is good because it helps you to focus. Unfortunately, Dale, I will not be able to attend this morning. Some matters came up this morning that I attended to, but now I am in traffic and there is no way I will be able to make it there until after the meeting is over."

"So I am going in alone?" Dale asked rhetorically.

"I am sure you will do fine," Egorov reassured him. "I know people who have done business with these investors before and I am sure you will find them quite pleasant and reasonable. I heard that they like punctuality and emphasis on meeting deadlines. Keep in mind that they represent an investor group from Russia that will want to see part of the company's efforts carried out in Russia. What you do not know is that for this purpose we will create a Russian company whose sole purpose is to carry out the clinical studies in Russia for us. This is not in the slides but it changes nothing, except it will make them more likely to invest their money with us. Do you understand what I am saying?"

"Sure," Dale responded. "To make them happy we form a wholly owned subsidiary company in Russia for the clinical trial work. U.S. companies do their clinical trials for drug approval in other countries by contract all the time because it is less expensive. This would probably be the same, except we form a company in Russia that we use to coordinate the clinical studies in the manner we planned to do anyway."

"Precisely, you have it exactly right," Egorov said, content to let Dale believe he was stuck in traffic when he was actually parked several hundred yards away in an office parking lot that had a clear view of where Dale was parked. "You will do fine. You should make sure everything is set up now, if you have not already."

"I am about to head in. I'll let you know how it goes."

"Thank you, Dale. I am sorry that I could not attend."

Egorov then watched Dale walk across the parking lot and into the medium sized but very nice three story hotel located near several office parks and not far from the local airport as well as the University. He had suggested to Dale that the meeting be held in a conference room there because of the business friendly atmosphere and the fact that the potential investors happened to be staying there.

As Dale walked the short distance from his car to the front entrance he felt his nervousness increase as it always did just before a presentation. Once inside, he approached the reception desk and said, "I have a meeting room reserved for Dale Wade."

The young woman behind the counter smiled at the tall handsome businessman, typed on her computer and replied, "Yes. Meeting room 3C. It's on this floor down the hallway around the corner to my left. Would you like to keep it on the same credit card it was reserved under?"

"Sure," Dale replied, and the woman printed out a receipt for him to sign. Dale saw that his hand was shaking while he signed the receipt.

Having taken care of the simple administrative matter, Dale walked down the hall and found the room easily. The meeting room was just as he had expected it would be, spacious with a large conference table. On the conference table was a video projector as he had requested, and along one wall there was an additional table that held an assortment of refreshments, including sodas and bottled water, and an urn of coffee. Dale plugged in his computer and attached the video projector to set up the presentation. Flipping through the presentation one more time to see it projected on the screen, Dale concluded that he was ready. The nervousness in his stomach suggested to him that maybe he was not.

Still being a few minutes early he began to pace back and forth in the room while he waited. The time he spent waiting seemed to stretch out interminably. When the potential investors had not arrived five minutes after they were supposed to, Dale thought nothing of it. When they had not arrived fifteen minutes after the scheduled time, he began to wonder what had happened, but thought better of calling to see where they were because that might set the wrong tone for the meeting. Instead he decided to put in a quick call to his girlfriend. "Hey babe," he said as she answered the phone.

"Use my name Dale," she responded light heartedly. "'Babe' was a pig from a cute movie. It's not my name. I thought you were supposed to be giving that presentation you've been obsessing about. What happened?"

Relaxing with the sound of her voice, Dale eased into one of the chairs around the conference room table, leaned back and put one hand behind his head. "They were supposed to be here almost twenty minutes ago. I really can't call them and say 'hurry up' so I figured I would give you a call instead. You were nice enough to give me a key to your apartment, so the least I can do is call and let you know how much I appreciate you."

"Sweet music that you know I want to hear. You're so full of it, but I love the way it sounds anyway. I'll probably get out of work early today, so, if you want to hang out at the apartment until I get home, I wouldn't mind."

"I have to meet with my business associate," Dale replied, using a mock officious tone, "but I am sure I can be around this afternoon."

"Good," she said in a way that hinted at what the afternoon might involve.

Seeing a man and woman in expensive looking business attire standing at the entrance of the room looking at him expectantly, Dale said into the phone, "Must flee. Guests are here."

Dale ended the call, stashed his phone in his pocket and stood up to greet the potential investors in one fluid motion that looked quite silly to the man and woman at the door. Stepping forward and offering his hand to shake, first to the man and then to the woman, Dale introduced himself. "Good morning. I'm Dale Wade. Please come in."

Chapter 14
(Tuesday: 8:20 a.m.)

Sacha Sidorov and Arina Nikitina each said "good morning" as they shook Dale's hand while entering the conference room and glancing at their surroundings. Dale guessed from the man and woman's open, friendly manner and appearance that they were colleagues of approximately equal status who had worked together for some time.

"Would you like some coffee or something else to drink?" Dale offered, gesturing toward the table with refreshments.

"No thank you," Sacha answered. "I have had enough coffee already. I am good."

"I have not, and I would like some," Arina answered, walking over and filling a cup.

The men paused for a moment while she poured. As she turned and stepped toward them Dale said, "Please have a seat. I appreciate your agreeing to an early meeting and I'd like for us to get started."

"It is not so early for us given the time difference, but thank you," Arina noted, as she and Sacha took seats near the end of the conference table away from the projection screen.

"Before we begin," Sacha suggested, "I would like to take a moment to describe our investment fund."

Dale realized that his nervousness had made him want to rush into the presentation when he knew these sort of first meetings generally started off with a "let me tell you about us" monologue followed by some light banter and a reciprocating description by the other person or group in the meeting. He knew it was a minor blunder but figured he could recover with little difficulty. Taking a seat next to Arina Dale responded, "Oh, of course. I am so excited by this opportunity that I'm getting ahead of myself. Please, by all means."

"As you may know, Russia is still transitioning its economy from the old way of doing things. It has been a long process and there have been successes. There are also areas we can still work on. One of the areas we are looking to develop is biotechnology and more specifically pharmaceutical development. The investment fund we represent was designed for that purpose. It was proposed by one of the thought leaders in developing Russia's economy and involves both private and government funding. The fund is quite large by our standards. We are looking to invest in companies that have a tie to Russia. Ideally the company will be a Russian company or have a Russian affiliate so the resources we invest will be used at least partly in Russia. That being said, the sources of our private funding are very interested in our investing the money in companies that will increase in value and be sold in five to seven years so they can receive at least a twenty times return on the investment in the ones that are successful. This way the ones that bring in a big return will offset those that fail and bring back nothing. Perhaps you can demonstrate for us that your company can satisfy both parts of what we are hoping to accomplish."

Dale recognized his cue and said, "We are confident that we can increase the value of HematoChem by bringing at least one lead compound forward through the USFDA regulatory process through Phase II clinical trials. We are inclined to partner with a large established company for Phase III clinical trials given the large expense involved in Phase III studies. Upon completion of the Phase II studies, which we can do with investment by people such as yourselves, HematoChem will be an attractive target for purchase by an established pharmaceutical company. On successful completion of Phase II clinical trials we are exceedingly confident that we will be able to sell HematoChem for an amount that will bring the early investors at least a thirty times return on the money they invest."

Dale felt that he was in his element as he continued, "And, HematoChem's initial investor, who has requested anonymity for the time being, is originally from Russia. He is very familiar with doing business in Russia and just this morning indicated that he would support our opening a Russian wholly owned subsidiary that would be located in Russia and would manage the Phase I and Phase II clinical trials under the guidelines and requirements of both the USFDA and the Russian equivalent. This way HematoChem can benefit from the tremendously lower cost of carrying out the studies in Russia, the resources will be spent in Russia, and by pursuing regulatory approval in both countries at the same time HematoChem will be able to enter the market and create jobs and revenue in both countries. Everyone wins."

Seeing that both Sacha and Arina where nodding their agreement, possibly without their even realizing it, Dale took the opportunity to move into his PowerPoint presentation. "By going through my presentation I'm sure I can flesh out how we are going to move the opportunity forward. If you would like for me to begin, I would be happy to."

"Of course, please proceed," Arina offered, leaning back in her chair and sipping her coffee. "We are interested to learn as much as we can about HematoChem and the opportunities you are preparing to pursue."

Dale stood up, walked to the other end of the conference room table and began going through the presentation he had rehearsed many times, including having presented it to his girlfriend twice. Arina and Sacha sat quietly taking occasional notes while Dale talked. They had sat through countless similar presentations and knew precisely what to look for. As Dale's presentation went forward they became more and more pleased with its content. The amount of money Dale was asking for to bring HematoChem forward seemed about right. They were looking to pull together an advisory board of experts in the field. The time and cost projections seems reasonable. The market size estimate was similar to the one they had developed in preparing for the meeting. Only one thing made Sacha and Arina look at each other. They both made note of it after sharing a knowing look.

When Dale signaled that he was finished by asking if they had any questions, Sacha spoke first, saying, "This was a good presentation. I am very pleased. I am sure my colleague is as well. You have clearly done your homework and the outcome is most impressive."

"There is one thing I am curious about and which gives me some concern," Arina said, leaning forward and looking politely but directly into his eyes. "On the slide where you described the technologies you have licensed in by contract from universities you described three that have already been 'locked up' and that the license contract for the technology you are most interested in pursuing first is still in negotiation and not yet complete. This could be an issue because under our fund's rules we must select a set number of opportunities to support and submit to our superiors three times per year. The next deadline is in about a week and if the most promising compound is not 'locked up' in a licensing contract then it is very unlikely that we can support investment in HematoChem. This is as people sometimes call a 'go-no-go' criteria because, if you do not have the technology exclusively by contract, then you do not have the opportunity yet in hand. I am sure you can understand our concern."

Dale actually paused for a moment, which he almost never did, before replying. "We have it covered. The license negotiation is going well. It turns out the licensing officer at the University is an old friend of mine, and we have a clear indication from everyone involved that it will be done very quickly. A week is shorter than we anticipated, but we can do it. Just in case, when is the next deadline after this one?"

"Not for six calendar months from this one because of the budgetary cycle of the source of government funding for the investment fund," Sacha replied. "We cannot guaranty that we would even be the people reviewing the opportunity at that time. If you can complete the license contract before our deadline, we can fully support your request and you will very, very likely be funded to the full amount of your request. If you cannot, unfortunately we do not know what will happen."

"Not a problem," Dale responded while offering his most confident smile. "We will have the license completed in time. You have my assurance on that." Dale believed he could work with Keith to get it done in time, but, more importantly, he knew that his other attempts to raise money had been entirely unsuccessful, except for Lenko Egorov, and that HematoChem would run out of money in about two months if this deal did not go forward. He was confident it would happen because he was going to make sure that it did happen.

"I appreciate your confidence," Sacha said. "If you can e-mail us by the close of business Monday pdf copies of the signed License Agreements for all of the technologies and a reasonably formal business plan consistent with your presentation today, then we can support your request for funding. Otherwise, you will unfortunately have to wait until the next deadline to apply for investment from our fund.

Dale beamed with confidence, offered again his most confident smile, and said, "It will be done."

With that Sacha and Arina stood and thanked Dale for presenting his company to them.

Dale responded, "Thank you for taking the time to meet with me. I am looking forward to taking care of that one last detail and getting the supporting documentation to you.

"We look forward to receiving it," Arina replied, nodding a goodbye as she and Sacha shook Dale's hand and left the room.

After his guests left, Dale poured himself a cup of the now merely warm coffee and drank it down in one long gulp. He was positive he had sold them on the opportunity. There was no question in his mind about it, and they even confirmed it with the single caveat of taking care of the licensing deal with Tailcrest. Collecting his things and heading toward his car, Dale focused his thoughts on his friend Keith and his need to get the license deal done very, very quickly.

Chapter 15
(Tuesday: 8:50 a.m.)

Lenko Egorov sat comfortably at a patio table of a sea food restaurant enjoying the warm sunlight while waiting to meet in person the woman he had recently met on-line. He had selected this restaurant because he had been there before and because the patio section provided the kind of atmosphere he wanted. Egorov was not surprised the previous evening when the woman who looked so lovely in the on-line picture had accepted his invitation to meet him early at the restaurant, but he was not new to on-line dating and figured a woman who would so quickly accepted his invitation would likely not be so pretty as the picture she provided. He also as a precaution had used an assumed name.

Leaning back in his chair and sipping his iced tea, Egorov observed the woman walk out onto the patio section of the restaurant and head toward him. On seeing her he stood, walked over to her and offered a handshake and a kiss on the cheek. "Good morning Kristeen. I am Ivan. Please come and sit."

She graciously accepted the handshake, kiss on the cheek and his invitation. "Good morning to you as well," she replied. "It is good to meet you in person. I must say that I am pleased that you look like your picture. I'm brand new to on-line dating, but I met a guy for lunch a few days ago and he must have used his son's picture because it was shocking to see the difference."

Egorov laughed at the image she had created and the surprised look she had affected when describing seeing the man for the first time. "I believe truth in advertising is the best approach. You are even more lovely in person than your picture would suggest, and you look very nice in your picture."

"Thank you, Ivan," she replied, smiling at his genuine compliment.

"Actually, I am brand new to on-line dating as well," he lied. "I was in a long term relationship, not married, but it ended suddenly two months ago. It is a long story but suffice to say I cringe when I hear the words 'personal trainer'."

"Oh, that had to hurt," she said in a comforting tone.

"Yes, but life goes on," he said, smiling warmly at her. "Now I am talking with a lovely woman who has already made me laugh. All things have silver linings."

Hearing this, she reached over and put her hand on his and gave a gentle squeeze. "You are a charmer, and quite handsome."

At that moment the waitress stepped up to the table and introduced herself. "Hi. My name is Veronica. I'll be your server this morning. Would you like something to drink ma'am?"

"Yes, diet soda," she replied.

She then handed each of them a menu and walked quickly away.

"Oh, before I forget, I received a text earlier indicating that I will be receiving a business call sometime this morning," Egorov said apologetically. "I will have to take the call, but I do not want to be rude."

"Not a problem at all," she replied. "I'm a real estate agent. I take business calls and texts all the time. I won't be offended in the slightest."

"Good," he replied. "Now let's see what is on menu –"

His phone rang before he could finish what he was saying. "Now I am psychic. I mention call and call comes in," he said, gesturing to make sure it was okay with her that he take the call.

She responded with a slight hand gesture and nod indicating it was okay to take the call. "Go ahead. I'll check my texts."

Egorov then answered his phone saying, "Good morning friend."

Sacha Sidorov recognized Egorov's overly friendly tone as some sort of signal. "Is there someone there with you?"

"Yes, but it is okay," Egorov replied, looking at Kristeen as she typed quickly with her thumbs on her phone's keypad.

"I am going to support HematoChem's funding request because of my stake in the outcome," Sacha said in a tone that was harsher than Egorov had expected, "and I believe my colleague Arina is mostly supportive based on HematoChem's merits and the presentation you obviously helped create."

"Good," Egorov interrupted. "So things are aligned in a positive way for success, no?"

"Mostly," Sacha responded, feeling his anger rise. "I can deliver on my end, but you must deliver on your end. The deadline for funding request submissions is just days away, and Arina and I just learned that the contract with the University for the nitrogen technology is not done yet. That is a crucial piece that needs to be taken care of, not just for the funding request but for the larger effort as well."

Egorov had anticipated some disappointment on his co-conspirator's part, and he was disappointed in himself for creating a potential bind by not pushing things forward much more quickly. Still, he was quite confident that he had the situation fully under control. "You have paid me well, and I will deliver," Egorov said into the phone while carefully maintaining a positive expression in case Kristeen looked up from her texting.

"I understand, my friend, and you have come through before, but you must understand that I have a personal stake in the development of the military applications of this technology, and there are people involved who will not accept failure." Sacha's words and tone were intended to convey to Egorov the seriousness of the situation.

Egorov continued to maintain his positive expression and tone, which irritated Sacha. "I do understand and appreciate the importance of what

KILLER DEAL: A TECHNOLOGY TRANSFER THRILLER

you are saying," Egorov said into the phone while looking into Kristeen's eyes as she had finished her texting and looked warmly at him.

"Yes, I hope you do. As you know we need the non-military development funded through our country's economic development program and a clean contract from the American University to ensure the appearance of genuine non-military development as cover for the development of the military applications of the nitrogen technology," Sacha said, even though Egorov was fully aware of what was required and why. "We need it done in time for the funding request to be approved by both me and Arina. She has no idea, and we cannot risk bringing her into the deal. As you and I have said before, my friend, times have changed and we do not steal technology when we can simply ask nicely. You must make it work or there will be problems for both of us."

"I will," Egorov said almost jovially while still looking at Kristeen. "Good day, my friend."

In putting his phone in his pocket Egorov also put the call and the very real threat of harm behind him for the moment, thinking to himself that, as with all other things, it was done and in the past. Speaking to Kristeen, who was contently smiling at him, he said, "I apologize for taking so much time for the call. Where were we?"

"I recall you were charming me with your lovely accent," she said, continuing to smile at him. "Tell me about where you are from."

"Oh this could take some time," Egorov said conspiratorily, returning her smile. "Are you free for the entire morning?"

"I am," she said in a way that made him think that this could turn out to be a very good day indeed. She did not let on that she had just texted her husband that a client had called and that she would be busy with house showings for most of the morning.

Chapter 16

(Tuesday: 9:00 a.m.)

Dennis and Keith were each in their respective offices in the Technology Transfer Office suite unaware of the other's having come into work. The white noise from the rain outside had provided enough background sound to prevent them from hearing the other's activities and from noticing that Carol had come into the office as well. Carol was sitting in her cubicle in the open space between the two men's offices when they both walked out into the common area in front of her at the same time, each carrying his leather briefcase and umbrella and looking surprised to see the other. "Good morning and goodbye gentlemen," Carol said as Dennis and Keith continued walking away from her.

"Good morning," Keith said in reply, while Dennis simply waved to Carol as they headed out the door. While leaving the suite, Keith made a point of allowing Dennis to go first, both out of courtesy and in deference to Dennis being his boss. Keith thought about how Dennis liked to be treated this way and recalled the advice he had received from a friend years before who had suggested that he forget the "stupid golden rule" because treating others the way you want to be treated is "dumb." His friend had then told him that it is better to treat people the way THEY want to be treated. This subtle difference in approach had seemed logical to Keith because it accommodated the differences in people's personalities and preferences. Keith had tried using the approach with Dennis since then and had noticed that it had actually helped make interactions with him easier.

While taking the stairs on their way down from their third floor office suite, Dennis asked Keith, "Where are you headed?"

"It just seemed like a good day to walk in the rain over to Aspen Hall to meet with Jason Roberts from the Legal Department," Keith responded. "Actually, our esteemed Associate General Counsel hasn't gotten around to reviewing several contracts I forwarded to him three weeks ago, so I got on his calendar this morning to put him on the spot. I figure he will either review the contracts in anticipation of the meeting or review them while I am there. Either way, they'll get to the top of his pile."

"Sounds like a good approach," Dennis said. "We could probably set up a scheduling process where a meeting is automatically set up a week after we send a contract over so he will be put on the spot for all of them in a timely manner. Let me know how it goes today. I'm not kidding about the automatic follow-up."

After taking a moment to navigate the doors at the front of the building, Dennis continued, "What contracts are being held up?"

"Just a confidentiality agreement we want a company to sign so we can show them detailed information about one of our technologies and two material transfer agreements that cover our sending biological materials to collaborating researchers."

Keith handled these types of agreements by the dozen, but much preferred working on the technology License Agreements he negotiated as one of the main parts of his job at Tailcrest Tech Transfer. "Nothing like the licenses I work on. Just run of the mill stuff. The only reason I have these contracts is because the collaborators work for companies as opposed to research institutions and Carol has been overloaded with work lately."

Stepping out onto the walkway and opening his umbrella Keith continued, "Where are you headed?"

"Same building, different floor," Dennis responded, opening his umbrella as well. "I have a meeting with Vice President Campanaro. It's my bi-weekly update on our office's activities. It's mostly a formality. He has zero interest in what we do. I don't think he reads anything I send him, and I'm lucky to get five minutes of his time."

"That's kind of sad," Keith offered. "If he took the time, he might find it interesting."

"That's only a tiny bit of the frustrations," Dennis added. "You see most of it. The administrative hassles of getting anything done in a University would never fly in industry, especially for negotiating contracts. We negotiate the contract, then have it reviewed by either General Counsel or the Associate General Counsel, then present the necessary changes back to the people we are negotiating with, then back to the Legal Department if there are any additional changes. It's a nightmare, and the kicker is that we are responsible for producing results when we don't have authority over what is necessary to get results."

Keith saw some truth in what Dennis was saying. "I like everyone in the Legal Department, and I admired Kaitlin quite a bit, but it has been frustrating trying to get contracts reviewed and approved sometimes," Keith said. "Like the ones I'm going to see Jason about now, he can read through them in a few minutes, but it takes weeks. I know he's busy, horribly busy, but it is still frustrating. Of course, part of me feels bad for him for having so much on his plate."

"I agree. Jason is too busy, and it's going to get much worse with the tragedy involving Kaitlin," Dennis said, leading into part of the real reason he was meeting with Campanaro this morning. "I think that our Technology Transfer Office should be able to review and approve its own contracts on behalf of the University like some other University's Tech Transfer Offices do. You're a lawyer and you know much more about these contracts than Jason does. I'm going to push for Campanaro to give us at least review and approval authority over contracts that we handle."

Keith remained silent after Dennis spoke and maintained a neutral expression. He was thinking that there was very little chance that Campanaro would give Dennis much of anything he wanted, given his apparent distaste for Dennis. Looking to change the direction of the conversation, Keith asked Dennis a question he had planned to ask Jason from Legal. "With Kaitlin's death who will be responsible for signing the contracts she used to sign? It's horrible to think about such practical questions so soon after her death, but, for example, who will sign the contracts I am meeting with Jason about?"

"Actually," Dennis said, pausing to look at a group of good looking female students who happened to look especially good soaking wet from the rain, "Campanaro has the same signatory authority that Kaitlin had. He just never wanted to be bothered. He will be signing documents in Kaitlin's place until they fill her position. Given how busy Campanaro is, and how little he knows about contracts, he will probably be relying heavily on Jason's 'reviewed and approved' stamp for the contracts he signs."

"It could be quite a while, given how long executive searches take up at that level," Keith said, shifting his umbrella as the direction of the rain shifted with the wind. "Do you know if they will be bringing in anyone to help Jason with the volume while they do the executive search?"

"Like who?" Dennis asked.

"Attorney's from the outside law firms Tailcrest uses could fill in," Keith offered, thinking about his own work within an outside law firm years earlier. "The only issue would be the hourly rate they would charge, probably around two hundred dollars per hour."

"That could add up quickly," Dennis said, trying to do some quick math in his head. "I don't know if they are going to bring anyone in to help Jason. If we could just take care of our own contracts ourselves, it would make things easier for everyone involved."

Keith thought about the possibility that the Tech Transfer Office would actually be given the authority to approve contracts and said, "But if they actually did that, we would be on the hook for every little thing that went through. It is actually helpful to have the Legal Department provide a second set of eyes to review the contracts, at least once, if you don't factor in the delays involved."

The two men stopped at the edge of a service road that had become a small pond from the hard rain, then shifted course to walk around it. The puddle was large enough that a number of students were working their way around it as well. Dennis and Keith's business attire stood out among the jeans and other casual attire worn by the students around them. Picking up the conversation where it left off, Dennis continued, "Yes, but the reality of Kaitlin being gone is going to make those delays even worse."

"You're right," Keith acknowledged. "I'm still absorbing the fact that Kaitlin is gone. It's so sudden; a bike accident. It's hard not to picture ways that the accident might have happed. They're all disturbing, especially since I knew her."

"Yes, it's strange that she is suddenly not there. You have to admit though, she was kind of stubborn and picky with contract approvals for everyone. She was at times frustrating for everyone who worked with her."

"I liked her," Keith countered, feeling compelled to defend her. "With my contracts at least she always had a reason for wanting the changes she insisted on, and she really cared about protecting the University's interests."

"Yes, I liked her too," Dennis lied, having always resented having to jump through her hoops to get deals done. "Services are tomorrow morning. I e-mailed you and Carol this morning in case you haven't seen it."

"Thanks," Keith replied, having not yet seen the e-mail.

Stepping under the overhang at the front entrance of Aspen Hall, the two men stopped, shook out their umbrellas and waited a few moments as they were early for their respective meetings. Recalling that he had not yet mentioned having Dale Wade over his house the previous evening,

Keith thought it would be best to mention it while he had the chance that morning. "Oh, Dale Wade stopped by my house last night and described the opportunity he is looking to go after and that he had already met with you about," Keith said. "Dale was a friend of mine from High School and it was good to catch up with him, although having not seen him since we were teenagers, it was almost weird talking with him with my kids right there. He seems pretty excited about moving forward with the company and his interactions with us."

Dennis made no effort to head into the building just yet. "I imagine that would be sort of strange," he said before switching quickly to the business part of the interactions with Dale. "The licensing deal with HematoChem is going to go forward, and I want the patent applications to be as solid as possible. The provisional patent application covering the invention Dale wants to license from us is due to be converted into a non-provisional and P.C.T. application pretty soon. I sent a note to Carol yesterday asking her to set up a meeting with you and the inventor to go over it. Obviously, we want to invest in keeping the patent application going. I want you to meet with the inventor as well to make sure everything is done properly."

"Sure," Keith said, knowing that his being asked to handle the patenting aspects of managing the inventions that went through their office was just part of his job. It had been that way ever since he joined the office and had been introduced to people as a patent attorney, even though that was technically not what he was doing for the University. "Do you want to be in on the meeting?"

"No, that's okay. Patenting is your thing," Dennis said, stepping toward the entrance to the building ahead of Keith. "I want you to have our outside patent attorney convert the application into a non-provisional and P.C.T. application right away. I have been meeting with Dale for several months, but I didn't know he was your friend. Make sure you are familiar with the details of the invention. In light of your licensing background and your being friends with him I'm going to want you to be very involved in this one."

Walking into the building and through the lobby toward the elevators, the two men saw that all of the comfortable chairs in the large lobby were, as usual, filled with students studying or talking among themselves. "All I see is women," Dennis said, feeling appreciative that the lobby had been set up specifically to be a meeting and studying area for the students and that it seemed to always be filled with them when it was open.

Keith smiled at the obviousness of Dennis' appreciation for the much younger college girls. "About half of them are guys, but apparently they are invisible to you," Keith offered in reply.

"Must be," Dennis answered.

As they walked among the students, Keith thought back to a decade earlier when in that same room he had been studying with friends when he met the pretty young student named Sharon who eventually became his wife.

Chapter 17
(Tuesday: 9:15 a.m.)

Dennis stood alone in the elevator in Aspen Hall waiting for the doors to open to the fifth floor. This was the one place in the University he did not like visiting. The fifth floor was the top floor of Aspen Hall and where Tailcrest's President, Provost and several Vice Presidents had their office suites. The elevator doors opened and Dennis stepped out into a large well lit central lobby that was usually accented by the natural light from the glassed atrium-like portion of the roof above the central portion of the lobby. Today the glassed roof feature provided a view of the rain falling onto it and running off the glass panels. In the center of the lobby was a short wall around a large square opening that allowed the natural light to reach the floor below, and allowed people in the upper floor's lobby a clear view of the lower floor's lobby, which had more sofas and chairs, and usually more activity. Walking along the short wall and toward the door at the far corner of the lobby, Dennis glanced down at the people in the lower lobby. Reaching the far corner, Dennis entered Vice President Campanaro's office suite.

Campanaro's suite was one of the larger ones on the floor, which reflected his relative importance within the University and the fact that he had three Assistant Vice Presidents, who more directly oversaw the various aspects of Tailcrest's research operations, and additional support staff. As the Director of the Technology Transfer Office reporting to Campanaro Dennis was technically at the same level as the Assistant Vice Presidents who had offices there, but, given the nature of his relationship with Campanaro, Dennis had always been pleased that the Technology

Transfer Office was located in a building relatively far from this office suite.

Walking past a small seating area and down the length of the office suite, which was essentially a wide hallway with administrative staff behind a short wall to the left and the Assistant Vice President offices on the right, Dennis came to the corner office with the name plate reading "Christopher Campanaro, Ph.D., Vice President for Research". The door was mostly closed so he asked the Administrative Assistant closest to him, "Is he in with someone? I am supposed to meet with him now."

"No," she responded, glancing momentarily up from her work. "He is expecting you."

Knocking lightly as he pushed the door open Dennis made a conscious decision to be positive and put aside for the moment his dislike for Campanaro's interactive style. "Good morning Chris," Dennis said as he closed the door most of the way behind him and took one of the seats in front of the Campanaro's desk.

Campanaro let Dennis wait while he finished reading the short memo he was focused on before responding. "What have you got for me today, Dennis?" Campanaro asked evenly, but in a way that conveyed to Dennis that his visit was a both to him.

"I know that you are very busy," Dennis said as an obvious lead in, "but I have two matters that I would like to talk with you about."

"You're right about my being busy, and it is only going to get worse now that Kaitlin has passed," Campanaro said, while deliberately looking at the multiple stacks of folders covering most of his large executive style desk. His slight smile while doing that was the first hint Dennis had seen of him being personable.

"The first one," Dennis continued, as he put a stapled stack of papers on the only open space on Dr. Campanaro's desk, "is this contract I need you to sign. It is a simple business development consulting contract to bring in an expert to help bench mark our efforts to create jobs in or region. I know a lot of the grants that have come through your office have been based on the promise of local job creation, and this will help us make sure we are doing everything we can do in our office so we can give good answers when we're asked where the results are from those grants."

"Good thinking," Camapanaro said, offering his first ever compliment to Dennis. "Has it been reviewed by General Counsel's office?"

"It was reviewed first by Keith Mastin from or office, who as you know is a lawyer, and then by Kaitlin who gave her verbal okay," Dennis lied in both respects. "Unfortunately her tragic death has impacted all of us and our efforts."

"Was it stamped 'reviewed and approved' before her accident?" Campanao asked.

"Unfortunately no, but they were both fine with it," Dennis went on with his lie, thinking it was okay because Keith was his employee and Kaitlin could never dispute what he said.

"Just this once," Campanaro said, while flipping to the signature page and signing the agreement on behalf of the University. "But, in the future you will need to get Jason to stamp every contract and put his signature over the stamp before I obligate Tailcrest by signing it myself. I don't have the time, interest or legal aptitude to review them, so until they replace Kaitlin, our Associate General Counsel is going to be even busier than I am."

"Thank you," Dennis said, seeing the opening he had been hoping for. This brings up my second item. There is an easier and more effective way than relying just on Jason, who I understand is swamped already."

Dennis then paused to give Campanaro a chance to react. "I am listening, and I am still very busy," Campanaro said. "Get to your point."

"Keith Mastin is a lawyer who knows this area much better than Jason and can more effectively and quickly review contracts involving technology transfer. Until the General Counsel's position is filled why don't we give Keith a 'reviewed and approved' stamp just like Jason uses and have him provide legal review for the contracts that involve our office. It makes sense and would save everybody time and hassle."

Campanaro thought about Dennis' suggestion for a long moment. He then announced, "Good idea. Have the Legal Department give you one of their extra stamps and have Mr. Mastin function as back-up to Jason for your office's contracts. Kaitlin had mentioned that he was good with contracts. I actually heard she was thinking about trying to entice him away from your office to work in the Legal Department doing just that sort of contract review and to work on other matters because Jason has been so overwhelmed lately. If it will save me time and hassle, let's try it out for now and see how it goes."

Dennis knew that Campanaro and Kaitlin had not gotten along very well, just as he knew that Campanaro did not like him. Dennis also knew that Campanaro's comment about Kaitlin enticing Keith away was both a jab at Dennis and a way to cover what Dennis suspected was Campanaro's real reason for going along with Dennis' suggestion, namely that there would be a new General Counsel coming in at some point and Campanaro probably wanted to start that relationship with the new person having to ask Campanaro to reconsolidate contract review authority under the General Counsel's office. Campanaro liked it when people had to ask him for things, and Dennis saw no reason why he, himself, should not benefit from that fact.

"Do you have anything else for me?" Campanaro asked Dennis, while looking over the top of his glasses at him.

"No. Thank you. I'll stop by Legal this morning to get the stamp," Dennis managed to say while standing, collecting the signed contract and leaving the room as Campanaro focused back on one of the stacks of papers on his desk.

While Dennis was walking out of the Vice President's suite past the Assistant Vice Presidents' offices, he thought to himself that he had won a long sought victory in gaining autonomy from the Legal Department for matters involving his office. Stepping out into the open fifth floor lobby and seeing the water rolling off the glass above him, Dennis felt quite pleased with himself.

Chapter 18
(Tuesday: 9:15 a.m.)

Keith thought he caught a glimpse of Dennis walking along the balcony of the floor above him as he crossed the lobby on his way to meet Associate General Counsel, Jason Roberts. Then while looking up at the glassed portion of the roof, Keith was mesmerized momentarily by the water running down the panels and nearly tripped over one of the couches in the middle of the lobby. Keith noticed that an older woman walking nearby had noticed him stopping just short of crashing into the couch and chuckled. Walking alongside Keith for a moment, after seeing his near collision, Bobbi said quietly to him, "People do that all the time. We used to have a weekly pool for crashes and wipeouts."

Keith had never met Bobbi before and didn't know that she was President Walker's assistant or that she was telling the truth about their having had a 'wipeout pool' some years ago, although people mostly just bumped into things. "I'd personally go for paper airplane accuracy contests from the balcony up there," Keith said, looking up again briefly and then smiling at the older woman who looked as though she probably had been quite beautiful in her younger years.

Before going in their separate directions she said, "Steven actually did that once, but don't tell him I told you."

Walking through the door that led to the Legal Department suite, Keith wondered who the Steven was who the woman had referred to.

A short hallway and a door later Keith entered the Legal Department suite. It had a simple layout with cubicles for a paralegal and an Administrative Assistant and three offices. One of the offices was for a Risk Management Officer, another was for Jason, and the third, which was open and unoccupied right in front of him had been Kaitlin Clark's. Seeing her empty office made it hit home for him that she was dead, just like that, gone. He walked to the doorway and looked inside, not sure why he did not want to enter the office he had been in so many times before. Then, to his left he noticed Jason walking over toward him. "Weird isn't it?" Jason said to Keith. "It's like she is about to walk in and scoot into her office like she usually did."

"She did move pretty quickly when she was going somewhere," Keith noted with a smile. "I've got some contracts I need feedback on. That's why I set up our meeting."

"I saw. I reviewed them this morning and made some edits we can go over, but otherwise they're ready to go," Jason said, while leading Keith into his office.

Jason handed Keith the marked up contracts and noted the minor changes he had made. Keith chose not to mention that the changes were needless and reflected wording preferences as opposed to substance. "This makes it easy," Keith said. "Would you be able to make clean printouts, stamp them approved and have them signed, I presume by Campanaro? Dennis mentioned that he would be signing things until the General Counsel position is filled."

"Yes, I can take care of that. I am sorry I sat on these contracts for so long. I've just been overwhelmed with other work."

The stacks of files on his desk and a side table evidenced the truth of his claim of being busy. Looking around at the stacks Keith said simply, "I hear you."

Jason looked at the piles too and said, "Dennis sent me an e-mail early this morning saying he was going to try to get you a 'reviewed and approved' stamp when he talks with Campanaro today. He wanted to give me a heads up on it and get my support in case Campanaro called me about it. He pointed out how it would make my life easier by taking some work off my hands. It actually would help me quite a bit."

"Dennis has always been big on getting signatory authority or at least review and approval authority for himself," Keith responded, leaning back in his chair, "but this is the first I have heard about him trying to get me a stamp."

"You didn't know that Dennis has been trying to get Kaitlin to give you a stamp for years?" Jason asked, genuinely surprised. "She wouldn't for political reasons involving Campanaro and Dennis. She wanted to keep review and approval authority just within the Legal Department."

"It makes sense that she would want that," Keith said, thinking that any General Counsel would want to control the review of contracts that could seriously impact their institution. "Misworded intellectual property provisions, especially if they involve rights to future inventions could have a pretty big impact on Tailcrest's research operations."

"I agree, but things are going to be different for a while now that Kaitlin is no longer here," Jason said, concealing the fact that he was looking forward to any change he could potentially take advantage of, even though he was saddened and deeply impacted by her death. "If you get the stamp, maybe your desk will start to look like mine."

"God forbid," Keith replied as he stood to leave, appreciating Jason's humor amid the heaviness of Kaitlin's loss.

"Just one more thing before I go," Keith said, having almost forgotten to bring up Dale Wade. "I have a friend from High School who has been meeting with Dennis about licensing one of our inventions into a new start-up company called HematoChem. His name is Dale Wade. He is kind of high energy and will probably want to move quickly on the licensing deal. If there is any way you can keep it on the top of the pile, or one of the piles, when it gets to you, I would appreciate it. It looks like it could be a decent start-up deal and could create jobs, money and good press for Tailcrest."

"I'll keep an eye out for it," Jason said as Keith turned to leave, not letting Keith know that he already knew quite a bit about Dale Wade and the interactions with HematoChem.

"Thanks," Keith said cordially before leaving Jason's office and glancing again at Kaitlin's office as he left the Legal Department suite.

Chapter 19
(Tuesday: 9:45 a.m.)

Keith had not seen Dennis on his way out of Aspen Hall or as he made his way back through the rain to the Technology Transfer Office's suite. He presumed Dennis' meeting had run long or he had other things to take care of. Walking into the office suite, Keith shook out his umbrella, waved to Carol, who was talking on her phone, and then went into his office. Tossing his umbrella on the carpet behind his desk, Keith entered the password for his computer and then looked at the small screen on his desk phone for voicemails before sitting down. The only call noted on the phone screen was from Sharon, but she had not left a message. His inbox showed several e-mails that he would have to get to but which did not require immediate attention. Having long been a member of the group of husbands who appreciated the importance of the expression "yes dear," he did what he thought was the most sensible thing and picked up the phone to call his wife.

"Hi, it's me," Keith said into the phone after Sharon answered. "I saw you tried to call. What's up?"

"I was just wondering what things were like there with the news of Kaitlin Clark having been killed in a bike accident. How do people seem?"

"I have only really talked with Dennis and our Associate General Counsel, Jason," he replied. "Both of them seemed sort of matter of fact about it, like it hasn't really sunk in. While I was in the Legal Department suite I looked into Kaitlin's office and it was kind of strange looking at her desk and her stuff on the shelves knowing that she wasn't ever coming back. There was sort of an ending and new beginning kind of feeling to it that made the moment of looking into her office sort of hang there, like it was one I will hold onto for a while."

"Wow, getting deep are we?" Sharon said, knowing exactly how to lighten her husband's mood. "I could tell you felt a connection of sorts to her, with you both being lawyers and all. Wives can tell. No, I wasn't jealous. It just seemed like you identified with her a little bit."

"Actually, she had a great ass and it made it hard to focus on anything else when she as in the room," Keith said, trying unsuccessfully to keep a straight face, and knowing exactly how to shock his wife into laughter.

The guffaw and laughter on the other end of the line signaled that he had hit his mark precisely. "I see how it's going to be," Sharon said. "Maybe I'll flirt with Dennis the next time I'm in your office. Better yet, I'll drop the boys off at Heather's house and not tell you where I'm going. We'll see how many times you call me on my cell phone while I'm out."

"Uncle, uncle," Keith offered in complete mock surrender. "You win. Actually, people seem mostly to be wondering who will be covering her work now that she is gone. You don't believe in jinxed files do you? Maybe one of the files is cursed and whoever works on it will be next. That could make for a good plot line for one of those horror movies you watch? Don't go in the law library, like don't go in the barn."

"Hate to break it to you," she said, "but, Kaitlin's tragedy aside, a movie about lawyers being killed would have the audience rooting for the killer and cheering him on. Remember how they applauded at that scene in Jurassic Park Two when the lawyer got eaten?"

"Yes, I recall," Keith said, leaning way back in his chair and putting his feet up on a short filing cabinet near his desk.

"Remember at that Meatloaf concert where he asked if there were any lawyers in the audience and you shouted out, and then he told you to 'Fuck Off' before going into that Lawyers, Guns and Money song?" She asked.

"I loved that," Keith said, looking up at the ceiling tiles. "He spoke directly to me during a concert."

"I'm not worried either way," she continued in jest. "I checked your life insurance and you are covered to three times your salary. That and Social Security survivor benefits for the kids and, hey, we could move to Tahiti."

Keith snorted a laugh.

"Now that you mention it," Sharon continued, feeling on a roll, "this is terrible, but we have some busy highways near our house. You could take up bike riding again. Tahiti is pretty nice year round I hear. Could do wonders for my medical condition. What do you think?"

Knowing how Sharon's medical condition had had her down so often, Keith was delighted that she was feeling well enough to engage their shared appreciation for over the top, really bad humor. Seeing little harm in pushing it, he decided to go for it. "Hmm, this sounds like a challenge," he said, grinning.

"What have you got?" she chided him, grinning on her end of the phone.

"Who, me? I'm just pleased that you're not painting graphic images of my demise in a future highway bike accident," he said, pausing for effect; "like my intestines getting snagged on a bumper of a moving car and stretching out behind it before snapping up and sticking to the window of another car, shocking the driver and causing another accident."

"Oh. Yuck. Good one. You're so gross," she said, pleased with their game. "You win. That image is going to be stuck in my head all day."

"I have to go," he said. "Fun game. It has been a while since we've done that. I should be home normal time."

"Okay, bye," she said, hanging up the phone.

On hearing the phone line close, Keith leaned forward to hung up his phone as well. Then his thoughts were drawn back to Kaitlin's office and the way her personal items were still there. He knew she had been married for a long time and recalled that some of the pictures in her office showed her with her husband. He tried to imagine what it must be like for him, and what it would be like when her husband went into her office to collect her personal items. Then he looked around his own office and tried to imagine what it would be like for Sharon if something happened to him. He knew the Tahiti joke was just that and that she would be devastated if anything happened to him.

Moments later Keith's quiet reflection was interrupted by a cheerful young voice. "Good morning!" Ginny said, popping into his office and beaming with the healthy energy students seemed to have in abundance. "Carol just told me we have a meeting in like ten minutes in the conference room. Something about an inventor meeting Dennis requested about converting a patent application."

"I didn't know it had been scheduled," he said, admiring the way her wet hair stuck to her face as she shook off her jacket without letting go of her bag. "It's simple enough. I'll be in there in a minute."

Folding her jacket over one arm she looked him in the eye and held his gaze for a moment, smiling at him. "I'm going to drop my stuff off and then hopefully we can go over any meeting materials before it starts."

"Sure," was all he could reply before she darted off to her cubicle near the conference room.

Turning to his computer screen Keith pulled up his calendar and saw that Carol had set the meeting up just as Ginny had said. Quickly printing three copies of the basic items that would be discussed during the meeting with Dr. Shen, the inventor of the technology Dale wanted to license into HematoChem, he grabbed a pen and note pad and headed into the conference room.

Chapter 20
(Tuesday: 9:50 a.m.)

Entering the Technology Transfer Office's conference room, Keith walked to the side of the room not visible from Carol's desk and took a seat at the middle of the conference table. While he put the stack of printouts he brought with him on the table, Ginny breezed in and took a seat to his right, pulling her chair close to his and making a point of leaning toward him so her shoulder touched his arm briefly. Keith welcomed the gesture of affection and looked sideways at her, offering a quick smile. Hoping to go over the meeting materials in the very short time before the scheduled start of the meeting, Keith jumped right in saying, "We only have a few minutes and you haven't been in an inventor meeting before, so I should go over the stuff quickly with you. Dr. Sean Shen is a brilliant researcher who loves his science, but this is the first invention he has brought to our office. English is also not his first language. When Dennis and I met with him about ten months ago, when he first talked to us about his invention, he was somewhat difficult to understand. He also didn't seem to know anything about patenting or commercializing inventions, which is fine because that is our responsibility."

"Where is he originally from?" Ginny asked.

"I don't know for sure," Keith responded, "but from his accent I presume China. On the invention disclosure form he submitted, he listed himself as a U.S. citizen. I also recall that last time he was late showing up so we may have a few extra minutes this time."

While they were talking Keith began splitting his stack of printouts into three piles, one each in front of himself and Ginny and the third in front of the seat across the table where Keith presumed Dr. Shen would sit. Picking up the document on the top of the pile in front of him, Keith said, "This one is the Invention Disclosure Form that Dr. Shen submitted to our office. You probably saw a lot of these while you were shadowing Carol. It basically describes the technology that the researcher considers to be an invention and lists any co-inventors, publication dates and funding used in creating the technology. Publication dates are important because of U.S. and foreign rules about when you have to file a patent application in relation to when an invention is disclosed to the public."

"This one says that it has not been published," Ginny noted while looking at the form.

"Yes, which means we did not miss any important deadlines. At least not yet," Keith replied.

"The technology Dr. Shen developed is really remarkable." Keith continued. "I'm sure you are familiar with 'The Bends'. When scuba divers come up too quickly after being down for a while the nitrogen gas that dissolved in their blood under the high pressure of being under water comes out as bubbles in their blood vessels and causes serious problems. Dr. Shen developed a small molecule, essentially a pill, which divers can take to prevent that from happening. It affects the nitrogen somehow so it stays dissolved in the blood for much longer and comes out slowly without forming bubbles.

As Keith put the Invention Disclosure Form on the table to the side with his left hand, Ginny reached across, tapped the next document on the pile and asked, "What is this one?"

Keith wondered whether Ginny found the information he was providing boring, but from her attentive look she seemed genuinely interested in what he was saying. "That one is the provisional patent application that was filed nine months ago," he responded. "Provisionals are basically place holders that get you a filing date with the Patent Office and give you a year to file a U.S. non-provisional application or P.C.T. international application, or both."

Putting that document to the side as well, Keith picked up the next document and said, "This is the prior art search we had done by a search company. It lists any articles, published patent applications and any other publications that are close enough to the technology that they may impact whether a patent can be granted. You cannot get a patent on something that was already published by someone else. It's called 'anticipation'. You also cannot get a patent if it would have been obvious to a person having ordinary skill in the art if all the published materials were right there in front of them. That's called 'non-obviousness'. The Patent Office has a lot of other rules too. I am going to ask Dr. Shen to review the articles listed in the prior art search before he meets with our outside patent attorney to go over what exactly is patentable before she writes the non-provisional and P.C.T. patent applications."

"Carol mentioned that you are a patent attorney. Did you work for a law firm and write applications?" Ginny asked, already knowing the answer.

"Yes," Keith responded. "I was with one of the larger law firms in the area doing patent work, licensing work and litigation. I liked all of it, especially being in a courtroom, but it was long hours and I never got used to tracking every tenth of an hour to bill the clients. When this position opened, up I went for it. I'm probably overqualified, and it was actually a lower salary, but I like it a lot and it has a much better working environment."

Ginny held his gaze and smiled at the way he emphasized the words "working environment," thinking correctly that the emphasis had been meant specifically for her.

Looking over at the clock, Keith shifted gears saying, "He's already late. What we want to get out of the meeting is to ask him to review the prior art publications and to let him know that we want to file a non-provisional

U.S. application and a P.C.T. international application so we can go into other countries later, and that we're moving more quickly than usual because a company is interested in licensing the technology."

Before they could say any more they heard Dr. Shen come into the office suite and say 'Hello" to Carol. They then heard Carol tell Dr. Shen that they were already in the conference room. As if acting on cue, Ginny moved her chair back to its normal place and took a more businesslike posture both because she believed it was what the office expected of her and also to signal for Keith that she intended to keep her affectionate interactions with him as private as possible.

Chapter 21
(Tuesday: 10:00 a.m.)

Dr. Shen entered the Technology Transfer Office's conference room and walked to the side of the table where Keith had placed the third stack of papers. He smiled broadly and said "Good morning" to Keith and Ginny.

"Good morning Dr. Shen," Keith said, standing and leaning across the table to shake his hand. "This is Ginny. She is an intern here in our office."

"Good morning," Ginny said politely, standing and shaking Dr. Shen's hand as well.

"I trust things are well with you since I saw you last?" Keith asked as they took their respective seats at the conference room table.

"Good. Yes," Dr. Shen responded. "My research has moved forward and I just had an RO-1 grant funded for a lot of money. Everyone is happy with me right now, mostly because of the grant money."

"Was any of your recent development work linked to the invention you brought to our office ten months ago?" Keith inquired.

"Yes," Dr. Shen replied, sitting down and pulling some papers out of a folding portfolio case he had brought with him. "This is new data that supports my earlier work. I used some of my grant funding to do initial in vivo animal studies using the hyperbaric chamber facility on campus. First I got University approval for the animal studies, which was not easy. The animals were not harmed. We adjusted the depressurization at varying rates intending to stop when the animals showed any signs of bubbles in their blood, but it never happened. Not a single animal experienced any signs of nitrogen narcosis. No 'Bends' in any of the animals at all. It was quite amazing. The data is right there."

"Can you provide the data to us in electronic form so we can forward it to our outside patent counsel, the one who will be writing the actual patent applications?" Keith asked. He made no effort to hide the fact that he was very pleased with the news of animal studies having been carried out and having been completely successful.

"Yes. I will e-mail them to you. How will this work with the patent lawyer? The last time when I met with her you were there for the discussion. Then she wrote the application that got filed with the Patent Office."

"It will be the same patent attorney who wrote the provisional application," Keith clarified. "She is already familiar with the technology and is quite good, so it makes sense to stay with her. This time she will want to meet with you in her office. I don't need to be there. She will probably ask you a lot of technical questions about the technology. Your answers will help her clarify what portion of it is new and patentable. She has to draft 'patent claims' within the application that clearly describe in words what the actual invention is. And, she has to make sure that the rest of the application has enough technical description to enable people to make and use the invention. The provisional application was a good start, but she still has a lot of work to do."

"I see," Dr. Shen noted.

"She will probably have questions about some of the documents I printed out as well," Keith continued, gesturing toward the small stack of papers all three of them had. "You'll recognize the Invention Disclosure Form you submitted to our office and the provisional application. What patent counsel will likely ask about is the one titled 'Technology Search'. We contracted out with a company that does prior art searches for inventions. We pay them to track down any published articles or earlier patents or any other published works that may reflect on the patentability of an invention. I have read the articles listed in the report and they look fundamentally different than what you have invented. We would like you to read them also so you can answer any questions our patent counsel may have."

"Yes," Dr. Shen responded while looking at the printout. "I recognize the first two articles and they are totally different. I will read the rest to be sure."

Ginny remained silent while following the conversation intently. She picked up her printout and reviewed it at the same time Dr. Shen reviewed his copy.

"Another thing patent counsel will want to know is whether your work has been published, and, if so, when," Keith said. "My understanding from when we last met was that you had not published any of it but you were considering submitting it to a scientific journal for publication. Have you done that?"

"No. I decided to hold off until after these animal studies where completed. I was also so busy writing grant applications that I have not published anything. After the provisional application was filed, I shared the basic concept of the invention with some people in the field without giving any details. They wanted to know more but I told them they had to wait."

"Good," Keith added. "That shouldn't be a problem at all. How about the new data from the animal tests? Did you share that with anyone?"

"No. I told Dennis from your office, but this printout is the first copy I have given to anyone."

"Excellent," Keith continued. "I have one more technical item. You are listed as the only inventor. Under patent law a co-inventor is someone who contributed to the conception of the idea. Did you discuss this or collaborate with anyone in developing this, maybe one of your graduate students? It is very important that the correct people be listed as inventors on the patent."

"No. I developed it myself. I even did most of the chemistry myself. For part of it I had my graduate student do some chemistry, but he did just what I told him to do. He did not contribute to the idea or even how to make it. I am very protective of this invention because I think it is a big deal."

"I agree," Keith responded, pleased that everything was lining up to make this invention straight forward and simple. "What we want to do is have patent counsel file both a U.S. non-provisional application and a P.C.T. international application as well so we can get patent coverage in the U.S. as quickly as possible and also go into foreign countries. The process can take years, but we want to take care of everything now so we can potentially get patents on this anywhere in the world. Patent counsel should contact you within a few days."

"I understand there is interest on the part of Dale Wade in licensing this technology and commercializing it. How familiar are you with that effort?" Keith asked, not knowing how involved Dr. Shen had been in any discussions thus far or how much he knew about the licensing process.

"I have met with Dennis and Dale Wade several times," Dr. Shen replied. "I think it is a perfect fit for Mr. Wade's company and I want it licensed into HematoChem right away. I met with Mr. Wade this morning in fact and he wants to move very quickly in putting together the License Agreement with your office. He said he has an investor deadline and that he and Dennis have talked in detail about the specifics of the agreement."

This was mostly news to Keith, although he knew that Dale and Dennis had been meeting about the technology. Keith suspected he would be brought into the licensing discussions with Dennis and Dale in due course, but later than he would prefer. "How familiar are you with licensing University technology to companies?" Keith asked Dr. Shen in as a respectful manner as he could.

"I know that you work out an agreement, the company gets the technology, you get some money at first and then maybe a lot of money later if the technology is successful. Other than that, I know very little about what is involved."

"Your description is actually correct," Keith added, pleased with Dr. Shen's basic understanding. "Once a patent is awarded it gives you the ability to block anyone from making, using, selling, offering for sale or importing the invention. A License Agreement is a contract where Tailcrest gives the company permission to use and commercialize the invention. Usually there is an up-front payment of money for signing the License Agreement and some payments, called milestones, while they are getting the invention ready for sale. They also share a portion of what they get for selling products covered by the patent. That last part is called 'royalties'. There is also sublicensing and sublicensing fees where the company can give other companies rights to use the invention while giving us part of the money they get for letting the other companies use it."

"This makes sense, but sounds complicated," Dr. Shen said. "But Dennis said you know this area and can take care of it."

"It is my area of specialty," Keith acknowledged, "but because it is very complicated and people have to agree on what will be included in the License Agreement, sometimes things go more slowly than people want them too. If everyone agrees, it can move very, very quickly, but there are a lot of things for people to disagree about and working through the disagreements can take some effort and time. I will talk with Dennis and Dale about this technology the first chance I get. It is very good that a company is interested in licensing your invention."

"I agree," Dr. Shen said. "I want to see this technology go forward and having a company involved is important."

"I'll do what I can," Keith reassured him. "I am supposed to have lunch with Dennis today. He'll probably want to talk about this technology when I see him. I'll bring it up regardless.

"Do you have any questions," Keith asked.

"No. I know what I have to do," Dr. Shen replied. "I will help in any way I can.

"Thank you." Keith said. "I think we are all set. If patent counsel hasn't contacted you within the next few days, let me know so I can help move it along."

Dr. Shen shook their hands once again as he left the conference room.

Keith then turned to Ginny, who was standing close to him, and said, "This is a really good one. Things could move really fast and, if you would like, you're welcome to be as involved as you would like to be."

From the way she looked at him, grinning just slightly, Keith realized she had read more into his statement then he had meant. Before he had a chance to say or do anything, Ginny stepped forward and hugged him tightly and just as quickly stepped back, winked at him and disappeared from sight.

Keith just stood there for a moment absorbing what had just happened before heading into his office smiling at the attention he was receiving from Ginny and feeling bewildered by what he had set in motion. He did not like keeping secrets from his wife, but he was absolutely sure that this was something he would keep from her. Trying unsuccessfully to get himself to stop grinning about the situation he had gotten himself into, Keith sat at his desk and started sorting through his e-mails and updating his to do list.

Chapter 22
(Tuesday: 12:00 Noon)

Stepping out of his office into the common area of the Technology Transfer Office to talk to Carol for the first time that day, Keith noticed that Ginny was not at her cubical. He had immersed himself in his work after their inventor meeting and had not noticed her leave. Carol had also been absorbed in her work but looked up from her computer when Keith came into her line of vision. It was only then that she realized that it was already noon and she would have to finish up soon if she was going to run some errands and still be on time for an off campus appointment.

"How goes the car search?" Keith asked her, knowing that she enjoyed searching for a car, mostly on-line, as much as owning one.

"I'm having a lot of fun with it," she replied. "I have narrowed it down to four models, but I'm having trouble picking one. My husband says I should just flip a coin twice and be done with it. Of course he still drives a Honda Civic that predates the Internet."

They both smiled at her reference to the old reliable car she had once driven to work when hers had broken down.

"Have you test driven any of them yet?" Keith asked.

"All of them," she replied. "I just can't make up my mind."

Just then Dennis stepped out of his office and said to Keith, "Ready for lunch? Bring a note pad."

"Sure," Keith responded before stepping into his office to grab his umbrella and his portfolio binder which had a note pad and pens in it.

"Albrecht's I presume?" Keith inquired.

"That is the plan. It will be a working lunch," Dennis said, meaning he planned to expense it to the University.

Leaving the building, they both saw that the rain had stopped for the moment. They remained comfortably silent while they walked the short distance across campus in the opposite direction from where they had gone earlier that day and arrived at Albrecht's Bar and Restaurant just as the lunch crowd was starting to fill in. Located just off campus, Albrecht's was an old style German bar and restaurant that had been in the Albrecht family for three generations. Being just off campus and having a lot of convenient parking and prices a little higher than the campus dining halls, the lunch crowd was mostly office workers from campus and nearby businesses with only a few students mixed in.

After being seated by a waitress who had known them as customers for years, they ordered from memory without looking at the menus.

"How did the inventor meeting with Dr. Shen go this morning?" Dennis asked while watching people be seated at tables nearby.

"Mostly uneventful," Keith responded while thinking of Ginny and keeping an absolutely straight face, as he had done so many times before as an attorney keeping client confidences. "We let Dr. Shen know that we would have outside counsel file the U.S. and P.C.T. patent applications from the earlier provisional and that the attorney would contact him about articles that the prior art search turned up. He seemed happy about it."

As the waitress returned with their drinks, Keith continued, "He also mentioned that he had met with Dale Wade about license discussions with HematoChem. He said that Dale had said something about an investor deadline and that Dale wanted things to move quickly. Do you know anything about that?"

"Some but not much," Dennis replied, bending the truth some. "I have been thinking about this licensing deal for a while now and I am convinced we should move on it fast and do whatever we can to get it done. Dale called me after his meeting with Dr. Shen and also mentioned the investor deadline he is faced with. Apparently it is a hard, solid date that I think is next Monday or Tuesday. They need an actual license signed by then or a whole lot of investor money will go away and nobody will be happy about it. It is a very tight timeline; but, if we and they are reasonable and work at turning the documents around the same day or the day after they are exchanged, I'm sure we can get it done. I've seen you review, modify and send back License Agreements the same day a few times so I know it can be done."

"You sure that was me?" Keith joked. "It could have been some guy who just looked like me."

"Nice try," Dennis replied, "but I want you to make this your top priority. Everything else can wait. Dale's investors apparently want a deal that is really favorable to them. No surprise there. I have thought about how we could put together a Term Sheet that they can say yes to without back and forth arguing. Got your pen handy?"

With exaggerated magician like flair, Keith palmed the pen out of his briefcase and presented it between his fingers as though he had conjured it out of the air. "Okay then," Dennis said, noticing that Keith was in a particularly good mood. "I want you to conjure up and send out a Term Sheet today. Use simple language so Dale maybe can skip having a lawyer review it. Once Dale agrees to the Term Sheet, or some variation of it, I want you to write and send out the License Agreement based on the Term Sheet right away. This could be in just a day or two if everything moves lightening quick."

Dennis had to pause as the waitress brought their orders to the table. "Enjoy," she said simply as she put their orders in front of them.

While she was placing the plates on the table, Keith had taken a notepad out of his briefcase and put it on an open space on the table. "You were saying," Keith said as he took a bite of his grilled chicken sandwich.

Dennis continued, "I have some specific things I want you to put into the Term Sheet that they should have no trouble agreeing to. Ready?"

"Shoot," Keith responded, putting pen to paper.

"Royalty bearing exclusive license," Dennis said as Keith wrote.

"Check," Keith said.

"Fully sublicensable without Tailcrest's prior approval of the sublicenses," Dennis said, watching for Keith's reaction, but seeing none. "I am sure they don't want to be bogged down with us reviewing their sublicensing contracts. Set the sublicensing rate at ten percent."

Keith wrote it down, but said nothing.

"Patenting costs to be reimbursed to Tailcrest out of royalties on sales of products by adding half a percent to the royalty until they're paid," Dennis said, again watching for Keith's reaction but seeing no visible reaction on Keith's face. "We don't want to tie up their available cash early on by making them reimburse the costs right away like we do with more established companies."

Keith wrote that down as well, took a deep breath and looked over at Dennis.

"Give them the option of acquiring future inventions Dr. Shen makes here at Tailcrest in the field of blood gas exchange for the next five years."

Keith made a note on the page while taking another bite of his sandwich.

Dennis took his first bite of his own lunch and then said, "For payments, write in a one percent royalty on product sales and a one-time milestone payment of twenty thousand dollars when they secure FDA approval to sell the compound to the public."

Having added the last additional note to the page, Keith finally spoke. "This is about the most favorable deal I have ever seen between a University and a start-up company," he said. "Frankly, I am not particularly comfortable with it. Especially since Dale is a friend of mine from High School. It's going to look like I am giving a sweetheart deal to an old friend."

"Relax. You worry too much," Dennis said. "I have instructed you to write it this way, so it's on me if anyone questions it. But they won't."

While chewing and swallowing, Dennis held up a finger, smiled broadly and said, "Besides, who knows where we'll be in five years anyway."

"Funny," Keith responded. "I plan to be right here if possible."

Changing the subject, Dennis then asked Keith, "Any new developments with your wife's health?"

Two years before, after a conversation with his wife where she agreed, Keith had started sharing with his immediate coworkers the mystery of his wife's health problems. Since then Dennis and Carol had heard about Sharon's evaluations for rheumatoid disorders, bacterial and viral infections, as well as numerous other possible disorders that might cause the ongoing and varying symptoms that had so badly impacted her health and quality of life. Responding to Dennis' question, Keith said, "The latest thought on the part of the doctors is that it might have an oncological basis. She is going in for a CT scan this week, but that is partly because of her migraines. There is a realistic chance, according to one current doctor, that it could in fact be a form of cancer. I don't think it is, especially because of the varying symptoms, but it is still uncomfortable to think about."

"That sounds scary. I hope everything turns out okay," Dennis said, feigning genuine concern.

"Thanks," Keith said. "I am more worried about the kids growing up with their Mom not being able to do much because of her migraines and persistent nausea. The 'C' word is not something I'm really ready to think about. I'm more inclined to think there is maybe some environmental factor like some bizarre mold in the basement or something like that."

Dennis was listening while he continued to eat his lunch.

Hoping to shift the conversation onto anything else, Keith opted to ask Dennis a loaded question about a topic he and others had nudged him about before. "So, you're still not looking to get married. Late forties is still young. I hear commitment is liberating, especially if you marry a rich girl."

"Divorce is liberating," Dennis responded, knowing full well that Keith was just messing with him. "Two of my daughters finished college and one is about to start. When she is finished, my financial obligations are over. After the last time, marriage simply will not ever happen for me."

Keith had heard the story second hand from two reliable sources and they were consistent so he presumed the version he heard was accurate. He had heard that Dennis had married young and had three girls in what he thought was a happy marriage. Years had gone by where his wife had stayed home and he worked, which had been fine with him until the kids started school. But, even after the kids went to school, his wife would not go to work and he was less okay with it. Then some years passed and he learned that she liked to spend money and had pushed up their family debt, mostly by pushing Dennis into medium and large purchases like a hot tub, a sun-room on the back of the house, expensive presents and other things that really weren't necessary. Then more years passed and he learned that in all the years since the kids had started school she had been entertaining other men in their home while he was working. By all accounts Dennis had done nothing wrong, but he still had to pay huge amounts for alimony, his part of their joint debt, half his retirement up to that point and child support for his three girls including most of their college costs. Everyone familiar with it thought Dennis had gotten a really raw deal, although no one would do anything more than tease him about being single. It was also common knowledge that, even with a good salary, he was not in a good place financially.

Dennis signaled to the waitress that he wanted the check and handed her his credit card. He then looked over at Keith and said, "A rich girlfriend might be okay. She could cover all kinds of costs and take me on vacation cruises. If you know any rich women, set me up with them."

"Will do," Keith said, handing Dennis a twenty.

They were quiet for a few moments while the waitress ran the credit card. Keith couldn't help but feel slightly complicit in Dennis' customary fraud. Whenever they went to lunch, Dennis would insist on putting it on his card and having Keith pay Dennis his half in cash. Dennis would then expense the lunch to Tailcrest, keeping the portion that was reimbursed for Keith's meal as well as his own. Keith thought it was petty, wrong and stupid of Dennis to make it a habit of cheating the University out of a few dollars every week or so.

"Your half with tip is nineteen dollars," Dennis said to Keith when the waitress returned with the bill. "I'll get you the dollar back at the office."

Keith knew he would forget about the dollar.

As they stood to leave, Keith said, "I am uneasy about the terms, but I should have no trouble putting a Term Sheet together this afternoon. Do you want to see it before I send it out?"

"No. Actually I have some things I have to take care of off campus so I won't be in at all this afternoon. Just write it and send it out."

With that they made their way out of the crowded restaurant and walked back to the office through the now heavy rain.

Chapter 23
(Tuesday: 1:00 p.m.)

Moments after Dennis and Keith returned to the Technology Transfer Office, Dennis picked up his briefcase and left for the afternoon. After Dennis left, Keith walked out into the common area of the office and realized he was actually alone in the office. With Carol's habit of coming in early and Dennis' habit of coming in and working late, Keith almost always had someone else there in the office with him. Keith took a long moment to enjoy the quiet, which was accented by the sound of the rain, before heading into his office and logging onto his computer.

With a few clicks of his mouse, Keith opened the electronic folder having the Non-binding Term Sheet template and License Agreement template he had created for the office some time earlier. Opening the Term Sheet template file and saving it as a new file, Keith recalled the political hassle his writing the templates had caused. He recalled how he had written them after Dennis had come to him with what he called a Term Sheet, but which was closer to a few ideas written on the back of a napkin, having already e-mailed people telling them the deal was basically done and that all that was left was for Keith to write the License Agreement. Keith then smiled as he recalled Dennis' reaction when Kaitlin had learned of the templates and insisted, not only that they be used for all technology deals, but also that all Term Sheets get reviewed and approved by the General Counsel's office just like License Agreements. Keith then recalled how Dennis resented Kaitlin for adding more bureaucratic hassle and started bringing his back-of-the-napkin discussion notes to Keith for him to fill in the Term Sheets before coordinating with Kaitlin's office and the target licensees.

Keith printed two copies of the Term Sheet template and stapled the pages together before bringing them and his note pad over to the table in his office. Sitting at the table in the relative quiet, Keith thought that one of the advantages of having their office suite in a building far away from Aspen hall was that the offices were bigger and nicer. His office was reasonably large and had room for his desk, credenza and a table with four chairs around it, which was well suited for meetings when the conference room was in use.

While he was transferring his notes, Keith heard Ginny come into the office suite and put her things down in her cubicle. After this morning he had not been sure what to expect the next time he saw her. Thinking of their interactions earlier in the conference room, he realized all at once that they were alone in the office suite and he had invited her to work with him on this project.

A moment later Ginny popped into Keith's office, saying, "Hi. How was your lunch?"

"Good," Keith replied, trying not to look at the Tailcrest University logo on her T-shirt stretched across her chest. "Dr. Shen's invention did come up. Dennis had some specific ideas and I am just starting to put together a Term Sheet. When the Term Sheet is finished, I'll use it to write the actual License Agreement to add standard provisions and more detail."

Sliding the extra copy of the Term Sheet template across the table, Keith then continued, saying, "If you have a little time, I can walk you through it."

"Sounds good," she replied, smiling in a way Keith wasn't sure he was comfortable with. She then closed Keith's door most of the way, picked up the form Keith had put in front of her and walked around the table to take the seat next to Keith. Moving the chair so it was right up against Keith's, she then sat down and slid over so she was physically up against him as fully as she could manage. She then tilted her head slightly while looking seductively at Keith and smiling hungrily.

Keith made no effort to dissuade her. At that moment Keith felt that his wife deserved better. He also felt that this girl was so appealing and assertive that he could not bring himself to make any effort to stop her. Focusing himself, Keith managed with some effort to keep himself from leaning over and kissing her.

Looking solely at the Term Sheet template in front of him, Keith attempted to focus on the work at hand. "It is probably easiest if we just go down the sections," he said, realizing too late that his choice of words was probably not the best.

"I would like that," she replied, shifting in her chair slightly to look at the papers in front of her.

Trying to focus his thoughts enough to read the words on the page, Keith imagined his wife's fury if she were to see them sitting together flirting like this. The image helped some and he was able to compose himself before describing the document.

Keith looked only at the document while Ginny smiled, knowing the effect she was having on him. Keith then said, "The purpose of a non-binding Term Sheet is so two entities can work out the framework of an agreement in reasonable detail without locking anything in place and without involving attorneys and a lot of legalese. The ones we use specify that they are non-binding and for discussion purposes only."

"The language down here," Keith said, pointing to the lower section of the last page of the document, "spells that out in bold type so there is no confusion as to whether this is an actual contract."

Reaching over and laying her hand on his as she pointed to the signature lines on the Term Sheet, Ginny asked, "Why are there signature sections if it isn't a contract?"

She then slid her hand slowly back across his hand, allowing her index finger to trace a line across the back of his hand. Not having the will to ask her to stop, he kept his eyes on the paper, but allowed himself a smile that she obviously saw. He knew that he was not handling this situation well at all and that he had already allowed things to go too far.

"The signatures give it an appearance of officialness that allows it to serve as a milestone in the development of the contract or in our case the License Agreement. Companies sometimes send out a press release announcing that a deal is in the works once a Term Sheet is signed."

"I see," she said very slowly, while sliding a finger up his forearm and shifting slightly in her seat so she was more facing him while maintaining physical contact from about their knees down.

Letting his smile turn into a grin at her advances, Keith said, "Once the Term Sheet is written and signed, both sides get the lawyers involved and they take the Term Sheet and convert it into a License Agreement which serves as a binding contract. The License Agreement has more specific wording and boiler plate legalese, and there can be a lot of negotiation over the details. The expression 'the devil's in the details' definitely applies to License Agreements."

"Makes sense," she offered. "Sounds sort of like starting a relationship. You figure out what each person would like and is comfortable with and then you move forward. Does that sound about right?"

Her meaning was clear as a bell to him and he could feel color rising in his cheeks as he smiled and looked down at the table. He tried to imaging his wife's fury again but couldn't. Sensing that Ginny was pleased with herself for triggering his reaction, he took a breath and looked over at her. Looking into her eyes he relaxed as he saw how much fun she was apparently having in enticing him this way. "Yes, that would be a good analogy. And, if either one isn't really sure what they want, it gives them the opportunity explore it more closely."

Ginny understood his meaning and did not feel at all dissuaded by his words. Keith looked back at the document and managed to continue his description, saying, "For the Term Sheet between Tailcrest and the new company that wants to license Dr. Shen's invention, Tailcrest would be giving the company rights under the patent we discussed this morning in exchange for money in the form of initial fixed payments and a portion of the money the company receives for selling things covered by the patents. The University is the 'Licensor' because we are offering rights under the patent, and the company is the 'Licensee' because they are receiving rights under the patent. The company usually has to pay for things like the cost of filing the patent, outside patent attorney costs, and their own costs for commercializing the technology. Each section of the Term Sheet addresses one of those items. The category is listed on the left, and the understanding of how they will arrange it is on written out on the right for each one."

Ginny patiently watched Keith while he spoke. When he finished she said, "I understand completely, but I do have a question. Would you look at me for a second?"

Keith turned his head and looked at her. She looked into his eyes and smiled seductively while sliding her hand slowly from his knee toward his waist. "Would you like me to close and lock the door?"

Keith was unable to look away from her. He was silent while her fingers traced a line, and then he replied, "Yes."

Chapter 24
(Tuesday: 4:00 p.m.)

Keith glanced at the small clock in the corner of his office computer monitor and saw that it was past four o'clock as he saved two files onto his computer and a flash disk. He then hit print twice and printed the two versions of the Term Sheet he had developed in a hurry during the hour and a half since Ginny had left. Picking both versions up off of the printer, Keith paced back and forth in his office looking at the documents and thinking about what he should do. In one hand he held a version of the Term Sheet that included everything Dennis had instructed him to put in it. In the other hand he held the other version, which he wrote in a way that included provisions he thought were reasonable for opening a negotiation with a start-up company. Recalling Dennis' instruction that he should send Dale a version having provisions Dennis preferred, for the second time that afternoon Keith felt conflicted about what he should do.

Carrying the two versions, Keith walked through the empty office suite to the paper shredder, thinking that he should probably shred the one including the provisions he thought were better and just do what Dennis had told him to do. Confident he was the only one in the office suite, Keith thought of his late father and wished he could talk to him about what he should do. Looking at the version that included all of Dennis' requirements and picturing his father in his mind Keith thought silently to himself, "Dale is a friend of mine from High School and I just drafted a 'give away' Term Sheet to open serious discussions in advance of a License Agreement that will bind the University. If I send this to him like Dennis wants me to, it will look like I am either trying to give an old friend a sweet heart deal or at best that I don't know what I am doing. Either way I am on the hook for Dennis' decision on how to handle the interactions with Dale."

Looking at the version which contained provisions he thought more reasonable, Keith then thought, "My version is more arm's length and reasonable. It is better for the University, would withstand criticism, and would lead just as easily to a better deal. Sending it to Dale would probably be insubordination and would definitely make Dennis angry. Certainly a bad idea in light of my preference for continued employment."

Holding both versions in front of him Keith continued his solo conversation in his head, "I was given verbal instructions during a lunch meeting that will likely be expensed to Tailcrest as a third party business meeting. With no written record that Dennis told me specifically what to put into the Term Sheet, I am not comfortable sending out a Term Sheet with what Dennis told me to put in it. I raised it at lunch but he dismissed it, and he is not available to speak with now, not that it would help."

Starting to pace in the office suite again, Keith continued, "Sending him an 'I don't agree with what you are telling me to do and I'm putting it in writing' e-mail would only tick him off. But, if the Term Sheet is criticized or challenged as too accommodating, Dennis would definitely have no recollection of telling me to do anything."

Standing in front of the shredder, Keith announced to the empty office suite, "This sucks!"

Reaching to put the Dennis version through the shredder, Keith had an idea and stopped. "If in doubt, delay," he thought, before turning and walking back into his office.

Putting both versions into his briefcase, Keith wrote a quick e-mail to Dennis. In it Keith indicated that he had completed a draft Term Sheet per the instructions Dennis had given him during their lunch meeting earlier that day, but that he wanted to meet with him early the following day to make sure the provisions matched what Dennis had instructed him to put into the document.

The situation felt more perilous to Keith than he knew it probably was, but he thought an e-mail record like he had just created might provide him some protection if an issue was raised by someone who had a problem with the deal. He planned to present both versions to Dennis in hard copy the following day and tactfully argue for their using his own version. If Dennis insisted on the give-away version, Keith planned to send a confirmatory e-mail with the Term Sheet attached to document Dennis' specific instructions.

Believing pretty solidly that Dale would be okay with Keith's version, Keith thought an informal meeting with him might help his discussion with Dennis the following day. After giving it another few moments' thought, Keith decided the best approach would be to have Dale stop by his house for another brief visit. Keith then dialed Dale's number.

Dale saw that it was Keith calling and answered by saying, "Afflack!"

"Afflack? Now you're an advertising duck?" Keith responded to Dale's startling version of "hello."

"One of the best advertising campaigns ever," Dale responded. "It's the company's name and millions of people went around saying it in a duck voice. It's absolutely brilliant marketing. If there were a Nobel Prize for marketing, they would probably win. What's up?"

"Dennis asked me to draft a Term Sheet for HematoChem but he and I are still discussing what should be in it. He has the lead in the negotiation and he's my boss so I have to go through him. However, I hear there are tight time constraints, and if you happened to stop by my house for a casual visit around seven o'clock and ask some pointed questions, I could answer them evasively and listen to your input."

"I understand what you're saying," Dale said, amused at Keith's surreptitiousness. "I'll be there at seven."

"Great, see you there," Keith replied.

Hanging up, Keith then dialed his home number. "Hello?" Sharon answered.

Keith could hear his sons arguing in the background. "It's me. I'm leaving in a little while and I wanted to give you a heads up that Dale Wade will probably stop by around seven for just a few minutes again this evening."

"Okay, no problem. Kind of busy," she said.

"Okay, bye," he replied, picturing her scolding their kids about arguing, especially when she was on the phone. All at once he felt terrible about letting the situation with Ginny take the course that it had.

Before locking the office suite to head home, Keith looked at the empty office and thought to himself, "What a day this has turned into."

Chapter 25
(Tuesday: 6:30 p.m.)

Aaron Konrad was sitting in one of the high-end patio chairs on the back porch of the home he had shared with Kaitlin and looking out over their landscaped backyard. He had insisted that his relatives, who had flown in to be with him, go out to dinner to give him the peace of sitting alone. Recalling many of the times he had enjoyed with Kaitlin there in the yard, he felt grateful for every moment he had shared with her. He also felt grateful to have people who cared about him and wanted to be there for him, but he found them to be somewhat under foot. He also couldn't help feeling like they were watching him and waiting for him to do something dramatic like collapse in a heap and start crying. Aaron hadn't even stopped working and he believed that he continued to think clearly and function normally, except for feeling overpowering feelings of loss that washed over him several times a day and caused him to sit and be still for surprisingly long periods of time. This had been one of those times. He had been out on the back porch for over an hour holding a drink that he had not yet taken a sip of when he heard the doorbell ring.

Aaron opened the door and saw Detective Baskin standing there with an officer he did not recognize. Aaron noticed that Detective Baskin looked slightly different than he had at the bridge. His expression and posture seemed curious to Aaron, but he couldn't be sure. "Please come in," Aaron said without any other formal greeting. "Would you like something to drink? My relatives have ensured that we are very well stocked."

"No thank you. We're fine. We just want to talk with you," Baskin said as Aaron led them into a spacious living room that looked like a page out of Better Homes and Gardens."

"Have a seat. I hoped we would be speaking more about Kaitlin," Aaron said while gesturing toward a couch and sitting in a nearby chair. He noticed that only Baskin sat. The other officer wandered around the room looking at his paintings and belongings, paying close attention to a shelf where Kaitlin kept Tailcrest University branded items she acquired as part of her efforts to enforce Tailcrest's merchandising contracts.

"I just have some basic questions for you," Baskin said. "You and your wife were getting along?"

"Yes. We considered ourselves fortunate that way."

"No indication of outside relationships or affairs."

"Kaitlin? No. Her moral compass was very strong and our relationship was good. I never doubted her."

"How about you?" Baskin asked.

"No. What are you getting at?" Aaron asked.

"Just some questions. Do you know of anyone who might want to harm either one of you or might have a serious grudge?"

"Kaitlin was General Counsel to Tailcrest University. There were lawsuits she managed, and she had mentioned some disgruntled employees, but they were angry with their Department Chairs or the Administration generally, not her. I have a business consulting firm where I advise clients about international shipping. I am an expert in customs and logistics. I have no enemies that I am aware of."

"Who arranged your vacation?" Baskin asked.

"Kaitlin did," Aaron responded. "She made the arrangements a while back and then had to slide the dates back because of a union negotiation she was participating in. We didn't receive any threats related to the negotiation and she said that all the issues were resolved within the collective bargaining agreement. I would like you to let me know where you are going with this."

"We looked through the resort security tapes," Baskin said, seeming to become more personable and less officious. "It was clear from the tapes that you and your wife kept to yourselves while you were in the main building and the restaurants. There were very few security cameras other than in those places. One near the main building did show her going by on her bike each morning at about the same time."

Aaron was trying not to become agitated at the Detective's disregarding his specific request for clarification about the direction of the questioning. "Yes, we kept to ourselves," Aaron said with a slight edge to his voice. "It was a vacation for my wife and me to be away together. Other than her bike rides we were together the whole time, and we didn't talk to any other guests that I recall."

The other officer then turned and looked at Aaron, but remained silent.

Baskin continued, asking, "Did you notice anyone observing you?"

"No. We had one of the more private cottages. Someone could have hidden in the trees, but we did not see anything unusual. We were simply enjoying our vacation. The only other person I recall talking to, besides the resort staff, was some guy in the lobby who offered some words of encouragement before your other officer picked me up."

The silent officer then took a thin a stack of photographs out of an envelope he had been carrying, thumbed through them and put a picture on the coffee table where both Baskin and Aaron could see it. "Is this the man you are referring to?" Baskin asked.

"Yes," Aaron replied, seeing an image of himself talking with the man. "He saw that I looked upset while I was waiting. I told him I was trying to locate my wife after a bike ride and he said something about her turning up with sore feet from the walk back. He seemed like a kind man trying to say something positive."

"Had you seen him before?" Baskin asked.

"No. Just that morning," Aaron replied.

"We spoke with the desk clerk. He flirted with her before he talked to you," Baskin offered. "He also paid with a corporate credit card from a company registered in Ukraine. We haven't traced it any further than that yet."

"I would also like to talk with you about the autopsy report. Would you be comfortable talking about that now?" Baskin said with an element of supportive warmth that Aaron found awkward coming from a detective.

"Yes. I want to know everything there is to know," Aaron replied, leaning forward.

"Your wife was an amazingly level headed and determined woman in the time before her life ended," Baskin said, while holding Aaron's gaze for emphasis. "The results show that your wife did not die from the bike accident or the fall. The Medical Examiner noted that her neck was broken and that her death was essentially instantaneous and painless."

Relief registered first in Aaron's expression, then confusion. "What do you mean? That doesn't seem possible, or I'm not hearing you right. Explain what you mean."

The silent officer had been focusing very intently on Aaron as Baskin provided this information and continued to watch his expression.

"Exactly," Baskin continued. "It doesn't make sense. It is very, very unlikely that the force of the impact and fall created the kind of aligned twisting force necessary to cause the specific break that ended her life."

"I still don't understand," Aaron said, becoming visibly agitated. "Are you saying she got up and fell again. What are you saying to me?"

"Your wife survived the fall. She was very badly injured, but she was alive and probably would have survived. This is where she had amazing presence of mind and determination. Injured but conscious, she recognized that she was in danger. The Medical Examiner took scrapings from under the fingernails of her right hand and found different materials under each. We collected samples at the scene and they matched. There was grass, dirt, and moss from a rock by the stream. Each was under just one fingernail. Another nail scraping had only human epithelial cells from her having scratched someone."

Aaron stared into Baskin's eyes. "You believe someone killed her," Aaron said. "Was the bike accident staged? Was she sexually assaulted? Tell me what happened."

"There was no indication of sexual assault," Baskin reassured him. "She may have been fleeing someone when she crashed the bike. We don't know. The way it looks is that she survived the crash and fall but was badly injured as I said. You said she was an experienced rider, so it might not have been an accident at all. She may have been knocked off the bike in an attempted assault. We have no way of knowing at this point. Then, badly injured but conscious, she saw her attacker and did the only thing she could. She left a message telling us that she survived the fall by scraping the different materials she could reach under each fingernail, and provided us a skin sample so we could try to match the DNA of whoever she scratched before she was killed. She was an amazing lady."

Dry eyed and numb, Aaron saw what looked like tears welling up in Baskin's eyes as he described Kaitlin's last moments.

Aaron smiled with pride. It was possibly the first time he had smiled since the event. "That is pure Kaitlin," he said, "stubborn, determined, clever and able to find a way to win, somehow, even if she didn't survive. That, gentlemen, is the woman I have been fortunate enough to spend my life with."

There was a long pause before Baskin said, "We've compared the DNA profile to most databases without a hit. We will let you know of our progress. I trust you will be staying here for a while?"

"This is my home," Aaron replied. "My business is established enough that I rarely travel. I don't have any trips planned currently."

"Have you ever been to Ukraine?" Baskin asked.

"No," Aaron replied. 'My clients do business primarily with companies in Japan, Taiwan, Hong Kong and the European Union. I have never been to Ukraine or any of the other former Soviet states.'

"Okay. If you think of anything or remember anything, no matter how small or seemingly irrelevant, call me," Baskin added.

"I'll do that," Aaron said, standing at the same time Baskin did. He then showed both officers to the door.

Watching Baskin and the other officer drive away, Aaron got the same wary feeling he always experienced around street cops. He then looked around his empty house and thought that his keeping to himself, other than his interactions with his family and work contacts, may have gone on long enough. Aaron decided to pick the brain of a federal prosecutor he knew to gain a better understanding of what Baskin was doing. He also decided that he should share more of the details of Kaitlin's death with people close to him; just not yet.

Chapter 26
(Tuesday: 7:00 p.m.)

Dale Wade parked his Chevy Camaro on the street in front of Keith's house fifteen minutes later than Keith had been expecting him to arrive. Having noticed that the garage door was shut, Dale walked up toward the front door and saw that the windows of the house had a noticeable mirror effect that he thought may have been from tinting or just the light at that time of evening. Dale rang the doorbell and a brief moment later Sharon answered door, holding Thomas on her hip while also holding a cell phone. Looking at Dale, Sharon held up one finger and said into the phone, "Mom, hold on. Someone's at the door. I know. Hold on."

Then, opening the door wider with the same hand she was holding the phone with, she invited Dale in and said to him, "He's on the back porch waiting for you. He's been absorbed in whatever you're here about since he got home. There's beer and soda in a cooler out there. Go on through."

Dale managed to say "Thank you" before Sharon's mother could be heard talking from the cell phone and Sharon resumed her conversation. Walking through the house, Dale noticed Heather in the kitchen with her little girl and Keith's son, Eddy. He couldn't tell what they were doing.

Stepping out onto the porch, Dale saw Keith and said, "Hey. What have you got there?"

"A beer for starters," Keith said, handing Dale a bottle out of the little cooler.

'Only half," Dale responded, accepting the beer. "I can only stay a little while and I don't want to make myself dangerous behind the wheel."

After Dale took a sip and sat down in one of the patio chairs arranged around a low patio table, Keith handed him a copy of the draft Term Sheet containing the provisions Keith wanted to work with as a starting point. "I didn't actually just hand you that, and I will need it back. It's just a draft anyway," Keith said, before continuing to talk while Dale read through the document. "Like I said on the phone, Dennis has the lead in the negotiations for our office. I haven't met with him on this draft yet and he will probably want some changes. Because timing is really tight and we have an obligation to negotiate what is best for the University I thought it might save some time to show you a working draft in case there were any problem areas that really jumped out. I don't want us to chew up time lobbing edited versions back and forth if there are deal breakers you could flag up front."

Keith then sat quietly while Dale read through the document and made notes in some places. As Keith saw Dale finish reading it he continued, "I structured it in a way that our General Counsel's Office has approved for previous deals. The provisions are reasonable, even generous, and there should be no trouble getting them to offer their legal stamp of approval. It really is a stamp too. They stamp and sign each contract indicating they have reviewed and approved it."

Dale thought to himself that Keith seemed to be babbling a bit and that he must be nervous about something. He also felt his own stress level increase because Egorov had described necessary deal terms that were much more favorable than what was written on the pages Keith had handed to him. Dale noticed that they were also inconsistent with Dennis' vague promise of "whatever terms are necessary".

"I am really squeezed on time by a new set of investors," Dale said. "I'm not posturing. They have a hard date they can't move. It is next Monday. I also see a number of potential obstacles in the Term Sheet. I put stars next to some important ones. Other people know more about these things than I do; particularly my investors, who are very interested in this deal. They are expecting a deal having terms that are much more favorable to HematoChem than what you have there. I, frankly, don't see anything really different than the earlier licenses HematoChem already has with other universities, but for this deal I think there are deal breakers in there. Everyone could lose out."

There was a long pause while Keith sipped his beer and Dale looked at him waiting for his response.

Keith remained silent while he put his beer down on the table. "Obviously not what I was hoping to hear, but still valuable input," Keith said, picking up the marked up draft and wondering how much of what Dale said actually was posturing. "Again I haven't met with Dennis to go over this draft yet, so he may want to change what I have in here."

While Keith was talking, his son, Eddy, came outside and sat in a chair next to him. "What that?" he asked his father while pointing at the papers in Keith's hand.

"Work papers," he answered, leaning toward Eddy and briefly tipping the papers to the side so he could see that they were filled with words before sitting back and looking at the sections Dale had marked.

Dale noticed that Eddy was sitting in his chair sort of like Keith was and that he looked a lot like Keith with some of Sharon's features evident too. While Keith was scanning through the brief notes Dale had made, Dale said, "There are a few sections noted with several stars that may be the toughest sticking points. For example 'Sublicensing' will be a problem. You have it listed that Tail-U will have the right to approve every sublicense deal in writing before we enter into it. That would be way too time-consuming."

"What's sublightning?" Eddy asked, thinking they were talking about lightning.

Dale smiled at the boy. "It's the little side pieces of lightning that come off of the big lightning bolt. The go zap instead of boom."

"Actually," Keith said, pausing and giving Dale a look that made it clear to Eddy that Dale had been joking, "the word was 'sublicensing' not 'sublightning'. Say I give you permission to use my table saw. That is like me giving you a 'license' to use it. If I give you permission to let other people use my table saw, that is like me letting you 'sublicense' my permission to them."

"Can I use your table saw?' Eddy asked.

"No, I don't think so," Keith said to Eddy, while wondering if he understood what he had just said. "I'd like you to go inside now. Your Mom probably wants to get you showered."

"Okay," Eddy said, climbing off the chair and giving Keith a hug before going back inside.

"I should get going," Dale said. "Please, talk with Dennis as soon as you can to see how flexible you can be on the sections I noted. I really need to get this through fast. Mind if I walk around the side on my way out?"

"Sure, go ahead," Keith replied. "Thanks for stopping by on short notice."

"No problem," Dale said, standing to leave and waving goodbye to Eddy, who was watching him from just inside the screen door.

Chapter 27
(Wednesday: 7:30 a.m.)

Aaron pulled his Mercedes into the parking lot of the funeral home where Kaitlin's wake was being held later that morning and for no particular reason parked in the same space he had used several years earlier when he and Kaitlin had attended her mother's services there. He recalled how hard it had been for her losing her mother after her father had died years earlier. He sat motionless for a time, playing back in his head how he and Kaitlin had gotten out of the car and walked slowly inside. Looking at the passenger seat, he thought to himself that now she was in there in her current state and he was going to walk that same way to go in and be with her. He felt no sense of hesitation or trepidation as he got out of the car and walked across the parking lot carrying a small CD player Kaitlin had bought many years before and kept in their kitchen. He was walking to be with Kaitlin, and that felt as natural and right to him as it always had.

Stepping into the lobby of the funeral home, Aaron experienced a sensation of hushed reverence like he should be quiet and step softly. He had felt that way every time he had ever entered the calming surroundings of a funeral home. This time the feeling was particularly strong as he was the only one in the lobby. Walking down a hallway toward the office where he had met with the funeral Director to make the arrangements, he noticed him coming out of one of the viewing halls.

The Director approached Aaron exhibiting a kind, supportive expression. "Hello. Kaitlin is this way," the man said, walking Aaron toward the viewing hall closest to the lobby. "Everything is set up just the way you requested."

Aaron followed without speaking. Reaching the door of Kaitlin's viewing hall the funeral Director touched a book on a small chest high table. "This is your guest sign in book," he said before pushing open one of the double doors to the viewing hall.

Stepping into the viewing hall, the first thing that came to Aaron's mind was how similar it looked to when he had been in this same room with Kaitlin for her mother's wake. The room was elegantly appointed, with seating, long drapes, discreet curved tables along one wall and soft lighting. At the far end of the room Aaron saw the coffin that he knew held the woman he had spent most of his adult life with.

The funeral Director had been watching Aaron's reaction as they entered the room and asked kindly, "Is everything consistent with what we discussed about the arrangements?"

"It's just right," Aaron responded, speaking more quietly than he otherwise would have.

Holding up the small CD player Aaron asked, "Are you sure that what we talked about is okay? It is probably an unusual request, and I feel like it may offend other people here."

"It's just us here," the funeral Director responded, smiling genuinely. "We have had much more unusual requests, and I think that this one is wonderful. Besides, if it is what Kaitlin requested and wanted, then it seems only right to honor her and her request."

"Thank you," Aaron said. The funeral Director took his cue and left the room.

Aaron felt no need to rush over to the casket. He knew Kaitlin was there. Walking slowly around the room, he stopped and looked at the Monet prints; then at the picture collage their relatives had created. Most of the pictures showed the two of them together, happy. One showed them at Machu Picchu. Another showed them standing on the Great Wall of China. Another showed them together in the hanging swing under an oak tree in their yard. Each picture brought back so many memories that he had to push himself to look at the next. Then he saw one of the pictures that showed just Kaitlin. He had taken the picture not long after they had met; right about the time had he decided he wanted her to be his wife.

After looking at all of the pictures in the collage, Aaron walked over to the open casket. Stopping just short of the kneeler that was positioned in front of the casket, he saw Kaitlin posed and made up like she was sleeping comfortably. Aaron saw that there was a heaviness to her makeup. He had no illusions about her essence or soul no longer being there in her, but this was Kaitlin and he loved her and wanted to be near her. Stepping partly on and partly around the kneeler he went closer to the casket, placed his hand on her upper arm and looked lovingly at her.

After a long moment he took his hand back, leaned against the coffin and did what he had always done; talked to his wife. "I feel like this is not real for me yet. I know you're gone, but I feel like we're going to wake up in our bed and everything is going to be like it was. I know that won't happen, but I feel like it will. You've been my life. I wouldn't change a thing we did together. I went through your Will and brought your old CD player. As you requested, I will always think of you when I hear that song by Trooper."

He stood silent for a moment recalling the words in his head, "raise a little hell, raise a little hell, raise a little hell," and how she always turned up the volume when it came on.

Looking at her again, he continued speaking to her. "We got your message. They took scrapings from under your nails and compared them to the ground where they found you. They also found the skin scraping under your one nail. We got your message. You want us to catch the person who did this to you. We will. I may take a while, maybe a long time, but you gave us what we need. The rest is up to us. You're amazing, and I am the luckiest man who ever lived."

"I am guessing that your unusual request in your Will is not only something you want just because of who you are but also so I will be more comfortable in this place, more like it's our home. You always thought of me, but I was surprised when I saw it in your Will. The funeral Director doesn't mind at all, and it will be a while before our friends and relatives start arriving. Now is as good a time as any."

Plugging in the little CD player and setting the volume to eight, Aaron rechecked that the CD Kaitlin had made as a compilation of her favorite classic rock and heavy metal songs was in place. Looking again at his wife, Aaron pressed play and the hall was filled with loud rock music that Kaitlin had listened to in their home more times than he could possibly recall. Aaron leaned on his wife's coffin and felt all the mornings, all the days, all the nights they had been together. Amid the music the emotion overflowed within him and his eyes welled up. He couldn't hold it back. His whole body shook as the emotion poured out of him through tears and a wailing sound that seemed wounded animal-like and sounded to him as though it was coming from someone else. His practiced reserved manner had been pushed aside by his fundamentally human reaction. The part moan, part scream sound he heard coming out of himself was only partly drowned out by the music, but he didn't care. His Kaitlin was gone.

He didn't know how long he had carried on that way, but when he found himself feeling calm, breathing deeply and looking at his wife, he reached over and turned off the CD player.

"That's what you thought would happen, wasn't it?" he asked her, not expecting an answer. "You wanted me to grieve fully, and you thought this would help, didn't you. I love you."

Unplugging the CD player and turning to carry it out to the car, Aaron saw the funeral Director standing in the door of the hall, looking on kindly from across the room. Aaron crossed the distance and patted the man on the arm. "Thank you for letting me honor her request," he said to the man.

The funeral Director had a look of genuine understanding and supportiveness. "If you need anything at all, I will be here the whole time," he said to Aaron before turning and heading back toward his office.

Chapter 28
(Wednesday: 8:25 a.m.)

Keith and Sharon pulled into the parking lot of the funeral home and found that the lot was already mostly full. They were running just a few minutes late because Sharon's normally punctual mother had been late in showing up to help with their kids. Keith believed that her mother was uncharacteristically late because it was an event linked to him, not Sharon. Keith found a parking space near the far corner of the lot and parked the car. Exiting the car, Keith and Sharon walked across the lot toward the entrance. It bothered him that Sharon's mother made them late, as so many of his mother-in-law's actions did, but Sharon was having a poor health day and was putting on a brave face to join him, so he decided it was best to just let it go.

They entered the crowded lobby and saw Kaitlin's name by the first viewing hall on the right. After a brief wait, while people in front of them signed the guest book, they too signed it and walked into the large relatively crowded room. Keith saw numerous people he recognized from Tailcrest, but whom he did not know. He wondered what sort of connections and interactions they'd had with Kaitlin. Moving further into the room, Keith saw through an opening in the crowd that Kevin Taft was having what looked like a serious conversation with President Walker. Kevin noticed Keith and looked over briefly and nodded slightly to him without missing a beat in his conversation with Walker. Keith also saw that a few yards behind Kevin was Aaron Konrad, who he recognized from pictures in Kaitlin's office, speaking with guests before they made their way up to the casket.

While Keith was looking in the direction of the open casket, Sharon nudged his arm and said, "I see Dennis and Dale Wade over there."

Following her line of sight, Keith saw his boss and Dale talking with Jason Roberts from the General Counsel's Office in an alcove-like section toward the back of the room. He also thought he saw Dr. Shen walking away from them, although he wasn't sure because people were partly blocking his view. Keith and Sharon headed toward the alcove through the people standing mostly in groups and talking. Stepping up to the three men, Keith said, "Dennis. Dale. Good morning. Jason, this is my wife, Sharon."

"Pleased to meet you," Jason said, shaking Sharon's hand politely, while noticing that she looked fatigued or like she wasn't feeling very well. "I work with Keith on his contracts. I'm with the General Counsel's Office and I read a lot of what your husband writes."

"So you worked with Kaitlin?" she asked.

"Yes, closely, every day," Jason replied. "We're still in shock and absorbing what happened. It's such a tragedy."

"Everyone is still sort of in shock," Dennis added, before looking specifically at Keith and continuing. "Carol is picking up Ginny. Her boyfriend apparently couldn't give her a ride. They'll be here a while later."

Keith was relieved that he would not have to introduce Ginny to Sharon, but wondered if Dennis was hinting that he knew something about Keith's interactions with Ginny. "We're going to head that way," Keith said, gesturing toward the far end of the viewing hall where the casket and Aaron were.

"It was nice to meet you," Sharon said to Jason as they made their way forward.

There was a line of people waiting to talk with Aaron, and Keith and Sharon joined it. After several people spoke with Aaron and moved reverently to pay their respects to Kaitlin, Keith found himself face to face with the man he had seen in several pictures in Kaitlin's office but whom he had never met. Shaking Aaron's hand, Keith said, "I am Keith Mastin and this is my wife Sharon. I worked with Kaitlin at the University. She probably never mentioned me, but I liked and respected her quite a bit. I am sorry for your loss."

"Thank you," Aaron said to Keith, looking warmly at both him and Sharon. "She did mention you several times. She liked your work and was thinking about trying to bring you out of the Technology Transfer Department and into hers. She would be glad to know that you are here. Thank you for coming."

Moving along in front of the open casket with Sharon next to him, Keith was still thinking about what Aaron had just said when he saw Kaitlin posed in the casket as though she were sleeping. He found it unnerving to see her like that. She was always high energy with a momentum and will that made her seem bigger than she really was. Now she was still. Keith then thought of Sharon's undiagnosed illness and what it could mean if the doctors gave her bad news after the CT scan. He then imagined what it would be like if he were the husband greeting guests and Sharon were the one positioned like that in the casket. He took Sharon's hand and felt a deep sense of loss. "Goodbye Kaitlin," was all he said before leading Sharon toward the exit.

Sharon guessed what Keith had imagined and saw how he was affected by seeing Kaitlin. Holding his hand, she said nothing while they walked among the people toward the exit. They both felt somewhat relieved to experience the natural light and gentle breeze as they stepped out of the building and into the parking lot.

Chapter 29
(Wednesday: 8:40 a.m.)

Each step away from the funeral home and toward their car helped Keith feel a bit more normal, like he could breath fully again. He knew the image of Kaitlin in her coffin would stay with him for a long time. They were almost to their car when Kevin Taft climbed out of a car, the make of which Keith did not recognize, and walked alongside them. "I am sorry Sharon. If you don't mind, I need to borrow Keith for just a minute."

"Not at all, Kevin," she replied honestly, looking expectantly toward Keith, who understood her meaning and handed her the car keys.

As soon as Sharon stepped away, Kevin got right to the point. "I thought you would like to know, and, while it's no secret, I'd prefer you not share this too broadly, but Kaitlin's death was not an accident. She survived the bike accident, which might not have been an accident, and then someone broke her neck by twisting it sharply. She saw it coming and scratched different materials under each of her nails to show she survived the crash, and they found someone's skin cells under one of her fingernails. She went down determined, if not actually fighting. Someone killed her, probably a man, given how she was killed, and he's still out there."

Keith adrenaline level and heart rate instantly skyrocketed. The normalness that Keith was beginning to experience evaporated immediately and completely. Keith was shocked by the news, especially having just seen Kaitlin in her casket. He then asked questions in rapid fire. "What do they know? Was it random? Was she assaulted? What caused the bike accident? Do they have a motive?"

Kevin fully appreciated Keith's reaction, having experienced a similar reaction not long before, when Aaron passed the news on to Walker and himself. "No motive, no sexual assault, no information on whether the bike crash was an accident, no ID on the skin cells, and they have probably ruled out Aaron's direct involvement, although even speculating about that would be absurd."

"So, if I understand correctly, they basically don't know anything except that she was killed after surviving a bike crash," Keith summarized.

"Yes, that's about right," Kevin agreed. "I introduced Aaron and Kaitlin a very long time ago. One of my dear friends has been murdered and another is left grieving her loss. I'm really angry and I'm going to see the guy put down like a rabid animal, literally. I'm going to be in the viewing room drinking a toast when it happens."

Keith knew Kevin well enough to know that he was absolutely serious, and that he was stating an actual intention that he planned to follow through on. "Is there anything we can do?" Keith asked, as the initial adrenaline rush subsided.

"Other than stay out of the authorities' way, unless we have a lead they can follow up on," Kevin answered, "no, there's really not much. Are you going to tell Sharon?"

"I should, but I probably won't. She has a lot of stress already. She has a CT scan coming up this week."

"Probably better to hold off then," Kevin said as he started heading back toward his car. "I'll let you know if I hear anything else."

"Thanks," Keith said as he started walking back toward his car, hardly able to think from the shock of what he just heard. Before opening the driver's side door he paused, recalling the image of Kaitlin inside the funeral home and whispered the words out loud, "Kaitlin was murdered."

Keith then slid into the driver's seat, turned on the engine and looked over his shoulder to back out. Sharon saw that he still looked upset and asked him, "What did Kevin want to talk about?"

"He's really broken up about Kaitlin," Keith answered. "He mentioned that he's known her and Aaron for a long time and that he was the one who introduced them. That was most of it."

Trying to rationalize that he had not technically lied to Sharon, Keith avoided looking at her by continuing to look over his shoulder while carefully backing the car out of the parking space.

Chapter 30

(Wednesday: 9:00 a.m.)

Driving away from the funeral home to bring Sharon home, Keith took a familiar route that would bring them by Green Lake Park. Part of his reason for bringing Sharon there right then was to try to focus on something positive and shake off the unsettling feelings of having seen his colleague in her casket and having learned that she was murdered. "The kids are excited about getting out on the boat this weekend at Green Lake Park," Keith said while driving. "I promised them that we could launch it this weekend last weekend when I told them 'no' because I hadn't made the new leeboards yet."

"I know" she replied, noticing that Keith was driving a back way that would bring them to the park, which was not far from the funeral home. "They keep mentioning it. They also like to climb in it. Heather and I sometimes invade your 'man cave' to let the boys play in it. Chrissy clings to Heather the whole time so we don't stay out there for long."

Keith started to feel better as he pulled the car into Green Lake Park. He parked in the mostly empty parking lot near the swimming area and nearer to where they planned to launch the little boat that following weekend. Keith always thought of this as a positive place, and it made him feel good to be there and to think of the good times he and his family often had there. It was a lovely park built around a good sized lake in a section of town that was more affluent then the section they lived in but close and convenient enough that they used it often.

They climbed out of the car and walked toward one of the benches near the water. As they crossed the short distance, Keith held Sharon's hand. He knew she liked it when he did that and that he didn't do it nearly enough. He recalled how they had been coming to this park since they bought their house six years earlier, and how about a year later when Heather and her husband moved in nearby that they had brought Heather there to show her the park. He then briefly thought about the one time he and Heather had slept together when Heather and her husband were going through a rough patch and how relieved he was when, after announcing that she was pregnant, she later told him privately that when they had been together she was already pregnant so there was no way the baby was his. Their one moment of weakness had been a non-issue between them during the entire time since.

Reaching the bench near the water, Keith pulled Sharon close to him as they sat down. While she was resting up against him, Keith noticed once again the difference in how she felt now as compared to before her illness. She was more frail; weaker than she used to be, almost like there was a malnourished quality to her. Being just inches from her hair, he could see how it had thinned out some, even though most people wouldn't notice any difference.

They sat in silence for a while, just enjoying the warmth and closeness in this familiar place. Keith did not want to bring it up, but he thought that Kaitlin's wake must be making Sharon think about her own mortality, especially given how her illness had progressed over time. He also wondered if something had changed recently. Sharon had always had a temper, but it was controlled and mostly just cute, but in the last few months though she had mentioned periodic mini-rages that made her just leave the room and wait them out. He speculated that this new symptom might be from depression or just a buildup of anger from the disappointments she faced having to deal with her illness.

Breaking the silence, Sharon said, "I miss working. I miss the students and the friendships. I miss having something to be in charge of. If not for Heather, I think I would lose my mind. She has been such a good friend to me."

"To both of us," Keith added. "She and Chrissy are like part of our family. Her husband is missing out on so much by always being at work or out on the golf course."

"Speaking of that," Sharon said, shifting the topic, "you've taken too much time off from work lately to go with me to my appointments. I don't trust Dennis not to use your absences to screw with your career somehow. I don't think he likes it when you get attention for your work and he may try to knock you down somewhat by using whatever he can."

"My work makes him look good," Keith responded. "Besides, they're not going to fire me for taking my wife to doctor's appointments. That just won't happen."

"You've taken more time than you should," she countered. "I can handle my CT scan appointment by myself. It's just migraines and I had a CT scan because of them once before after I first started getting sick. They're no big deal and I don't want you to miss any more work."

"Granted, ours is the only Technology Transfer Office within driving distance, but they're not going to fire me," Keith said. "Even if they did, I could go back into private practice. I would probably make more money by hanging a shingle and starting my own law firm. It would take a lot or work and time, but I could do it if I had too."

"Still," she said, "I would rather you skip my appointment and go to work instead."

"We both know that if the disease is something really scary like cancer, the CT scan would probably show that. I would kind of like to be there," Keith said gently.

Sharon replied, "The results won't be interpreted right away anyway. You can come with me for the follow up appointment."

"If it would make you more comfortable, okay," he said. "I'll skip this one. I'll just call you every five minutes until the procedure is done."

She turned and gave him a look; then smiled, saying, "We should probably get me home so you can get back to work."

"Okay, okay," he said, faking a cross look. "Work, work, work; I see your plan. Work me to death and collect the life insurance. I guess that's how it's going to be."

She smirked at him, then replied, "Better that way than that highway splattering image you created for me on the phone the other day. That was really gross."

"Thank you. I take pride in my creativity," he responded as they got up and walked toward the car holding hands.

Chapter 31
(Wednesday: 9:50 a.m.)

Keith and Sharon drove home in comfortable silence, each absorbed in their own thoughts. Pulling into their driveway and parking, Keith asked rhetorically about his mother-in-law, "So, you think she is going to have anything nice to say to me?"

"She was nice enough to watch the kids this morning. You know I don't like it when you criticize my mother," she replied, showing her disappointment in her expression.

"She's mean to me," he offered in his own defense. "Do you also not like it when she criticizes me?"

"Of course. I've talked to her about it. But, you took away her little girl by marrying me. Even worse you insist on privacy and autonomy in our running of our household. She finds that simply unfathomable when you so obviously need the benefit of her greater wisdom and experience."

Keith chuckled at Sharon's accurate description of her mother's mindset. "Shall we go in so I can gain the benefit of her greater wisdom and experience before going in to work?"

"I could just bring your stuff out to the car so you can slip away quietly into the morning mist," she said, playing along.

"No, no. Dealing with her provides contrast so I can better enjoy the good things in my life," he said before opening the car door and walking with Sharon around the front of the house to go inside. "Besides, no mist."

Entering their home through the front door, they immediately saw the fold out card table Sharon's mother had set up in the middle of the living room, and her and the two boys sitting around it. From the looks of it she was trying to play cards with them, even though her past attempts to teach them how to play were unsuccessful because they were still too young.

"I see you're back from that work function. How was it dear?" she asked Sharon, while not looking at Keith.

"Just like all the other work funerals we go to. Thanks for asking," Keith said, being more harsh and direct than he had intended to be.

"It was fine, Mom," Sharon added. "People were nice and we didn't stay too long anyway."

"Well the boys were angels while you were gone," Sharon's mother continued, speaking only to Sharon. "We played cards, had a snack and played games. They kept asking to go out in the garage to play in that boat, but their FATHER keeps all those tools out in the open so they couldn't play out there safely."

Keith heard her tone and recognized the non-verbal attack for what it was. "Well boys, maybe GRANDMA should have asked whether you've been taught to stay away from the tools when you're out there. THEN she would know it's okay; maybe next time."

Sharon's mother went on as though the retort hadn't happened, saying, "If he would only build something to put them in, it would be SAFE for little children. Everyone knows little children need to be SAFE."

"They need to know that people will behave respectfully toward their parents too, because they identify with their parents and attacks impact them. Parent alienation is a nasty practice that I am not going to put up with," Keith said much more harshly and aggressively than he had intended.

Sharon's mother bristled at being confronted directly.

Quickly stepping between Keith and her mother, Sharon said, "Let's get your things for work. I know you're running late."

"Yes, that would probably be best," he replied, glaring at his mother-in-law before retrieving his briefcase.

Sharon walked out with him to the car and gave him a hug before asking, "What was that?"

"Partly, it was my being wound up because of this morning," he said, breathing deeply and nuzzling her hair, "but partly it was the fact that she was criticizing me in front of our kids. I am not going to put up with that. If she keeps that up she will not be welcome here. I don't care that we'll have to pay a sitter sometimes. I will get in her face and keep shouting at her until she leaves. I am not okay with what she just did."

Sharon squeezed him a little tighter. "She's my mother. She cares about me, but I agree that she was out of line today. I'll talk to her. Now you have to go to work."

"I'll call you later," Keith said before kissing her on the side of the neck, climbing into the car and backing out of the driveway.

While driving toward the University campus, Keith realized that he was experiencing a whole lot of stress between knowing that Kaitlin was murdered, worrying about Sharon's health, his mother-in-law's obnoxiousness, the developing situation with Ginny and all the more normal things in his life that he always worried about. Driving his normal route to work without really paying attention to his speed, Keith focused on the thing that was bothering him more than anything else. He said it out loud again so he could hear himself say it, "Kaitlin Clark was murdered."

He knew he would keep the information Kevin shared with him secret and act as normally as he could until the word got out through other channels. A few minutes later, as he drove through Tailcrest's main entrance with its red brick square pillars with decorative tapered walls and prominent Tailcrest University signage on each side, he tried to put Kaitlin's death out of his mind so he could focus on the tasks before him and so he could try to act normal.

Chapter 32
(Wednesday: 10:40 a.m.)

Keith walked into the Technology Transfer Office suite and noticed that Carol was at her desk typing, but that Ginny's cubical was unoccupied. He could not tell whether Dennis was in his office because Dennis' desk was positioned in a way that it could not be seen from out in the office's common area. "Good morning," Keith said to Carol as he walked into his office to put his things down and sort through his to do list. Carol heard Keith and nodded while she continued typing.

Keith quickly scanned his e-mails and looked over the files he had splayed on his desk like a deck of cards. He then went out to talk with Carol. He waited a moment until she finished typing, then tried to focus their conversation on work. "The contracts I went over with Jason were signed by Vice President Campanaro and sent to the other parties by the Legal Department. They copied me on the e-mails. I'll forward them to you for the database."

"We just missed you at the wake this morning," she said to him, not wanting to avoid the topic that was no doubt being discussed in offices all over campus. "We saw you talking with Kevin and then getting into your car just as we were pulling in. It didn't look like you noticed us."

She paused to take a drink of her coffee, then continued, saying, "It was really strange being at Kaitlin's wake with so many people from Tailcrest. It was surreal to see her in her coffin. Ginny stayed with me and I introduced her to some people, but it's hard to make a positive introduction at a wake."

"I imagine," Keith said, agreeing.

"I've been to a lot of funerals over the years but this was the first one for a coworker," she continued. "We only stayed a little while. Then I dropped Ginny off at her dormitory and came in to get some work done and get my mind off poor Kaitlin. She was just riding her bike."

"Sounds like you are still wound up about it," he said, trying to be supportive. "I am too. I am still absorbing it all and seeing her there..."

"I know," Carol said, "It's like she's supposed to be in her office, not there."

"Yes," he agreed, "that captures it about right."

They were silent for a moment. Then Carol sighed and smiled crookedly at Keith. "On a separate topic, we seem to have a school girl crush going on here in the office," she said, watching for any reaction on his face.

"I haven't noticed anything," Keith replied convincingly. "What makes you think that?"

"Well, Ginny was kind of giddy, even though we were going to a wake. She kept asking questions about you. Where you were from? What kind of things do you like to do? Do you talk about her at all? Let's see, when I mentioned your wife, she changed the subject. And, when we saw you in the parking lot, she brightened up and started waving to get your attention like she had just seen her beau. Does that seem like enough evidence?"

"Wow," he responded, trying to look surprised. "I hadn't noticed anything other than that she usually seems to be in a good mood."

"You may be the source of her good mood," Carol offered. "Please try not to give her any mixed messages. She's a really nice person and I wouldn't want her to get too built up and then disappointed. I also wouldn't want your wife to kill you. You remember that joke where the last thing the husband heard was his wife saying 'how do I reload this thing?'"

"I've heard that one; and it definitely would apply in Sharon's case. I like Ginny too and I don't want to see her get hurt."

Carol then did something Keith had never seen her do before. She looked right at him and raised one eyebrow in an inquisitive look. The gesture was very clear. She was looking to see if anything in his expression would reveal whether there was anything going on between him and Ginny. Keith responded by meeting her gaze evenly and warmly, giving her absolutely nothing to work with.

Switching gears, Carol said, "Before I forget, Dennis wants to see you right away when he gets back. I talked to him at the wake and he asked me to let you know if I saw you first. He said it has to do with the man who is interested in licensing Dr. Shen's invention into his start-up company, Dale Wade."

"Did Dennis say when he was going to get back?"

"He didn't say, but I had the impression he was coming right back to the office. I expected he would be here by now."

"There is apparently an urgency to license Dr. Shen's invention into Dale Wade's company," Keith said. "Dale actually stopped by my house and we talked about it. He was a friend of mine back in High School. He was over earlier in the week too. It was good to catch up."

"I didn't know he was your friend," Carol said, surprised by the coincidence. "Dennis has been meeting with him for months and he never mentioned it."

"No one made the connection until I saw him at the Inventor's Award Ceremony," Keith said while shrugging his shoulders. "He was a good friend until his family moved away. We used to hang out a lot. I got the impression that he hasn't changed much since then."

"Some people are like that, especially if they don't get married," she said, recalling several of her own friends who had avoided growing up by staying single. "If your connection helps make the deal happen, I'm sure

Dennis will be happy about it. He mentioned that he feels pressured to make the office's numbers look better for Vice President Campanaro."

Stepping toward his office, Keith then said with well faked incredulity, "You really think Ginny has a crush on me?"

"Do you really expect me to believe that you haven't noticed?" Carol replied without hesitation.

Keith chuckled and broke into a broad smile as he disappeared into his office.

Chapter 33
(Wednesday: 11:00 a.m.)

Keith was working at his office table, seated facing the door so he could keep an eye out for Dennis. He had read through two technology transfer contracts that were unrelated to the HematoChem matter before he saw Dennis enter the suite looking somewhat stressed. Keith then waited a few minutes out of courtesy before grabbing copies of the two versions of the Term Sheet and walking over to talk with Dennis in his office.

Keith sat in one of the chairs across from Dennis' desk and asked, "What's up? Carol said you wanted to see me about the negotiation with Dale Wade. He actually stopped by my house last night and we talked about it a little bit."

"He told me about that," Dennis responded. "He said you were feeling him out about the Term Sheet provisions and it made him anxious that you might get things hung up over some provisions his company can't accept. I told him you're not like that and that you were probably just testing the waters. I told you what provisions to put into the Term Sheet and I expect you to follow through on that."

Keith remained silent, partly because he did not want to openly disagree with his boss about the Term Sheet and partly because he sensed Dennis had something else he wanted to talk about.

"This is for you," Dennis said, while tossing Keith the "reviewed and approved" stamp he had gotten from the Legal Department.

Keith caught it and read the backwards lettering on the stamp. "Why are you giving me one of the Legal Department's stamps?"

"I had a conversation with Vice President Campanaro," Dennis replied. "He has faith in our office and, more specifically, he knows you are a lawyer. He also knows that you know more about this area than Jason ever will, and that Jason is overloaded already and that it will only get worse. His solution was to have you be able to review and approve contracts coming through our office just like the Legal Department can. Jason still can review our office's agreements, but I don't see any reason why he should. We can finally get things done without having to wait weeks for our contracts to be read. Things will work much better this way and I think the University will benefit."

"Campanaro also reminded me that it is time for me to do your and Carol's annual employment evaluations," Dennis continued. "I really don't have time for them but I have to have them done in the next week or two. You'll have to put together a list of accomplishments like last year. That's not as important right now as the Term Sheet for HematoChem."

Keith continued to listen quietly, knowing that Dennis sometimes did one way conversations where interjecting was futile, and that this was one of those conversations.

"Actually, I am so overloaded right now that I don't have time for anything. I want to make the Dale Wade negotiation my top priority but I have to deal with prima-donna researchers, Deans and Vice Presidents who think their worthless inventions are the best thing ever and more important than anyone else's. I also have to work with Carol to put together our end of the fiscal year numbers to submit in a few weeks. It's an administrative nightmare."

"I would be happy to help," Keith offered. "Lawyers and paperwork kind of go together."

"What I want you to do is clear your desk of everything other than the Dale Wade negotiation and get it done. I want you to get this one done quickly, even if you have to give it away. The terms I gave you yesterday will be acceptable to them. Be even more generous if you have to. The dollars are only part of it. We have a local entrepreneur starting a company that will aid in the University's economic development efforts and create local jobs. Everybody wins. Tailcrest gets a positive press release for the local paper and our office's performance looks much better because we have a completed start-up company based on Tailcrest technology. We haven't had one yet this year so this one is even more important."

Keith understood very clearly what Dennis was saying and he appreciated the faith that was being put in him, but he also saw what to him looked ridiculous from a University perspective. "So, if I understand this correctly," Keith said, leaning back in his chair, "I can negotiate the Term Sheet, write and negotiate the License Agreement based on the Term Sheet, stamp it reviewed and approved, and Vice President Campanaro will sign it basically without reading it. That would certainly be efficient from an administrative standpoint. Wow."

"Exactly, wow," Dennis repeated. "Finally we can get things done efficiently, and I need you to get this one done quickly. Dale has his investors to deal with. We have our annual reports to turn in. I gave you the terms to put in the Term Sheet. Now it's your responsibility to get it done."

Keith could see from Dennis' manner that he was genuinely stressed and under pressure. Trying to lighten things, Keith opted for humor. "So, if I'm hearing you correctly, you want me to, um...get it done?" Keith said, cracking a smile.

Dennis responded with a withering look before saying, "I'm not joking around on this one. It is your responsibility."

Keith nodded his acceptance and walked back to his office. Crossing the distance, Keith couldn't help thinking that Dennis had just metaphorically turned him into a micromanaged sock puppet and possibly a rubber stamp for what Dennis wanted. Sitting back at his own desk,

Keith went over it in his mind. He felt incredulous that he had been instructed verbally about what terms to negotiate into a Term Sheet and put into a License Agreement and then told that it was his responsibility to make it happen and approve it under his own name. Keith knew he was being leaned on to do it Dennis' way while assuming responsibility for the deal if it failed or was viewed unfavorably. Keith's concerns were heightened when an e-mail from Dennis popped up reiterating how it was Keith's project and his responsibility to move it forward. Keith did not like the situation he found himself in, but couldn't see a way out of it. Recalling a lovable bear from a cartoon his sons loved to watch, he leaned back further in his chair and said to himself, "Think, think, think," but nothing came to mind.

Chapter 34
(Wednesday: 11:45 a.m.)

Keith entered the campus coffee house and found it crowded with students standing in groups, lounging on soft couches or sitting in the chairs around short tables. Most were holding large cups with sleeves around them. The background music in the coffee house was unusual but pleasant and Keith wondered whether it was a corporate product that came with the franchise package. Before Keith could get in line to buy a cup of flavored coffee, he saw a group of students get up from around one of shorter tables along a wall close to where he was. Keith moved in and put his leather briefcase with his lap top computer on the table and hoped that people would not take the seats or the laptop while he was in line. Getting in line, Keith kept himself positioned so he could see his things just in case.

A few minutes later, after purchasing a cup of hazelnut coffee, he returned to his table and took a seat facing the counter. His positioning gave him a clear view of the entrance so he could watch for Ginny. He had left a message with Carol that he would be at the coffee house and asked that she send Ginny over when she got in around noon.

Keith sipped his coffee and watched the students while he waited for Ginny. His attention stayed focused on a group of pretty girls in line in front of a plane looking boy who obviously wanted to talk to them. Keith watched the girls chatting quickly with each other and positioning themselves physically so the boy had no chance to join their conversation. As the girls got their drinks and left, Keith wondered if girls' social cliques provided evolutionary advantages in light of how universal they were among teenage girls.

Not long into his observations of the students Keith saw Ginny come through the front door. Ginny saw him immediately. She smiled broadly as she walked over to him, put her Tailcrest University emblazoned bag under the table and pushed a chair closer to him. "Are you trying to frustrate me?" she asked, looking at him seductively.

Keith blushed and looked down for a moment before looking at her and saying, "I just need to be able to focus. If we were to meet about this in my office or the conference room I would probably lose the power of speech, let alone my ability to concentrate."

"That would be okay," she said, leaning toward him briefly and touching the back of his hand before leaning back in her chair. "What would you like to go over?"

"The Term Sheet we started going over yesterday," he said, handing her the two versions of the document he had created the previous afternoon. "I made two versions. I'm not sure which one I want to send out. I was hoping you would read through both and let me know what you think about each. They're not long. It will only take a few minutes, and I can answer any questions you have. Would you like me to get you a coffee while you go through them?"

"No thanks, I'm fine," she said, holding both documents in front of her and quickly reading a section at a time of one and then the correlating section of the other.

While she read, Keith watched her and took in the lines of her face, how her hair fell to one side as she tipped her head slightly as she read, and the warmth and excitement in her eyes, even though she was reading documents that would be considered boring by most anyone.

"They're mostly the same so far," she said, peeking up to look at him while he watched her. "Exclusive license means they are the only ones we will let use the invention, right?"

"Yes, under whatever rights we own in it," he confirmed.

"Reservation of rights for educational and research purposes means we can still use it?"

"Yes," he replied. "We need to make sure we can still accept research grants and do further research. Companies never mind that and we would insist even if they did."

"What is sublicensing again and why do we need to approve it in writing in this first one and not in the other. Why is it thirty percent of sublicensing fees in the first one and ten percent in the second one?"

"Sublicensing is permission to transfer the license rights to others," Keith replied, recalling his poor attempt to describe the same concept to his son the previous evening. "If my giving you permission to use my computer is a license to use it, then my giving you permission to let other people use my computer is my letting you sublicense that permission to them. Prior written approval allows us to prevent them from giving permission to people we don't want them to or in ways we don't want them to. There are ways to play games with sublicensing that could cut us out of receiving money under the license."

"Okay," she said. "Considerations I know are the payments Tailcrest gets under the license. Here they are broken down in the first version into three one hundred thousand dollar payments as they reach different stages of FDA approval, annual minimum payments and a four percent royalty on sales once they start selling a product."

"That is relatively standard," he said.

"Okay, so why does this other version just say they have to make a single twenty thousand payment on final FDA approval for sale to the public and pay just a one percent royalty on sales. The second one is so much less. I don't know what's normal but one percent of what they sell the product for seems like a very small percentage."

Keith looked down at the Term Sheets. "Yes, the second one is much more favorable to the company."

"The second one also has other things that are more favorable too," she said, reading through several of the sections again while she spoke, "like patent cost reimbursement, future patent rights. From the looks of this one Term Sheet, it looks like a lot is sort of being given away."

"You have identified the nature of my dilemma," Keith said, taking a sip of his coffee. "The second one includes terms that Dennis wants me to use. The first one has terms I would be comfortable using as an opening position with a start-up company before adjusting them during the negotiation."

"So," she said, picking up his coffee cup and taking a sip while looking over the rim at him, "you're not sure if you are going to go with what you want or with the one Dennis wants? He is your boss. Seems like an easy decision."

"One would think so, but there are two other factors. One, Dennis gave his instructions verbally over lunch, and I doubt he would back me up if anyone questioned why the deal was so incredibly generous. The other is that Dale Wade, the Licensee, happens to be a guy I was good friends with back in High School. The deal Dennis wants me to go with will look like I am giving a sweetheart deal to an old friend. That could be bad for me, very bad."

"I see your point," she said. "Have you talked with Dennis about it?"

"Yes, unfortunately I have" he replied. "He thinks it is no big deal and has dropped the whole thing in my lap while telling me he wants me to get it done his way. I am really tempted to do it my way, even if it ticks Dennis off, because my name will be on it. If I go against Dennis, and I might, I will involve you in everything else I do in the office, but not this one anymore. I wouldn't want Dennis' reaction impacting you at all."

She looked sweetly at him and said, "As long as it is everything else you do at the office, I'm completely okay with that."

Keith blushed again because it was clear to him what she meant. She smiled, showing distinct pleasure in being able to trigger this reaction in him. Ginny then started to say something else, but Keith gave her a sharp look and then looked toward the door. Right then Ginny's rather plain looking boyfriend walked up to their table, obviously concerned that they were meeting at the coffee house. Ginny reached up and squeezed her boyfriend's hand when he reached them saying, "Hey babe. Glad you found me. Keith and I were going through these Term Sheets and we're pretty much done. I wanted to leave early so I tracked Keith down here. Keith, do mind if I take off?"

Keith noticed that Ginny's boyfriend's expression turned to one of relief when he heard what she said and saw the papers on the table. "Sure," Keith said, impressed by Ginny's improvisation, before making a point of nodding politely to her boyfriend. "Go ahead. Thanks for your input on the drafts."

Keith picked up his coffee cup and took a sip as the two walked away. While her boyfriend was reaching for the handle of the door to open it for her, Ginny looked back at Keith and winked at him without her boyfriend noticing. Keith watched her until they were out of sight, then thought of his wife and how enraged she would become if she ever found out how he interacted with Ginny. A momentary image entered Keith's mind of his wife going ninja on him and Ginny and violently killing them both. His guilt pangs increased as he leaned back in his chair and drank more of his coffee.

Chapter 35

(Wednesday: 12:20 p.m.)

Keith looked around the coffee house and saw that a group of five college students at a nearby table had observed his interactions with Ginny and the way she had winked at him as she left the coffee house. It was clear to Keith that they were talking about him. The two young women in the group looked at him pleasantly but with matched expressions that he could not read, while the guys in the group looked reasonably impressed. Keith looked at each of them, then smiled innocently and shrugged. This made them smile. He then turned his focus back to the papers in front of him and the dilemma he was faced with.

Keith felt distracted and wished he had more opportunities to interact with the students. He admired their energy and how they seemed so alive. Recalling his own student days at Tailcrest, he thought about how they were all going somewhere, even if they hadn't decided where that somewhere was yet. He then thought about a friend of his from Tailcrest's Law School who had invited him to teach a course on Technology Licensing. He wondered what it would be like walking into a classroom in the Law School he had graduated from as an adjunct professor teaching about the area he practiced in. He knew he was well qualified in the subject area and that putting together a course syllabus was a lot of work, but that he could do it. He also knew that decisions should not be made when someone was under stress, and that he was definitely under stress right then. He decided to continue waiting, at least a few more weeks, before making any commitments on the teaching front.

Keith then collected himself, took a sip of his coffee and pulled his laptop out of his briefcase. First he checked the major news outlets for the news of the day, noting the obvious political bias each exhibited in presenting variations of the same news stories. Then he checked his e-mails and responded quickly to several that were routine or simple inquiries regarding matters being handled by the Technology Transfer Office.

Then Keith picked up the two Term Sheets and scanned through them, not really seeing the words because he already knew their contents completely. Looking at one and then the other Keith said, "Damned if I do, damned if I do, really damned if I don't."

Hearing himself say those words, Keith got a strong feeling that there was something strange about this deal. Keith stopped and thought about the situation and how Dennis had gotten him the "reviewed and approved" stamp and e-mailed Keith that it was his responsibility to get it done after telling him to do it a certain way. Keith concluded that it just wasn't right.

Keith then crafted a cover e-mail to Dale Wade explaining that he was attaching a draft Term Sheet to further the discussions about licensing Dr. Shen's technology into HematoChem and that he understood there were time constraints and looked forward to speaking with him further. Relying heavily on his gut feeling that something was not right, Keith made a decision. He attached an electronic copy of the Term Sheet containing the provisions he thought appropriate, took a deep breath while looking around at the many students, and hit "send" on the e-mail.

Chapter 36

(Wednesday: 12:50 p.m.)

Dale Wade had been out late with his girlfriend the previous evening. Then he had been up even later with her once they had gotten back to her apartment. He hadn't heard her get ready for work or leave. He hadn't heard much of anything until he woke up around eleven thirty that morning in her apartment. After a two mile run through his girlfriend's neighborhood, he showered, left a voicemail for her and then turned on his laptop.

He saw that Keith had sent him an e-mail but did not open it until he took care of all his other messages. Finally opening Keith's e-mail, Dale thought it strange to see professional writing from his old friend. The message was straightforward and he went right to the attachment to see what Keith had put into the Term Sheet.

Scrolling through the Term Sheet he was disappointed to see that it appeared to be exactly like the one that Keith had shown him at his house, even though he had told him portions were unacceptable. Dale understood full well that he did not know enough about this subject area to write even a minimally functional counterproposal. He also knew that even if he could, he wouldn't without sending it to Egorov first because Egorov was actually dictating everything that happened with HematoChem and the negotiations.

Taking a few minutes to read through the entire Term Sheet in detail, Dale then forwarded it along with Keith's e-mail to Egorov. Dale's cover note indicated that he had just received it and that it looked like there were things in it that were very different from what he and Egorov wanted.

Laying back on the couch after hitting "send" on his e-mail to Egorov, Dale felt the anxiety he had somehow been keeping at bay creeping in as he waited for Egorov's reply. Dale was finding this negotiation more and more stressful for a number of reasons. He had been expecting more favorable terms based on his conversations with Dennis Gearin, especially given how close they were to the investor's deadline. He was worried that his situation depended on things mostly beyond his control, particularly securing an agreement acceptable to the University and Egorov within the short time line the investors had given him. He was also worried about Egorov for reasons he did not want to think about.

After about ten minutes waiting without a reply from Egorov, Dale decided to call him. When Dale dialed the number, Egorov answered almost immediately. "Did you get what I sent?" Dale asked without any greeting of other pleasantries.

"Yes, I am making changes to the document now," Egorov replied, sounding like he was paying more attention to the document than the call.

Dale continued, saying, "I looked through it and it looked mostly okay, but it also looked like there where some things that need to be changed."

Egorov sensed Dale's stress and focused his full attention on the call. "You think it is mostly okay only because you are not me, my friend. I see many things that need to be changed, and I will change them. This is the way these things are done. I am making important and not so important changes so that we can give in on some things while getting the things that are very important to us."

"We have basically no time," Dale replied. "Dennis assured me that things would go through smoothly and quickly, but these terms really aren't close to what he described."

"I do not think Dennis Gearin is the obstacle here," Egorov observed. "He has good reasons to give us very favorable terms. I think it is Keith Mastin playing a negotiation game. I have played these games many times before, my friend, and I always win. We will win here too and we will all benefit. I assure you."

Dale was silent for a moment before Egorov continued, saying, "Do not worry about these things. I brought you in and I will make you rich because you are good with people and you communicate very well. I will send you the modified Term Sheet in a few minutes. When I do, you will write an e-mail making it look like you made the changes after a conversation with your investor and you will send it to Keith Mastin and copy Dennis Gearin. Then you will forward to me what you sent. Do you understand?"

"Sure, I get it," Dale replied. "I'll make it look like I was the one who made the changes. I will also stress the time constraints."

"This would be good too," Egorov replied. "Now wait for what I send you."

Dale heard the call end and felt his anxiety building even more. He recalled advice he had received from his former mentor about heading up a start-up company; basically that what is required is tenacity, endless self-confidence and a very strong stomach.

While he waited, Dale thought about how little he actually knew about Egorov; the man who knew so much about so many things and who had provided access to a source of capital for the company. Dale recalled the numerous times he had been amazed by how brilliant he was; whether the subject involved technology, business, finance or anything else. Dale also recalled a look Egorov sometimes got that gave him the creeps, like Egorov was angry and had no sole, and wondered whether it was a mistake for him to have become involved with him at all. Dale's train of thought was interrupted when the e-mail came in with Egorov's modifications to the Term Sheet. There was no cover e-mail and the e-mail account it was sent from was different than the one Dale had sent the earlier draft to, but Dale knew that Egorov habitually used several e-mail addresses concurrently.

Opening and then saving the attachment on his computer, Dale then wrote an e-mail back to Keith, copying Dennis and attaching Egorov's modified document, making it look like he had made the changes himself. He again stressed in the e-mail the need for fast action to get the deal completed. Hitting "send," Dale then quickly forwarded the e-mail to Egorov at both e-mail addresses Egorov had used that day.

Chapter 37
(Wednesday: 1:15 p.m.)

Back at his desk, after taking his time enjoying a julienne salad at one of the dining halls and walking through the Law School, Keith noticed that Dale had already replied to his message, and that the reply had an attachment. Opening it, Keith saw that somehow Dale had already modified the draft Term Sheet and sent it back, copying Dennis. Dale's modified version included extensive, detailed redlined modifications. Keith immediately thought that either Dale had understated his skill in this area or someone else had made the changes. Looking more closely at the detailed wording and nature of the changes, Keith concluded that Dale must have shipped it off to a licensing attorney who was willing to work through lunch. It was clear to Keith that whoever made the changes really knew what they were doing. Keith also knew that Dennis would see the wording that had been changed and be ticked off that Keith had gone with his own way instead of doing what Dennis had insisted on.

Keith barely had time to print the modified Term Sheet before Dennis came into his office carrying his own copy and sat down at Keith's table. "Let's go through this," Dennis said, not showing the anger that Keith expected.

"Sure," Keith replied evenly as he took a seat opposite Dennis. "Their pushback was even more than what you had wanted. There are things we shouldn't accept no matter how important it is for us to close the deal before the end of Tailcrest's fiscal year."

"That's for me to worry about," Dennis replied, somewhat curtly. "Now, the way it looks to me, they pushed back to just about where I had wanted you to position it in the first place and added some things that aren't great but should be acceptable."

"Dennis, they wrote in that we pay for future patenting costs, while they guide the patenting effort, and they only reimburse those costs out of whatever royalties they get from sales of products, if there actually are sales on products," Keith pointed out. "That's like giving them a blank check to spend huge portions of our patenting budget, and we would be contractually obligated to let them spend as much of it as they want, or more than what is actually budgeted. If they insist on filing patents in multiple countries on the current invention or any of the covered future inventions, it could be hundreds of thousands of dollars per invention. Agreeing to that would be nuts."

"For that one we should try for language that says 'reasonable patent costs after consulting with' our office,'" Dennis responded. "That should soften it."

"That really doesn't change anything," Keith countered. "And for the future rights section they changed it to say any future invention of the entire University 'relating to or based on' the inventions covered in the license and that those new inventions would serve as the basis for their having rights to further future inventions 'relating to or based on' those future inventions as well. Their future rights could expand like a funnel and cover researchers other than Dr. Shen. They also extended it to twenty years. Agreeing to this would also be nuts."

"Try to change it to 'relating directly to' and 'based directly on' the invention or improvement inventions to limit what is covered," Dennis said. "That should keep it to a dull roar. Besides, Dr. Shen and his grad students are the only ones working in this area at the University anyway. There really isn't much at stake. Dr. Shen also mentioned to me that Dale had offered him both a consulting contract for his company and money to fund research at Tailcrest once the deal goes through and HematoChem raises money. Tailcrest will benefit in the long run."

Keith realized that he wasn't getting through to Dennis and leaned back in his chair. "I would like to insist on more standard provisions to protect the University's interests," Keith said evenly, trying to mask his feeling of exasperation at the approach Dennis wanted him to take.

"That's not what we are going to do here," Dennis replied, equally evenly. "This deal has to go through quickly. I expect you to write a draft License Agreement based on their version of the Term Sheet, with the adjustments we just discussed, and get it out to them today. There is plenty of time this afternoon. You're quick with these agreements. You just take what's in their version of the Term Sheet and cut and paste its sections into the License Agreement template you wrote with the boiler plate legalese in it, make some adjustments so all the defined terms line up and it will be good to go. You should have no trouble getting it done and out today."

Keith remained silent.

Dennis sensed that Keith was annoyed at being given such a specific directive and affected warmth that was not actually there, saying, "Look, who knows where we will be in five years anyway, and no one is going to be talking about this deal even six months from now. Jason took a few days off to deal with things because of Kaitlin's death and we need to get this done now. Sometimes the agreements won't look exactly like we want them to. That's just practical reality. You need to be more flexible, Keith, if we are going to get anything done."

"I'll get a License Agreement out to them today," Keith said, implying but not stating that he would go along with what Dennis wanted.

"Good," Dennis said before standing and walking out of Keith's office.

Chapter 38
(Wednesday: 1:45 p.m.)

After Dennis left his office, Keith felt highly agitated. He knew that he was a skilled professional capable of exercising independent judgment in furthering and protecting Tailcrest's interests. He also knew that Dennis had authority over the Technology Transfer Office and his actions because he was his boss. Dennis could fire him, and he knew that, if pushed, Dennis would. He also knew that Dennis was directing him to do something he believed was detrimental to the University and possibly to his reputation and his career.

Without offering a word to Carol Keith got up and walked out of his office and out of the office suite thinking that a walk through the campus might calm him down and help him to think clearly. Heading in a direction that would lead him away from their building and Aspen Hall, Keith found himself walking faster than usual and consciously slowed his pace. He then tried to slow his breathing and calm himself down. He found that it worked some but not much. As the path he was walking along brought him past the undergraduate dormitories, he observed students sitting on the grass studying, some alone and some in groups. He saw couples going in and out of the dorms, and guys playing Frisbee, showing off near girls who were pretending to study. Seeing all this, Keith relaxed some. He did not understand why.

Walking a little further to a bench near the paved walkway he was using, Keith sat down and decided to call Sharon. Before dialing her number, he stared at the phone as he thought about what he should say. He thought about how just days ago, with Kaitlin around, this would not have been a problem. He could have used Kaitlin as a backstop, either convincing Dennis that she would never approve the terms he was proposing or by bouncing the Term Sheet to her and letting her block the problematic terms without a word from him. He thought in retrospect that the hassle and delay had been worth not finding himself in the position he was in now. Now it was on him to write the License Agreement and approve it, knowing that Campanaro would simply sign it without even reading or understanding it. Keith started to feel genuine resentment toward Dennis for putting him in this situation, specifically for the way he was directing Keith's efforts without any clear paper trail. He thought it was flat wrong for Dennis to guide his efforts with such specificity and delegate responsibility without giving him actual authority over his actions. It particularly irked Keith to know that, if the deal were criticized, Dennis would literally point to Keith and say, "He's the lawyer," and wash his hands of any responsibility for anything, especially since Keith also knew that at the same time Dennis would take full credit for working another start-up license deal without mentioning Keith's efforts.

Taking a deep breath and taking in the scene in front of the dorms for a little while longer, Keith called Sharon. She picked up on the third ring. "Hello," she said, seeing from the caller ID that it was him.

"I have to make a decision that could affect our family and I want to get your thoughts," he said before continuing without giving her a chance to ask what it is about. "Dennis has put me in a tough spot. He is directing me to send a really bad License Agreement to Dale Wade, and I know he won't back me up. I also think that he will screw with my employment evaluation if I don't do what he wants."

"He's a scumbag and a snake," Sharon said without hesitation. "I've never liked him. I want you to do it your way. If he gives you grief, tell him to put his directives in an e-mail to you or he can bring it to that Jason guy from the Legal Department. He is such a prick."

"I was hoping you would see it that way," Keith said, knowing that dropping the negotiation on Jason wouldn't work because he had taken time off, but feeling very pleased to have Sharon's support and reassurance. "I may be home a little late."

"No problem. I love you. See you when you get home," she said, hanging up the phone.

Looking at his phone, Keith felt amazed at how much better the brief call had made him feel. Walking back toward his office, Keith realized that he had been so wrapped up in his work that he was just now noticing that it was a warm, sunny day like so many he had enjoyed when he was a student living on campus.

Chapter 39

(Wednesday: 4:00 p.m.)

Keith walked back into the Technology Transfer Office suite feeling considerably better than when he had left. He walked straight into his office, waving briefly to Carol as he went by. He closed his door most of the way, which signaled that he wanted to be left alone, signed onto his computer and opened a web link to his favorite local radio station to listen to some music while he worked. Setting the volume low to avoid disturbing Carol, he then pulled up a copy of the License Agreement Template he had created for the office and saved a copy under the file name "HematoChem License Agreement v1."

Keith then hunkered down and set about tailoring the License Agreement, taking a step-wise approach while not really hearing the music coming out of the speakers behind his computer.

He started by filling in the caption section at the beginning of the document, which identified who the parties to the contract were. Then he glanced over the Whereas clauses, which he knew were not meant to include any substantive provisions but which were instead intended to give someone reviewing the agreement a contextual overview of what the contract was about. After entering the patent application filing number and name in the Definitions section, which comprised a list of capitalized words having a specific meaning each time they were used in the agreement, Keith then moved on to the Grant section, which described the nature of the license rights HematoChem would be receiving from Tailcrest.

Keith adjusted the wording of the Grant section just slightly, then saved the changed document and leaned back in his chair while scanning the few changes he had made so far. Taking a deep breath and exhaling before leaning forward over his keyboard, Keith then filled in the Considerations section, which described the money Tailcrest would receive from HematoChem and when Tailcrest would receive it. Keith then reviewed or modified the remaining sections of the License Agreement, including the sections addressing sublicensing, patent cost reimbursement, representations and warranties, indemnification, export control, and the standard boiler-plate provisions.

Keith then paused in his efforts and took a moment to go into the common area of the suite and fill a cup of coffee before returning quickly to his office. Sitting back in his chair, Keith thought about how he had often been teased about "going into the cave" when he worked and how the description might be accurate.

Sipping his coffee while reading the entire License Agreement off his computer monitor, Keith took his time reading every word of the fourteen page document to make sure everything was accurate.

Keith then wrote two e-mails which he knew he would feel good about sending, and which he intended to send out simultaneously. The first e-mail was to Dale and indicated that the attached draft License Agreement was for his consideration and that he appreciated Dale's time constraints and looked forward to meeting with him to go over the details at his earliest convenience. He then typed in Dale's e-mail address, attached the draft License Agreement, and moved on to the second e-mail. The second e-mail was to Dennis and indicated that Keith believed that sending to Dale the attached draft License Agreement was the best way to protect and advance Tailcrest's interests, that it had just been sent to Dale Wade at HematoChem and that he would, in light of the timing relative to the end of the year and its being a start-up company, not object if Dennis wanted to handle the negotiation himself and have the License Agreement reviewed and approved by Jason in the Legal

Department. Keith then entered Dennis' e-mail address and attached the draft License Agreement.

Keeping both draft e-mails and kept open on his computer, Keith moved the cursor over the "send" button of the first e-mail, but then held off, choosing to call Kevin Taft before sending either one.

Chapter 40
(Wednesday: 4:40 p.m.)

Kevin had just gotten home and was near the top of the stairs from his car port to his house when he heard his cell phone ring and saw that it was Keith. "What is it Keith? I'm at home and I'm on a tight schedule," he said, while waving "hello" to his wife and walking toward her. She got up very slowly from the couch to greet Kevin, limited severely by her rheumatoid arthritis.

"Sorry to bother you. I'll be quick," Keith replied. "I just wanted to give you a heads up and do a spot check to make sure I'm doing the right thing."

"Fair enough. Shoot," Kevin said, while giving his wife a very gentle hug, being particularly careful to avoid causing her pain or aggravating the arthritis that had swollen her joints and bent her fingers like a storybook witch, but which had not affected her smile or the warmth in her eyes.

"The short version," Keith continued, "is that Dennis used Kaitlin's death to convince Campanaro to give me review and approval authority over our contracts just like the Legal Department has, and now Dennis is pressuring me to give a sweetheart looking deal to Dale Wade's company so our office's yearly numbers will look good. It counts twice because it is both a start-up company and a technology license."

"What?" Kevin said rhetorically, feeling repulsed by Dennis' apparent attempt to exploit Kaitlin's death.

"Yes," Keith replied. "I now have a 'reviewed and approved' stamp just like Jason from the Legal Department, and the provisions Dennis wants me to put into the License Agreement are pretty terrible and I think they are against Tailcrest's interests."

Dennis thought for a moment while watching his wife cross the distance into the kitchen, then asked, "Is there an e-mail trail where you can object to what Dennis is trying to get you to do?"

"No," Keith responded. "Dennis dumped it on me in an e-mail saying it was my project, but gave me very clear verbal instructions to write the license his way. It's like he's trying to distance himself from it at the same time he's telling me what to do with it."

"That part doesn't really surprise me," Kevin offered. "By micromanaging you this particular way, if people don't like the deal, he can just blame you and somehow not recall what he had instructed you to do. You're definitely in a difficult spot."

"It gets even better," Keith continued. "Even if he put his instructions in writing or wrote the contract himself I would not be okay with approving the provisions he wants in there."

"So what is it you're about to do that you want me to spot check you on?" Kevin asked.

"I just wrote a License Agreement that is more in line with what our office usually does and which goes specifically against what Dennis told me to do. I am about to engage in an act of blatant insubordination by sending it to Dale Wade. Then I am sending it to Dennis with a note saying that this is how I think it should be done and that, if he wants to take it over in light of all the circumstances and have it reviewed by Jason at the Legal Department, that would be okay with me."

"Interesting approach," Kevin said. "Hard for him to go after you for insubordination by claiming that you didn't follow verbal instructions unless he puts those instructions on the table, which would subject those instructions to criticism, which he wouldn't want. And, you will have already focused the issue by sending it to Wade. I think the military expression is that you are putting Dennis in a 'cross rough.'"

"I haven't heard that expression before, but it sounds exactly like what I was thinking in taking this approach," Keith said, not at all surprised that

Kevin would see the underlying strategy. "But, before I hit 'send' and really tick off Dennis, I was wondering if you have heard anything about this deal that would warrant us treating it differently and whether you think what I am about to do is nuts?"

"Well, yes, its nuts," Kevin replied honestly, "but it's probably your best option to avoid being caught in the middle any more than you already are. The only potential complication is that I heard that Jason is taking a few days off to deal with Kaitlin's passing. I doubt he would stay out more than a day or two though. I also heard that Campanaro may be leaving for a vacation soon to recharge before the end of the fiscal year push. I don't know when or for how long."

"So it sounds like you agree that I am in a tough spot and this is a reasonable way to address it?"

"Sure, I think it's your best option," Kevin answered, while sitting on the steps of the stairs that led up to their guest bedrooms, "but what is bothering me is the fact that Dennis would use Kaitlin's death to undermine the Legal Department's role and pressure you. Even for Dennis, that's a bit too much. It is for lack of a better word, scummy."

"That's kind of how Sharon saw it too," Keith added, "only she used the word 'scumbag.'"

Kevin remained silent for a moment watching his wife make tea for both of them. Keith waited, knowing that Kevin sometimes paused like this during conversations while he was thinking. Kevin then took a breath and continued, saying, "It's Dennis' department and he can do what he likes, but I think he may have crossed a line with this. I am glad that you are pushing back. If it kills a bad deal, so be it. He is probably going to be a bastard to you. It's annual evaluation time and he may use that to take a swing at you. If he does, I think you should be direct and clear in your evaluation response and point out how he exploited Kaitlin's death and pressured you verbally. I will mention it to a few people in due time.

This way, if he tries to put you out of your job, he might find that he is mistaken about which way the metaphorical gun is pointed."

"I appreciate that. Thanks," Keith said. "I've kept you too long already. Sorry."

"Not a problem. Keep me posted. And don't worry about your job," Kevin added. "You know someone who owns a big stake in several technology companies that could use your expertise. Take care."

When the line went dead, Keith collected his things so he could make a quick exit, and then hit "send" on each of the e-mails before locking his computer for the evening. Taking a deep breath and feeling good about the approach he was taking, Keith then walked quickly out of his office and toward his car.

Chapter 41
(Wednesday: 6:00 p.m.)

Dale was seated at a table and sipping white wine at a seafood restaurant that Egorov had insisted upon for a meeting to discuss the situation with the University. Dale's earlier light dinner with his girlfriend had been interupted when Keith's e-mail came in with its attached License Agreement. Against his better judgment and his girlfriend's wishes, Dale had opened the e-mail during dinner and scanned through what Keith had written into the agreement. The initial result was that Dale had been distracted during the rest of his meal because portions of the License Agreement bore no resemblance to the terms in the Term Sheet Egorov had modified, and which Dale had sent to both Keith and Dennis. Dale had been instantly troubled when he saw Keith's draft License Agreement because Dennis had called him earlier that afternoon and assured him that Keith would send a License Agreement that looked like Dale's Term Sheet. Bowing to his girlfriend's insistence during the earlier meal, Dale had held off until they had finished their dinner before forwarding the document to Egorov and calling Dennis. Dale was regretting having waited because in the time since then he had not been able to get in touch with Dennis, and he wondered whether he might have been able to catch him if he had called earlier.

Dale noticed that Egorov was late, and recalled that he usually was late for their scheduled meetings, even when, like then, Egorov had suggested the time and place. Taking another sip of his wine, Dale tried again to call Dennis. This time the call went through and Dennis answered.

"Dale, Hi, I see you tried to call several times. I have been away from my phone," Dennis lied, having simply ignored Dale's earlier calls. "I am guessing you want to talk about the License Agreement."

"I am waiting to meet with my primary investor. He could be here any minute. What the hell happened? You told me you would get Keith to deliver a Term Sheet that was at least close to what you and I have been discussing for weeks and he sent me something this afternoon that is totally different."

"I know," Dennis replied. "He sent a copy to me too saying it's what he thinks is best for the University."

"Didn't you tell him what to put in it?" Dale asked.

"Yes, I did," Dennis responded. "This afternoon I told him very specifically to send a draft License Agreement to you based on the wording of the Term Sheet you sent to both him and me. I thought he understood and agreed when he told me he would get a draft license out to you today."

Dale thought of his old friend's habits and said, "If that's what he said, then he was being cute. He did get a draft license out to me today, just not the one you expected."

"There is another issue you might not know about yet," Dennis said with an almost weary tone in his voice.

"What is it?" Dale asked, not sure if he really wanted to know.

"Vice President Campanaro is currently the only one who can sign this agreement, other than President Walker, who simply won't, and I just heard that Campanaro is getting on a plane for a two week vacation either Friday night late or Saturday early. He will be completely off the grid the whole time so he can come back rested for the hellish end of the fiscal year work during the weeks after he returns."

"So what are you telling me?" Dale asked.

Dennis offered the obvious answer to the question, "We have two just over two days to get this deal done and signed by Campanaro, or there will be a two week delay, which would mean your missing the investor deadline you've been all but screaming about. Are you sure there is no flexibility in their timeline?"

"Absolutely sure," Dale responded.

"Look," Dennis said, "I want this deal to go forward just as much as you do. I will lean heavily on Keith tomorrow. His wife doesn't work. Threatening his job should give him all the encouragement he needs. It's also time for annual employment reviews and he knows it, so I am sure I can be persuasive. I may even bring in Dr. Shen to point out how much he wants HematoChem's consulting money for himself and sponsored research money for his lab."

"Keith can be really stubborn if he thinks he's being bullied. Reason and an emotional appeal would probably work best with him," Dale offered. "But it sounds like you have already taken that approach.

"This is the first I have seen of him being inflexible," Dennis replied. "I'll do what I can to get him to adjust his approach and approve something you can work with. You should maybe do whatever you think will work too."

"I have to go. I'll follow up with you," Dale said before hanging up the phone as Egorov walked up to the table and sat down.

"Who was that?" Egorov asked Dale, somewhat presumptively as a waitress walked up and handed them both menus and asked if Egorov wanted anything to drink.

Before Dale could answer Egorov looked at the waitress and said, "Something diet; whatever you have."

As the waitress made a note on her pad and walked away, Egorov looked back at Dale expectantly. "It was Dennis Gearin from Tailcrest." Dale responded. "He is not at all pleased with Keith Mastin's draft License Agreement. He said that Mastin is acting not only on his own but against Dennis' specific instructions. Dennis is going to lean on him tomorrow, maybe threaten his job to make him change it to look like the modified Term Sheet we sent them."

"That would be good," Egorov said, looking over the menu, "because we have done quite a bit to move it along this far and we are very close to running out of time. If this Keith Mastin is permitted to dig in his heels and force too much delay, that would be very bad for all of us. You would agree?"

"Of course," Dale said, not entirely sure what Egorov was implying.

"Good," Egorov said with a harder edge than Dale had expected.

"As I understand it from an earlier conversation with Dennis," Dale said, "Jason from their Legal Department, who could also review the contract, took off for a few days after their General Counsel's accident. It apparently affected him deeply and no one is really sure where he is. But, before that happened, Dennis managed to get Keith Mastin approval authority on the technology transfer contracts. He can't sign them, but, if he approves it and literally stamps and initials it, then their Vice President for Research will sign it, just like if it had been approved by their Legal Department. When Vice President Campanaro signs it, we are all set."

Egorov frowned, "So the only path forward is to get this Keith Mastin to stamp his approval on a License Agreement, and he is fighting his boss because he does not want to sign off on our deal terms. My friend, it looks like the entire effort is going to shit while we wait and do nothing!"

"Not necessarily, but maybe," Dale replied, embarrassed because some people in the restaurant had turned to look at them. "There is still some time, but there is another element we have to factor in to get it done."

"Please tell me," Egorov said sarcastically. "I am in mood for more good news."

"The Vice President for Research, the one who has to actually sign it, he is going on two week vacation and will be unavailable during that time. He is getting on a plane Friday night late or early Saturday, so for us to meet our deadline he has to sign it before he gets on the plane," Dale said in a matter-of-fact manner. He then waited for Egorov's response.

Egorov looked intensely angry for a few seconds, and his expression had a coldness to it that made Dale start to sweat. But then Egorov's expression changed completely. To Dale's astonishment Egorov laughed heartily and then smiled and said, "You impress me. I would not have expected you to be able to say that with such a calm expression."

Dale continued to feel himself sweat, not at all from the temperature but from the feeling he had gotten from the way Egorov had looked at him.

"Perhaps you will talk to Keith Mastin soon," Egorov said, almost cheerfully, "maybe this evening after we enjoy our meal?"

"I'll do that," Dale said, consciously breaking eye contact with Egorov and looking down at the menu.

While Dale studied the menu, Egorov decided what he would order from his near perfect recollection of the menu from his last visit to the restaurant. Before the waitress returned, Egorov had also already thought through several things he intended do to help the negotiation move forward to completion in the very little time they had left to get it done.

Chapter 42
(Wednesday: 7:15 p.m.)

Keith was washing the dishes in his kitchen when he noticed Dale pull up in his car and park on the street in front of his house. Shaking the water off his hands, Keith walked to the screen door by the back porch to tell Sharon that Dale was there. When Keith reached the screen door he saw Sharon holding Chrissy on her lap, reading her picture book with some words while Heather was in the yard easily outmaneuvering Eddy and Thomas with a soccer ball.

"Dale's here. He's going to want to talk about the Hematochem negotiation, and he's probably not very happy about what I sent him," Keith said through the screen door to Sharon. "I am going to need a few minutes without the kids to talk with him."

"We're fine out here," Sharon replied, looking over her shoulder at him. "He doesn't have Dennis with him I hope."

"No. Just him," Keith said as the doorbell rang.

Keith had anticipated that Dale might stop by and was ready to talk with him. Grabbing printouts of the draft License Agreement out of his briefcase while he headed toward the front door, Keith opened the door and welcomed Dale in. "I thought you might stop by. Come on in. Would you like a drink?"

"No thanks, Keith," Dale responded, sounding different and a little harder edged than he had during his previous visits. "I am under the gun and I need to talk with you about the document you sent over. I shared it with my initial investor and we have some real issues with it. Is now a good time?"

Holding up his copies Keith said, "Yes, definitely. I am all set. The dining room is probably best."

Keith sat at the end of the dining room table as Dale sat diagonally across from him. Keith thought briefly about the subtle power politics of who sat where in business meetings and thought it odd to be having a business meeting where he and his family had just enjoyed their evening meal. Dale took out his own copy of the draft license which included hand notes that Egorov had written on it during their dinner meeting. Egorov had used the dinner meeting to mark up by hand a printout of the draft license and to explain what changes he wanted for each section and why, and what concessions they could comfortably make. Egorov had explained to Dale that this should be presented as a "take it or leave it" position for the deal and that they just had to make sure that Keith would take it.

Dale put a copy of the draft license with Egorov's hand notes on the table in front of him. "I have gone over this in detail with my initial investor," Dale said, gesturing to the hand written notes, "and there are real issues that we need to work through to get the deal to a point where he is okay with it, and where my new investors will be okay with it."

Keith remained silent, allowing Dale to lead the discussion.

"First, there are several things that we can accept," Dale said, using the easy "gives" to lead into the "gets." "Patent cost reimbursement. We can pay you for existing patent costs right away. It is not much anyway. We can also reimburse within thirty days for ongoing patenting costs."

"Okay," Keith said, anticipating that these concessions were just a lead in to the more important issues.

"Reporting on a quarterly basis not just on sales activity but also on what we are doing to develop the technology and get regulatory approvals, no problem," Dale said.

Keith remained silent, waiting to see what else Dale would concede on.

Wrinkling his brow, Dale continued, "We can give you HematoChem's corporate formation documents, it's an LLC, and list of owners after the deal is signed. You wrote it in there as upon signature, but it will change almost immediately once the new investors come in. Also, my initial investor is a very private person and he does not want people chasing him down to have him invest in their companies."

"Actually," Keith countered, "I want to see the business formation documents and list of owners before it is signed. I can hold it confidential, but I think it is important for the University to know who it is doing business with."

"How about we come back to that," Dale said. "For sublicensing, it has to be the way we had it in our version of the Term Sheet. Having to get prior written approval for each sublicense would be a deal killer for us. My investor is insisting, and my new investors will insist on unrestricted sublicensing with the Sublicense Agreements surviving termination of the actual License Agreement and the University getting twenty five percent of sublicensing fees. I am going to act in HematoChem's best interests to make money, and Tailcrest would get twenty five percent of that sublicensing money. That should be okay, and I don't see any problem with it."

"I do," Keith responded. "What if your new investors get majority ownership in HematoChem, replace you, and then sublicense the rights to one of the other companies they have invested in for, say, a dollar, leaving both you and us out in the cold?"

Dale paused, then continued, "There has to be some other wording to address that without making us get your written approval every time, but let's come back to that too."

"We can add that our approval will not be unreasonably withheld and that we only have thirty days to review each one, but prior written approval is something I am going to insist on," Keith added.

"How about an easy one," Dale said, offering a hopeful smile. "The wording we want for export control just says we will comply with all laws for exporting the technology and you will comply with all laws for exporting technology. That makes good fair practical sense."

"Devil is in the details," Keith responded.

"I don't understand why you would have a problem with our version," Dale said, feeling exasperated. "Ours should be fine. You put in wording that requires as a condition of the license that we will ensure that all technology you provide us will be received by a U.S. citizen or permanent resident and that we will perform export searches and get export licenses. We can't even give the technology to our own employees until we have gotten necessary approvals. That seems kind of ridiculous. Even our own employees who are covered by confidentiality agreements saying they cannot disclose anything to anyone outside of HematoChem? You have to be willing to be flexible on this one."

"Unfortunately no," Keith replied. "This one is actually sort of important. I have been told that transferring technology to non-U.S. citizens is a 'deemed export' which is treated just as seriously as shipping the technology oversees. The quirk, as I understand it, is that if we send technology to a U.S. company knowing that a foreign national will be receiving it, we have to apply for the export license with the U.S. Department of State or U.S. Department of Commerce. The wording I put in there puts the burden on you and protects us. And I think it is fair because you would be the ones hiring and managing any foreign national employees."

"I think I followed that," Dale said, realizing that he was not making any progress.

Keith saw his friends look of frustration, "Dale, even though this is 'business,' I am not trying to screw your company. I want to put this deal through on terms I can sign my name to."

"I get that," Dale replied. "But I have to get this deal done in a way my investors are okay with, apparently in the next two days, or it's my ass. I have committed a lot of my time to this and I have a lot riding on it."

"I understand your point," Keith said.

Moving to the next hand note on Dale's printout, Dale said, "How about future invention rights? My investor is adamant about using the wording in our version of the Term Sheet where we get future inventions in this field. It is very, very important to him. Can you explain your version?"

"What I put in there is that any inventions made by the same inventor, to the extent not covered by other contracts, during the next five years will be included under the license if they are covered by the current patent rights."

"Exactly," Dale said, wrinkling his brow. "Is there an English translation of that?"

"Sure," Keith replied, realizing that he had unintentionally talked over Dale's head. "A patent for a drug or compound covers all uses of that drug or compound. But, a new use of that drug or compound can potentially also be patented. So that new invention would be an invention in its own right but would also be blocked or 'covered' by the earlier patent on the drug or compound. The wording I put in gives you rights to that type of invention by the same inventor for five years. It is probably more than most universities will give you."

"I followed that, but there is no way it is going to fly with my investors." Dale looked stressed and frustrated and wasn't showing any of the warm charm that usually filled any room he was in.

Keith saw Dale's stress. "The deal I am offering is probably better than market rate and quite reasonable. If anything, the fees and royalties I put in are too low and the due diligence obligations are too minimal. At some point I am going to be called out to explain why the terms I put in there are so generous to HematoChem, and I feel terrible about the position it puts you in."

Dale's expression had changed some and Keith saw that there was growing anger mixed in with his frustration. "Look, I am in a tough spot and so are you," Dale said with a harder edge to his voice. "We may be at an impasse, but do you want to be the one who explains to Dennis and everyone else that the deal fell through because you got hung up on a few items. The goal for us is to get a deal our investors can live with. The goal for you is to get licenses and money for Tail-U. How about we all focus on the goal and put this through with the terms my investors can accept. We'll even add another twenty thousand dollars as an upfront payment before your fiscal year ends"

Keith felt bad for his friend but was going to stand his ground. He also recalled how Dale's anger back in High School could sometimes be explosive, so he decided it was time to end the meeting. Keith stood up and picked up his papers as a cue, and said, "I agree that we are at an impasse. Hopefully your investors will see the value in the terms I put in there."

"This really sucks," Dale said, while collecting his things and walking with Keith toward the front door.

"I agree," Keith said, as he opened the door. If it would help for me to speak with them directly in a meeting, I would be fine with that if you can arrange it."

"I'll let you know on that, but it's unlikely," Dale said. "Chances are we'll send you a draft license as a counter-proposal later tonight or tomorrow morning. I'm sure we'll talk more in the next few days."

"Bye Dale," Keith said before closing the door.

Keith felt terrible about the position Dale was in but he was equally sure that he was doing the right thing. He didn't realize how long he had been standing by the door thinking about the situation until Sharon had walked up behind him and held Chrissy out past his shoulder so he would see her big eyes looking at him. Seeing Chrissy, Keith made a silly face, and Chrissy giggled and pulled back toward Sharon. That looked really tense through the window," Sharon said.

"It was," Keith replied. "Dale is in a really tough situation and so am I. I guess this is why we make the not so big bucks," Keith said.

"Things work out. You and Dale will stay friends. Whatever happens with Dale's company will happen. Relax and come outside," she said, tugging gently on his shirt. "The boys are really active and, if we don't give Heather a break, she might collapse in a miniature heap."

"Okay, okay," he said, realizing that Sharon's encouragement and her petite joke about Heather had helped cheer him up.

Chapter 43
(Thursday: 7:45 a.m.)

Keith arrived at his building on campus earlier than usual in hopes of taking care of some administrative matters before all hell broke loose with Dennis because of the position he was taking on the negotiation with HematoChem. Walking down the corridor toward the Technology Transfer Office's suite, Keith paused and took a deep breath when he saw that the outside door was already open and the lights were on. Walking through the office suite's common area toward his own office, he saw that his office door was open as well and that Dennis was sitting at his work table with Dr. Shen.

"Good morning," Keith said cheerfully to both men as he walked past them, sat in his desk chair and swiveled around to face them from across his desk. "Things are going okay with the negotiation with HematoChem, but they are insisting on terms I cannot accept. So, while I remain hopeful, unless they come around on some things that are really not acceptable, the negotiation may be delayed or even collapse. I know you both really want this to go forward, but I can't sign off on things that are bad for the University. I presume that is what you are in my office to talk about."

There were several seconds of complete silence in the room. Dennis broke the silence while speaking in an even but clearly angry tone, "I got a voicemail from Dale Wade last night saying that he met with you and that you were being intransigent on everything. He went on to say that there was no way his investors would accept the terms you wanted. And from what you sent out and copied me on yesterday I am not surprised at his reaction. I told you specifically to be more accommodating so we can get this deal done."

"Dennis," Keith said, "like I said, they are insisting on things that are completely unacceptable. I would like to be accommodating, especially since Dale is an old friend of mine, but there are things the University simply should not do. Signing on to the terms they want would be in that category."

Dennis' expression turned more angry as he said, "I am the Director of Technology Transfer and I decide what deals go forward and on what terms. I told you to be more accommodating and you are being insubordinate."

"I respect your role," Keith responded. "I have no problem with writing a draft license with any provisions you put in writing in an e-mail to me. I have done that many times. Before Kaitlin's death, either I would negotiate and write the license and then send it to Legal for review and approval, or you would negotiate terms and then give them to me in writing and I would write the license and send it to Legal for review and approval. Here it is different though."

"I don't see any difference here," Dennis snapped at Keith. "I want you to do the deal like I said."

Keith noticed that Dennis was choosing his words carefully, and this reaffirmed for Keith that Dennis was trying to be slick with him. Instead of replying Keith chose silence as his answer.

After a long and awkward silence, Dr. Shen spoke up. He was clearly concerned that the deal might be in trouble and angry at Keith because he believed that Keith was just being difficult, based on what Dennis had told him. "I invented this technology and I should have a say in what happens with it."

"I agree completely," Keith replied earnestly. "My understanding is that you want us to license the technology to HematoChem and that is what we are trying to do."

"Let me be clear," Dr. Shen said to Keith, his frustration and anger showing more in his face. "There are not many opportunities to have one's invention licensed to a company. I receive forty percent of whatever the University receives under the License Agreement based on Tailcrest's invention policy. I have a financial stake in your getting this deal done. I want you to do what Dennis says and have the deal signed. He is your boss and you should do what he says. If anyone in my lab acted like you, I would fire them. If this deal falls through, I am going to contact everyone who will listen to me in the Administration, and the Deans, and tell them how much of an obstructionist you are and why the deal failed."

Keith had not expected Dr. Shen to be so assertive, and he tried to be understanding and patient. He surmised that Dennis had primed him somewhat. "I am only going to sign off on deals that are good for the University. Kaitlin would have flatly refused to sign what they proposed and would have insisted on terms more stringent that what I have proposed. I am not being in any way unreasonable."

Dr. Shen was not even slightly deterred. "You are standing in the way of my being able to receive a portion of royalties under the license, and HematoChem and I are working through a consulting agreement where I will be working as a paid technical advisor. Your refusing to sign off on this license will cost me a lot of money. It's not your money you're playing with. Also Dale Wade told me HematoChem will want to do funded research at the University through my lab as the commercialization effort goes forward. I would not be Principle Investigator managing the funded research because of conflicts of interest, but a colleague of mine would. Our lab and the University could receive substantial amounts of money in grants. You are holding that up too. How do you think Vice President Campanaro would view Tailcrest losing out on hundreds of thousands of dollars of sponsored research funding because you decided to get in the way of a deal your boss told you to sign off on."

"The consulting and sponsored research funding are not news to me," Keith said calmly. "It doesn't change anything about the acceptability of the terms or what I can sign off on, but it would certainly be a positive outcome."

Dennis chimed in, "It certainly would be a positive outcome, and it is another good reason to accommodate Dale's position on the license. Dr. Shen is also absolutely right about how Campanaro would view lost funding for sponsored research."

"Like I said," Keith countered, 'it doesn't change the acceptability of the terms."

Dennis seemed even more angered by Keith's response. Leaning more forward toward Keith, Dennis said in a serious tone, "I hope you appreciate what you are doing in holding up this deal and what it means to our office, to Dr. Shen, to the University and to your continued employment here in our office. I had every intention of giving this one to Jason in the Legal Department. Dale and I had talked about it, specifically about having Jason review it because he is more flexible than Kaitlin was, but instead I saw an opportunity to let you expand your role and get our office more freedom from the Administration's bureaucracy. I didn't have to do that. If I had given it to Jason without expanding your role, it would have been done by now. You blow this one and that stamp goes away and our office has to go back to dealing with the Legal Department and jumping through whatever hoops they want."

Keith thought for a moment; then said, "There is a solution in what you just said. You put in writing to me the changes you want made. I make the changes and send it back, noting my objections. Then you bring it to the Legal Department and get Jason to sign off on it. This way, it gets approved, if Jason will actually sign his name to it, which I doubt, and nothing else changes. The other solution is that we continue to negotiate. Hopefully they will come to their senses and accept deal terms that are reasonable, or at least minimally acceptable from the University perspective."

"There are some things you should know," Dennis replied through gritted teeth, "First, I don't appreciate being told to put things in writing. Second, Jason took several days leave to deal with Kaitlin's death and he did not tell anyone where he was going. He is not responding to cell calls, e-mails or texts. Apparently he is pretty broken up about it. The third thing is that Vice President Campanaro is catching a flight out on Friday night for a two week break before the end of the fiscal year crunch. He will be unavailable during that time. Today is Thursday. Friday night is tomorrow night. Since Dale's investor deadline is, I think, Monday, that means you have two days to 'come to your senses' and get this deal done and signed by Campanaro."

Keith looked sternly at Dennis for a long second, then said, "Something is not right about this."

Before Keith could say anything further, Dennis said to Dr. Shen, "Let me walk you out."

As the two men stood to leave, Dennis looked at Keith with an expression Keith could not read, and said, "Just get it done."

Keith kept an even expression when Dr. Shen gave him an openly scornful look while he was leaving Keith's office.

Thinking that the meeting could have gone worse, Keith remained in a good mood while making instant coffee using hot water from the water cooler and one of the Tailcrest University mugs he kept in his desk. He noticed that Dennis had left the office with Dr. Shen and guessed that he would not be back for a while.

Chapter 44
(Thursday: 8:15 a.m.)

After the difficult meeting with Dennis and Dr. Shen, Keith took a moment to appreciate the quiet and stillness while sitting at his desk alone in the office suite. He then walked to his window and looked out over the students heading to their classes. "So many students," Keith thought to himself, half-wishing he could be one of them again. After a minute or so watching the students he smiled, realizing that he was mostly checking out the really attractive females among the many students outside. Finding amusement in his own behavior and the fact that the University was affectionately known as Tail-U, Keith stepped away from the window, thinking that he should get started on his work.

Sitting back down at his desk, Keith logged onto his computer and scanned his e-mails. He immediately saw that Dale had sent an e-mail with an attachment late the previous evening. Seeing that it had been sent close to eleven thirty at night, Keith wondered whether Dale had gotten an attorney to work late into the night or if, possibly, his initial investor had worked on it. Opening the attachment and reading through a few of the red-lined modified sections, it was clear to Keith that the changes had been made by someone very skilled in crafting legal wording and that the changes were probably well beyond Dale's capabilities. This made Keith suspect more strongly that Dale's initial investor was giving Dale considerable intellectual capital in addition to his investment capital.

Sipping his coffee, Keith hit "print" and waited for Dale's version of the draft license to print out. He knew he would not be able to accept their version, just from the small sections he had read through, but he also knew he had to review every detail.

After spending quite a while reading every word of Dale's version, including the portions that were not redlined as having been changed, Keith leaned back in his chair, having observed, as he expected he would, that Dale's version was unacceptable for numerous reasons. Keith concluded that they were at a true impasse, that the deal would likely fall apart, and that he would be blamed for it.

Setting the printout aside to work on the other administrative matters he had come in early to try to take care of, Keith took a moment to reread Dale's cover e-mail. Dale was quite stark and clear in how he expressed that these were the necessary deal terms for the license to move forward and how he hoped Keith would reconsider his intransigence and be flexible enough to let the deal move forward so that everyone could benefit. Keith knew that Dale was saying "take it or leave it" without actually using those words.

Keith felt compelled to answer Dale's email, so he wrote a quick response. In it Keith thanked Dale for sending over their draft and indicated that they were still quite far apart on many of the deal terms and that much of what they were proposing was unacceptable. He also put in the e-mail that, if Dale was willing to be flexible regarding the University's requirements, then he would be more than willing to accept the changes he could agree to as incorporated into his earlier draft License Agreement and to meet with him to discuss how to find areas of agreement in the very short time frame created by HematoChem's funding requirements. Keith was careful to make it professional and polite, and also clear that Dale was being intransigent regarding the University's requirements, at least as Keith viewed it. Keith then adjusted the draft license he had sent Dale the previous day to incorporate those of Dale's changes he could accept, attached it to his he reply e-mail and hit "send."

Keith then took care of his other e-mails and administrative matters. He read several confidentiality agreements and two material transfer agreements that Carol had put together and negotiated. Finding Carol's agreements acceptable, he stamped each "reviewed and approved" and initialed them, using his stamp for the first time. Using the stamp felt strange to him. After initialing his approval on each of the agreements, Keith twirled the stamp between his fingers, thinking that it was remarkable how something so small could be a source of so much stress.

Having caught up on his work Keith leaned back in his chair and sipped more coffee. Noting the time, Keith realized that while he was having his challenging discussion with Dennis and Dr. Shen, Sharon was undergoing her CT scan to see if there was any physical basis for her migraines. He knew that he should have insisted on going with her to the appointment, but he also knew that she was right about Dennis' possibly using his excessive leave time against him in his evaluation. She had told him earlier that morning to focus on his work and that she would call him on his cell phone when she was done. Keith thought that Sharon probably should have been done with the appointment by then and wondered why she hadn't called. Putting down the urge to call and possibly interrupt her appointment, he put his cell phone on his desk and looked at it, waiting for it to ring.

For several minutes Keith replayed in his mind the progression of Sharon's disease while he stared at the phone on his desk. Pulling his awareness back into the present, he reminded himself that her migraines were just one of the symptoms and that many people had migraines. He also acknowledged to himself that he was trying to block out what he was really worrying him, specifically that the CT scan might show that her disease was something life threatening like cancer. Taking a deep breath, he then drank the rest of his coffee and noticed that his hand was shaking. It occurred to him then that he really was afraid of what the CT scan might show.

Chapter 45
(Thursday: 8:45 a.m.)

Keith saw no point in sitting there in his office stressing while he waited for Sharon's call. He decided to go for a walk instead and picked up his cell phone as he got up from his desk. He hadn't heard Carol come into the office suite but noticed her in her cubicle as he walked by. "I am waiting on a call from Sharon," he said, holding up his cell phone as he went by. "I'll be back in a while."

Carol looked up from her work and gave a quick wave before going back to what she was doing.

Keith left the building and headed toward a section of campus he had not been to in a while. The place he had in mind was near several dormitories and had a man-made lake with a bridge to a small island with benches that he used to visit quite often. Today he felt that he wanted the familiarity of that scenic part of campus.

Keith allowed his stress to hasten his pace and he quickly reached the walking bridge to the little island. He paused at the top of the arched walking bridge to take in the view. The dormitories and a dining hall were all connected. A grassy courtyard fronted the structure, and students made almost constant use of it. The dormitories and the courtyard all faced a man-made lake that covered about three acres, and which was a well-disguised part of the drainage and water management system, complete with large weeping willow trees along the shore. The result was a beautiful collegiate scene.

Keith had been leaning on the rail of the bridge for some time when his cell phone rang. Seeing that it was Sharon he answered quickly, choosing to use humor to cover his stress. "Hi Sharon," he said. "Any new telepathic powers from the CT scan?"

"Wow, what planet are you on?" she replied. "It was just a CT scan."

"Is the CT scan the one where anything metal can be pulled into the tube like a bullet?" he asked, trying to keep it light.

"No, that's an MRI," she replied, "which uses big magnets. This was just a CT scan, which I think is like a bunch on thin sliced x-rays stacked up. But you know this stuff better than I do. You're just messing with me, aren't you?"

"Of course I am," he answered. "So how was it?"

"It was just like the last one I had, only this time I waited and waited. Then I had the scan and I drove home."

"I should have called before I left, but then I was driving. Then I got talking with Heather, and then I was taking care of the kids. Now I feel really bad that I made you wait and didn't call you sooner."

"I was really stressing," he said.

"Ouch, sorry," she replied, feeling bad that she had forgotten to call.

"Did they give you any feedback on the scan?" Keith asked.

"No, actually," she said. "It was just the technicians. The scan will be read by a doctor in the next few days. We'll get the results at my appointment next week."

"So there is no news at all, other than nothing having been sucked into the tube because CT scans don't do that?"

"Well, there were two weird things, but they're not related to the scan, unless the scan is making me hallucinate."

"It's those new telepathic powers," he joked.

"Seriously, it was just after Heather left. The phone rang and I answered it thinking it was either you or my mom, but it was a guy who said 'Tell him to knock it off, now.' That was all that the guy said before he hung up."

"Did you check the caller ID?" Keith asked.

"Yes, the number showed up as blocked."

"Could have been a wrong number," Keith said, thinking out loud. "Didn't sound like Dale, did it? No, that would be unthinkable. He's just not like that. What did the guy sound like?"

"Hard to describe," she replied. "It was definitely not Dale. It just sounded like a guy. That's not the really weird part though."

"That's not weird enough? What else happened?"

"This is the part where I am not sure if I am imagining things," she said. "It was barely a minute after the call. I noticed a man walking past the house and I swear he stopped right in front of our house and turned toward the house and looked at each of the windows and then started walking again. I have never seen this guy before in my life and I only saw him for a few seconds but it was really weird, especially right after the call. Maybe I was just weirded out because of the scan and the call. People walk by every day. Maybe he knew the previous owners. I don't know. It was just strange."

"How long ago was this?" Keith asked.

"A while ago; I am not sure," Sharon responded. "I am making the kids play inside and I'm keeping the doors locked just to make myself feel better, even though I think I am being ridiculous."

"How about I come home right away," Keith offered. "I'm not kidding. There are crazy people out there."

Sharon thought his offer was sweet but declined, saying, "I think the only crazy person around here is me. I am sure it's nothing. I am stressed about the scan and your problems with Dennis and my Mom's attitude and lots of other things. What are the chances that I am going to think something is weird right after I get back from having my head examined? Pretty good I think."

"At least your sense of humor is intact," Keith said, looking at the ripples in the water below him. "You sure you're okay? I would like to come home, no matter how much crap Dennis will give me."

"No," she insisted. "You stay there and deal with Dennis. I'll guard our castle from curious pedestrians."

"Okay," he said, "but do me a favor and turn on the internet video surveillance system we put in when you first got sick. I would feel better if I could see from my computer, at least the parts of the house that are visible from the mini-cameras."

"I will, but if the kids are in another room I might flash you," she said playfully.

"I would like that, but please don't. There are things I would rather Dennis and Carol not see if they happen to come into my office. Actually, as much as I prefer not to have to deal with your mother, you could take the kids there for the day until it's time for me to come home."

"Now you're the one being silly," she said. "I will stay with the kids here until you get home. We'll just spend the day inside. No big deal. Now get back to work. I'll talk to you later."

"Okay, Bye."

Keith felt like his capacity for worrying was being stretched past its limits while he put his phone in his pocket and walked further along the footbridge toward the tiny island.

Taking his time walking around the island and then back to his office, Keith wondered if his wife actually had hallucinated about the man looking at the house. He knew the windows were sort of mirrored, so a passerby might find the reflections interesting even though they could not see in. He had, however, never seen anyone do that in all the years he had lived in the house, and he knew that stress and extreme sleep deprivation could make people hallucinate. When his office building came into view, he thought about the negotiation with HematoChem and briefly entertained the thought that the call could be linked to the negotiation. He quickly dismissed the thought as ridiculous.

Chapter 46
(Thursday: 9:10 a.m.)

Standing in her living room, after hanging up with Keith, Sharon felt like she was being hugely paranoid while she watched her boys watching television. She knew the call was probably meant for someone else, and that the guy who walked by was probably just a guy walking by. She was also a protective mom though, and she hadn't let her sons out of her sight since seeing the man outside. This had been easy for her because not much time had passed and Eddy and Thomas never minded watching kid's shows.

Sharon then went into the computer alcove near the front door of their house, while still keeping the children in sight, and turned on their computer. While the computer was coming on she took out her cell phone and called Heather, who had left earlier to take Chrissy to a well visit doctor's appointment. "You aren't in with the doctor, are you?" Sharon asked when Heather answered the phone.

"No, we are just waiting here in the well-baby waiting room," Heather answered. "I like the way this doctor's office has two waiting rooms, one for well visits and one for sick visits. Make's me almost comfortable enough to let Chrissy play with the toys they have set out."

"I noticed you said 'almost,'" Sharon said, teasing her friend because of her germaphobic nature when it came to Chrissy.

"She's just comfortable on my lap. If she wants to play with the toys, I'll think about it," Heather replied, chuckling lightly.

Sharon then jumped right into the reason for her call. "I had two really strange experiences right after you left, which were probably nothing, but which were still, well, weird."

"What happened?" Heather asked.

"First I got a call and it was some guy who said 'tell him to knock it off, now' and then hung up."

"That must have felt creepy," Heather said as she shifted Chrissy from one knee to the other.

"Then, like a minute later I saw a guy walking past our house stop right in front of it, turn fully toward the house and then look at each of the windows before turning back and continuing to walk past. It was probably just a guy looking at the house while he was out for a walk, but seeing that right after the call felt really unsettling to me."

"I can see why," Heather replied. "Everything is probably fine, but those two things together would weird anyone out. Did anything else happen?"

"Other than my locking the doors and calling Keith, no," Sharon answered. "I'm stressed about the CT scan and Keith's work and so many other things that I'm probably just losing it a little bit. Still, if there was some creepy guy watching our house, he might have seen you and Chrissy. And who knows, there are some really strange people out there."

"Then it's our responsibility to be even stranger," Heather said, trying to make her friend laugh.

"Sure, okay," Sharon said, smiling at the attempt at humor. "Let's team up and stalk some guys while they're doing yard work."

"Actually," Heather said, smiling at the thought, "that could be fun. Of course it would be hard for us to be menacing while they're inviting us in for a drink."

"Thanks," Sharon said.

"For what?" Heather asked.

"I feel better," Sharon replied.

"Good, because I have to go," Heather replied. "We're being called in."

"Okay, bye," Sharon replied.

Turning toward the computer Sharon searched for the program that would turn on the internet video surveillance system. It had been quite a while since they had used it, and it did not have its own icon on the screen. She went to the "all programs" section and tried to remember its name. While she was searching she remembered how she had first met Kevin Taft the day he had come home with Keith to install this program and set up the tiny cameras. She recalled that he was a little older and not a very large man; and that he had a very self-confident manner and was consciously gracious. She also recalled that he had spent quite a while setting up the software and installing the impossibly small cameras that day. What she remembered most about that day was his surprising answer when she asked how he knew so much about surveillance equipment. She had figured he would say that he had a similar system in his own house or that he was a technology buff or something like that. She had been taken aback when he answered that one of the companies he owns sells state of the art surveillance equipment to the military and private security firms. She had been similarly surprised later on when she learned from Keith that Kevin had neglected to mention anything to him about his owning a surveillance technology company, and that he had only told Keith that he had an extra system and insisted they take it because he had no use for it.

Finding the program, Sharon opened it, entered the very basic password they had set up and clicked the activate button on the screen that turned the system on. She then closed out of that program and went to a news website to check out what was going on in the world outside while she, Eddy and Thomas were spending the day inside until Keith got home.

Chapter 47

(Thursday: 12:30 p.m.)

Keith had spent the last hour in his office watching his family on the internet surveillance system Sharon had activated. He had not intended to spend that much time watching them, but, once he had opened the site on his computer and set it to display on his monitor, he could barely pull himself away. The twelve squares in the window on his screen showed most of the interior of his house; and in two of them were his family. Other than a few interactions with Carol and making coffee, Keith had watched continuously. Part of the draw was that every now and then Sharon would look at the nearest camera and wave like she knew Keith was watching. Mostly, he was just anxious and felt compelled to watch over his family, even if it was just images of them on a computer screen.

It had been mostly a slow e-mail day until Dale's newest e-mail came in. Keith opened it and saw that it had as an attachment the same version of the license that Dale had sent previously. Keith was surprised to see that the cover e-mail Dale had sent to him was rude to the point of being unprofessional and went on to list everything Tailcrest might lose if Keith did not stop being "intransigent." Keith also saw that the e-mail copied in Dennis. There was no question in Keith's mind that Dale's strategy was straight forward pressure. This aggravated Keith enough that he thought that writing an immediate reply would be a bad idea because he hoped to stay positive and professional regardless of how rude or aggressive Dale became. Instead of responding right away, he decided to call Sharon and tease her about the way she had been waving to him through the cameras.

When he dialed his home number, Keith saw Sharon walking from one room to another to answer the phone. "Hello," she said on the third ring.

"I am watching you," he said, using his normal voice so as not to alarm her. "You're standing in the kitchen right now."

"You are, are you? Have you been watching us all morning?"

"I did peak in now and then," he fibbed, "at least enough to see you wave a few times."

"Sure," she replied, not believing him. "You've had it up your screen the whole time like you used to do, haven't you?"

"Maybe," he said. "It has made for some interesting viewing. Especially the way you have been waving every few minutes the whole time."

"Why aren't you out getting lunch?" she asked.

"I'll get to it," he said, "but first I have to e-mail Dale back. His most recent e-mail to me was strategically rude and I wanted to talk to you to cheer me up so I can reply without matching his rudeness. It would be bad form and eventually used against me by somebody. So I am calling to say 'hi.'"

"So basically you are using me for your own purposes, not concerned about cheering me up at all, just wanting to make yourself happy so you can work more effectively."

"Yes. Talking to you makes me happy, and I wanted to feel happy," he said sweetly.

"Good recovery," she replied, knowing that he knew that she loved it when he said sweet things in the middle of their bantering. "So you think you feel good enough to write back to Dale yet?"

"Almost," he answered. "How are you doing after this morning?"

"Still weirded out some, but I feel better. No more calls, except some mystery caller who said he was watching me."

"Maybe this new mystery caller has been waiting for you to flash him."

"Oh really?" she asked while turning toward the camera and quickly lifting her shirt and bra and then pushing them down again. "That's all you get for now."

"Okay, that's more like it!" he said, feeling much better than he had before. He knew how modest she was and what it must have taken for her to do that.

"You realize that I am going to be watching the monitor all day hoping that you are going to do that again," Keith said, grinning at her surprising move.

"Not a chance," she replied. "Now go write a polite e-mail telling Dale off and then get some lunch. I want to get back to the kids."

"Okay, talk to you later," he said, watching her wave to the camera and then flash her chest at him one more time before she walked back in by the children.

Feeling upbeat and amused by Sharon's antics, Keith opened a blank e-mail and attached his version of the draft license to it. He then wrote a polite and professional message saying that the attached draft license is one that he can approve and that he cannot approve the changes Dale had requested. He also said in it that if they could accept his version they could have an agreement signed very quickly, but otherwise he would be pleased to discuss ways to move forward in securing an agreement. He then copied Dennis on the e-mail and hit "send."

Chapter 48

(Thursday: 4:00 p.m.)

Keith filled the quiet afternoon reviewing patent related correspondence and billing statements forwarded to their office by their outside counsel patent attorneys and occasionally looking out the window at the campus and the students walking by. Keith had come to half-regret having initiated a policy where any correspondence between their outside law firms and the patent office had to be copied to their office so they would have a record of what was sent back and forth, and so that he could review what they were doing. This gave Keith a solid understanding of the patenting efforts for Tailcrest's inventions and allowed him to answer inventors' questions easily. The downside was that there was a lot of complex, heavy reading that made the minutes pass by more slowly. Just as Keith was picking up the last Office Action from the U.S.P.T.O. to review, Dennis stepped into Keith's office and asked him curtly, "Have you approved the license yet?"

Keith concluded from the question that Dennis had not yet read the e-mail Keith had sent out earlier. Putting the office action back down on his desk, Keith braced himself for some unpleasant treatment and decided to choose his words carefully. "I sent them a license that I can approve earlier today, but I haven't heard back from them yet. Hopefully they will allow the agreement to go forward. I would really like the deal to be completed," he said, knowing that Dennis would be very bothered by the underlying message. "You were copied on the e-mail. I sent is around lunch time today."

"I'll read it," Dennis said tersely, before walking out of Keith's office.

Keith piled up his folders of correspondence from the patent office because he knew Dennis would be back shortly and he would have little chance to go through the remaining material or even put it away. Keith barely had time to straighten the stack of folders before Dennis was back in his office looking very angry. "I read it and it looks like your telling Dale off."

"I did no such thing," Keith contested. "You must be misinterpreting what I wrote. I was careful to be professional and polite."

"It's the meaning of the message you sent more than the actual words you used," Dennis said. "I told you to get it done and instead you are killing the deal by insisting on things they have made clear they cannot accept because of their investor's requirements."

"I am being entirely reasonable in the negotiation," Keith replied, "and they are insisting on things that are totally unacceptable. I sent them a draft license that I can okay on behalf of the University with no problem. I also invited discussion, but they have not replied yet."

"You know exactly what you are doing," Dennis said louder than Keith had ever heard him speak. "Your evaluation will definitely reflect your lack of cooperation and inability to come to terms on this deal. I handed this one to you and made it your responsibility, and you are refusing to approve a decent License Agreement because you are objecting to a few terms that shouldn't warrant you blocking it."

"You entrusted me with it and you are welcome to take it back," Keith shot back. "You approve it and get someone from Legal to sign it. I am not putting my name on their version with what is written in it. They have my version, which they should be able to accept. This is just another negotiation, so let me negotiate it or take it back."

Dennis was incensed by the way Keith was speaking to him and got red in the face. He then yelled at Keith for the first time ever, "If this deal falls through, you better polish your resume. It's on you and you'll have to account for your actions."

"You know what," Keith said, managing not to shout back, "my wife had a CT scan today and I came in here to take care of this instead of going with her, even though she's stressed out and not feeling well. I have lots of personal time stored up. I'm taking my laptop and the file with me so I can take care of her and my kids and get the deal done in a way that works for the University. Like I said, take it back or let me do it."

Dennis was shocked at Keith's response and calmed himself down with some effort. "Just get it done, even if it means signing off on their version," Dennis said firmly before leaving Keith's office, entering his own office, and closing his door.

Keith and Dennis did not notice but Ginny had come into the office and was in her cubicle listening to the exchange between Dennis and Keith. On hearing the back and forth, she was surprised at how heated it became and thought it was probably good that Keith had chosen to leave her out of this part of the negotiation. After Dennis went into his office and closed the door, Ginny stood up and walked just inside Keith's office doorway. He noticed her standing there and paused, offering her a warm look while wondering how much of the exchange with Dennis she had heard. She gave him a supportive smile. He couldn't help but smile back at her. "How much of that did you hear?" he asked quietly.

"All of it," she answered softly while smiling more broadly at him and tilting her head slightly. She then made a twisting gesture with her hand and whispered the question, "Would you like me to lock the door for a quickie?"

Keith blushed at her question and couldn't help but grin. He then whispered his answer, "I have to go."

Ginny was obviously pleased by the reaction she had triggered but disappointed that he had to leave. She replied initially by making a sad face. Then she smiled and said "bye" slowly, winked at Keith and left his office. Keith watched in pleasant amazement as she left his office, holding his gaze until the last possible moment.

Chapter 49

(Thursday: 4:15 p.m.)

Keith was experiencing more simultaneous emotions than he could process while he was putting his laptop and the Dale Wade file into his briefcase. He was feeling the stress of the negotiation and dealing with Dennis, the excitement of a new romance and all the guilt of knowing that he was cheating on a woman he loved. He couldn't help being delighted by Ginny's flirty teasing. He also felt that he was being a terrible husband and father for encouraging Ginny's attention, and for liking the smell of her hair and the feel of her skin. Just as Keith was picking up his briefcase, his cell phone rang. Figuring it was Sharon wondering when he would be home he answered it. "Hi Sharon. I'll be home in a little while. I'm just leaving now," he said into the phone without looking at the incoming number.

"It's actually Kevin Taft," Kevin said in reply, finding Keith's presumption amusing. "I just got a call from Dale Wade asking me to pressure you into accepting their deal terms and the draft license they sent you and to encourage you to get it signed by Campanaro before he gets on a plane tomorrow night. He seems seriously concerned that the deal will fall through if you don't sign off on what he gave you."

"Interesting that he would call you," Keith said in reply.

"Even better, he called me on my cell. I am presuming you didn't give him my number, which means Dennis must have because not many people have it."

"I haven't given it to him, and I wouldn't give it out," Keith replied. "Did Dale say anything else?"

"Not really," Kevin answered. "I told him I would speak with you, but that I wouldn't pressure you one way or another. I let him know that I didn't much appreciate his request, but I explained that I could understand the pressures he was under and why he would do whatever he could to make the deal work. He seemed genuinely stressed and I don't think he was posturing. What is the current status on the negotiation and how is Dennis treating you?"

"Well," Keith said, taking a deep breath and exhaling before continuing, "We are at an impasse in the negotiation. They sent over a draft license that ignored everything I have said and which has a lot of things that I think are completely unacceptable from the University's perspective; really bad. Dale's cover letter basically said, "take it or leave it." I sent back to them a draft that I can sign off on, which is actually quite generous to HematoChem, and invited further discussion. They have been silent since then. I sent it around noon. Dennis has continued to pressure me verbally to sign off on their version, without putting anything in writing. He is basically telling me my evaluation is going to be negative because of my intransigence and that, if the deal falls through, I may as well start looking for another job. Dr. Shen has also threatened to go after me if he loses out on sponsored research funding and consulting money that Dale apparently promised him."

"Wow, is that all?" Kevin asked rhetorically.

"If only," Keith replied before continuing, "Sharon had a CT scan this morning and, after she got back, she got a strange call that was probably a wrong number saying 'tell him to knock it off' and she thinks she saw a guy staring at the house right afterward. She's a little freaked out about it but is maintaining her sense of humor. I've heard that all stress is cumulative, and at this point there is a chance I may burst into flame."

Kevin laughed at Keith's comment. "You'll get through it. Bottom line has to be whether the deal is good for the University. If there are things in there that won't fly, then you are obligated to say 'no,' and to keep the dialogue open. You're doing exactly what you should be doing. Dennis is really being an asshole to you. In getting you that 'reviewed and approved' stamp he expected you to literally be a rubber stamp for what he wanted to do. The fact that he isn't putting anything in writing also suggests he's putting you out on the tree limb all by yourself. That is not very kind of him. I think it's important that you stand your ground."

"I appreciate that. Thanks," Keith said, thankful for Kevin's support. "The other part that is gnawing at me is that there was no way Kaitlin would have signed off on a number of things they want, and I don't think her death should change our approach. It would be like a slap at her memory, and I'm really not okay with that part."

"I was thinking the same thing," Kevin agreed. "Unfortunately, Dennis doesn't see it that way, and you're in the thick of it. This too will pass, and Dennis will be dealt with eventually.

"Dennis being Dennis aside," Keith said, "there is something strange about this one. It's like it's moving too fast with too much urgency. Maybe I am just feeling the stress from Sharon's health and everything else. Any more information about what you said about Kaitlin's 'accident?'"

"I haven't heard anything since I talked to you about it, other than what you just told me," Kevin replied, saying the last few words slowly. "But, sometimes it takes a while for word to get around. I am sure more will come out."

Keith noticed Kevin's choice of words and manner of speech and asked quite seriously, "What do you mean 'other than what I just told you'?"

"I don't want to alarm you, especially since you are doing the right thing and there is probably absolutely no connection whatsoever," Kevin said.

"But?-" Keith prompted.

Kevin paused for a moment because he knew what he was about to say would probably upset his friend, possibly unnecessarily, and would at best sound paranoid. "The person who would most definitely have gotten in the way of the deal was murdered a few days ago and now you are being pressured to sign off on it, and you are resisting the same way she would have. Those are known facts. You mentioned that someone called your house today saying 'tell him to knock it off' and that Sharon though she saw someone staring at the house. You also said that you felt there was something strange about the urgency of this deal."

"You don't think…" Keith started to speak and trailed off, but then the small but real possibility of a connection registered in his mind and he stood stone still.

Kevin sensed the impact the thought was having on Keith. "It is overwhelmingly likely that there is no actual connection at all. In all honesty I am probably grasping at imaginary straws to try to find an explanation for why Kaitlin was murdered. Just in case, I would be a little more careful than usual."

"Someone did call my house using a blocked number with the message 'tell him to knock it off.' Sharon did say that about a minute later a man walking down the street turned and faced our house and appeared to look at every window visible from the street before continuing to walk on. Kaitlin would definitely have blocked the deal terms I am being pressured to sign off on. Kaitlin was murdered in a way that made it look like an accident. I really don't like the plausibility of this connection and what it means for my family and me. If this notion is correct, than a murderer may have talked to my wife on the phone and then stood outside my house today while my family was inside."

"The notion is probably NOT correct," Kevin offered, "but if it is, yes, that is probably what happened."

Keith felt sick. "This is really giving me the creeps right now. I am going to head home, but I want to talk this through some more. Mind if I call you back once I'm in my car?"

"I'll be waiting," Kevin said. "I would like to explore this more too."

Keith picked up his briefcase and headed out through the common area to leave. Part way through the common area he saw that Ginny had looked up at him from where she was sitting in her cubicle. He stopped and walked over to her. While she looked up at him he leaned down and kissed her very gently, then looked into her eyes and said, "Be safe."

"I will," she said sweetly, not knowing why he had chosen those specific words.

He then turned and walked out of the office.

Chapter 50

(Thursday: 4:25 p.m.)

Keith walked the distance from his building to his parking lot quickly, barely noticing the students around him. Stepping into the parking lot he found himself very aware of small things in front of him; the look of the pavement, the way the lines for the parking spaces were faded, and he realized that he was experiencing stress overload. Willing himself to breath deeply and slowly while he crossed the remaining distance to his car, he felt calmer by the time he unlocked his vehicle and climbed in. He then started the engine, turned off the radio and attached the hands free earpiece to his cell phone. Dialing Kevin's cell number, he started pulling the car out without waiting for Kevin to answer.

Kevin saw that it was Keith calling and didn't bother with pleasantries. "You're back, good."

"I am just pulling out of the parking lot," Keith replied. "I am feeling more than a little stressed thinking that there may be some connection between Kaitlin's death, the HematoChem deal and some guy who may be stalking my family. Also, I don't want to put this on Sharon if I am just being paranoid. She has enough stress already. What are your thoughts on how they could be connected?"

Kevin was in his spacious but sparsely decorated office in Tailcrest's Technology Incubator. He had closed and locked his door so no would interrupt him. "I don't know what the connection would be or if there actually is one. Money or the promise of it can make people do strange things, but murdering Tailcrest's General Counsel is more than a little extreme. Kaitlin's murder could have started as an attempted assault but ended up with her attacker killing her to avoid identification. There may be no connection at all."

"In a sick sort of way that makes me feel a little better," Keith said, "but let's think through what connections there may be."

Kevin remained in his office chair leaning forward over his desk, not at all convinced that Kaitlin's murder was related to an attempted assault. "Everyone knew that Kaitlin was a stickler for contract provisions. She had quite the reputation for getting in the way of agreements going forward in all parts of the University unless they were worded the way she wanted them to be. If there is any sort of connection between her murder and the guy telling you, through Sharon, to knock it off, it would have to be linked to something in the deal, something they want that Kaitlin would have gotten in the way of and that you are getting in the way of now."

"That makes sense. Kaitlin would have objected to a lot of things in this agreement. Probably more than I am," Keith replied.

"What are the main ones?" Kevin prodded him.

"Considerations is one," Keith replied. "They want a one-time small milestone payment and a one percent royalty. That is all they are willing to pay, besides patent cost reimbursement. It is not something we would normally consider."

"Don't you usually get several hundred thousand dollars in milestone payments and about a four percent royalty?" Kevin asked, recalling a license Keith had shared with him previously.

"Yes, for a technology like this that would be more usual," Keith answered. "Rights to future inventions is another one. They want it to be way too broad. Most licenses don't provide any rights to future inventions, but they not only want them but want them to be unbelievably broad."

"Future rights are very valuable to a start-up company for business to business deals, especially if the start-up is looking for investment money,"

Kevin offered. "Why is it different for a university; and why would Kaitlin object to that part?"

"For a lot of reasons. It's complicated. It messes up the University's ability to accept future funding of research from companies because the rights to the inventions have already been given away. There are tax law issues too. Anyone skilled specifically in university licensing would have a conniption seeing what they want. Campanaro would obviously sign off on it without reading it, but that is just him. Kaitlin would have probably thrown it on the floor and stepped on it."

"What else?" Kevin asked.

"Another one is the sublicensing terms," Keith said, pulling to a stop at a red light just outside the University's main entrance; not really noticing the car in front of him or the other cars around him. "They want an unlimited right to sublicense the rights under the agreement to others. I am insisting on the University having to give prior written approval for any sublicense of the rights under the license. We can say that the approval shall not be unreasonably withheld, but Kaitlin and I were both sticklers on this one in the past. There is another way to do it that is sort of in between, but I want us to have prior approval for this one. They should be willing to accept it."

"So why is this so important?" Kevin asked.

"We get requests like theirs every now and then, but the companies always adjust to our position. The wording they want would allow them to transfer the license rights to another entity right down the street or anywhere without us being able to do anything about it. And the way they want it, these third party sub-licenses could be difficult or impossible for us to collect money from, even if the sublicensee breached the agreement and even if HematoChem went out of business. We do not enter into contracts that leave that possibility so wide open."

"That makes sense, sort of," Kevin said. "What else?"

"There are other changes that stand out," Keith said, "but one that Dale specifically called out was insisting on their wording for export control as opposed to ours. Theirs just says that each party will comply with applicable laws, while ours is more specific in requiring them to take specific steps to comply with the laws. There are subtleties to the differences that are important for the University's protection and mean more work and risk for them. If they want to do development work in other countries, then they have to bear the risks and costs of getting export permits so they can share the technology with foreign nationals here or abroad. There can be million dollar fines and jail sentences if this stuff is messed up too badly."

"Could this technology be dual use technology or have some export restrictions on it?" Kevin asked.

"Yes, actually it could. Its development was funded at least in part by a grant from the Department of Defense. Because it helps to prevent The Bends for scuba divers it could potential help people in submarines or people like Navy Seals with rapid assents. That is why I want wording that says they will search out and comply with every restriction as a condition of the agreement. They want softer language. The costs of searching for restrictions and applying for the permits can be substantial, so my presumption is Dale wants to minimize his costs."

"Another less important sticking point is that I want to see the corporate formation documents and a list of investors before it gets signed," Keith continued. "Dale says the investors like their privacy and that he will forward the documents and investors only after the deal is done."

"I like my privacy too," Kevin said. "Still, it is important to know who you are doing business with."

"So, basically, we don't know if there is any connection between Kaitlin's death and anything involving this negotiation," Keith said.

"That is how it looks," Kevin confirmed. "However, just because we can't point to it, doesn't mean it's not there. I would continue to be careful just in case."

"That is not an issue. We will be on edge for a while I imagine," Keith responded, chuckling in spite of the seriousness.

"I think it is important that you stand your ground in the negotiation," Kevin said seriously. "If there is some connection to Kaitlin's murder and this negotiation was part of their motivation, I will learn of it eventually. I am asking this as a personal favor. Do not cave in to Dennis' or anyone else's pressure. I will back you all the way to President Walker and to the University Counsel he reports to if necessary."

"I am not caving anyway," Keith replied, while passing a slow moving car, "so you won't owe me a favor. I really do appreciate your support though."

"Good, keep me posted. I have to take care of some things now," Kevin said, pleased with Keith's answer as he hung up the phone and leaned back in his office chair.

While Kevin was looking up at the ceiling in his office, he thought about Dale Wade and the brief interactions he had had with him. Then he realized that he had never read through the papers he got Heather to copy as part of the "protocol" game he played with her that day when Dale was at Keith's house. He recalled that he had tossed them on a pile of trade journals on one of the tables in his home office. Smiling at the memory of his game with Heather and at the fact that the papers she copied may prove helpful, he stood up from his chair and left his office to head home and see what information they contained.

Chapter 51

(Thursday: 4:45 p.m.)

Keith pulled into the driveway of his home just a few minutes after his call with Kevin had ended. As he sat in his driveway Keith wanted to reassure himself, and thought to himself, "I have seen nothing in the license negotiation that would warrant someone killing Kaitlin because she would get in the way, even if someone did learn of her reputation as a General Counsel who blocked agreements over small details. I have seen nothing to solidly link the strange call and the man looking at the house to anything other than a wrong number and Sharon's stress levels. The only thing I can point to that ties all the individual elements together is that they all happened very close in time. That is not enough to conclude anything."

Sitting in his driveway, Keith remained mostly motionless in the driver's seat, holding the remote garage door opener while he thought about how to approach Sharon. He recalled that he had not told Sharon that Kaitlin had been murdered, and he was on the fence about whether the call today and her seeing a man outside made it more important for him to tell her or more important for him to keep the information from her. Unable to decide what to do, he pushed the button to open the garage door.

As the garage door slid up, Keith saw Sharon standing in the open doorway to the main part of the house. His son, Eddy, was looking out from alongside her. Seeing them there and noticing that Sharon had cleared space in the garage so he could pull the car in, he was filled with guilt for having kissed Ginny just a little while earlier. He pulled the car into the garage and climbed out as Sharon pushed the wall mounted button that caused the garage door to start closing.

"Why didn't you call?" she asked as he cleared the short distance and entered the main part of the house.

Before answering he gave her a hug and kissed her deeply, causing Eddy to look at them awkwardly and say, "Daaaad."

"What was that for?" Sharon asked.

"I don't know," Keith replied before answering he first question. "I was on the phone with Kevin Taft at the office and then in the car. I should have called in between, but I was distracted with everything going on. Sorry."

"It's okay," she said. "What were you and Kevin talking about?"

"The HematoChem negotiation," he answered. "I told him about the call today, your seeing a man outside and how it is probably nothing but that it is making us uncomfortable."

"You told Kevin Taft?" she asked, surprised that he had shared that information with him.

"I also told him how Dennis is pressuring me and how the negotiation is at an impasse and how the timing of the call, which probably was a wrong number, was close enough to make it look like a very unprofessional attempt at intimidation."

She looked at him in a way that showed that he was not making her feel reassured. She then said, "Putting it that way makes it sound like it really was an attempt at intimidation to get you to sign off on the deal you're working on."

"I know, but that kind of thing just does not happen in technology licensing," he said, trying to un-ring the bell he had just rung. "Still, I think we should be cautious for a while, just in case I am wrong about that."

"What do you have in mind?" she asked.

"I don't know really," he answered truthfully. "Just the basics I guess. Lock the doors. Keep the kids inside unless there are several adults there.

Be mindful of our surroundings when we go places. Sleep indoors, no napping on park benches. Avoid wearing blindfolds outside. Refrain from excessive public nudity. You know, that kind of thing."

"The last few should be easy to take care of. No problem," she said, smiling at the humorous images he had created for her.

"And I am going to start carrying my SeaCamp just to make myself feel better, even though I know you don't like it."

"You're right. I don't like that little gun even being in the house," she said, referring to the tiny thirty two caliber silver pistol Keith had carried in his pocket for years until she demanded he keep it locked up when Eddy first learned to walk. "But in this case I don't mind as long as you guaranty that the boys won't even see it."

"I promise," he answered. "With the laser site attached it looks like a smartphone in my pocket anyway."

"Good," she said leaning in and giving him a hug.

Keith smiled and held her close, then whispered, "So I guess I can't carry my H&K P2000 forty caliber with an extra clip?"

"Only if it's locked in the car trunk on the way to the shooting range," she whispered back without missing a beat.

"You have to admit, it's a cool weapon," he said smiling.

"Cool yes," she said. "Unlocking it in our house, no, I don't think so."

"Fine," Keith said in mock irritation.

Keith then went around the first floor of house and the basement checking all of the windows and doors to make sure they were locked. When he finished checking, she walked up to him and said, "You're really worried, aren't you?"

"I am under a whole lot of stress and checking everything makes me feel better," he replied. "I'm just being paranoid, and I would rather be cautious when our family is involved."

Checking to see that that their kids were still firmly ensconced in front of the television, they went up to the bedroom so Keith could change out of his work cloths. Before changing, Keith leaned into his closet and unlocked the gun cabinet where he kept the two guns they had discussed along with some ammunition. He then took out his little SeaCamp pistol and six shells, put the shells into the clip and chambered a round. Sharon watched Keith put the pistol on top of his dresser. She then continued to watch it as though it was going to fire on its own. "It's an inanimate object. It's just going to sit there," he said while taking out jeans and a T-shirt to change into, "just like me when it comes to household chores."

Stepping in between Sharon and his dresser and holding her gaze he then undressed in front of her. She enjoyed watching him undress, and she always had. It was one of their private activities that they had maintained throughout the years of their marriage. When he was fully undressed she walked over and hugged him and kissed him deeply, like he had done with her minutes before. She then stepped away and said, "I'm going to check on the boys and then keep going on dinner."

Pulling on his jeans and sliding the SeaCamp into his front right pocket he said, "Suit yourself."

Sharon then disappeared downstairs while he finished getting dressed.

Once downstairs Sharon peeked in on the boys and saw that they were still in the exact same place as when she went upstairs, watching the television as if hypnotized. Sharon then went into the kitchen to finish making dinner. Walking into the kitchen the stress and anxiety and physical discomfort weighed especially heavily on her and she folded her arms on the counter, put her head down and quietly cried, hoping no one would see.

Chapter 52
(Thursday: 5:15 p.m.)

Keith finished changing out of his work clothes and went downstairs to help Sharon with dinner. When he walked into the kitchen, he saw her emptying canned fruit into bowls on the counter near a strainer filled with salad that had not yet been rinsed. He also saw that the oven lights were on, and, although he could not see it, he guessed from the smell of the seasoning that dinner was baked chicken.

"If you could set the table that would be great," Sharon said, without turning to look at Keith. "We still have a few minutes."

"Okay," he said, reaching to open a cabinet to start taking out dishes.

Sharon then took her cell phone out of her pocket and said, "I'm going to call my mom."

"Give her all my best," Keith said in a softly sarcastically tone, just in time to see Sharon wrinkle her face at him in a pretend sour look as she disappeared out of the room.

"Hi mom," Sharon said when she heard her mother come on the line.

"Sharon, it's good to hear from you. How are you feeling?" her mother replied.

"Not great, actually, but that's not why I called" Sharon said. "We got a strange call today. Some guy just said 'tell him to knock it off' and hung up. Then I saw a man out front that looked like he turned and looked at the house before walking on. The combination really freaked us out. It's nothing, but it feels creepy, like there is someone stalking our family."

"That's awful. What did your husband get you involved in that you're getting that kind of call?"

"Mom, it was just a wrong number and some guy out for a walk."

"I know dear. You had a CT scan today and your husband didn't go with you," her mom said. "You must have been so stressed. He should have gone with you instead of going to work."

"Mom, this doesn't have anything to do with Keith not going with me. I insisted he go to work," she protested. "He wanted to go with me, but I wanted him to be able to take time off to go with me to the appointment when I get the results."

"He should have insisted," her mother retorted. "I worry that he isn't taking good enough care of you and I think you deserve better, that's all. I have said that since you first started dating him."

"I know mom, and in spite of everything you said I chose to marry him. Then I chose to have two wonderful children with him. And the whole time he has been wonderful to me."

"I know you like him, dear," her mother said. "I just worry about you."

"Why do we have to do this? I called because we are actually worried about the strange call and we both wanted to let you know about it so you could watch out for anything strange just in case. There are crazy people loose in the world and who knows."

"I appreciate the warning Sharon," her mom replied, "but I'm more worried about you and how well you're being taken care of. Maybe if I was over more to help out I would feel better about it."

"We're fine mom. I am doing okay and my friend Heather is here almost all the time to help out. You have nothing to worry about," Sharon said, thinking that it would an emotional and marital nightmare if her mom and Keith were in the same place more often. She thought the occasional interaction they both endured currently was bad enough, especially after what happened the last time they were together.

"Suit yourself dear. I have to go now," her mother said.

"Bye mom," Sharon replied, wishing she hadn't bothered to call her at all.

Looking over at the kids and then at Keith, who was walking back and forth between the kitchen and the dining room setting the table, she decided to send Heather a quick text message. They talked so often that they rarely texted and it was usually a fun diversion when they did text each other. "Nothing new on the weird call. Stay safe. Keith is home."

Within seconds her phone buzzed with Heather's reply text which read, "Lucky. My husband's still out. Hope he stays out if he's going be as negative as usual. We're fine here. Nothing strange. Relax and enjoy."

"Thanks," Sharon texted back before walking into the kitchen to finish making dinner.

Chapter 53
(Thursday: 8:30 p.m.)

Dinner for Keith and his family had been the usual routine of conversation, teasing, and Sharon and Keith trying to encourage the boys to use good manners. Sharon and Keith had struggled some with Eddy's habit of trying to cut meat by holding the fork like a dagger, stabbing straight down into the meat and then using the knife to try to cut. This caused the meat to pivot around the fork without being cut effectively at all. By the end of the meal, after much encouragement and some laughter, they had gotten Eddy to cut the meat correctly. Keith and Sharon knew, however, that he would probably go back to his way of cutting, just like he had done each of the previous times they had worked with him on it.

After dinner, Keith took care of the dishes and put away the leftovers while Sharon brought the boys into the living room and read books to them. Sharon sat on the living room carpet with one boy on each side of her. She read slowly to them, pointing to the words as she went along. The boys sometimes said the words on the page before she did, as though they could read, but she knew it was a convincing illusion because they had memorized what she had said the previous times she had read the books to them.

Keith finished with the dishes and joined his family in the living room. Sitting on the couch, Keith leaned his head back and closed his eyes for a moment before looking toward Sharon. She had just finished one of the story books and asked the boys, "Do you want to watch Pablo be a secret agent?"

Hearing a clear affirmative from both boys, she pulled up the show on their entertainment system and then sat with Keith on the couch. With the boys electronically entertained, Sharon moved close to Keith and he put his arm around her. They sat comfortably like that, without bringing up any of the stressors they both faced, long enough for several episodes of the show to play through. Keith occasionally stroked Sharon's hair, but mostly they just enjoyed being together with her, home with their boys.

When another episode of the show ended, Sharon announced, "Time to get ready for bed."

The boys protested, but only a little because they were tired. Keith and Sharon then ushered the boys upstairs, partly by Sharon challenging Eddy to a race up the stairs. Keith carried Thomas up the stairs behind them.

While the boys were going through their evening ritual of tooth brushing and changing into pajamas, Sharon brought up part of what she was stressing about. "I am really worried that the CT scan will show something bad. I have no family history of cancer, but what if? A friend of mine in college lost her father to cancer and it was the most god-awful thing imaginable. I am so tired of being sick. I can't stand not knowing what it is, but at the same time, if it is something horrible, I don't want to know."

"I can only imagine what you're going through," Keith said, trying to be supportive but not knowing what to say. "I feel totally helpless. I want to do something to fix it and make your feel better, but I am absolutely powerless to do anything. It really sucks for me, sometimes, so it must be terrible for you."

"Some days it feels like a slow motion nightmare," she said as tears welled up in her eyes. "But there is so much good too. And sometimes I feel perfectly fine for a while, but then it comes back."

"That must be hard," he said.

"It is," she replied. "And now I have to wait until next week to get the results of the scan. It's like having to wait a week for a jury verdict when one of the possible outcomes could be the death penalty."

"It's not going to be that," Keith replied, trying to reassure her while knowing she could be right, even if it was unlikely.

"And if it isn't," she continued, "then we still don't know what it is. It could be Lupus. It could be something like fibromyalgia, or some other autoimmune condition. Being sick, dealing with all of it and not knowing the cause is driving me nuts."

Keith couldn't think of anything to say so he just gave her a hug, held her close and nuzzled her hair. He was worried that maybe she was becoming genuinely and justifiably depressed. He knew that grieving could happen for the loss of anything, especially health, and that for a long time she had been showing some of the signs of clinical depression and sometimes the anger stage of grief. He was sure that she would not hurt herself or mistreat the boys, ever, but he also knew that she was suffering and had no outlet to deal with it.

They ended their hug when Eddy came out of the bathroom with a big smile and toothpaste smeared all around his mouth. "Let's clean you up," Sharon said, walking Eddy back into the bathroom.

Sharon then marched both boys off to bed while Keith waited. "Night Dad," the boys each said in turn as they went into their rooms.

"Goodnight," Keith replied, wondering how much Sharon's illness would affect them through their lives and whether they would even remember her ever not being sick.

Having tucked each boy in, Sharon came back over to where Keith was and put her finger to her lips and then pointed downstairs, signaling that she wanted Keith to be quiet until they got downstairs.

Once downstairs Keith poured each of them a glass of wine and joined Sharon on the couch. "The strange call and the man who looked at the house still have me creeped out," Sharon said, "but what I am more worried about is how this Dale Wade thing is going to affect your job. Dennis is probably going to go after you, and he is your boss."

"I am worried about that too," Keith replied, sipping his wine. "But I am getting the feeling that Kevin Taft may have more influence over my job than Dennis does, as strange as that sounds, since Kevin is not even in my reporting line."

Taking another sip of his wine, Keith wondered whether he should tell Sharon that Kaitlin was murdered. He thought again about the person who would have been reviewing the contract for the Dale Wade negotiation having been murdered, and how it is was now on him to review it and the potential inference of a connection. He knew it was probably unrelated, but felt that he should tell Sharon. He decided he had no right to keep this information from her. "You know," he said, "the call and the man may actually be part of a negotiation strategy for the HematoChem deal."

Sharon laughed, "I don't think so. Dale's easier to read than a children's book. He's a smooth talking charmer who is more interested in checking out Heather than working on whatever business deal you have going. It was definitely not him on the phone or outside, and I would be shocked if he would play that kind of game. It wouldn't fit with his personality."

"I agree," he replied. "Although Dale does have a nasty temper that gets really bad really fast. Back in school I saw him get ugly quick a few times, but he always calmed down within a little while. At his worst he'll get up in your face and yell at you, and with how big he is I imagine that is pretty awful, and he might hit, but that would probably be the extent of it."

They each took a sip of their wine. Sharon shifted closer to him as they enjoyed the quiet of the house. "Dale's deal sure seems to be making a mess with your work," Sharon said, leaning her head on Keith's shoulder.

EDISON DALY

"Yes, it is," he agreed. "I am holding out to do what is right. That's important to me."

Sharon looked at him and smiled crookedly.

"See that picture of my father over there," Keith continued, pointing at one of the framed pictures displayed on a shelf that had souvenirs, the old Tailcrest beer mugs they had bought and used as college freshman and several family photos. "I am doing what he would have done, and what I hope the boys will do some day if faced with a similar situation."

Sharon's smile broadened as she said, "You mean jeopardize their family's income and financial stability?"

"Yes, that is what I mean entirely," Keith replied, smirking at Sharon's obvious humor. "Actually, Kevin is looking into other angles related to the company and the deal. If there is anything to find, Kevin will find it. If Dale or anyone else involved in the deal is pulling a fast one and I approve it, it could put me in just as much risk of losing my job as going against Dennis currently is. I don't want to put my job in jeopardy by giving in to Dennis' or anyone else's bullying."

He noticed that Sharon was smirking at him as she said, "So your noble quest is actually an attempt to save your ass."

"Yes, yes it is," he replied, appreciating the way the mood had lightened. He then decided that he should hold off for now on telling her about what really happened to Kaitlin.

Keith then kissed her gently on her head, which was a gesture that had long before become their unspoken signal that he wanted to go to bed, and they got up from the couch and headed up stairs. Keith put their empty wine glasses on the shelf near his father's picture as they went upstairs. Glancing over at the picture as he walked by, Keith wondered how his father actually would have handled the current situation.

Chapter 54
(Friday: 2:30 a.m.)

Keith and Sharon had drifted off to sleep quickly and slept soundly for several hours. Sometime in the middle of the night Keith realized he was awake and watching Sharon breathing lightly while she slept. Getting out of bed as gently as he could, Keith checked on the boys and saw that they were each sleeping quietly. Padding barefoot back into his and Sharon's room, he slipped back into bed. He slid over close to her and held her while she slept. He felt her hair on his face as he breathed through it and took in her scent. He stayed like that for a long time, feeling her warmth and the rise and fall of her breathing while she slept. Recalling something he had read about hypnosis, he whispered very quietly, "With each breath, good feelings and love for me in, bad feelings out."

Without giving any indication that she was not still sleeping Sharon said, "You're weird."

Keith didn't know whether Sharon had actually woken up so he decided to test it with humor. Whispering just as quietly as he had before, he said, "Every time you hear me say the word 'grapefruit' you will experience an overwhelming need to have sex with me. This need will be more powerful than anything you have ever experienced."

Expecting her to laugh or snort or something, Keith was surprised to see that she just kept breathing easily and lightly while she slept. He struggled against an impulse to push it by whispering other phrases that might cause her to do all sorts of interesting and pleasurable things. Winning the fight against his impulse he continued to hold her close while he tried unsuccessfully to fall back asleep. He rested there awake for quite some time and he found that his thoughts had drifted to Ginny and what it would feel like to hold her close. Letting his imagination wander in ways he knew Sharon would be enraged by, he found himself drifting off to sleep. Then he heard a loud BANG on the glass back door of the house and was instantly awake and on his feet.

In the quiet of the night the noise had seemed as loud as if a car had crashed into the back of the house. "I'll check the kids," Sharon said as she zipped past him while he was pulling on his jeans. A moment later, Sharon had collected the boys in bed with her, and Keith was partway downstairs, gun in hand.

Reaching the bottom of the stairs with his SeaCamp held out in front of him, Keith flicked on the lights and looked into the space of the living room and out through the windows to what might be visible outside. Continuing his scan of the first floor and checking the locks, Keith found nothing out of order. Calling up to Sharon, Keith said, "Nothing down here. Everything is still locked too. Must have been outside."

Sharon herded the boys onto the landing at the top of the stairs. "Stay right here. I am going down into the living room, but I will stay where you can see me," she said too them, looking at each of them reassuringly, even though she had been rattled by the sudden, loud sound.

Reaching the base of the stairs in a heartbeat, she saw Keith, shirtless, gun in hand looking out through the back windows. "I can't see anything from in here," he said, opening the sliding glass door and stepping out into the night.

"Don't," Sharon started to say, but Keith was already outside padding barefoot through the yard trying to find any sign of who or what had made the sound. Using the light from the house, he checked for footprints but found none. He looked for any sign of anything that might have been thrown at the glass door, and again found nothing. He then walked the perimeter of the yard, staying about ten feet back from the wooded section, looking for any sign of anything. He found nothing and backed toward the house while Sharon watched him through the glass back door.

Satisfied that there was nothing much to find outside in the yard and having found nothing visible in the darkness, he inspected the back door where he thought the loud bang had originated from. Looking closely, he saw that there was a smudge on the outside but nothing else. He then looked at the back of the house near the back door and saw nothing out of the ordinary at all.

Walking back into the house and closing and locking the door behind him, Keith wiped his bare feet and the carpet mat near the back door and said to Sharon, "Nothing, just a smudge on the outside of the door that could have come from almost anything."

"You shouldn't have gone out there," Sharon said, tears welling up because she had really been frightened.

"I know. I'm sorry," Keith replied. "I don't know what I was thinking. I just needed to see what was out there, but there was nothing. We're fine."

"Back to bed boys," Keith said to Eddy and Thomas, who had come downstairs and were watching him, wide eyed from behind Sharon. "It was probably just a deer who ran into the back door because it couldn't see the glass. Deer do that sometimes because they don't know what glass is. Everything is fine. Go back to bed."

Sharon went upstairs and tucked the boys back into their beds and then came back downstairs. "I don't like this," Sharon said quietly to Keith.

"Me either," Keith replied. "I think we should call the police. Between the call and the man outside and this tonight, I think it is time."

"I don't want the police here," Sharon said wearily.

Keith gave her a perplexed look and she continued, "I don't care what the neighbors would think about police cars being here. It's not that."

"What are you talking about? The call, the guy outside and now this. Why not?" Keith asked, not following what his wife was saying.

"I don't want to sound like a crazy person," Sharon answered. "Really, what would we tell the police? That you're involved in a negotiation at work and I got a weird call, and I thought I saw someone turn and look at the house and now tonight we heard something go bump in the night?"

Keith saw where she was going and realized she had a point. "It was a really loud bump," Keith protested weakly while giving her a look that communicated clearly that he thought she was probably right.

After again checking to make sure the back door was locked, they went back to bed. Both of the boys were already asleep in their beds. Neither Keith nor Sharon could fall back to sleep easily after what had happed. After some time, Keith noticed that Sharon had finally drifted off to sleep. He couldn't though and kept playing over in his mind the events of the last few days and worrying that there might be some connection between Kaitlin's murder, the Hematochem negotiation and the events at his home. The fact that Kaitlin was murdered kept reverberating in his mind.

Chapter 55

(Friday: 2:50 a.m.)

Lenko Egorov had been standing in the darkness, shadowed by the trees not twenty five feet from Keith when he came out and looked into the darkness. Egorov had looked right at his backlit form, unable to clearly see his face because of the lights from the house. He recognized the small silver gun in Mastin's hand as a virtual replica of the old Czechoslovakian made CZ45 that was currently being sold in the United States. He knew that its short barrel made it ineffective at anything other than very close range. He felt no fear. Egorov stood very still and watched Keith as he came out into the yard after the loud noise. Egorov had used a fallen branch wrapped in cloth to wake them by hitting the glass hard without breaking it. He was pleased to see that his effort seemed to have achieved its desired effect. To Egorov, Keith seemed shaken by the disturbance at his home and his woman seemed even more so. Egorov saw that she also looked sickly, which surprised him.

Egorov observed the conversation between Keith and his wife inside the house and noted that neither picked up a telephone nor took out a cell phone before going up stairs and turning off the lights. Egorov concluded that the authorities had probably not been contacted and that he had nothing to be concerned about as he made his exit. He slowly made his way back through the wooded area he had used to approach the house. While he walked, he unwrapped the cloth from the branch with his gloved hands and simply put the branch down amid the trees. Egorov was convinced that he had not been observed at any point during his visit to the Mastin residence. But he was mistaken.

When she received the call and request from Kevin Taft, Heather thought it was odd, even for Kevin. He had told her that there was a small chance that someone dangerous might approach Keith and Sharon's house. Kevin had elaborated that they might approach from the back street through the wooded area behind their house or they could simply park nearby and walk up the street out front. He told her that he would be dropping off a camera that worked in the dark without a flash and asked her to park on the road near the treed section behind Keith and Sharon's house and photograph anyone who walked by. He had been quite explicit about keeping the car doors locked and the key in the ignition and that she was "to get the hell out of there if she was noticed." Even though Kevin had stressed the danger involved, Heather had agreed immediately. After meeting Kevin and listening to his instructions on how to use the camera, she parked on the back street and watched.

She had waited nearly three hours when she saw someone approaching. She saw a man walking along the street toward the treed section from down the street. Instantly awake, she snapped several pictures with Kevin's small camera that made no sound as the man walked by, just fifty feet from her car.

Not satisfied with the distant shots and pumped up on adrenaline, she waited for the man to pass and enter the woods. Then she very quietly opened the door of her car, climbed out and used her hip to quietly nudge the door shut. Jogging silently in her sneakers, she quickly closed the distance between herself and the man, thinking that following him was crazy, but feeling confident that she could outrun anyone if it came down to a chase.

Pausing at the edge of the wooded area, she peered into the well treed section and saw the man moving silently forward. Her heart was racing as she followed him through the darkness. She knew what she was doing was reckless and stupid, but she wanted to know what he was doing and she couldn't stop herself.

Pausing every few yards to listen and snap another picture, she kept a reasonable distance between them. When he approached Keith and Sharon's back porch carrying what looked like a log, she couldn't help herself. She walked into their backyard and snapped several photographs of the man as he walked up to the back of the house and slammed the piece of wood into the glass back door. As she realized he was going to turn around, she scurried back into the wooded section and quickly crouched down with her back against a large tree just a few feet into the wooded section. She wanted a clear photograph of the man's face. She peered around the tree and saw him quickly walking right toward her. She took one picture and then ducked back into her hiding place, desperately hoping that he had not seen her.

Barely a moment later, Egorov walked right past her, close enough that she could have grabbed his pants cuff. He stopped about ten feet past her and calmly turned around. She couldn't breath. By then the house lights came on and provided just enough light for her to see that he was looking at the house and not at her crouched in in the dim shadow of the big tree. Raising the camera very slowly, she took five clear shots of the man's face as he stood there placidly watching the house for several painfully slow minutes. She didn't dare move to see what he was looking at.

Then, after the lights in the house had been turned off, Egorov turned and headed back in the direction he had come. The instant he disappeared from her sight, she suddenly felt alone and terrified. She imagined herself as a lone swimmer in the water with a shark she could not see. She then made a snap decision to do the only thing that made sense to her in her frightened state. She chose to keep the man in sight. Standing, she silently followed him, wondering if he actually had seen her and was looking for an opportunity to circle around and attack her. She believed he had probably not seen her, but she was not going to give him any chance to get the upper hand. They both silently walked forward through the dark woods; Heather making sure she kept a good distance between them.

Egorov was relaxed and unaware that anyone was following him. Heather could feel the adrenaline rush as she pursued the man from whom she wanted to flee.

When Egorov reached the road he turned left and walked along like he was on an evening stroll. Heather waited, heart pounding, until he was a good distance away and then bolted for her car. She got into her car and immediately locked the doors just as she saw car lights just up around the curve of the road. By the time she started her car and pulled around the curve, the man had disappeared.

Satisfied that she had done all that she could, and that the pictures she had taken could probably help Kevin in whatever mischief he was up to, and maybe help protect Keith and Sharon, she drove off. For several blocks she kept her lights off, only turning them on when she reached a main road that had traffic even at this time of night.

Once home, she checked on Chrissy and her husband and was relieved to see that they were both still asleep. Then she downloaded the pictures and e-mailed them to Kevin with a note that read, "Back home. Safe."

Within a minute she received a reply which read, "Excellent job! Thanks. Way too dangerous. Thank God you're safe!"

Chapter 56

(Friday: 5:30 a.m.)

"Wake up," Keith said to Sharon as she lay sleeping next to him in their bed. "There's something I have to tell you."

Groaning and stretching, Sharon peeked over at Kevin, barely opening her eyes. "Its five thirty and we had a really rough night. Unless you have proof that you're pregnant, I want to wait until six or six thirty to talk about whatever it is." She then squeezed his hand and closed her eyes.

"Sharon?" Keith said a moment later while looking right at her.

"What?" Sharon responded, sounding irritated that he was not going to let her sleep.

"It wasn't an accident," he said.

"What, last night?" she asked, yawning. "How do know it wasn't a demented raccoon?"

"That's not what I am talking about?" he replied.

"Then what wasn't an accident?" she asked pulling the covers up close around her neck.

"Kaitlin," Keith said simply.

"What are you talking about?" she asked, confused. "Are you sure you're awake?"

"I'm awake," he replied, pausing for a moment before continuing. "Kaitlin's death wasn't an accident."

"How do you know?"

"Kevin Taft told me," Keith responded.

"How does Kevin know?" she asked, feeling suddenly more awake.

"I saw him talking to President Walker at Kaitlin's wake. He heard it from him or Kaitlin's husband, Aaron," Keith answered, not fully understanding the nature of her question.

"No, how do they know it wasn't an accident?" Sharon asked, being very specific and feeling annoyed that Keith wasn't understanding her. "Are you saying she committed suicide or that someone killed her? And how do they know?"

"I am sorry I didn't tell you sooner. First I was just absorbing it. Then I held off because I didn't want to upset you. Then last night was so strange and I didn't want to frighten you."

"Tell me what you're talking about right now or I'm going to beat you with the alarm clock," Sharon said in frustration.

"Kaitlin was murdered," Keith said calmly. "They don't know whether she crashed her bike or was knocked off or why she was attacked. There was no sexual assault, but she was badly hurt by the bike crash. They don't know whether it was a failed attempt at a sexual assault. What they do know is that she survived the bike crash and that someone snapped her neck in a way that couldn't have happened in the bike crash."

"How can they know that for sure?" Sharon asked, not wanting to believe what she was hearing.

"According to Kevin, the nature of the neck fracture was enough, but apparently Kaitlin told them, sort of," Keith said. "Apparently she survived the crash and was conscious enough to know she was in trouble. She used her fingernails to leave a message. She scraped different things she could reach under each nail individually, essentially telling the medical examiner that she survived. I think Kevin said dirt, grass and moss."

"Why would she do that?" Sharon asked. "Unless maybe she knew she was going to die."

"She wouldn't have been able to do that with a broken neck," Keith said, looking into Sharon's eyes as she looked back at him, her face partly obscured by the edge of her pillow. "Apparently her other fingernail had only human skin cells under it. And her neck was broken, ending her life and making her unable to control her hands. This suggests -.''

Sharon gasped lightly with the realization of what Kaitlin's last moments must have been like and tears came to her eyes. "She saw him and knew she was about to die. That poor woman. Oh my God. I can't imagine."

"Exactly," he said, reaching over and holding her hand. "Unless it was a bizarre 'signature' her killer left, which seems really unlikely, she probably experienced that in her last moments. If you think about it, if that's the way it happened, then she went down asserting control, fighting. And if she managed to scratch the guy, then she got his DNA. I think she was saying 'Here he is, get him.'"

Sharon lay there quietly sobbing, thinking about Kaitlin's final action and picturing in her mind what Kaitlin probably experienced.

Keith just held her hand until he sensed that she has had calmed down some. Sharon then squeezed his hand and said, "Why did you think that would frighten me?"

"Because Kaitlin would have been the one reviewing the HematoChem License Agreement, and now I am reviewing it. And because you got a strange call and saw a guy outside, and I am getting pressure to approve the contract. And because there is a tiny chance that the guy who killed Kaitlin might have banged on our door in the middle of the night."

Sharon sat upright in bed, then squeezed his hand again and quickly got out of bed to check on their boys. Seeing that the boys were comfortably sleeping, she climbed back into bed. She then snuggled up close to Keith. He held her close while she thought about what he had said. Holding her in the darkness, Keith said softly, "I am not comfortable leaving you and the boys alone today. I would rather not, but I will probably have to go into work at some point. I think it's best if you and the boys spend the day at your parents' house, maybe even do an overnight."

"Okay," Sharon said. "I would like to go there now, right now."

"That's fine," Keith said in reply as they both got out of bed.

They packed overnight bags for Eddy, Thomas and Sharon. While Keith put the bags in the car, Sharon woke the boys, made them use the bathroom and helped them brush their teeth. Eddy was midway through brushing his teeth when he asked, "Why are we up so early?'

"Because we are going to visit Grandma," Sharon answered, thinking it best to just keep the answer simple.

"Can we use the playground?" he asked hopefully. Eddy loved the playground near his grandparents' house.

Knowing they would all be staying inside, Sharon said, "Maybe, we'll see."

Keith carried Thomas as they went out into the garage and got into the car. Once everyone was settled, Keith locked the car doors, used the remote to open and close the garage door as he pulled out, and then drove into the pre-dawn darkness.

Keith decided on a roundabout route to his in-laws house after mentally asking himself, "What would Jason Bourne do?" While he zigzagged through suburban neighborhoods, Sharon made a quick call to her mother. "Hi Mom. Sorry to call so early, but we're stopping over for a visit."

"When will you be here?" Sharon's mother asked, surprised by the call and Sharon's announcement.

"In a little while," Sharon replied.

"Is everything okay?" he mother asked slowly.

"Mostly," Sharon answered, not wanting to say too much in front of the boys. "We're just coming over for the day, maybe a sleepover tonight if you don't mind."

"Of course we don't mind. I will see you when you get here," Sharon's mother replied, her tone reflecting concern.

"Thanks mom," Sharon said before ending the call and starting on a text message to Heather.

In her text to Heather Sharon said that they were staying over at her mother's house at least for the day and that they had to adjust their plan for Heather and Chrissy to come over. Within moments Sharon's phone buzzed with Heather's reply that she wouldn't mind bringing Chrissy over to join their visit with Sharon's mother if it was okay. She also asked if there was anything new about the weird call. Sharon texted back with her parent's address, that there was news to share in person and that she was sure her and Chrissy visiting at her parents' house would be fine.

Keith had been alternately watching Sharon texting, peeking at their boys dozing in the back seat and keeping an eye out to ensure that they weren't being followed. Convinced, incorrectly, that they were not being followed, Keith said, "I'll just drop you off and head back home. I really don't want to deal with your mother at all this morning," His tone made it clear that it was not up for discussion.

"That's okay," Sharon said, smiling at him in the dashboard light. "I don't want to deal with you dealing with my mother this morning either."

Hearing Sharon's normal jabbing humor made him feel considerably better, and they rode the rest of the way in relative silence.

Chapter 57
(Friday: 6:15 a.m.)

It was still dark when Keith pulled into his in-laws' driveway. Keith had pulled into that same driveway, which ran along the side of the modest house, so many times since he first met Sharon when she was a college freshman that it was automatic to him. This particular morning he didn't care that he had never felt welcome there. He had more important concerns.

As Keith opened his car door, Sharon's mother and father both stepped out of the side door into the driveway. Her mother had her arms folded, and would not look at Keith. Her father was holding the door open and looking warmly at Sharon. To Keith the man looked much older and worn down than the last time he had seen him. Keith wondered what the poor man must have endured living with Sharon's mother for nearly thirty years. Sharon smiled as she opened the door and gave her father a hug. "Sorry the get you up so early," Sharon said to her father.

"Nonsense," her father replied. "I'm up this early anyway. What's the occasion for your visit?"

"I will tell you once we are inside," Sharon replied, picking up Thomas and handing him to her father.

Keith picked up Eddy and carried him into the house, while his mother-in-law held the door and gave Keith an accusatory look.

By the time Keith carried Eddy inside Sharon and her father had already put Thomas, who was still sleeping, on a couch and covered him with a blanket. Keith put Eddy on the other end of the couch, pleased that he too was still asleep. Sharon put a blanket on Eddy as well, and the four adults made their way into the kitchen.

"So what have you gotten our daughter and grandchildren involved in now?" Sharon's mother asked sharply, speaking quietly so as not to wake the children.

"Drug money. They're after us," Keith responded evenly, as though he were serious.

The eye popping look on Sharon's mother's face suggested that she was considering whether his statement was true. Sharon tried unsuccessfully to suppress a smile as she stepped in between Keith and her mother. "It's not that at all," Sharon said. "I got spooked yesterday when I got that call that was probably a wrong number and thought I saw a man looking at the house. Then last night there was a sound like a deer ran into the sliding glass door in the back of our house. Deer do come through our yard from the wooded section out back, but after the earlier part of the day, I am really spooked. I thought I would be more comfortable having the kids here for the day and maybe for a sleepover. I am sure it's nothing. I hope you don't mind."

"Of course not, dear," her mother replied. "You and the boys are always welcome here. I wish you would come over more often."

"Oh, I told my friend Heather she could stop over later with her little girl, Chrissy," Sharon continued, noting her mother's sudden frown. "I am sure that, if you spend some time with Heather, you will see why I like her so much. Chrissy is a doll too. Dad, just so you know, Heather is very pretty."

"All the better," her father said. "It's settled then. We'll have a busy house for a change."

"I should go," Keith interjected, before giving his wife a hug and stepping toward the door. "I will keep you posted on my work schedule for today and tonight."

Sharon walked out of the house with Keith and gave him a kiss as he got back into the car. "I take it you aren't big on sleeping here if it turns into a sleepover," she said, smiling crookedly at him.

"I'll take my chances with the deer who head-butted our door," he replied.

"Thought so," she said as he started to back the car out of the driveway.

As he waived to his wife and drove off, Keith got a sick feeling in his gut like something was really wrong and he should be staying with them. He knew his family would be fine at Sharon's parents' house, but something was still making the hairs on the back of his neck stand up.

Taking a direct route back to his house, Keith sped down a section of highway that was already showing signs of morning traffic. He had no need to get home quickly but he found himself speeding and weaving between the lanes, passing car after car. Seeing the speedometer reach eighty, he consciously slowed the car down to avoid causing an accident or getting a ticket. A few minutes later his house came into view. He backed his car into the driveway and put it in park while he looked around him. Everything seemed normal to him, except that his family wasn't there.

Using the remote switch he opened the garage door, backed the car in and closed the garage door behind him. He then climbing out of the car and looked around at his tools and the newly completed boat. Trying to relax, he focused on his breathing and took in the smell of the sawdust, concrete and damp wood. Walking around his "man cave," he felt like escaping into a focused effort on a project using his tools. However, in addition to having no projects in the works other than the boat, he knew he had other matters he needed to focus on. Escaping into a project would have to wait.

Taking his little gun out of his pocket, Keith entered the main part of the house and went quietly room to room making sure he was the only one there. Satisfied that the house was clear of intruders, Keith concluded that he was acting a little bit like a grown version of a kid who was afraid of the dark. Putting his gun back in his jeans pocket, Keith took one of their many Tailcrest University mugs out of his kitchen cabinet and made instant coffee before walking upstairs to take a shower. Sipping his coffee while taking out a fresh change of clothes out of his dresser, Keith then walked into the bathroom, closed and locked the bathroom door and put his gun on a tissue box within easy reach of the shower. The shower's hot water relaxed him and made him feel more normal.

Finishing his shower and dressing, Keith felt like his head had cleared and that this was like a one of the occasional days off he used to take back when Sharon worked and the boys spent more time over at Sharon's parent's house. He recalled that it was one of those days years before when Heather had stopped by and they shared a drink and had let one thing lead to another, just that once. It was a mistake he recalled vividly and fondly. He was still thinking about their "mistake" a while later when he was making himself a cup of hazelnut coffee, which he planned to take his time enjoying. This time, he used their new Keurig one cup coffee maker.

Sipping his coffee while he walked, Keith grabbed his briefcase, which contained the papers for the HematoChem negotiation, and went into his dining room. He then spread the papers on the dining room table and sat in his usual chair. Keith leaned back in his chair, recalling how he had sat in the same chair when he was discussing this particular negotiation with Dale Wade just recently. He then sipped his coffee and paused to enjoy the flavor. He felt good knowing that he was not going to let Dennis or anyone else bully him, even if it was going to cost him his job. He also knew that he had at that moment an unusual opportunity to relax in his own home without anyone around. He sipped more of his coffee and thought about the only thing on his to do list; calling Dennis later to tell him he was going to be working from home that morning.

Chapter 58
(Friday: 8:30 a.m.)

Keith had been sitting on his couch with his hands folded behind his head for a while waiting for the clock to flip to eight thirty. As the seconds ticket toward precisely eight thirty, Keith took out his cell phone and dialed Dennis' number. Dennis picked up on the third ring. "Dennis Gearin, Tech Transfer," Dennis answered.

"Dennis, it's Keith," Keith said, expecting grief once he gave Dennis a chance to respond. "I had a rough night and I am not feeling too great right now. I'm going to work from home this morning and come in this afternoon to take care of things. I can do everything I need to do from here."

"I don't care if you had a rough night," Dennis replied. "I want you to get in here and do your job. You have a responsibility to get into this office and take care of the Dale Wade negotiation the way I told you to. Get in here and take care of it or it's your ass. Do you understand me?"

"Sorry, what? I didn't catch that," Keith said, taking affront at the way Dennis was speaking to him.

"I expect you to get in here right now and resolve the HematoChem matter," Dennis said, not appreciating Keith's response. "I have been absolutely clear on what my expectations are as your direct supervisor and you are putting your job in jeopardy by taking the approach you are stuck on. Keep it up and you're gone. I will fire you. I have worked with you a long time, but you have been difficult and insubordinate and now you are refusing to come into work at a critical time in a negotiation. Get into work now."

"I will be in this afternoon, and I have not been insubordinate," Keith replied calmly. "You indicated that this was my responsibility and I am taking care of it. Responsibility and authority go hand in hand and I am taking care of my responsibility, fully and diligently. You are welcome to take it away from me, negotiate it yourself and give it to the Legal Department to review and approve it. Be my guest."

"I told you why I can't do that," Dennis replied, surprised at Keith's assertiveness. "You have to take care of it and, frankly, you're screwing it up. You are going to get hung out to dry if you don't get it done today."

"I will approve it when it is approvable," Keith offered back calmly. "Between now and then I am encouraging them to move toward a position that is approvable. Brinksmanship in this particular negotiation is the only thing that will work."

"Try getting your ass into work and getting the deal done."

"Look Dennis," Keith said in a more conciliatory tone, "I really did have a rough night, I really do feel like crap, my wife had a CT scan of her head yesterday and we won't know the results until next week. Someone called our house yesterday saying 'tell him to knock it off' and my wife thought she saw a man watching our house. Last night, here's the kicker, someone pounded on our back door in the middle of the night, but when we got there no one was around."

"Yes," Dennis said, "sounds rough. Now get in here and make the deal happen."

"I can make the deal happen from here, so long as they come around," Keith countered. "I don't have any need to come in until this afternoon when things will have been sorted through more fully. I am not coming in this morning, and I wouldn't recommend firing a man who took part of a day off after his wife had a CT scan to help diagnose a debilitating illness. Recall that joke about what you should do if you hit a lawyer with your car? The punch line suggests that you back up and make sure that he's dead. Don't hit me with a car Dennis or the gloves will come off. I don't appreciate your threatening my job."

"You know what," Dennis said, seething with anger, "I am going to save your career by initialing your approval on the document based on our conversation right now and send it off to Campanaro for his signature. I will tell him that you are home sick and that you told me to put it through for his signature because of time constraints. You can actually take the rest of the day off. In fact I insist on it. We can talk more about your career on Monday."

Keith replied very clearly while taking his smartphone out of his briefcase, "No, you may not initial my approval on the license."

Feeling thankful that he had left his smartphone on and that the battery was not dead, during and awkward silence in the conversation Keith quickly typed and sent an e-mail to Dennis saying, "To be clear, I am NOT approving the HematoChem license. I hope we get an acceptable deal today. KM."

Dennis swore when he saw the e-mail pop up on his computer screen; then said into the phone, "Cute Keith, real cute. I'm not in the mood for games."

Then Dennis hung up the phone loudly and Keith was once again alone in the silence of his home.

During the telephone conversation, Keith had clicked into what he sometimes called "lawyer mode" and had remained internally calm in spite of the heated conversation. Keith then put his cell phone on the couch next to him, leaned back and thought about whether there might be other reasons why Dennis was so focused on getting this deal done. Keith then closed his eyes for a moment and pictured Dale sitting at Keith's dining room table. "What's your relationship with Dennis, Dale?" Keith asked himself before remembering something Dale had said sort of as a joke several days earlier. He recalled that Dale had commented about giving him an ownership stake in HematoChem so they could both get rich. Keith wondered if Dale had said something similar to Dennis and whether Dennis had taken him up on it. Keith knew it would be very easy to write Dennis into the deal by giving him part ownership of HematoChem in exchange for Dennis using his influence to push for a quick deal on very good terms for the company.

"That would be a clear violation of conflicts of interest rules and laws," Keith said out loud to no one. "Would Dennis take a payoff like that to get a sweetheart deal for Dale? Yes, he would, but only if he could make it look clean by having me do the deal and by being really quiet about his ownership in HematoChem."

Keith took another sip of his coffee and considered his new theory about Dennis' possible motivation for pushing so hard for a bad deal. At first he thought his theory had merit because it fit with how Dennis was behaving. Then he thought about how valuable ownership of HematoChem would be to Dale, and how unlikely it would be that Dale would actually give up part ownership of the company just to grease the skids on the deal. Giving it more thought, Keith could not decide whether Dale would actually give up something so valuable, but his gut said that maybe he would.

Chapter 59
(Friday: 8:45 a.m.)

Lenko Egorov had slept on and off for most of the previous day and had remained awake with little difficulty throughout the night. After his late night visit to the Mastin's backyard he had spent a good portion of the early morning hours watching their house from his car, which he had parked a discreet distance away. The adrenaline and anxiety of the current situation were sufficient that he would not have been able to sleep even if he had not rested the previous day. He knew that he had to make things happen today or all his preparation and risk would have been for nothing, and dangerous people would hold him accountable for his failure.

When Egorov had seen Keith pull his car out of his garage with his wife and children in it earlier that morning, he simply followed them at a reasonable distance to see where they were going. When he later saw them pull into an unimpressive neighborhood with small houses and then pull into the driveway of one of the houses, Egorov presumed Keith was dropping his wife and children off with a friend or relative. This provided Egorov a small sense of satisfaction because he believed that Keith's bringing his family elsewhere probably meant that his own efforts were having an impact. Egorov thought that Keith was very likely feeling pressure from the things Egorov had done the previous day and during the night, and that with some additional persuasion he could be made to do what Egorov wanted. Egorov was convinced that Keith would approve the License Agreement exactly the way Dale had presented it to him. Egorov had then forced himself to picture in his mind Keith putting a stamp on a document and initialing it as approved and having it signed by an official at the University. This image represented exactly what Egorov wanted and he fixed it in his mind, knowing that he would do anything he had to in order to make it happen today.

Egorov had watched Keith and his wife bring their children into the house from their car and realized that he was parked physically too close and might be observed unintentionally. He decided to find a better vantage point and to spend some more time in this particular neighborhood keeping an eye on the house where Keith's family would likely be spending the day.

When Egorov saw Keith pulling his car out of the driveway without his wife and children, he crouched down in his car to avoid being seen. Egorov then waited five minutes and pulled out to go find a better place to wait and watch.

Egorov had not travelled more than fifty yards before he saw what would likely be a suitable place to observe the house and its occupants. He had almost missed it, but what he saw was a narrow paved pathway that led to a children's park located behind several houses across the street from the house he intended to watch. After parking further up around a curve in the road of the small residential block, he entered the children's park and simply dragged one of the park benches part way across a grassy area to a place where he could see the house clearly. Looking like a relaxed man taking a day off, Egorov sat down at the picnic table and pretended to read a thin novel he had brought with him.

After quite some time watching, and seeing only Keith's wife and two older looking adults occasionally walking passed the front window, Egorov decided that his efforts might be better directed elsewhere. He also decided that he wanted to allow himself to be observed like he had attempted to do previously at Keith's house when only his wife and children were there. Standing and pocketing the thin novel he had been pretending to read, he lit a cigarette and casually strolled back toward the playground entrance.

Before he had walked twenty five feet, his cell phone rang. It was his Russian investor contact, Sacha Sidorov. He answered on the first ring.

"Hello Sacha. How are you today?" Egorov said in greeting as though everything was moving right on schedule. While talking, he continued to stroll toward the exit of the playground on his way to walk past the house he was watching.

"Lenko, I have not heard from you in several days and I want to hear from you that everything is in order regarding the University license deal. I trust everything is completed or almost in place?"

"Yes," Egorov said honestly, focusing in his mind on the word "almost." "Everything is in place, except there is just needed one final approval from their tech transfer lawyer for the document to be signed today to bind the University. Once it is signed, then it will have been taken care of completely and the necessary rights will have been locked in."

There was a long pause on the line while Sacha Sidorov silently counted to five before replying, "I thought this would already be taken care of because of the arrangements you made. You are aware of the deadlines we face and the importance of having a clean contract from the University. Tell me what has happened now to keep things from being completed."

Egorov exited the playground showing an outwardly calm manner as he replied, "A lawyer from the Tech Transfer Office who reports to someone we have some influence over is being momentarily stubborn. He is being as inflexible as the woman lawyer was known to be, but he is being leaned on and he will bend very soon."

"Are you sure that this person will do as you wish?" Sidorov angrily asked, more as an accusation than as a question.

"Yes, he will. I am sure of it," Egorov replied, as he passed in front of the house where Keith had dropped off his wife and children. As he had previously done at Keith's house, he conspicuously looked into the windows. "Do not worry my friend. If he does not bend in the next few hours I will adjust my approach and break him. The document will be signed today."

Egorov could tell from Sidorov's tone that he was intensely angry at hearing the disappointing news. Egorov also knew that Sidorov could be an exceedingly dangerous man when he did not get his way, even on matters much less important than this. "I am relying on your personal assurance that it will be done. I will pass this along to other people who are interested in this deal. Do not fail my friend," Sidorov said. "Do you understand?"

"There is no need to threaten," Egorov replied warmly, even though he knew just what Sidorov's words meant. "I have not failed in any matter I have put my efforts toward, and I will not fail here. I will let you know when the matter is completed. This should be within the next twenty four hours."

"I hope so," Sacha replied. "Goodbye Lenko."

As he ended the call, Egorov felt a wave of coldness wash over him. He continued to stroll around the small rectangular shaped residential block that surrounded the playground on his way back to his car. Having been intently focused on the call with Sacha Sidorov, Egorov had not noticed whether anyone in the house had seen him walking by or looking into the windows. He hoped that they had and that it would quickly get back to Keith Mastin. He picked up his pace as he thought about how the one person who needed to sign the License Agreement to bind the University would be getting on a plane later that night. Egorov also knew it was up to him to convince Keith Mastin, his way, to approve the contract before the Vice President for Research boarded his plane. Egorov knew that he could not rely on Dale to provide any meaningful help in delivering Keith's approval with so little time remaining.

Egorov reached his car quickly, after the brief walk around the block, and climbed into the driver's seat. As he started the car, Egorov sensed that he was being followed. After carefully looking around, he decided that the stress was affecting him and that he was imagining things. He then pulled out and drove out of the modest suburban neighborhood.

Egorov had in fact been observed outside Sharon's parent's house, while he was walking to his car, and while he was driving away. But he had not been observed by anyone inside the house. This time, Heather had used her cell phone to capture pictures of Egorov walking past Sharon's parents' house and looking at just that one house. She had also gotten pictures of him getting into his car and a clear image of the license plate number. Taking a few minutes to send most of the pictures to Kevin's phone, Heather then pulled away from the curb feeling pleased that she had noticed the man from the previous night and had been able to get these additional pictures for Kevin.

A minute later, Heather parked out in front of Sharon's parents' house, woke up Chrissy, carried her up to the house and knocked. When Sharon's mother answered the door, Heather smiled cheerfully and said, "Hi. You may remember me. I am Heather and this is my daughter, Chrissy. Sharon said we could stop by. I hope its okay. We don't want to intrude."

"Its fine," Sharon's mother replied, offering a smile that Heather recognized as artificial and cold.

"Come in," Sharon's mother continued. "They're in the living room. Sharon mentioned that you might be stopping by for a short visit."

Heather carried Chrissy into the house while feeling clearly unwelcome. Heather understood more clearly why Keith was not fond of Sharon's mother. She decided right then that she would extend the visit to Sharon's parents' house as long as she possibly could in defiance of the clear insistence on her making it a short visit.

Chapter 60
(Friday: 9:00 a.m.)

Keith paced slowly back and forth in his living room while his stress escalated. Sleep deprivation and caffeine were having their effects, but he was troubled mostly by the idea that Dennis might be playing both sides of the HematoChem negotiation; taking an ownership stake in the company and at the same time pressuring Keith. Keith knew that the notion was probably incorrect, but something was wrong with the deal, and he couldn't put his finger on it. He knew he was being inappropriately pressured by Dennis to approve it when it was bad for Tailcrest. Keith eventually concluded that Dennis had more likely than not had been "bought" by Dale, but he just didn't want to believe it.

"If Dale bought off Dennis with an ownership stake in HematoChem, how would he have done it?" Keith asked out loud in his empty house while he continued to pace.

Answering his own question, Keith said, "It's structured as an LLC, so he could just add Dennis to the Ownership Schedule of the LLC Operating Agreement. But then Dennis' name would show up on the ownership documents, which he probably would not want because it would be obvious once the documents were shared with Tailcrest Tech Transfer."

"Is there a way around that?" Keith pondered out loud.

"Yes," he said, again answering his own question. He then stopped pacing and stood very still, thinking how easy it would be for them to hide Dennis' part ownership of HematoChem.

There were things Keith wanted to do, but only after he had a conversation with Kevin Taft. Resuming his pacing, Keith kept unconsciously putting his hand in his jeans pocket and holding the handle of his SeaCamp pistol. While he paced, Keith recalled Kevin's often stated rule that no one should ever schedule a meeting or call him before ten in the morning because that was when he got his actual work done. He wondered whether he should break that rule this morning, but decided to wait just a while longer.

To occupy his mind while he waited, Keith went upstairs and started cleaning his boys' rooms. Not yet old enough to be diligent about putting things away, the boys' rooms were always littered with toys, books and stuffed animals. The physical act of putting the boys' things in their proper place was very familiar to Keith and he did it almost automatically. While he was making the bed in his Thomas' room, he noticed out the window that Dale's car was pulling up in front of his house.

At first Keith thought that this was a good development and that he could use the opportunity to confront Dale about whether or not he had "bought" Dennis. But then Keith saw the way Dale pulled in fast and braked hard before pulling to a stop, and how angry he looked as he walked across the lawn. Recalling how intensely aggressive he had seen Dale get in the past when angry, Keith instantly decided to not deal with Dale in his present state. Keith was confident that Dale could not see in through the windows because of their mirroring effect, but more importantly, he felt that this was his home and that he had no obligation to interact with anyone who showed up unannounced looking angry, even an old friend. Choosing to remain silent, Keith did nothing when Dale pounded on the front door.

"Keith, I need to talk to you about this deal," Dale shouted at the closed door before pounding on it again.

Hearing no reply, Dale pounded on the door again. "Open up you asshole!"

Keith could hear Dale's breathing from the other side of the door. He could tell without question that Dale was furious and knew that if he were to open the door, he would be putting himself in physical danger. Keith wanted to talk with Dale and explain what he was doing, but not while he was enraged like this.

Still not hearing a reply, Dale pounded the door a third time. This time Dale shouted louder than before, "You're going to kill my fucking deal you prick. At least you can fucking talk to me about it. Shit!"

Keith then heard Dale try the doorknob to see if it was unlocked. This was seriously crossing a line. He would not tolerate anyone trying to invade his home. Not being able to open the door, Dale walked around the house trying to look into the windows. Dale first tried to look into the kitchen windows, which were set relatively high. Dale could almost reach because of his considerable height. Keith stepped away into the living room so he would be less visible just in case Dale could see in. Then Keith saw that Dale was heading around the corner of the house. He guessed that Dale was going to check each of the doors and look in each of the windows. Keith hoped that Dale would not do something stupid like break a window to get in. He knew Dale might really hurt him. He also knew that, even if he were to pull his gun on Dale, he probably wouldn't be able to bring himself to shoot him no matter what he did.

When Dale left Keith's field of vision, Keith wondered how Dale could be so sure that Keith was in the house. He concluded that Dennis had probably told Dale not only what approach Keith was taking with the deal but also that Keith was probably home. Keith then adjusted his vantage point so he could see more clearly into the backyard. He saw that as Dale cleared the corner of the house heading into the backyard he kicked one of the children's toys out of the way. He also saw that Dale had hurt his shin in the process. Dale came onto the porch and put his hands up to the glass like pretend binoculars so he could see in without the reflective effect of the glass. Dale saw no one though because Keith had stepped into the kitchen just in time. Dale tried the handle of the back door before walking off of the porch.

Keith then looked out the back windows and front windows. He saw that Dale had gone back to the front of the house. A moment later, Dale stopped, took out his cell phone and dialed Keith's home number. Keith let it ring and go to voice-mail while he set the ringer on his cell phone to vibrate. The land line phone stopped ringing, and a moment later he saw Dale dial again. Keith then felt the phone in his hand begin to vibrate. Choosing not to answer it, he saw Dale's look of frustration at not being able to see in, get in or contact Keith. Keith wondered whether Dale had begun to doubt whether Keith was even there. Then Dale put away his phone and took out what appeared to be a sticky pad and wrote something on it. Dale then walked up to the kitchen window and slapped a sticky note hard onto the glass. Keith could see that Dale had written his phone number on this inside of the sticky note so it was visible from inside the kitchen. The message was clear, "Call me."

As Dale stormed off, Keith realized that Dale was acting just like he did when they were both in High School. Keith was sure that now, like then, Dale would cool off within about an hour. Even as he watched Dale speed away in his car, Keith felt strangely reassured by Dale's display because it solidified in his mind the idea that Dale was not the one who had banged on the door the night before. The apparently quick communication between Dennis and Dale, suggested by Dale's showing up when he did, made Keith wonder even more about how closely they were linked in this deal.

Chapter 61

(Friday: 9:25 a.m.)

After Keith saw Dale drive off, he sat on the couch and called Sharon. As he waited for her to answer, he thought about how they had been cuddled up on the same section of the couch just the night before. He found it strange that something that had occurred just hours before felt like it had occurred much longer ago.

"What's up? How are you holding together," Sharon asked in greeting, while hoping that Keith would reply that he was bored and that the deal had been taken care of the way Keith wanted.

"Well," Keith answered, suggesting that the answer to both was not ideal.

"What?" Sharon pressed.

"Let's see, Dennis tried to force me to come into work, basically threatened to fire me, and then tried to shove the deal through claiming that I was verbally approving the deal when I wasn't."

"Holy snikees!" Sharon replied, using the more polite term they had adopted for use in front of their children.

"It gets better. While he was saying that he was sending it through for signature claiming I had approved it, I typed out and sent him an e-mail saying that I did NOT approve it, which blocked him and really, really ticked him off."

"Oh," Sharon said sympathetically. "Sounds like you really need to start looking for a new job because he is going to get back at you for that."

"Yes, I think you're right," Keith agreed. "Of course I did threaten him."

"What?" Sharon blurted out, not sure if Keith was joking with her. "Run that by me again."

"Well, Dennis was basically threatening my job and I mentioned that joke about hitting a lawyer with your car."

"You mean the one where you are supposed to back up and make sure they are dead because, if they are still alive, they will come after you and make your life miserable?"

"Yep, that one," Keith replied. "I don't have much to work with, other than his lunch reimbursements, but he doesn't know that. I figure that if he is willing to scam on lunch bills, pretending that I am a potential licensee so Tailcrest will pick up the whole bill after I have paid my half, then there probably are other things he has done that he suspects I may know about. It is those things he probably doesn't want brought to light. I am blackmailing him on a bluff."

There was silence on the line long enough that Keith wondered if the call got dropped. "You disapprove?" Keith asked, hoping she wouldn't be ticked off and blame him for any resulting hardship their family might face if Dennis used his comment to hurt his career.

"Are you kidding?" she replied, beaming with pride. "It took balls, and it was exactly the right thing to do. I am proud of you. I am absolutely proud of everything you are doing with Dennis and this weird deal. And you know what? I bet Kaitlin would be proud of you too."

Keith could not have been more pleased with the support and praise he was receiving from his wife. He smiled for possibly the first time that day and he wondered if Sharon knew how much her words meant to him right then. "Thank you," he said simply before moving on to the next thing he wanted to mention to her. "There's more."

"What else happened?"

"I am presuming that Dennis got on the phone with Dale right after I hung up and told Dale that I was here and that I was going to stand my ground on the deal terms. It wasn't long after my call to Dennis that Dale came tearing up in his car and pounded on the door demanding to talk to me and shouting that I was going to 'kill his fucking deal,' and he tried the doorknob to see if he could get in. He was really angry."

"Did you let him in?"

"Hell no! I didn't even give any indication that I was home. I once saw him beat the crap out of a kid back in school because the kid had asked out a girl Dale was interested in. He was that angry again today, maybe more so, and I was not going to put myself in harm's way. There was no way in hell I was going to open that door."

"Would it help to talk with him by phone?" Sharon asked.

"Yes. I plan to later today, but not just yet."

"So I take it he left without setting the place ablaze?"

"No damage. He left just as angry as when he showed up, but I am sure he will cool down and feel really bad about it later. That is just the way he is."

Sharon could hardly believe the things she was hearing and tried to continue to be supportive. "Sounds like you are having a really rough morning. What are you going to do now?"

Keith took a deep breath before responding. "I am going to talk with Kevin Taft. He asked me not to cave in to the pressure, and I won't, but I also got the impression that he was up to something. I really need to talk with him before I do much of anything. If I don't hear from him in the next few minutes, I am going to call him."

"I hope he is up to something good," Sharon offered, "because the 'snikees' we are dealing with is kind of wide and deep."

"Snikees palooza," Keith agreed.

"So you are going to be home for a while?" she asked.

"Yes, at least until I talk to Kevin," Keith answered. "But this afternoon is anyone's guess depending on what happens. For all I know I could end up driving the License Agreement out to the airport tonight to get Campanaro to sign it before he goes through airport security."

"I think we should take a vacation," Sharon suggested out of nowhere. "If Campanaro can, so can we, right?"

"It's a deal," Keith replied. "One way or another, we're going on vacation after this crap is over. So, how are things going over at your parents' house?"

"You would love it," Sharon replied seriously.

"Really?" Keith asked, surprised by Sharon's answer.

"Yes, definitely. Heather is being sweet and polite and is charming my dad, and its driving my mother nuts. My mom is pissed off and Heather is ignoring her rude comments and not giving her anything to work with. I love my mom, but this is really beautiful to watch."

"I agree. I would love it," Keith replied, wishing he could see it himself.

"Anything else I am missing?" he asked.

"Not really?" Sharon replied, not wanting to admit how much she was enjoying spending time with her parents and seeing their kids interacting with her father. "If anything comes up, I will call you from my cell."

"Sounds good, bye," Keith said, still feeling pleased by Sharon's support.

"Bye," Sharon said back before hanging up the call and going back to enjoying her time at her parents' home.

Keith then put his phone in his pocket and looked at the clock, wishing Kevin would just call. To give himself something to do, Keith decided to go into the garage and rearrange his tools and boat equipment.

Updating Sharon had lightened his mood, but rearranging his things in his garage gave him a sense that he was actually doing something. It let him see the results of his efforts in real time. He also found that it took just enough focus to take his mind mostly off of the stress of his situation. His rearranging had taken very little time but Keith was satisfied with the results. Leaning against the tall whiteboard, he looked at the now cleaner and more open space in his garage and then at the small boat he had designed and built and which he had planned to launch the following day.

He wondered if it would still be possible to launch it this weekend while things were still so up in the air. Then, as he had so often done during the last year or so, he let his mind wonder into imagining design enhancements for the little craft. While he was imagining a design for a long detachable bow sprit and a proportionally sized flying Dutchmen sail, his cell phone rang. It was Kevin Taft. He answered immediately. "Kevin, Hi. I have been waiting for you to give me a call."

"Anything new on your end?" Kevin asked.

"Other than someone pounding on my back door in the middle of the night, my dropping my family off at my in-laws, Dennis threatening my job and Dale Wade pounding on my door screaming for me to open up, well, not much," Keith said all in one breath, expecting Kevin to be surprised by the events.

"Wow, Wade tried to confront you this morning? Did you talk to him?" Kevin asked.

"No. I refused to even answer. He was in quite a hostile mood and, friend or not, I was not going to deal with him when he was worked up like that."

"Probably a good thing," Kevin said. "Where are you now?"

"I am at home, but I will probably have to go into work in a while," Keith answered.

"Don't," Kevin said seriously. "I have some things I want to show you. I will be over in a few minutes. Stay inside."

"Okay," Keith responded, before hearing the line go dead and not knowing exactly how to take what Kevin had just said.

Believing that Kevin would not have told him to stay inside without a good reason, Keith decided to clear room for Kevin to pull his car into the garage. He then rearranged a few things and flipped the boat onto its side, making enough space for a normal sized car to fit in next to his own.

Chapter 62
(Friday: 9:40 a.m.)

Keith remained in his garage organizing and reorganizing his things for several minutes before going into the main part of the house to watch for Kevin to pull up. A few minutes later, Keith saw Kevin pull into his driveway in a car that Keith had not seen him use before. Keith opened the garage door by hitting the button as he stepped out into the garage. Kevin recognized the invitation and pulled his car into the open space. Keith closed the garage once Kevin pulled in and found himself admiring the car Kevin had chosen to use that day. It looked brand new, but Keith recognized it to be an Alfa Romeo from the nineteen eighties.

"Nice ride," Keith said, clearly admiring the lovely car.

"I bought it new quite a long time ago, but I don't use it much because my wife finds it uncomfortable to ride in," Kevin replied, as he climbed out wearing his usual jeans and polo shirt and choosing not to elaborate about his wife's debilitating arthritis.

"We have much to discuss," Kevin continued, before walking around the back of the car and putting a number of papers and pictures on the side of the small upturned boat, arranging them like a deck of cards.

Keith came around the front of the car and glanced at the papers and pictures Kevin had begun putting down and noticed that one man was featured in most, if not all, of the photographs. Who is that?" Keith asked, picking up the picture closest to him and looking at the handsome man's facial features.

"He is the man who wrapped some kind of cloth around a branch and used it to harass you by slamming it into your glass sliding door last night," Kevin said, while handing Keith a photograph that showed enough background for him to recognize his own backyard.

"How did you get these pictures?" Keith asked, staring at the image of the man walking casually across his backyard.

"I had a very brave friend watch your house last night as a precaution. I have friends and contacts with influence and people who owe me favors. I hope you don't mind. I acted on a hunch."

"Hardly," Keith responded, "I'm grateful."

"Good. For now just remember his face. More about him in a minute."

Kevin then pointed to the first document he had put on the boat. "This is the LLC Operating Agreement for HematoChem, or at least one version of it. It describes who owns the company and the way the business is set up."

"How did you get that?" Keith asked, smiling at Kevin's resourcefulness.

"Quite by accident," Kevin replied honestly. "That day I met Dale here at your house I grabbed the papers out of his briefcase and had Heather photocopy them while you were talking to him. It was just a mischief game where I put her on the spot. I have messed with her like that ever since she was a little girl. This time it bore fruit."

"How do you mean?" Keith asked.

"See Appendix C there?" Kevin said, handing Keith the Document.

"Yes," Keith answered. "It lists several corporations as the owners of HematoChem. It looks like every other one I have seen, pretty standard."

"I agree," Kevin said, his expression shifting into a smile. "And that is what anyone reviewing it would think, but there is more to it."

Keith recalled his line of thinking about Dale possibly buying off Dennis by giving him part ownership in HematoChem and said, "Dale had joked with me about making me a part owner so we could both get rich. I laughed it off, but if he was serious and offered an ownership stake to Dennis in exchange for Dennis pushing for a sweetheart deal, and, if

Dennis had accepted the offer, it would explain a lot of his behaviors lately. Are you suggesting that they gave Dennis an ownership stake in HematoChem and hid it behind a separate company name?"

Kevin smiled more broadly, pleased that Keith had pieced together what he was getting at. "The second company listed is an S corporation owned in its entity by Dennis Gearin. Dennis' shell corporation owns ten percent of HematoChem, so Dennis owns ten percent of HematoChem, and as such he has been pressuring you to give a ridiculously good deal to a company he co-owns."

"Oh my god," Keith said. "That was really stupid on Dennis' part, but, if you think about it, who would even know? Maybe it wasn't so stupid. Maybe he has done it before."

"We will have to look into that eventually. Normally no-one at Tailcrest would ever think to check," Kevin said, "but I did check and these papers are proof. Dennis has stepped in it big time, but I suspect it is even bigger than Dennis thinks it is."

"How so?" Keith asked.

"The first part, which Dennis probably already knows about, is that this first company on Appendix C is also an S corporation, but it is owned in its entirety by Jason Roberts from the Legal Department. He also owns ten percent of HematoChem, which may partly explain why he took off after Kaitlin was murdered."

"Does Jason know that she was murdered?"

"I told him myself," Kevin offered, "not long before he chose to take a few days off."

"I can almost understand Jason's financial motivation in getting involved in this kind of ownership self-dealing, even though he is probably putting his license to practice law in jeopardy; but how does Kaitlin's murder tie in with Jason taking off this week? He could just be upset. They worked closely together for a long time."

"Timing. I checked with Campanaro. He had approved that 'reviewed and approved' stamp you have sooner than when Dennis gave it to you. I don't know how they tie together, but I think Jason does and that he is hiding out until the deal is done. I do know that Dennis gave you the stamp and the assignment about the same time that Jason sort of disappeared. Jason has apparently been in contact, but no-one seems to know where he is. I think that his sudden unavailability is telling, especially since he is the only other person with one of those stamps. I just don't know for sure what has been going through his head."

Keith thought about what Kevin was saying and replied, "I have no idea, but two things do make sense. One is that Jason would not look as bad if I approve the deal for a company he owns than if he approved a deal for his own company. The other is that Dennis would not look as bad if he dumped the negotiation of a deal with a company he owns on me so later on he can wash his hands of it saying, 'He's the lawyer, and I stayed away from it.'"

"I agree," Kevin responded, "that would explain why they are putting the approval of the deal on you. Maybe Dennis would have put the negotiation on you anyway, and maybe Campanaro's willingness to give you the stamp was just lucky for Jason so he wouldn't have to approve it himself. I think something changed when Kaitlin was killed."

Keith thought for a moment. Leaning on the edge of the boat, Keith then said, "If it was a standard market rate deal, Jason might have gotten it past Kaitlin and gotten her to sign it by offering assurances that it was fine, waiting for her to read it and sign it. She always read everything, no matter who handed it to her."

Kevin nodded. "That would be a logical way for Dennis and Jason to scam Tailcrest and cash in, potentially to the tune of millions of dollars in a few years, if or when HematoChem increases in value and is sold. If I were to invest in Wade's company right now and basically buy a ten percent ownership stake like each of them has, I would have to pay about two hundred thousand dollars. In other words, Dennis and Jason are scamming Tailcrest and enriching themselves to the tune of about two hundred thousand dollars each."

Keith continued, "What does not make sense is that they could have put through a reasonable, more market rate deal and Kaitlin would have approved it and signed it or, even now, I would have approved it and Campanaro would have signed it. No-one would have known any difference, including us. Why are they insisting on deal terms that Kaitlin would never, ever have accepted and that I won't approve?"

Kevin and Keith looked at each other for a moment. Kevin then said, "Are you sure the deal terms are so bad that Kaitlin would never have approved them?"

"Absolutely," Keith replied. "I am one hundred percent sure that she would have blocked the deal. I know that, Dennis knows that and Jason would, I presume, know that. Anyone who knows technology transfer licensing well and worked with Kaitlin on contracts would know that she would have hit this deal with a flying tackle."

Kevin's expression turned momentarily grim, then softened. "You are supposed to be a rubber stamp and approve the deal, but you are spoiling their fun. Dennis and Dale have been pressuring you and it may get worse in the hours between now and when Campanaro gets on his flight tonight. I do know for certain that President Walker would have a real problem with Tailcrest doing any deal with a company that operates like this, especially with the taint from Dennis' and Jason's involvement. If I had authority over it, I would shut down the negotiation and fire them both."

Kevin then continued, "Now for the bad part."

Keith's brow furrowed as he asked Kevin, "What do you mean?"

"You see the third company listed on Exhibit C?" Kevin asked.

"Sure," Keith replied. "It looks like another holding company, probably owned by the initial investor Dale mentioned or by an investment fund that is managed by the initial investor, or something like that. It says that it owns sixty percent of HematoChem, leaving Dale with the remaining twenty percent. So, the owner or owners of the holding company have majority ownership and control over HematoChem. How is this the bad part?"

Kevin paused for a moment then spoke evenly. "That holding company, the one that owns sixty percent of HematoChem and has control over it is one hundred percent owned by a Russian national by the name of Lenko Egorov. I had to do some digging and call in some favors to get information on the holding company because it is a Delaware corporation that is owned by a New York corporation that is owned by another corporation that is incorporated in Russia. Egorov owns one hundred percent of all of them and he is a bad, bad guy."

"How bad?" Keith asked.

"Bad enough. I will get to that," Kevin replied, "Now, I know how to start and build companies and structure corporate relationships, but technology transfer and intellectual property licensing are your areas. I need your help to sort through how to fit some pieces together for this deal and Egorov's involvement."

"I am as in as I can be," Keith replied. "What do we know about Lenko Egorov?"

Kevin looked at Keith and held his gaze, then said, "For starters he is the man in these pictures. He was here last night."

Keith felt his face flush and was suddenly more aware of the saw dust and wood smell of his garage as he unconsciously put his hand in his pocket and gripped the handle of his Seacamp pistol.

Chapter 63
(Friday: 10:00 a.m.)

Keith took several deep breaths while silently absorbing all of the information Kevin had provided him. Most difficult to absorb was the fact that the man in the picture was the majority owner of HematoChem, had been there at his house the previous night and had apparently taken several bold steps in harassing him and his family. Kevin calmly observed the way Keith was taking in the news and gave him a moment to process it mentally before stepping over toward the large whiteboard mounted on the wall. Moving two boxes to the side and picking up a dry erase marker, Kevin gestured toward the whiteboard and asked, "Do you mind?"

Keith smiled at the humor in Kevin's exaggerated politeness under the circumstances. "By all means," Keith responded, while nodding slightly.

"Dale, Dennis and Jason are in bed together, so to speak, regarding HematoChem. This much we know without question," Kevin said, while writing their names on the whiteboard.

He then put another name on the whiteboard, Lenko Egorov. "Egorov used several straw companies to hide his ownership of HematoChem. He is actually the majority owner, which means he controls it. Dale basically works for him. Egorov has taken an active role in pressuring you into okaying a deal that you know is problematic and that Kaitlin would have blocked had she been given the opportunity to read it. Since it is a License Agreement, she would most definitely have had her eyes on it within the Legal Department while she was there."

He then put Kaitlin's name on the board and said, "I suspect that Egorov may have killed Kaitlin to get her out of the way of this deal, as strange and excessive as that sounds. I would like for us to sort out the connections and why he would do something so overboard."

While Keith was focusing on what Kevin was saying he was diverted momentarily by the thought of how naturally Kevin, a multi-millionaire businessman, and himself, a technology transfer attorney, were sliding into the use of business meeting practices amid the tools and supplies in his garage. Keith then raised a hand. "Devil's advocate for a moment; Egorov could, conceivably, just be a strange aggressive guy who operates like a business savvy and corrupt thug. He used Dale to buy off Dennis and Jason so he could get a really good deal for HematoChem. We know that is probably what happened. He could also just be really pissed off at me for getting in the way of the deal and harassing me because he wants his candy and I am not letting him have it. There may, arguably, be no connection to Kaitlin's death at all."

"That is plausible," Kevin offered, "but I don't buy it. Granted, the accumulation of wealth in Russia may involve more rule bending and force than it does here. I honestly don't know. But, when you look at the pictures of him coming here last night something jumps out. He's relaxed. He doesn't hurry. He waits. Then he strolls away like he is walking through a park. That is not normal, and neither was the way Kaitlin was killed."

Keith felt a chill through his spine as he walked over and looked at more of the photographs. Kevin was right about Egorov having been relaxed and unhurried.

While Keith looked more closely at the pictures, Kevin continued, "Kaitlin would have definitely gotten in the way of this deal and she was definitely murdered. She also had time to leave a message before she was killed. It wouldn't have taken her long to scrape different things under each of her fingernails, but she was so injured that it would have taken effort and thought. There was time between her realizing that she was going to be killed and it actually happening. I think her killer walked up calmly, maybe spoke with her, and then reached down, snapped her neck and disappeared, not realizing she had scratched him to collect evidence for the authorities to find."

Kevin then stepped over to the pictures and picked up one that clearly showed Egorov strolling away from Keith's house looking calm and relaxed. "He had just slammed your glass door loud enough to wake up your family, and he is not even in a rush to get out of your yard. He then waited and watched. If you had come out, he might have harmed you. I think he killed Kaitlin, and I think the reason has something to do with the HematoChem deal."

Keith picked up another picture and saw clearly the cold malevolence in Egorov's eyes and then saw the small time stamp at the lower edge. "I did come out. I walked along the edge of the yard. He was watching me from not twenty five feet away when this picture was taken. I think you're right. I think he that he is a cold predator and that he killed Kaitlin just to get her out of the way of this deal."

"Okay, back to the whiteboard. What do we know?" Keith asked.

Kevin summarized what little they had. "Kaitlin would have blocked the deal they want, and she was murdered days before they started pressing hard to get it through in a way that would be bad for the University. There were skin cells under one of Kaitlin's fingernails from a man, not her husband, who does not show up in any available DNA database. Lenko Egorov is taking an active thug role in pressuring you to okay the deal the way they want it. They are claiming that there is a hard date deadline coming up very soon for funding from an investment firm. The person who can sign the deal before the hard deadline for investment funding passes is getting on a plane tonight. You are holding up the whole deal by refusing to okay the deal in the form they want. And, it's a sleazy deal because Dennis and Jason have taken ownership interests in HematoChem while supposedly being on this side of the negotiation table. Did I miss anything?"

"Not really," Keith replied. "Except maybe that Egorov's getting at Kaitlin while she was on vacation would have required that he know when she was going on vacation and where."

"Who would know that?" Kevin asked, while the answer came instantly into his head.

"Jason," Keith said without hesitation. "He shared an office and a secretary with her. He would have had access to her calendar, and chances are she would have told him where she and her husband were going whether he asked or not. He could have mentioned it to Dale, who would have passed it along to Egorov. It still seems excessive to kill someone. I am not sure why Egorov, or anyone, would consider doing that."

"You're right of course," Kevin said. "Something may have gone wrong. Maybe she saw his face when he didn't want her to and he was concerned that she could identify him. I don't know, but something about this deal is important enough for Egorov to take extraordinary steps to get the deal done their way. If there is something they want in the deal that was important enough for them to kill her or even hurt her to get her out of the way, then it probably involves something that you have found objectionable in their version of the License Agreement. Does this make sense?"

"Yes, I follow your logic," Keith said, wondering what could possibly be in the deal terms that would be important enough for Egorov to go after Kaitlin and then harass him. "There are several serious sticking points."

"I recall you mentioning some but what were they again and why might they be very important to Dale or Egorov?" Kevin asked, holding the dry erase marker at the ready like a business meeting facilitator.

Keith then listed the main sticking points slowly enough for Kevin to write them out on the whiteboard. "Future intellectual property rights, sublicensing rights, milestone payments and royalties, and export control compliance," Keith said. "They are all very technical legal provisions. Of course, there was also my wanting them to show us the corporate documents and list of owners, but you have taken care of that."

"They don't know that we know about their ownership stakes in HematoChem, but covering up a corrupt sweetheart deal would hardly be enough of a motive," Kevin said. "Besides, they hid their ownership stakes well enough that no one would have noticed, at least probably not initially. What is the difference in your and their positions on the other things?"

"For future rights, I am trying to limit what future inventions are covered by this contract," Keith said. "They want basically everything invented in this technological area at Tailcrest. I want to limit it to five years and only inventions made by this particular inventor in this field during that time."

Kevin wrote notes on the board; then paused. "What's the practical difference?"

Keith shrugged, "It is a tremendous difference in value, although it is impossible to tell until the inventions are made. In all likelihood the bulk of any new inventions HematoChem would be interested in would be made by the same inventor in the next five years anyway. They shouldn't care much, other than having a better selling point for investors. What they are getting is already really good."

"You said milestone payments and royalties?" Kevin added.

"Yes," Keith answered. "They want to pay one minimal milestone payment upon FDA approval of the technology, and just a one percent royalty on sales. This could add up to a lot of money. However, if it is commercially successful, there would be plenty of money for everyone. It doesn't make sense to risk much of anything over a few percent royalty obligation on sales and keeping milestone payments low."

"What about sublicensing?"

"That's more complicated and more interesting," Keith answered. "I want to have the University preapprove in writing all sublicenses.

Basically, if HematoChem wants to transfer the rights under the license to any other company, they would need our written approval to do so. What they want is to have an unlimited right to sublicense any of the rights under the License Agreement to any other company without us having any say or even seeing it. They also want the sublicenses with other companies to stay in effect even if HematoChem ceases to exist or we terminate the License Agreement that the sublicenses were based on. What they want for sublicensing is simply not okay, and arguably a deal killer, but again, it's not worth hurting anyone over. Companies ask for variations that are less stringent than prior approval sometimes, but they always come around to our position."

"So," Kevin said while drawing three circles with an arrow connecting each to the next, "the way they want it they can get the rights from you and right away transfer them completely to some other company, and there would be nothing you could do about it?"

"Yes," Keith said.

"Even if HematoChem goes out of business?" Kevin asked.

"Yes again."

"Even if HematoChem is in Russia?" Kevin continued.

"Yes," Keith said, looking at Kevin and wondering where he might be going with this. "Why are you focusing on this part?"

"I'll get to it," Kevin replied. "The other one you mentioned was export control. What is the deal with that?"

"Export control is a very technical, complicated and difficult to understand area of law," Keith answered, trying to think of a way to simplify it. "The United States Departments of State, Commerce and Treasury all have their own restrictions on what technologies can be sent out of the country. The Treasury Department's rules are mostly for embargoed countries. The State Department and Commerce Department's each have detailed control lists describing what technologies cannot be sent to other countries without permission in the form of an export license. There are also bad guy lists that have to be checked. This is very serious business when you are dealing with things that can be used by our enemies to harm us. For example, sending night vision technology to Iran would be very, very bad, and would probably include a jail sentence and a fine of up to a million dollars per violation. I wouldn't sell them on E-Bay."

Kevin nodded, "I deal with some of this in my businesses. I have a law firm in Washington, DC on retainer that evaluates every product we sell outside of the U.S. We also do all of our technology development work in the U.S., and mostly with U.S. Citizens or foreign nationals who are permanent residents. How does the University handle it?"

"It depends," Keith said. "I know that is a non-answer but it does depend on the situation. In this one it is supposedly a U.S. company owned by U.S. citizens. I am insisting that all technology be received by a U.S. Citizen at HematoChem and that they evaluate it before allowing any non-U.S. person or company access to it, and that it be a strict condition of the license. I am also requiring that they certify compliance every six months as a condition of the license. I know Dale plans to run clinical trials in Russia because it is cheaper, so I want his company to be fully responsible for export compliance."

"Okay. What do they want?" Kevin asked.

"They want basic language saying that each side will comply with export rules," Keith replied, "which is not sufficient to protect Tailcrest."

Kevin folded his arms and leaned back against the white board. "I think I see what Egorov may be up to. Say for argument sake Tailcrest entered into the license."

"Okay."

"You mentioned the other day that part of the technology was funded by a grant from the Department of Defense and that preventing The Bends could have military applications especially in the Navy."

"Yes," Keith replied.

"What would happen if Lenko Egorov used his majority ownership of HematoChem to insert himself as CEO?"

"He would control all aspects of HematoChem. He essentially does anyway, but that would solidify it."

Kevin then continued, "Then what would happen if Egorov sublicensed the technology to a Russian company that intends to develop both civilian and military applications of the technology, with the military applications going to the Russian military?"

Keith understood Kevin's point. "Potentially bad things. Egorov could then stay in Russia and guide the efforts of HematoChem, probably out of reach of the U.S. Government. And, at least on the surface it would look like a clean transfer of technology from Tailcrest to HematoChem and then from HematoChem to the Russian company. Not good. It would be almost invisible to our office for a while, especially if they described what they were doing using non-military terms," Keith said. "And, even if we were able to terminate the license to HematoChem, the sublicense to the Russian company would likely still be valid unless we make some argument about it being against public policy. By the time we noticed and sorted it out the military applications would likely already have been developed for the Russian military under color of a valid contract with Tailcrest."

"Complicated stuff," Kevin said.

"Yes, yes it is," Keith replied, nodding.

Kevin then looked Keith in the eye. "So the real question is whether Egorov would view the development of the military applications of the technology for the Russian military under color of a valid contract as being important enough for him to harm the people who might get in the way of the contract. He went so far as to hide his ownership in HematoChem behind two corporations and he visited you last night. I don't think he would have hesitated to injure a female lawyer who would have spoiled his plans. What do you think?"

"I think you're right," Keith answered. "I think he killed Kaitlin, and I think I am in considerable danger."

Kevin smiled, "Yes, but there is a silver lining to this knowledge. A devil we know is better than a devil we don't. He killed someone very dear to me, and this knowledge may help me show my appreciation for his efforts."

Chapter 64
(Friday: 10:25 a.m.)

Egorov stood very still in the wooded section behind Keith's house smoking a cigarette while shielding the cigarette's bright tip with the palm of his hand. Egorov had positioned himself so he could see the back of Keith's house as well as the garage door on the side and most of the front yard. Thus far he had only seen an older man in an expensive car pull into the garage, which had been opened and closed so he could pull in. Egorov guessed that the garage door had been opened by Keith from the inside and that Keith remained in the house with his visitor. Snuffing out his cigarette on a tree trunk and placing the filtered butt in his pocket, Egorov then took out his cell phone and called Dale.

"Lenko, I was going to call you in a few minutes," Dale answered, after nodding to the bespectacled, short, blonde hostess who had just signaled for him to follow her to his table in the chain restaurant known for its eggs and ham breakfasts.

"Good, have you learned of any progress since we last spoke?" Egorov asked more quietly than felt natural to him.

"Unfortunately, no, quite the opposite," Dale replied, unsure of how Egorov would respond as he sat down in the booth the petite hostess had led him to. "I spoke with Dennis and apparently Keith has dug his heels in on the deal and is insisting on working from home. When I heard, I drove over to his house and tried to talk with him, but he wouldn't even answer the door. I have seen what Keith is like when he gets stubborn. I am worried that he won't budge on the deal terms."

"You worry too much my friend," Egorov said reassuringly. "People have a way of changing their approach when there is a gun pointed at their head. You just relax and call me if you hear anything else from Dennis Gearin."

"I will," Dale replied before Egorov ended the call, leaving Dale to wonder if he was speaking literally or figuratively about putting a gun to Keith's head.

Egorov returned his phone to his pocket, then continued to watch the house, wondering how long it would be before the visitor left so he could deal with Keith his way, get the deal done and get back to his own home.

Chapter 65
(Friday: 10:25 a.m.)

Kevin picked up a rag near the whiteboard and used it as a makeshift eraser to wipe off the writing. He then started to collect the papers and pictures he had set out on the side of the small boat. Handing two pictures to Keith, one showing a close up of Egorov and one taken from further away, Kevin said, "It is really quite brilliant on Egorov's part. The United States and Russia are on better terms now than during the Cold War. Why steal technology when you can push through a complicated contract that makes everything look okay and where things are so complicated from a technological and relationship standpoint that no one will bother to look or question anything."

Glancing at the pictures Kevin had handed him, Keith replied, "I agree. Tailcrest Tech Transfer personnel would be the only ones who would monitor the license contract, and Technology Transfer Offices are generally not very diligent about that sort of thing. In this case the Technology Transfer Office's Director has been 'dirtied up' by taking an ownership interest in the company. Dennis would be the one to put resources toward looking under HematoChem's skirt, so to speak, and he is not going to do that when he is hiding the fact that he is a co-owner of the company."

"You're right," Kevin concurred. "Egorov had every angle locked down. The only things that got in his way were Kaitlin and now you."

"Now me," Keith agreed.

"I am guessing there is even more to it," Kevin continued, while straightening the papers and pictures in his folder by tapping the edges on the side of the boat. "Russia has stimulus funds that are sort of like the massive U.S. stimulus from a while back, only not as large and they blend private and public money. I would not be surprised if getting the license from Tailcrest would make the deal clean enough to apply for investment by a Russian stimulus fund for the open development of the non-military applications of the technology while using the development results to advance the military applications."

"That would explain the deadline Dale and apparently Egorov are so concerned about. Dale mentioned a hard date based on requirements from an investor."

Kevin smiled. "Most investors do not have actual hard dates where things must be submitted to them by a certain time. Some investors may set artificial deadlines, but realistically most all private investors are relatively fluid and will bend their own rules if a good opportunity presents itself. Now, government bureaucracies do set hard dates. A Russian public-private fund's having a hard date makes sense because of the government bureaucratic element."

"So if I have this right," Keith said, "we could be looking at a Russian stimulus fund paying for the development in Russia of military and non-military applications of technology initially developed using funding by the U.S. Department of Defense?"

"Yes," Kevin agreed.

"And the Russians will get the military applications and the U.S. won't?"

"Yes again," Kevin said. "It's an interesting new world where you can hide things like that in plain sight."

Keith thought for a moment about the earlier part of their conversation, then said, "If the military applications are what they want, wouldn't it make sense for Egorov to scuttle HematoChem, which is actually Egorov's company, by breaching the agreement and then just developing the military applications in secret?"

"Not if you look at it practically," Kevin replied. "If there is publicly available investment money and a solid market for the non-military applications, why not move forward with that part too? This way you have a cover for the military development and legitimate funding for the non-military technological development, which just helps with the military part. Egorov, or the Russian military, or whoever is involved in developing the military applications, would save a boatload of money. And, the civilian applications may actually be huge money makers that can make all of the investors rich.

"This is making way too much sense, and is making me even more concerned about Egorov's having been here last night."

Kevin straightened his posture and said, "Well counselor. You are a lawyer, right?"

"Yes, but I haven't been in a courtroom in a very long time."

"In summation," Kevin said in a mock officious tone before returning to his more normal speaking voice, "under your version of the License Agreement the American people are protected as fully as possible. Under their version of the License Agreement they are not, and there is a loophole that would allow for Russian military development of technology funded by the U.S. Department of Defense. And furthermore, henceforth and in perpetuity, you are going to stand your ground and not authorize the contract to go forward."

"You make a persuasive case, counselor, and I will comply fully with your request," Keith said, appreciating Kevin's caricature of an attorney. He then looked again at the pictures of Egorov he was holding in his hand.

"Good," Kevin replied. "They are not playing games with this, and neither are we."

Chapter 66
(Friday: 10:35 a.m.)

Kevin collected all of the papers and pictures, except the two pictures Keith was holding, and put them in his worn leather briefcase. He then put the briefcase on the passenger seat of his car through the open passenger side window. While Kevin did this, Keith wrinkled his forehead and said, "You know, your having discovered those documents and tracked all this information down clearly makes it impossible for me to approve this deal no matter what, which is good."

Kevin saw that Keith was leading into something and said, "But-"

"Now there is probably a brilliant homicidal foreigner, who has killed before and who has visited my home, out there somewhere. He knows I am the only thing standing between him and what he has already killed to make happen."

"This concerns you?" Kevin asked, breaking into a supportive grin.

"Just a bit," Keith replied. "He may try to harm me or, God forbid, my family to get me to approve the deal. He doesn't know that I am not going to approve it no matter what or that you have those documents showing the ownership scheme or the pictures showing him at my house. He thinks he is operating completely in the clear so he has no reason to slow down or stop trying."

"Well," Kevin said, pausing for effect, "if he goes after you, you could try to get a DNA sample. That would actually help us prove the connection to Kaitlin's murder."

"Are you planning to use me as bait?" Keith asked, half wondering if Kevin would do that to catch Kaitlin's killer.

"Of course not," Kevin replied.

"Good, because as much as I liked Kaitlin, and as much as I want to see her killer caught, I have no desire to be anywhere near Lenko Egorov, at least not until my children are grown and no longer need my guidance."

"Hate to break it to you," Kevin said, "but once they're grown, they'll still need your guidance. I know that first hand."

"Then it's settled. I never see Egorov, ever."

Kevin chuckled lightly, knowing there were still two important things he had to do before he left. "In all seriousness there is an issue in there. We don't know where Egorov is and, other than being able to prove harassment using these pictures, without a DNA sample I don't think we have any evidence that he has committed any real crimes. Others may, but we don't yet. That's a detail I am working on. No, it does not involve using you as bait."

"Why am I thinking that it means our holding off on making noise about Dennis' and Jason's having been bought off until you have dealt with Egorov somehow?"

"It does, but I will explain more on that in a bit. It really does not involve using you as bait. Trust me on that."

Kevin then stepped past Keith as though he was going around to the driver's side to get in his car, even though that was not yet his intention. "There is something else."

Keith rolled his eyes. "What else could there possibly be, aside from the murderer and the fact that my boss will most definitely fire me, if he ever gets the chance?"

"Look closely at the pictures," Kevin said in a soft, even tone.

Keith looked more closely at the two pictures he was holding. First he focused on Egorov's face in the close-up and did not notice anything he had not seen before. Then he looked closely at the other picture and noticed the background behind Egorov. At first he did not see anything unusual, but then he saw that in the background were several ordinary looking houses including Sharon's parents' house. Keith's face turned pale and he made a beeline for the driver's side of his own car. Kevin deftly stepped in front of Keith and, using positioning and a grip of his arm, stopped Keith where he was, even as Keith tried to push past him.

"Your family is safe, perfectly safe," Kevin said to reassure Keith.

"What do you mean?" Keith asked him, stepping back and looking at him curiously.

"I mentioned that I have friends with influence and people who owe me favors," Kevin said. "I made a few calls this morning. Just because we have very little on Egorov, it doesn't mean he has not made mistakes in his past. Turns out that there are people who would really like to talk to him about some other matters involving the transfer of technology to places it should not have gone."

"Kevin, my family is involved," Keith said. "I would like some more detail than that. How do you know my family is safe?"

"There are two armed government good guys on foot watching the house where your family and Heather and Chrissy are," Kevin said. "And there are two more in a van not far away. I am not taking chances with your family or Heather or Chrissy."

Keith knew that Kevin had an emotional bond with Heather that was like a father's with an only daughter. He also knew that Kevin would move heaven and earth to protect her and Chrissy. If only because they were with Heather and Chrissy, Keith felt reassured that whatever steps Kevin had taken would keep his family safe. Keith took a deep breath and let it out slowly. Then he said, "You could let Egorov take out my mother-in-law."

Kevin took Keith's attempt at humor as a sign that he had calmed down. "That would be tricky to pull off without putting others at risk, but I understand the sentiment. Now, there are two parallel objectives in this effort. One, keep you, Sharon, Heather and all the kids safe. Two, deal with Egorov before he realizes the situation has collapsed and he disappears."

"You did a strategic planning and project management outline for this, didn't you?" Keith asked, having observed the approach Kevin used in his University efforts.

"Well, actually, yes," Kevin replied, amused that Keith had guessed what he had done.

Kevin then took a folded envelope out of his back pocket and handed it to Keith. "In here is an address. When you call Sharon and fill her in on more of the details, just tell her that there is a van with federal law enforcement officers waiting to take everyone in the house to a very safe place. All she has to do is literally wave something by the front window and the van will pull up."

"And me? What do I do?" Keith asked.

"All you have to do is make the call to Sharon, maybe grab a day or two's extra cloths for the kids, then get yourself to that address."

"I can do that," Keith said. "They keep a change of clothes here for Chrissy too. I'll grab them as well."

"Good. Now the Egorov part. I am going to get a DNA sample from him, maybe even today. I am going to connect him to Kaitlin's murder, and I am going to change his life forever," Kevin said, smiling in a way that Keith thought made him look kind of evil. "My plan for getting to Egorov today is to be myself, just differently. You see, I am a ruthless investor, and I managed to figure out that there is a potentially financially lucrative back deal going on, and I have documents and pictures. Do you follow where I am going with this?"

"No, no I don't, Keith replied.

"Well, Dale keeps calling me to get me to talk sense into you, so you will accept their deal. They know we are friends and they think I can sway your opinion. I plan on floating a business proposition to them that they have to act on quickly. I'll propose that they cut me in on the ownership of HematoChem, claiming that they should have paid off the right people in the first place, in exchange for my delivering your stamped approval on their version of the License Agreement and my agreeing to hand over the documents I have and never think of the matter again. I will also insist as an absolute requirement that I meet the man in the picture in person because I always meet the people I do business with. That part happens to be true. When I meet Egorov I get a DNA sample, even if I have to scratch him myself."

"That could work," Keith agreed.

Kevin then walked over to Keith's tool bench and picked up a flat ten inch pry-bar that Keith used to pull out nails. "This could help. Mind if I borrow it?"

"Not at all," Keith said, both impressed and pleased with what Kevin had in mind.

"I am going to clue in an old friend I trust so I am not implicated in actually trying to get in on the corrupt dealing, and then I will set some things in motion. Let me know when you get to that address," Kevin said, patting Keith on the arm and heading toward his car.

Chapter 67

(Friday: 10:50 a.m.)

Keith pushed the button to open his garage door and then watched Kevin pull his car out before pushing it again and waiting for the door to fully close. Keith then took a picture of the close-up photograph of Egorov using his cell phone. Satisfied that the image on his phone was clear enough, Keith forwarded it to Sharon's cell phone with a text message noting the address of the safe-house. He then waited, knowing that Sharon would reply quickly.

Over at her parents' house Sharon felt her phone vibrate. She saw that a text message had come in from Keith and that it comprised just an address with an attached picture. She then opened the attachment and froze in place when saw the picture. What she saw was an image of the man who had turned and looked at the windows of her house the day before. She quickly waved Heather over and showed her the picture. "It's from Keith," she said. "He just sent me this. This is the guy I saw outside my house. I am calling Keith right now. Stay here and listen."

"Okay," Heather said, not letting on that she had been the one who had taken the picture they were looking at nor that she had seen the same man this morning outside the house they were currently in.

About twenty seconds after sending the picture, Keith answered Sharon's call. "Is the guy in the picture the same guy you saw outside the house?" he asked.

"Yes. How did you know? Where did you get this picture?" Sharon asked.

"From Kevin Taft. He was concerned about us and had an amazingly talented surveillance person watch our house last night and take this picture and several others."

"Last night?" Sharon asked, feeling her anxiety level rise. "So this is the man who made the noise that woke us up last night."

"Yes. He apparently used a branch to slam the sliding door without breaking it. Kevin has a lot of pictures showing the whole thing."

"Okay, I am really worried and kind of freaked out right now," Sharon said while glancing at Heather and holding her gaze as she spoke.

"First, the good part," Keith said. "You and Heather and all the kids are perfectly safe. You have nothing to worry about."

"How do you know?" Sharon asked, worried and confused by his statement.

"Kevin is very resourceful, and he is protective of the people in his life, including us," Keith said. "And you know Heather is like a daughter to him."

Sharon continued to maintain eye contact with Heather while asking Keith, "How does Heather's safety tie into this? She is right here with me."

"To answer that I have to give you more of the good part and some of the bad part," Keith continued. "The good part is that there are several federal law enforcement officers watching your parent's house right now to ensure everyone there remains safe and to keep an eye out for the man in the picture. His name is Egorov."

"What's the bad part, and why would they be watching my parents' house?" she asked, breaking eye contact with Heather and having already guessed the answer.

"Egorov followed us this morning. Kevin showed me a picture, taken this morning showing Egorov walking casually past you parents' house. He knows you are there."

Sharon felt a wave of cold fear run through her, and she looked over at the three children sitting in front of the television near her own parents. "Why is this guy harassing our family and what can we do about it?" she asked, feeling afraid and angry.

"It's about this deal I am in the middle of. There is a lot more to it. This Egorov guy is really creepy. He actually looks relaxed in all of the pictures, like what he was doing last night was no big deal. Even more concerning is that he may be the one who killed Kaitlin, and he may be targeting us to pressure me on the HematoChem deal. Kevin is working on a way to get at this guy, but our part is to just 'lay low' as they say."

"I don't like this," Sharon replied.

"Me either," Keith said, "but we're safe. The officers are literally watching your parents' house right now. They are outside and there is a van nearby waiting to take everyone in the house to a safe location. It's the address I sent you. Kevin gave me the address and a Mapquest printout before he left just a minute ago. All you have to do is wave a cloth or a towel or something by the front window and the van will pull up and pick you all up. I am going to grab some cloths and toothbrushes for us and the kids and I will meet you at that address as quickly as I can."

"I still really don't like this," Sharon repeated.

"Which part," Keith asked, smiling to himself, "the creepy guy stalking us or having to convince your mother to get into the van?"

"You're an ass, Keith, but I love you," Sharon said into the phone. "I'll get things moving here, with or without my mother. You just get yourself to that address. I don't like you being by yourself at our house right now."

"I love you too, and I will. Bye," Keith said, hanging up the call and putting his phone in his pocket.

Sharon put her phone away as well and then looked at Heather and asked, "Did you hear all of that?"

"Sure. He said he loves you," Heather said. "I can just pick Chrissy up when it's time to go. How can I help with the boys and your parents?"

Sharon looked over at her mom and tried to imagine her reaction at hearing that Keith's work had created a dangerous situation, that there were officers watching the house and that they all had to go to a safe-house right away. Picturing her mother's probable reaction, Sharon covered her mouth with her hand tried to suppress a building laugh. After a moment tears welled up in her eyes while she covered her mouth with her hand trying not to laugh. Heather mistook Sharon's reaction for genuine crying and asked quietly, "Are you okay?"

Moving her hand away from her mouth Sharon tried to speak, then paused, then tried again. "I have to convince my mother to get into a police van," Sharon said quietly to Heather before bursting out laughing.

Heather then laughed too, appreciating the situation and feeling glad about Sharon's reaction to it. The two women then looked at each other and laughed even harder when they heard Sharon's mother call in from the other room, "What's so funny?"

Sharon wiped the tears from her eyes and walked over to talk to her mother, pulling Heather along by the wrist. Looking back at Heather, Sharon whispered, "Stay close," and burst out laughing again.

Chapter 68
(Friday: 11:15 a.m.)

After talking to Sharon, Keith headed into the main part of house to collect things to bring to the address that Kevin had given him. Without realizing it Keith was keeping his right hand in his jeans pocket on his pistol and tapping the trigger lightly as he moved through his house. He moved quickly upstairs and grabbed a duffle bag out of his closet before shoving suitable cloths for himself and Sharon into the bag. He then grabbed the change of clothes Sharon kept for Chrissy and clothes for the boys, tooth brushes, tooth paste and a hair brush. Thinking this was probably enough to bring with him, he tied the bag at the top and headed down stairs holding the duffle bag in his left hand.

Nearing the bottom of the stairs, he again slipped his right hand back into his jeans pocket and onto the handle of his gun. Crossing his living room on his way to his car, Keith looked up and stopped short. He stood frozen, staring at Lenko Egorov who was standing in Keith's living room and pointing a black handgun right at his face. In that first instant Keith saw that Egorov had a placid expression on his face and appeared comfortable and at ease holding his gun in a two handed grip out in front of him, looking at Keith with both eyes open. Keith also recognized from the squared off barrel that the gun was a Glock pistol and guessed from the size of the barrel that it was a .40 caliber.

In the next moment Keith regained the ability to breath and realized that, even with his right hand literally on his gun in his pocket, he had no chance at all to outgun Egorov. He knew that if he tried to pull his pistol, he would be dead in a few seconds.

Egorov then did what Keith thought was a curious thing. He smiled at Keith like they were old friends. "You are under a lot of stress lately," Egorov said. "You are imagining things: a bump in the night; a man pointing a gun at you; reasons to hold up a technology licensing deal that can help everyone involved."

Egorov then paused like he was waiting for Keith to say something, but Keith remained silent, hoping Egorov would lower his gun even for a second. Keith saw that Egorov's weapon did not move or shake or wobble at all. Egorov also showed no sign that the weight of the weapon was having any effect at all while he stood there pointing it at Keith.

Egorov then continued to talk to Keith conversationally, "You will lose your job. Unemployment is hard on a family, no? Your wife, she is ill? She did not look well when you dropped her off this morning with your children. Better to approve the deal and make everything go smoothly for everyone. If you approve the deal in the next few hours I would have no reason to visit you or your family again. If you do not approve the deal today, or if you involve the police, I will most certainly visit your family. It is remarkable just how easy it is for people to have unfortunate accidents. Did you not lose someone in your Legal Department to an accident recently?"

"Did you kill Kaitlin?" Keith asked evenly, surprising himself that he could speak at all.

Egorov ignored the question. "Don't make me hurt your family Mr. Mastin," Egorov said, closing one eye and sighting his weapon specifically at Keith's right eye for added effect.

Keith registered the threat against his family and for the first time felt a genuine urge to kill another human being. He also experienced a curiously calm rage. Keith then pictured in his mind the two of them sitting across a conference room table from each other, sneared at Egorov and said in a professional tone, "You realize of course that you are going about this the wrong way. You don't need to threaten my family or point at gun at me, and I would prefer that you didn't," Keith said, hoping to convince Egorov to lower his weapon so Keith would have a chance to shoot him.

"What do you mean?" Egorov asked.

"I am negotiating the deal the way I negotiate deals," Keith said. "I needed to flush out the real decision maker. Obviously it is not Dale, and I prefer to be discreet. It would have been easier if you had just knocked on my door last night. I would have welcomed you in so we could discuss this over a drink."

"What are you saying, Mr. Mastin?" Egorov asked.

Keith continued talking; hoping Egorov would lower his weapon. "I have a colleague named Kevin Taft who I rely on for certain things, and I help him in certain ways. He just left, and I had him hold on to the approval stamp that I will use to approve the deal once a suitable accord is reached so Kevin benefits personally. After Kevin benefits, he will arrange things so that I will benefit too, just very discreetly. No one will know the difference and it will be sufficiently separate that no one would be able to prove it, even if they suspected a connection."

"I may have misjudged you, Mr. Mastin." Egorov said. "What is it you intend?"

"It was simple for Kevin and me to figure out that Dale had approached the person who he thought could move the deal, Dennis, and offered him something to sweeten it. Then the situation changed. I am the person who can move the deal forward now, and Dennis has no power at all, other than to fire me. Frankly, I don't care if he does. I think this technology has promise and I would like to own part of the company, but I cannot because I am too close to the deal. That's where my friend Kevin Taft comes in. He can very cleanly own part of HematoChem. Perhaps later he will share some of his ownership with me or give me something else of value. I do not get involved in these things directly, but, if Kevin is satisfied and says to approve the deal, I will approve it."

"Why should I accept your conditions?" Egorov asked.

"Because if you don't, or if you show up near my family or you harm me, you will not get your deal today, or ever," Keith said, meeting Egorov's gaze coldly as though the gun was not pointed at his face. "Kevin Taft will contact Dale Wade to make arrangements. Oh, the part about pretending that Wade was the one negotiating the terms of the license didn't work. It was obvious that someone else was pulling the strings. Kevin will also insist on meeting you in person, just so you know. He meets everyone he does business with. That is a well-established fact."

"Very interesting Mr. Mastin," Egorov said, not shifting the gun at all. "Let me put it this way. You will approve this deal today or one of your children will die. Would you like to choose which one? I understand that you want us to accommodate your personal interests. That is a reasonable request. I will speak with Dale Wade about coordinating with this Kevin Taft. Understand, however, that you will approve the deal today, one way or another, or one of your children will die."

Keith remained silent while fighting the urge to pull his pistol and try to get off an accurate shot before Egorov knew what happened. "Good," Egorov said. "I believe we understand each other."

With that Egorov nodded slightly and backed out through the sliding door onto the porch without lowering his weapon. It was not until Egorov was more than half way across the yard that he lowered his weapon, turned and walked quickly into the wooded area at the edge of Keith's yard. Keith knew that he had no chance of getting off an accurate shot before Egorov was gone into the woods. He also knew that, if he were to follow him or try for a lucky shot, it would end badly. Keith fumed, put down a powerful urge to chase him into the woods, and stayed in his house.

Chapter 69

(Friday: 11:25 a.m.)

After Egorov disappeared from view, Keith thought there might be a small chance that Egorov was watching from the woods like Keith knew he had done after his previous visit. He quickly closed and locked the sliding back door and pulled the vertical blinds shut to help ensure that Egorov could not see into that portion of the house. Keith then checked the locks on all of the doors and windows to be sure, while wondering how Egorov had gotten in. He then returned to the living room where he had left the duffel bag. As he reached to pick up the duffel bag he thought of his children's cloths being in it and how Egorov had just threatened to kill one of them if he didn't approve the deal today. The blended fear and anger of what had just happened opened up in him and he experienced such a powerful sense of rage that he felt he understood how people could "lose it" and kill. Keith paced back and forth in his living room clenching and unclenching his fists and his jaw, trying unsuccessfully to calm himself down.

After almost two minutes of pacing, his breathing slowed slightly and he was able to relax his fists and his jaw. Then, abruptly, his expression changed and he grinned widely when he had a sudden realization. He shot over to the computer nook near his front door and logged into his computer. "Please be there," he said to himself as he worked the keyboard and mouse.

"YES!" he shouted more loudly than he had intended when he saw the recorded images from his home security system, which had been left on from the day before.

Right there in front of him was an electronic recording of the events from when Egorov entered his home until he left. Keith was mesmerized watching the video showing Egorov enter through the front door of his house, put something in his pocket, which Keith presumed was a lock picking device, and then relock the door and wait behind a wall as Keith went upstairs. He continued watching and saw how Egorov then calmly opened the back sliding door, took out his gun and waited for Keith to come back downstairs. The images of Egorov pointing his gun at Keith were as clear as could be and Keith knew they would provide enough evidence to put Egorov in jail for maybe a few years, if they could just catch him.

Breathing deeply and relaxing somewhat more Keith took several cell phone pictures of the images on the computer screen and used a feature on the security system to e-mail copies of the video recording to both of Kevin's e-mail accounts as well as his own and Sharon's so there would be copies available no matter what. He then used his cell phone to send one of the images to Kevin's cell phone with the message, "He just left. Sent video to your e-mail."

Keith then took several deep breaths while looking at the portion of his living room where Egorov had been standing and played over in his mind the whole interaction, start to finish. Forcing himself to focus on the present, Keith then decided to hold off on telling Sharon about Egorov's visit for a while. He then shut down his computer, grabbed the duffel bag and headed out to his garage. After climbing into his car and starting the engine, Keith used the garage remote in his car to open the garage door. He pulled out quickly and waited in the street until the door had fully closed again. Driving very aggressively, he looked alternately at the road and the Mapquest printout while finding his way toward the safe address and his family.

Before he made it far out of his neighborhood, Keith's cell phone rang and he saw that it was Kevin. He quickly plugged in the hands free earpiece and answered the call. "Kevin, I met Egorov."

"I can see that," Kevin said, while he too was driving through traffic, pleased that Keith seemed okay and surprised that he had gotten the video of Egorov.

"But I didn't get a DNA sample," Keith continued. "He picked the lock and waited for me, then kept a gun at my head the whole time. I had no chance of getting anywhere near him, and he was wearing gloves.

"Not to worry," Kevin said. "This will be enough to have him arrested and convicted, if we can entice him to show up somewhere where we can catch and restrain him. After that a DNA sample will be easy to get. You did good."

"Thanks, but we need to do a lot better. He threatened to kill one of my kids if I don't approve the deal today. If I could have gotten a shot off, I would have. I really wanted to kill him."

"You carry?" Kevin asked.

"Not on campus, but yes, sometimes," Keith replied. "It didn't help. He didn't move his weapon at all. I would have been toast if I pulled my SeaCamp out of my pocket."

"He didn't know you had it?" Kevin asked. "How small is this gun?"

"About the size of a smartphone. It was in my jeans pocket when we were talking this morning."

"Wow, pretty small. Umm...Keith?" Kevin said.

"What?" Keith replied.

"How fast are you going?" Kevin asked. "I think can hear your car's engine whining."

Keith looked down and saw that he was going eighty seven miles per hour down the uncrowded highway. "Shit. Thanks," Keith said, easing off the gas and allowing the car to slow down. "I am still a little wound up. It shouldn't take me long to get to the address you gave me."

"Try not to blow past the exit," Kevin chided him. "Did Egorov say anything other than threatening your family if you don't sign off on the deal?"

"This is where it gets good," Keith said, keeping a close watch on his speed. "You are going to like this. I played on your idea and told him that you take equity in my deals to sway my efforts and share the benefits with me in a way that cannot be easily connected, and that, since they want me to okay the deal, my interests should be accommodated."

"How did he respond?" Kevin asked.

"He said it was a reasonable request and that he would talk with Dale. I also told him that we figured out that someone was working the negotiation at a higher level than Dale was capable of and that you are going to talk to Dale about meeting him, Egorov that is, because you always meet the people you do business with. I did not let on about how much you figured out."

"What did he say about the meeting?" Kevin asked.

"He didn't say anything about the meeting, other than saying that he would talk to Dale about accommodating my interests by giving you something. So, I don't know whether Egorov will agree to meet with you. He basically said that whatever else happens, if I don't okay the deal today, he is going to kill one of my kids, but that he will talk to Dale about throwing me a bone by tossing the bone to you. I went into lawyer mode for the discussion with Egorov and did not yield or even look away, even though it was strange looking past his gun. I gave him no indication that I would okay the deal unless he did whatever you wanted. I was clear that I would kill the deal if he came near my family."

Kevin had the unusual experience of feeling utterly surprised. "What I am hearing is that you refused to yield and basically stared down a murderer with a gun in your face while he was threatening to kill your kid, and that you instead demanded he pay you off through me. HOLY SHIT!"

KILLER DEAL: A TECHNOLOGY TRANSFER THRILLER

"I was angry. I wanted to put a bullet in his head. Very few people have actually seen me angry. It doesn't happen very often," Keith said.

"I never thought I would say this, Keith, but remind me never to piss you off."

"Funny," Keith responded. "I am coming up on the exit I need to take. Is there anything for me to do?"

"Not a thing," Kevin replied. "Just get to that address and be safe with Sharon, Heather and the kids. Oh, one more thing."

"What?" Keith asked.

"HOLY SHIT, Keith," Kevin added one more time for emphasis.

"I know. Bye," Keith said before hanging up the call and taking the off ramp from the highway to go be with his family.

Chapter 70

(Friday 11:30 p.m.)

Kevin hung up from his call with Keith and pulled his Alfa Romeo over to the side of the road not far from his home so he could dig out Dale's phone number. Then, remaining parked in the scenic neighborhood, he placed the call to Dale and listened. Dale was in his girlfriend's apartment waiting on calls from both Dennis and Egorov when his cell phone rang and he recognized that it was Kevin Taft calling.

"Dale," the voice answered in a friendly, business-like tone.

"I had a long talk with Keith and I think I have talked some sense into him," Kevin said, before pausing to let Dale ask for more information.

"Did you get him to accept our version of the deal and sign off on it?" Dale asked hopefully.

"In a manner of speaking," Kevin said, again pausing to let Dale ask for more information.

"In what manner of speaking?" Dale asked. "Did you get him to okay the deal or not?"

"Well, you see, Dale, his okaying this deal creates risk for him, and my putting my support behind it creates risk for me."

"What are you getting at Kevin?" Dale asked, not sure what Kevin was implying. "I want this deal done today. Campanaro gets on a plane tonight. We are out of time and Keith is being a prick. Do we have a deal or not?"

"Well, Dale, that depends on you and one other person, not so much on Keith," Kevin answered without offering clarification.

"Please just put it to me straight, Kevin. What do I have to do to get this deal done our way today?" Dale asked in a serious tone, while looking around his girlfriend's apartment for a pen and paper.

"I am glad you asked," Kevin said breezily, as though he were strolling across a golf course on a Sunday afternoon. "You see, you are a businessman, and I am a businessman. We understand risk and reward. Keith is a technology licensing person. He thinks in terms of shared risk. That's why the licenses have the licensee obligated to share a percentage of their gross sales with the licensor. More sales by the licensee, more money to the licensor. Less sales, less money to the licensor. It is all about being compensated for the risk you take. Now, the way Keith and I see it, we are taking a risk in getting behind your version of the deal. I have my credibility and standing with the University. Keith is literally signing off on it, and every finger in Tailcrest will be pointing at him if people question it. My question to you, Dale, is where is the reward to Keith and me for taking this risk?"

"Are you serious?" Dale asked. "Are you looking for a payoff at the last minute? How much do you want? I can talk with someone."

"No, no," Kevin answered, "nothing that direct and provable. There are much better ways. I propose that I invest in HematoChem. A simple fifteen thousand dollar investment, a token really, in the form of a convertible note discounted seventy percent to the Round A investment, accruing fourteen percent interest or, at my sole option, convertible to an ownership of ten percent of HematoChem either six months after the investment or after you have raised one million dollars in outside investment.

"Wait," Dale replied, "in plain English you want to own ten percent of HematoChem after I have raised a million dollars? The people who invest the million will want to own a percentage of the company, which will diminish the portion the rest of us own, and you want to come in after that and own ten percent? You would end up owning almost as much of HematoChem as I do. This is outrageous."

"It is about risk and reward, Dale. Besides, this is to accommodate the risks that both Keith and I are taking. It is not just me."

"It's too much. There is no way it is going to happen," Dale protested

"Okay, I see your point. We all want it to go forward," Kevin continued, "so I will knock it down to eight percent, but there is an additional condition for the deal to move forward."

"Eight percent is still outrageous, but may be possible, but there is no way we could get the paperwork together today. It would take at least a week, and we do not have a week," Dale said. "How do you propose we do this, if it is even possible?"

"That is why I bring up the extra condition, which is simple. I meet the man behind the scenes, Lenko Egorov, and show him the paperwork I have showing you paid off Dennis Gearin and Jason Roberts with ownership in the company. Then I make clear that if you make good on your commitment to me, I do not dry up further investment money by showing the documents to the newspapers and anyone else that may be interested. Do we have a deal, Dale?"

"WHAT THE HELL?" Dale shouted before composing himself. "How did you-"

"None of your business Dale," Kevin cut him off. "Now, Dale, you are going to arrange for Lenko Egorov to meet me at two forty-five this afternoon on that little island with the walking bridge on campus near the dormitories. I have several things to take care of at the University for my day-job between now and then. That will give Mr. Egorov plenty of time to find a parking space and get to the little island. If he does not show up and agree to my proposal, the deal will not go forward. If he does show up and agree to my proposal, the deal will go forward exactly as you requested. It is that simple Dale. Are you absolutely clear?"

"I have it written down," Dale said bitterly, "but I can't guaranty that he will show up."

"Well Dale, he is a businessman like you and me. He will show up. It has been nice talking with you," Kevin said before hanging up the phone and smiling about what he actually had planned for Lenko Egorov.

Chapter 71
(Friday 11:40 a.m.)

Dale sat on his girlfriend's couch for several minutes brooding about the call from Kevin and thinking that it may have been a mistake to get involved with Egorov and this deal. The down to the wire brinkmanship was causing him so much anxiety that he was feeling continuously nauseated. Now he was being shaken down for part ownership of HematoChem by a guy who apparently thought nothing of talking down to him. He had already handed over much more of the company than he wanted to, and now the way he had gone about that was being used to blackmail him. "This is outrageous," he muttered as he stood up and walked around his girlfriend's femininely furnished apartment.

Grabbing one of his girlfriend's Fruitopia drinks out of the refrigerator, he walked over and looked out the front window toward where she usually parked, wishing she would come home from work so he could distract himself from the situation with the HematoChem deal by undressing her and enjoying himself. He tried to keep his mind focused on the last time they had been together that way and how eager to please she was, but his stress about Egorov and the deal blocked his concentration.

He recalled that when he had spoken with Egorov earlier that day, Egorov had said that he was going to pressure Keith in his own particular way and had said something about how people tend to change their way of looking at things when you hold a gun to their head. Dale kept getting hung up on the possibility that Egorov may have meant that he was literally going to point a gun at Keith's head and how badly things could go if he did that. He also did not know how Egorov would react to Kevin's wanting to meet him in person to arrange a side deal. Walking back over to the couch and sitting precisely where he had been before, Dale sighed as he thought about how much he really did not want to make the call to Egorov to explain Kevin's new requirements. "Focus on the positive," he mumbled to himself, hoping that Egorov would appreciate the positive aspects of Kevin's presenting a way for the deal to go forward.

Dale dialed Egorov's number and waited. Egorov answered on the first ring. "Dale, I was going to call you in just a moment. Your timing is good. Have you heard yet from Kevin Taft about their desire to have their personal interests addressed in the deal? I understand he will be contacting you."

"I just got off the phone with him," Dale replied, startled by Egorov's question and the positive tone in his voice. "How did you know that they wanted a payoff to make the deal go forward?"

"I had a good conversation with Keith Mastin. He told me that he and Kevin Taft have an arrangement where Taft accepts payoff's for deal favors from Mastin to make the payoffs invisible. It is a good way to extort bribes."

Dale responded by asking, "What did Keith say that they wanted?"

"He did not say," Egorov replied. "He said that Taft makes the arrangements and then gives word to him to go forward. Did Taft tell you what he wants in exchange for the deal going forward on our terms?"

"Yes, he wants to invest fifteen thousand dollars in exchange for eight percent of the company after we have raised a million dollars in private funding," Dale said. "He wants to bury it in a convertible note agreement that has extraordinary provisions."

"This is not so unreasonable," Egorov replied, "but the paperwork will take time. He will trust us or he wants some assurances?"

"He said that he wants to meet you in person because he always meets the people he does business with," Dale said. "He used your name and claimed he had documents showing the arrangement with Dennis and

Jason. I don't know how he got any of that, but he seemed confident that he had enough leverage to ensure that we will fulfill anything we commit to. He threatened to go to the media and others to try to dry up future funding."

Egorov felt himself go cold as a smile came to his lips. "That is interesting to know," Egorov said. "I will meet with him. Did he provide a time and place?"

"Yes," Dale replied. "Two forty-five this afternoon on the small island with the walking bridge on Tailcrest's campus. Do you know where that is?"

"I have seen it before. I am sure I can find it. Call Taft and tell him your associate will meet him at two forty-five by the island. I will update you after the meeting."

"Okay," Dale said before hearing Egorov end the call.

After dialing Kevin Taft's number and waiting through four rings, Dale heard Kevin answer, "Hello Dale. Any news?"

"My associate will meet you at two forty-five by the small island on campus," Dale said curtly.

"Good job, Dale," Kevin said before hanging up on him.

Dale felt his anger rising, and he tried his best to suppress it. His brief interactions with Kevin had left him feeling belittled, and he found it infuriating. That and everything else about the deal made him want to throw his girlfriend's coffee table into a wall. He was also worried about how Egorov would react if the deal fell apart. He hated admitting it to himself, but he was deeply afraid of Egorov, and terrified of what he might be capable of doing to him if things didn't work out. Abruptly, Dale made a decision to grab some things from his own apartment and prepare to make himself very hard to find for a while just in case things went very badly.

Standing up from the couch, he went over to his girlfriend's little whiteboard on the back of her apartment door and left a note saying he had to take care of some things. He then collected the few items he had brought with him and left the apartment, heading for his car. He planned to go to his own apartment to pick up several changes of cloths, his important documents and the fifteen thousand dollars in cash he kept in his safe, and to then go for a very long drive.

Reaching his car Dale thought to himself that, if things went well, he would get the call on his cell phone and he could simply drive back. And, that, if things went badly, he would have everything he needed to disappear for a while.

Pulling away from the curb, he looked back, wondering if he would be back to see this apartment or his girlfriend anytime soon.

Chapter 72

(Friday: 12:00 Noon)

Kevin pulled his Alfa Romeo up in front of a downtown office building having a decorative fountain with a modern art statue that evoked images of two people embracing. Seeing no available parking near the building, he used a pedestrian walkway to pull his car up onto the building's open front area and parked near the fountain. As he walked toward the building entrance, he noticed people admiring the car and how it looked with the fountain as a backdrop. He also found it amusing how his casual clothes made the suited professionals around him chose not to notice him, as though he were invisible.

Kevin entered the building and took the elevator to the twentieth floor, where Aaron Konrad's office was located. He had called ahead and been informed that Aaron was in a meeting. His walking into the well-appointed lobby of Aaron's office wearing jeans and a polo shirt caused the receptionist to look at him oddly. "May I help you?" the lovely middle aged woman asked in a professional you-don't-belong-here tone.

He had not met this particular receptionist before and assumed that she must be new to Aaron's company. He also thought that if she was aware of his relationship with Aaron, she would have been much more welcoming. "I am Kevin Taft. I need to see Aaron Konrad right now," Kevin said. "Can you bring a note to him?"

"I am afraid that is not possible Mr. Taft," she replied. "He is in a meeting. If you would like to wait, there is seating over there, but he will likely be some time as the meeting will not be over for at least forty-five minutes. Perhaps you can arrange an appointment."

"I'll wait," Kevin replied.

"In that case, may I get you some coffee?" she asked. "It could be quite some time before he is available."

"Yes, coffee would be nice. Thank you," Kevin replied, feeling angry about how he was being treated.

As she walked over to a small alcove just off of the lobby where Kevin knew they kept a coffee maker, Kevin stepped around the reception desk and walked quickly up the hall to where the two conference rooms were located. Seeing that the first was empty, he headed for the other one just as the receptionist called after him. "Mr. Taft, you cannot go down there. You must wait in the lobby or I will call security."

She caught up to him just as he reached the door of the second conference room. As she took a breath to speak he gave her a menacing look that made her pause and turn pale. He then opened the door and stepped into the conference room where Aaron was conducting his meeting.

When Kevin walked into the conference room he saw Aaron seated at the head of the large conference table speaking to a group of nine people seated around the table and wearing expensive suits. They all turned and looked at the casually dressed man who had interrupted the meeting some of them had travelled great distances to attend.

Aaron smiled at the oddity of Kevin's intrusion and chose to roll with it. Speaking to the group, Aaron said, "Gentlemen and ladies, this is my good friend and business associate, Kevin Taft. I am sure you recall my having mentioned him. I invited him to stop in to meet you on his way to a family outing if his very tight schedule would permit it. Kevin has one of the most agile minds I have ever encountered and a gift for business."

"It is very nice to meet you all," Kevin said to the group, "but I am afraid a personal matter of considerable urgency has arisen, so I cannot stay to spend time getting to know each of you. I would very much like to when the opportunity presents itself. Aaron's assistant can coordinate our schedules. I must also ask Aaron to do something he would normally never consider, and that is to interrupt his meeting and come with me to address the personal matter that has suddenly arisen. I know he places tremendous importance on etiquette and being respectful of people's time and their commitments to meet with him, so I apologize and beg your indulgence just this once."

Kevin then held up for Aaron's view a picture of Egorov. Aaron saw the picture and immediately recognized the man he had spoken with in the lobby of the hotel the day Kaitlin was killed. He then looked at Kevin and saw him nod slightly. Turning back to the group, Aaron said, "As you know I recently experienced a family tragedy. I believe it is necessary that I acquiesce to Kevin's request and join him. I am very sorry. My assistant will schedule a time for us to reconvene as soon as possible during your visit, hopefully before dinner this evening."

In response an older looking man seated in the middle of one side of the table said, "Aaron, we know you lost your wife. Please do not apologize. We're here for several days, and we will arrange our schedules around yours. We'll meet whenever you would like."

With that Kevin made eye contact with the man who had just spoken and nodded his appreciation. "Thank you," Aaron said before he and Kevin left the room and headed down the hallway past the dumbstruck receptionist. Entering the lobby and pushing the button for the elevator, Aaron spoke first. "I talked to that man the day Kaitlin was killed. He walked up to me in the lobby and was friendly and supportive and joked about her walking back from her bike ride with sore feet after I told him why I was waiting there. What does he have to do with her death?"

"His name is Lenko Egorov and he very likely is the one who killed her," Kevin said calmly as the elevator doors opened and they stepped in. "I plan to get DNA from him and ensure that he stays around long enough to be held accountable. You said he was friendly and supportive?"

"Yes, he was cheerful and positive. Seemed like a nice guy who saw that I looked upset. You are now saying that earlier that morning he killed Kaitlin, which means he probably knew who I was and was there to gloat."

"I would guess he is a sociopath," Kevin offered. "He looked calm and relaxed in photos of him walking up to the Keith Mastin's house in the middle of the night last night when he went there to harass him. He is very intelligent, but something is wired wrong in him."

"Mastin's the one from the Tech Transfer Office at Tailcrest, right? Why would this man kill Kaitlin and then harass Mastin?" Aaron asked as the elevator doors opened and they stepped out into the busy lobby of the office building.

"It's about a technology licensing deal, apparently," Kevin said as he pulled up a picture on his cell phone showing Egorov pointing a gun at Keith Mastin and showed it to Aaron. "He is quite serious about making sure the deal goes through his way."

Aaron was startled by the image. "Is Mastin hurt?" Aaron asked, while holding open the door for Kevin as they exited the building.

"Keith's fine," Kevin replied. "He apparently ignored the gun and kept negotiating. Egorov threatened him and then left."

"What did you just say?" Aaron asked, as they walked up to the sides of Kevin's car and got in.

"Yes, we have video proof," Kevin replied, starting the engine. "While Egorov was pointing a gun at him, Keith negotiated to have Egorov meet with me for a sham payoff as a condition of the deal going forward."

Aaron heard the words and then looked solidly at Kevin. "You are meeting with Egorov?" Aaron asked, wanting to confirm that he had heard Kevin correctly.

"Today at two forty-five, on campus. I have a plan. We have much to discuss and not much time," Kevin said, pulling the car slowly through the people on the sidewalk and easing it gently onto the street before pulling out into traffic. "I understand you spoke with Karl Taylor."

"Yes. I called him to pick his brain about what the Detective was and should be doing to solve Kaitlin's murder," Aaron replied. "Karl is a federal prosecutor, so it made sense to call him. He didn't seem particularly impressed with Detective Baskin's efforts. He did say that Baskin seemed to be doing a 'competent' job."

"I spoke with Karl too. He is already involved in what I have set in motion to capture Egorov," Kevin added as he made an illegal U-turn, accelerated and weaved through traffic. "He mentioned Baskin and said that he would let the Detective know how things went after we have Egorov in custody. Karl doesn't know all of what I have in mind for Egorov though."

Aaron looked over at Kevin and saw the confident, determined look in his eyes. "I'm in, whatever it is," Aaron replied, looking forward to hearing more.

Chapter 73

(Friday 12:45 p.m.)

Kevin drove alone onto Tailcrest's campus and parked in his normal parking space outside the Technology Incubator building. Looking around, Kevin noticed that, while his car stood out, it was not the only high end vehicle in the lot. This made perfect sense to him as some of the business owners who rented space in the Incubator for its combined business office and wet lab space for their start-up companies were serial entrepreneurs like himself and had already accumulated considerable wealth. As he made his way through the parking lot, Kevin admired some of the other vehicles and thought of an irony peculiar to Technology Incubators; that part of the draw of Technology Incubators for new entrepreneurs was access to the experienced entrepreneurs who used the building, while the experienced entrepreneurs were even more drawn to the energy and excitement of the new entrepreneurs who were starting out fresh.

Kevin entered the building and said "hello" to several people as he made his way into his office, carrying his leather briefcase packed mostly with the papers and pictures related to the HematoChem deal. Taking a quick look at his e-mails and responding to a few before turning off his computer, Kevin then picked up his briefcase and left the building. Walking casually across campus, Kevin took his time heading over to Aspen Hall to meet with his old friend, President Walker.

Kevin was alone in the elevator as he took it up to the lobby outside Walker's office suite. The doors opened and he stepped out into an open space he had walked through countless times before. Making his way past the open space in the center of the lobby, where the floor below was visible, he glancing up at the skylight feature and recalled a more light hearted visit there, years before, when, after a late night meeting, he had convinced Walker to try out a tube shaped paper airplane design that could fly thirty feet straight up if thrown correctly. He recalled how they had competed to see who could bounce the planes harder off the skylight before they curved down to the floor below through the open space, and how they had recruited Bobbi to throw the planes back up to them from the floor below. Opening the door to the President's suite, Kevin thought about the contrast between that time and the seriousness of what he had planned.

"Hi Bobbi," Kevin said to her as she looked up to see who had entered. "Thank you for setting this up on no notice. I know how busy he is, especially with it being so close the end of the fiscal year."

"Are you kidding?" Bobbi beamed at him. "He would much rather meet with you than deal with all this 'end of fiscal year horse shit,' as he calls it. Each year dealing with the backbiters and suck-ups during the budget cycles seems to annoy him a little more."

"Good thing he loves the rest of it," Kevin replied.

"He does," she agreed. "You can set up in the conference room over there if you would like. He will be here in a couple of minutes. Would you like some coffee?"

Thank you, no," Kevin said, declining politely. "It's good to see you. We should have you and Steven over soon. It has been too long."

"We would love to," she replied as her desk phone rang. He nodded an unspoken "thank you' and walked toward the open conference room as she answered the phone.

Kevin entered the conference room and took most of the papers and pictures out of his briefcase, setting them up in the middle of the conference table like a deck of cards similar to the way he had done on the side of the boat in Keith's garage. He also used the computer in the room to access his e-mail and activate the media projector and screen for later use. He then reclined in one of the leather chairs and waited for Walker to arrive.

A few minutes later, Walker entered the room and greeted Kevin with a warm handshake. "What have you got for me today, Kevin? Something sordid I hope. Security cameras captured sorority girls doing something interesting again?"

"No, but I still have that video," Kevin replied. "It's amazing what sorority pledges will do outdoors. Today it's something more serious, and I need to bring you into the loop."

"Okay, what have you got?" Walker asked.

"A killer deal," Kevin replied seriously. "Let me lay it out using these documents."

Kevin picked up the first document in his deck and put it at one edge of the table. "A researcher here at Tailcrest invented technology that prevents 'The Bends,' which has civilian and military applications; submariners, Navy Seals, that sort of thing. It was partly funded by the U.S. Department of Defense."

"Okay, I am with you so far," Walker interjected, glancing at the document.

Kevin then picked up the next document in deck and said, "Our Technology Transfer Office is licensing the intellectual property rights to a new start-up company called HematoChem that was formed by an entrepreneur named Dale Wade. I have met him. He is a big guy but sort of a lightweight. Someone else is pulling the strings."

"Okay," Walker offered. "Is the license done? I heard that Dennis Gearin is ticked off that Keith Mastin is holding up this deal over some details."

"Thankfully no, it's not done. Keith has been standing his ground, and I have told him to keep it that way, and that I would back him."

"Interesting. I sense intrigue," Walker added.

Kevin then turned to the exhibit at the back of the document in his hand and tapped three others on the table. "Yes, that's putting it mildly. HematoChem is pressing for a sweetheart deal that Keith balked at. Keith is being pressured by Gearin to accept it when, get this, HematoChem is partly owned by Jason Roberts from our Legal Department and Dennis Gearin. Dennis and Jason hid their ownership behind simple corporate entities that each of them own and which were recently set up. It is a self-dealing scam, or a conflicts of interest scam, at Tailcrest's expense. Dennis put Keith right in front of it and is now pressuring him hard to accept the sweetheart terms while creating a minimal paper trail. It is really scummy, but that's not the worst of it."

"How can it get much worse than that?" Walker asked, furrowing his brow. "It's appalling."

"I'll show you," Kevin replied, picking up one of the documents he had tapped on the table. "This one holding company here in the exhibit owns a majority stake in HematoChem and controls it. I did some digging. It is owned by one person who used several corporate entities to hide his ownership. He is a Russian national by the name of Lenko Egorov. He is the one pulling Dale Wade's strings for the start-up company. I think he is using HematoChem and Dennis' and Jason's willingness to be bought off with partial ownership to enter into a cleverly structured and clean looking contract with Tailcrest to bring the military applications of the technology into Russia in such a way that no-one would even think to look too closely at what HematoChem is doing."

"Wow, how did you come to that conclusion?" Walker asked, amazed and concerned.

"Keith and I went over the sticking points in the deal. The things Keith is standing his ground on, and the things they are demanding, don't make sense for a legitimate start-up company to go to the mat on, and they are consistent with Egorov getting the technology very quickly into a Russian company by contract with essentially no legal recourse on Tailcrest's part.

If the deal goes through, Tailcrest will have facilitated the transfer to Russia of DOD funded potential military applications of the technology under a supposedly clean contract. It could be very bad press for Tailcrest and almost everyone involved in negotiating the deal, and it may violate federal law, not to mention the impact of the potential military uses of the technology."

Walker looked at Kevin and added, "And because of the potential bad press and violation of law almost everyone involved would be incentivized to keep everything quiet. And, if it were to blow up in the media or the courts, it would be viewed as Tailcrest's fault for letting it happen. Wow."

"Yes, but it gets even worse," Kevin continued, putting the documents down on the table. "Chris Campanaro gave in to Dennis' request to give Keith a 'reviewed and approved' stamp like the Legal Department uses for License Agreements, so now all eyes are on Keith to approve the deal today so Campanaro can sign it before he leaves for vacation."

Walker smiled and said, "But that is not going to happen now, is it? So what is the problem?"

"Lenko Egorov is the problem," Kevin replied, showing Walker pictures of Egorov outside of Keith's house and in front of Keith's in-laws' house. "Egorov is harassing Keith and trying to physically intimidate him into okaying the deal. Kevin then turned over several photographs. This was taken very late last night. Egorov woke Keith's family in the middle of the night. This was taken this morning at a house where Keith's family was visiting. Egorov must have followed Keith when he dropped his family off there."

Walker furrowed his brow further and said, "This is creepy."

"It gets more so. Keith's home security camera caught this earlier today," Kevin said before activating the video system and playing the soundless video of Egorov entering Keith's home and pointing a gun at him while they talked.

"Oh my god!" Walker said, while watching the video. "Did Keith call the police?"

"Thankfully no," Kevin replied. "If he had, Egorov likely would have just walked away and we wouldn't have any chance of catching him. He called me instead and sent me the video."

"Why did he do that?" Walker asked.

"Ah, that brings us to the really important part," Kevin said, smiling devilishly. "Keith knows I want Egorov here and alive so I can get a DNA sample and link him to Kaitlin's murder."

Walker looked at Kevin with a serious expression when he mentioned the connection to Kaitlin's death.

"Yes, I think Egorov killed Kaitlin and made it look like an accident because he knew she would get in the way of the deal he is pressuring Keith about now. He may have initially intended only to hurt her but he went on to kill her. Keith managed to stand his ground with a gun in his face and demand that Egorov meet with me to arrange a fictional side deal."

"What do you mean, 'fictional side deal?'" Walker asked.

"Before Egorov showed up at Keith's house with a gun, I had talked with Keith about convincing Dale Wade that they had paid off the wrong people, and that they have to pay off Keith and me to get the deal done on their terms. And, that my meeting Egorov in person had to be part of it. Keith used Egorov's invading his home to set that in motion."

"That's what he is doing in the video?" Walker asked.

"Yes, I am set to meet with Egorov here on campus by that little island at two forty-five this afternoon. I have made arrangements with a federal prosecutor named Karl Taylor from the U.S. Department of Justice to coordinate a law enforcement effort to capture Egorov. The Justice Department takes the export of controlled technologies very seriously. Karl has accepted my one request; that any Tailcrest involvement be kept out of the media."

Walker held Kevin's gaze for a long moment thinking about everything that Kevin had said and showed him. Walker then said, "I am going to want to meet this Karl Taylor as soon as possible, but, if Egorov killed Kaitlin, I want you to get him in any legal way you can."

"I will, Steven, probably later today," Kevin said. "I will have Karl call Bobbi to set up a meeting. Aaron was a witness on one of Karl's cases a while back. He is solid."

"That is good to know," Walker said. "Is there anything I can do?"

Keith smiled, having known Walker would offer to help. "Yes, if you have a few minutes, there is," Kevin said.

Chapter 74
(Friday 1:00 p.m.)

Walker was pleased to think that he could maybe help with Kevin's efforts to catch Egorov. He looked at Kevin and asked, "What do you have in mind for me to do?"

"I have a plan, a trap of sorts," Kevin replied. "There are four players in the deal that we know of; Dennis, Jason, Dale Wade and Lenko Egorov."

"Okay," walker said.

"If Egorov killed Kaitlin, and I am convinced that he did, then it was because he knew she would get in the way of this start-up deal, and he knew where she and Aaron were vacationing. That information probably came from Jason or maybe Dennis. I would like for us to inspire conversation among them about their back room dealings and maybe their roles relative to the situation with Kaitlin."

"How do you propose we do that?" Walker asked.

Kevin replied, "We have already thrown a monkey wrench into their plan by insisting on a meeting with Egorov and demanding a payoff. Now, if we can make them think the deal will be done once I have met with him, they will hopefully talk to each other about it and offer comments that can be used against them. I have already talked with Karl Taylor about it and he thinks it is worth a try. The wire taps are already approved and in place to the extent they can identify ways that they will communicate."

"Good. By the way what is Keith Mastin doing?" Walker asked. "Is he okay? His encounter with Egorov looked frightening."

"Keith's fine, maybe a bit angry at Egorov," Kevin replied. "He and his family are staying at Karl Taylor's home, at least for today, and maybe tomorrow."

"So how can I help inspire conversation?" Walker asked.

"By making two phone calls," Kevin replied. "One to Dennis Gearin, and one to Dale Wade. The gist of each call would be that you talked to me, that you know there is an important deal that Keith is holding up, that Keith has just been under a lot of stress because his wife is having some health issues, which is true, and that I will get him to sign off on the deal today, once I am satisfied. Maybe you can make Dennis think that the blame for Dale's frustration will fall on Keith. Dale Wade would probably like to be thanked for his patience. It may be good to add that you don't know enough about the deal to sign off on it, but that there is time to have it signed through the normal process."

"I am sure I can make the calls and be persuasive," Walker said confidently. "Should be no problem at all. Do you have their numbers? I can call them now."

"I have them right here," Kevin replied, handing Walker a sheet of paper.

Reaching for the phone in the conference room, Walker then paused. "I don't know what kind of caller ID they may have. Might be better if I call from my desk phone."

"Good Idea," Kevin replied, pushing the papers and pictures into a pile and gesturing toward the door. "After you, Steven."

Chapter 75
(Friday 1:15 p.m.)

President Walker's office was thoughtfully appointed in a way that made it look and feel the way visitors would expect when entering a University President's office. It had a large mahogany desk with a credenza and darkly stained wooden bookshelves, a high back leather executive chair, plants, large windows, several pictures of Walker with national and world leaders and Tailcrest University's logo displayed on several items. It also had an eight seat conference table and a coffee and refreshment station that was continuously stocked. For people who had not spent considerable time there, as Kevin had, it could also be imposing and intimidating. Walker strode into his office and turned his swivel chair while sitting down at his desk. Kevin pushed one of the chairs from the conference table over near Walker's desk and sat down, fully expecting an expert performance on Walker's part. Kevin had always marveled at his friend's communication ability, especially when he was communicating a bold faced lie or manipulation. Walker had often joked that it was his gift.

Walker dialed Dale Wade's number first. "Hello," Dale said.

"Is this Dale Wade?" Walker asked with considerable warmth.

"Yes, who is this?" Dale responded.

"This is Steven Walker. I'm Tailcrest University's President. It has come to my attention through a personal friend of mine, Kevin Taft, that you have experienced some frustration with one of our employees in the Technology Transfer Office, Keith Mastin, regarding a negotiation with a your start-up company, HematoChem."

"Yes," Dale replied. "I have actually known Keith for some time, and I consider him a friend, but he is being completely unreasonable. We are about to lose a great opportunity for ourselves and for the University because we are faced with a deadline and Keith is being intransigent. If there is any way you can help, it would be good for us and the University. If we can get the deal done today, it will mean research money for the University and jobs right here in the community. If you could talk to Keith, that would be a great help."

"Actually I can do even better than that," Walker said, smiling at Kevin. "Kevin Taft knows Keith Mastin better than anyone here at Tailcrest. When I spoke with Kevin he said he was going to meet with someone from your company, he may have meant you, and then talk sense into Mastin. I told him to meet with whoever he has to meet with and then to tell Keith that, unless there is something really wrong, he better get the deal done or he won't be working for Tailcrest University any more. This community needs technology start-ups and jobs. The community has invested in our University and expects job creation. We cannot have a headstrong employee blocking a deal where everyone would benefit. Have your people meet with Kevin Taft, and then I am sure he can get Keith to do whatever he does to approve the deal."

"Thank you," Dale said, pleased that the University President was apparently on board.

"No thanks necessary. Tailcrest needs this sort of thing. I am going to send a note to our public relations director asking her to put together a press release announcing the deal. Presuming everything goes well we should be able to get it into this Sunday's business section. It has been good talking with you Dale."

"Likewise," Dale replied before the line went dead.

Grinning at Kevin, Walker then put the phone dawn and said, "What do you think, convincing?"

"Yes, completely," Kevin replied truthfully.

"Now on to our ethically challenged colleague," Walker said, while dialing Dennis Gearin's number.

"Dennis, this is President Walker," Walker said in a gently commanding manner. "I talked with Kevin Taft earlier. Apparently Keith Mastin has gone off the ranch so to speak in blocking a deal. I also just spoke with a Dale Wade from HematoChem. The way we are going to handle it is to have Kevin Taft meet with someone from the company and then with Mastin. Unless there is something that is a real problem, Kevin Taft will tell Mastin to approve the deal. I know you are the Tech Transfer Director, but Mastin knows that Taft and I have known each other a long time. Hearing it from Taft will have more impact."

Dennis took in the new information that Walker and Kevin Taft had known each other for a long time with some surprise, then replied, "It may be easier if we just approve the deal. I think it is fine. Keith has let his new approval authority go to his head. I really wonder if he is a good fit with the University given the way he has been acting."

"I'll keep that in mind," Walker replied, "but we have an approval process for a reason, and our auditors look closely at our processes. So, unless we follow our process, it could mean more paperwork and hassles. None of us wants that. Let Taft talk to the person from HematoChem and then to Keith. If it falls apart I will know you have done everything you can. Don't worry about it."

"Thank you," Dennis said.

"You're welcome," Walker replied before hanging up the phone and leaning back in his chair, clearly pleased with his own performance.

"Good enough?" he asked Kevin.

"Better than I could have hoped for. Thank you," Kevin answered before standing to leave. "Those copies of the documents and pictures in the conference room are for your records. I suspect there will be a file or two opened on this in the very near future."

"Yes, I would suspect so as well," Walker replied, amused by his friend's understatement.

Walker then walked with Kevin out of the office suite and to the elevator. As the elevator doors opened and Kevin stepped in, Walker said to him, "Be careful. This Egorov is dangerous."

Kevin smiled at his old friend and, as the doors started to close, he winked and replied, "It's just a little mischief."

Chapter 76
(Friday 1:20 p.m.)

As the elevator doors opened to the lobby of Aspen Hall, Kevin stepped out and affected a relaxed, businesslike manner as he crossed the lobby amongst the many students and exited the building. He then walked casually over toward Tailcrest Commons, taking his time, stopping to check the contents of his briefcase, and smiling at some female students who made eye contact with him as they walked past. To anyone who saw him he appeared like a relaxed administrator or professor who had plenty of time to get where he was going.

Entering the Tailcrest Commons with its garden courtyard appearance and wrap-around, U-shaped building, he saw the University Bookstore, the small fast food restaurants packed with students and the benches positioned near a central fountain designed with a flat bench-like edge so people could sit at the edge of the water. He then bought a cup of black coffee in the campus Subway shop and found a seat on an open bench near the fountain. He felt very much at home, as these surroundings had been familiar to him since Tailcrest Commons was built back before most of the students around him had entered kindergarten.

Outwardly appearing completely relaxed and comfortable, Kevin gazed at the fountain and at some girls who were particularly pretty. He recalled the many times he and Kaitlin had sat at the edge of the fountain, long before she had become Tailcrest's General Counsel. She would tell him about the things going on in her and Aaron's lives and what they had planned for themselves. With each recollection, Kevin felt his adrenaline rising.

Kevin had not chosen this particular location to spend time before the meeting with Egorov because of its connection to Kaitlin. Many places in the University had a similar connection to her. He had chosen this spot because he guessed that Egorov had already gotten his picture from Tailcrest's website and would try to seize control of their interactions by changing the plan. Kevin was intentionally staying out in the open, hoping that Egorov would see him before their meeting. He was actively, but subtly keeping an eye out for any glimpse of Egorov amongst the students.

As the minutes past, Kevin continued to recall many of the interactions he had had with Kaitlin over the years. His mind kept going back to seeing her in her casket. He felt a profound anger that continued to build and rise toward the surface. Egorov had done something infinitely unacceptable to Kevin in ending Kaitlin's life, especially the way he had done it. Kevin looked forward to coming face to face with the man very soon. He found that he was not thinking of Tailcrest or Keith or Aaron or really anyone, just his need to face Egorov and hurt him badly.

After nodding politely to a woman who gestured that she would like to sit on the open part of the bench Kevin was using, he thought about how he had always gotten this way when people mistreated people he cared about. He knew it was the one thing about himself he could not effectively control. He recalled occasions, going as far back as his youth, where he acted in ways that, if discovered, would have shocked people close to him and probably jeopardized his freedom. He had always been careful to arrange things so his actions appeared justified or would never be discovered. The expression "benevolent predator" came into his mind while he gazed at the people sitting on the edge of the fountain and pictured Kaitlin sitting among them. That was how he thought of himself when he was angry and focused like this, like he was hunting prey that deserved to be hunted. There was no question in his mind that he was "hunting" Egorov, very much like the times he had hunted before.

Finishing his coffee, Kevin noticed the time. He stood up and tossed his empty cup in a nearby trash can. He then picked up his briefcase, smiled at the woman who had sat down near him and began his casual walk toward the scheduled meeting place. Subtly glancing around as he strolled along, he hoped that Egorov was watching him.

Chapter 77
(Friday 1:40 p.m.)

Kevin had just cleared the edge of the Tailcrest Commons building when he caught a glimpse of Egorov. It was just a glimpse, but he could see that he was dressed casually, looking very much like he could be a parent of any one of the students or maybe a professor. Kevin saw that Egorov was watching him, looking directly at him. Without looking back Kevin started walking along the paved jogging path that wound a roundabout path past a small stream near the edge of campus and would, after quite some distance, lead to the island where he was supposed to meet with Egorov. The plan set up with Karl Taylor was that Kevin would simply go to the island and wait for Egorov, and that FBI agents would take Egorov into custody as he approached the island. Kevin liked the plan's simplicity, but he had something very different in mind for Egorov, if he could just get Egorov to follow him.

After Kevin had walked about two hundred yards at his casual pace he looked to the side and noticed out of the corner of his eye that Egorov had started walking along the same path behind him. Shifting his briefcase partly in front of himself while he walked, Kevin unzipped it and slid his hand inside to get two things and then zipped it shut again. He liked to keep things simple when he could. What he had in mind for Egorov was no exception. "Come along, Lenko," Kevin said to himself, while he continued to walk along the path.

After covering another hundred yards, Kevin had reached the portion of the trail that went through a scenic wooded section of campus by the stream. He could smell the stream and the distinct peat-like, earthy scent of the woods near the path. Glancing to the side again, he saw that

Egorov was still walking behind him and had closed the distance between them to less than a hundred yards. Looking ahead, Kevin could just see the portion of the path he had in mind. It was heavily wooded on both sides and was near the part of the stream where there was a small footbridge to a residential development just off campus. Kevin felt relieved that Egorov had chosen to follow him, especially since there was a shorter route from Tailcrest Commons to the island that Egorov could have taken. Kevin was also pleased to see that this portion of the path was not well travelled by students on this particular day and that he and Egorov would soon be basically alone and shielded from view by the trees.

Once Kevin reached the portion of the path that rounded a curve where he was blocked from Egorov's view by the trees, he quickly stepped far enough into the woods so he would not be seen, and then waited for Egorov to walk past. After observing Egorov pass by, Kevin stepped back out onto the path and walked silently behind Egorov for about fifteen yards. Kevin then shouted harshly, "LENKO EGOROV!"

Egorov whirled in place and saw Kevin standing there with a broad smile on his face. "Good afternoon Lenko," Kevin said in a more businesslike tone. "We are here to do some business."

"So I am told," Egorov replied, looking at Kevin with completely cold eyes. "What do you have to offer me and what do you believe it is worth?"

"Well, for starters," Kevin said while taking a few steos toward Egorov, "I have documentation showing that Dennis Gearin and Jason Roberts are co-owners of HematoChem while Gearin is pushing for a sweetheart deal to be approved by his subordinate."

"So?" Egorov replied.

"So," Kevin explained, "I can kill this deal with a phone call, and I can back it up with documents Dale Wade left lying around. Or, I can make a call and make it happen the way you want it to."

"What do you want in exchange for your favorable treatment of HematoChem and ensuring that the deal is completed today?" Egorov asked.

"Eight percent ownership of HematoChem after you have raised one million dollars in private investment money," Kevin replied.

"This would not be so unreasonable I think in another case, but here it is not worth what you are asking," Egorov replied, looking steadily at Kevin. "Perhaps less would be acceptable. More importantly, once you call Mastin and get the deal done, how will you be assured that we will follow through? I think you are maybe not serious in your request, or you would ask for money in cash up front."

Egorov paused waiting for Kevin's response, but Kevin placidly said nothing while moving steadily closer toward Egorov.

Egorov then continued. "A few side deals, you call them conflicts of interest, are really nothing. You have nothing. Mastin will approve the deal today or I will do what I told him I would do."

Kevin smiled while holding Egorov's gaze. "I have more."

Egorov squinted at Kevin. "This will maybe be more interesting. What else do you have to make sharing part ownership of HematoChem worthwhile?"

"Ah, Lenko, as you no doubt know there is a way to scam in every situation," Kevin said, grinning menacingly as he moved closer to Egorov. "And, if you can figure out a scam, you can get in its way and extract payment. Would you agree with that, Lenko?"

"I am not a fool," Egorov replied, irritated at the way Kevin was speaking to him. "I understand this well and have used it myself. What is your point?"

"I traced your ownership stake in HematoChem to a Russian corporation," Kevin said, easing his way even closer to Egorov.

"Yes, and you learned my name and probably realized I am Russian. But this you could have learned by asking me. What is this thing you have that is supposedly so important?"

"Well, Lenko," Kevin said, now standing just a few feet from Egorov and watching for an opportunity to attack him, "you are structuring the licensing deal so the license can be very quickly sublicensed to another company without the University's review. And the export control provisions you are insisting on seem to put the burden of compliance on the University. And, you want rights to future inventions. And, this part is important Lenko, the technology covered by the license has military applications and probably requires a separate export license from the United States government before it can be released to HematoChem because it is foreign owned by virtue of your owning a controlling interest."

Egorov's posture changed slightly as Kevin spoke. "These are technical matters that are of concern to no one. You sound like a government bureaucrat. How does this relate to what you want and why I should give it to you?"

"Glad you asked Lenko," Kevin said, easing his phone out of his pocket and getting ready to activate the video record feature. "You see, I was on a commercial flight to New York with some friends and their young children during the long weekend before the September Eleven attacks. I pointed out the Twin Towers to their little boy out the window. Then the attacks happened and I thought about the families with children on those planes, Lenko."

"Most unfortunate, I agree," Egorov said. "You could perhaps get to your point, Mr. Taft."

"My point, Lenko, is that you will be transferring to me a twenty percent ownership stake in HematoChem, non-dilutable until you, we, have raised one million dollars in outside investment capital. And, I will be blocking any transfer of the technology until the paperwork is done.

And, I will talk to Dale Wade, Dennis Gearin and Jason Roberts to install me as the President of HematoChem so I can ensure that you and all other foreign nationals have no access to the technology because of its military applications. You and whoever you are working with to get this military technology into Russia will be excluded from access. Do you understand, Lenko? Your efforts to get this military technology into Russia have failed, and you are going to help me with the paperwork. How does that make you feel Lenko?"

Egorov's faced tightened into a mask of cold rage as he absorbed what Kevin had just said. Kevin activated the video record feature of his phone just as Egorov pulled out his pistol and pointed it at Kevin's face. "I do not respond well to threats, or to people getting in my way," Egorov said, holding the gun steady with both hands.

Chapter 78
(Friday 1:50 p.m.)

Amidst the light breeze and pleasant smell of the woods and nearby stream, Kevin was able to maintain eye contact with Egorov, even as Egorov pointed his gun at him. Seeing the gun only peripherally, Kevin could still tell that it appeared to be the same gun Egorov had pointed at Keith Mastin earlier. Egorov was so angry and focused on Kevin's face and upper body, drawing his weapon and holding the gun pointed straight at Kevin's chest, that he did not notice Kevin recording video footage with his phone and then returning it to his pocket.

"We are now going for walk," Egorov said, momentarily glancing to the side toward the wooded areas nearer to the stream to signal the direction.

Kevin nodded his understanding and then began walking into the woods, keeping himself positioned on an angle so he could see Egorov while they walked. Once they were a dozen yards into the woods, Egorov spoke again. "Continue walking toward the little river. When we get further in you will make a call to Keith Mastin. You will tell him that we have reached agreement. You agreed to receive eight percent ownership of the company, non-dilutable until we raise one million dollars. You will also tell him that he must send you a picture of the agreement signed by your Vice President within forty five minutes or a member of his family will die, and that he must get an original signed agreement to Dale Wade within one and a half hours. You may also wish to let him know that, if he does not do this in this time, you will die too. I leave up to you whether to inform him of that last part. Do you understand?"

"I understand that you are going to kill me no matter what I do, so there is no reason for me to do anything. You can go fuck yourself, Egorov," Kevin responded, knowing full well his statement was incorrect.

"Not if you can deliver Mastin and the signed agreement," Egorov responded in an almost friendly businesslike tone. "Yes, if you and Mastin do not deliver, then I will kill you and then a member of Mastin's family, and then Mastin himself. But, I am a businessman with no desire to kill unnecessarily. Why take the risk and draw the extra attention? No, if you deliver on the contract, I will not kill you or any of Mastin's family, but you and I will be spending time together, perhaps a week, while all information about the technology is transferred to HematoChem and then into Russia. After that I will return to Russia, assume a different identity and you will either keep your mouth shut because you are implicated in making the deal happen or you will cause problems for only Dale Wade and the others. Either way, you will not be able to influence me in any way. You see, either I win, or you die. It is a very straightforward proposition."

"Clear as a bell," Kevin responded, stopping near a rock outcropping not far from the ten foot drop to the rocky edge of the stream. "I will call Mastin."

"Good," Egorov replied, watching Kevin take out his phone and dial a number.

"Oops, misdialed," Kevin said, while forwarding to Keith the video of Egorov pulling his gun on him.

"Okay," Kevin said, dialing again.

"Keith," Kevin said as Keith answered his phone. "I'll talk, while you listen. Egorov is here with me. He is being quite reasonable. He agreed to what we wanted initially, eight percent non-dilutable. So do exactly as we agreed. Also, if he does not get a picture of the signed agreement via your sending it to my cell phone within forty five minutes people will die, someone from your family actually. He is quite serious. If it is done and a signed original is in Dale Wade's hands within an hour and a half, no one will be harmed and he and I will spend about a week together conferring on the collaboration and everything will be fine. Do you understand completely?"

"Yes, I do," Keith replied. "I will do exactly as we agreed."

"Good," Kevin said, hanging up the phone. Kevin then offered to hand the phone to Egorov as a way of both stepping closer to him and distracting him.

"No, you hold it," Egorov said, just as he heard a loud branch snap twenty feet behind him.

Whirling around and pointing his gun in the direction of the sound, Egorov saw Aaron Konrad standing there, pointing a gun at him while his foot rested on broken branch that had been placed against a rock. In that moment of recognition Egorov realized that he had been set up and immediately closed one eye to aim at Aaron. In that same instant Kevin slid the flat, mettle pry bar he had taken from Keith's garage out of his sleeve and into his hand and slammed the tool, hatchet-like, into Egorov's wrist. Kevin broke Egorov's wrist badly and caused the weapon to fire wide and away from Aaron. Continuing his attack, Kevin then slammed the thin edge of the improvised weapon into Egorov's knee, breaking it, and then slammed the flat side of the pry-bar into Egorov's face, shattering and flattening his nose. Egorov crumpled to the ground as blood poured out of his face.

Kevin then kicked Egorov's gun to the side as Aaron walked over. Putting his own gun in his waste holster and snapping it shut, Aaron took a gallon sized plastic freezer bag out of his pocket and, turning it partly inside out, collected Egorov's gun inside it without actually touching the weapon. Aaron then placed the bagged gun back on the ground and took two more steps toward Egorov. Looking down, Aaron then gazed into the eyes of the man who he knew had killed Kaitlin. Aaron experienced a moment of stillness, like time had stopped, where he could feel and smell and taste everything in the present more fully than he ever had.

"I believe you two have met," Kevin said, breaking the silence partly because he believed there may be little time before the video he had forwarded to Keith disclosed their location. "Aaron, would you like to kill him quickly or slowly?"

Egorov heard the words and believed he was about to die.

"Slowly," Aaron replied, stepping closer to Egorov. Aaron then grabbed Egorov's unbroken wrist and sat on Egorov's chest so he could not inhale.

For a full two minutes Aaron sat there looking into Egorov's shocked eyes as he struggled to get out from under Aaron's weight. Aaron watched Egorov slowly pass out. Aaron saw bloodshot star-like shapes appear in Egorov's eyes as blood vessels broke. After a few more moments, Aaron then asked Kevin casually, "Think he has had enough?"

"Yes," Kevin replied simply, and Aaron stood up, allowing Egorov to breath and slowly regain consciousness.

As Egorov's eyes began to refocus, Kevin took out a small old fashioned tape recorder having a mini-cassette ready to record once he hit a button. Looking into Egorov's eyes Kevin said, "You are going to tell us how you killed Kaitlin Clark and why, and that you pointed a gun at Keith Mastin and why. If you do not, he will sit on your chest again, and this time he will not get up. Do you understand?"

"Yes," Egorov said, sounding different because of his smashed nose.

Kevin then hit record and held Egorov's uninjured wrist as Egorov spoke. "I killed Miss Kaitlin, Kaitlin Clark, by breaking her neck. I tried to make it painless for her. I first knocked her off her bicycle. My intention was to disrupt the University's system so she would not review the license contract. I entered Keith Mastin's house today and used my gun to threaten him to approve the license deal."

"Very good Lenko," Kevin said as though speaking to a small child after stopping the recording. "Now you are going to give me the name of your

Russian collaborators, the ones who would receive the technology and develop it for military applications."

"No," Egorov said defiantly. "You may as well kill me. I would be a dead man anyway."

"Okay," Aaron said, stepping forward.

"Wait," Egorov said, believing absolutely that Aaron would kill him. "I will tell you, but you must protect me. I have much knowledge to share for protection."

"No promises," Kevin said, "but we'll put in a good word."

Kevin then pressed "record" again on the tape recorder and held it toward Egorov. "I was paid to get the nitrogen technology and how to use, make and develop it to Sacha Sidorov from Russia. He has contacts in Russian military who want to develop military applications for use in our Navy."

"Very, very good, Lenko," Kevin said, after turning off the tape recorder and placing it in his pocket. "Aaron, time for you to disappear."

"Goodbye Lenko Egorov," Aaron said before turning and walking across the rocky ground back toward the footbridge he had used to come unnoticed onto campus.

"Now, Lenko, it is just you and me," Kevin said, smiling menacingly at Egorov.

Chapter 79

(Friday 2:00 p.m.)

Kevin took several deep breaths while staring at Lenko Egorov laying on the ground. Egorov was staring back at him with an expression of blended fear, anger and outrage. The combination of Egorov's expression and his smashed nose looked grotesque to Kevin. After waiting a moment to ensure that Aaron was a good distance away, Kevin stepped over by the bagged gun, picked it up and wiped the outside of the bag on his jacket to eliminate Aaron's fingerprints. He then placed the bag and gun back down where it was and walked over toward Egorov.

"What now?" Egorov asked. "You kill me so I cannot tell about the deal you wanted?"

"Not yet," Kevin replied. "I want to talk to you first."

"What do you want to-" Egorov started to say before Kevin kicked him hard in the mouth, knocking out most of his front teeth.

Kevin then watched Egorov spit out teeth and blood. While Egorov winced in pain and put his usable hand to his mouth, Kevin picked up one of the teeth and put it in a small plastic bag he took from his pocket. "DNA sample," Kevin said to Egorov as he put the bag and tooth in his pocket.

"What for?" Egorov spat from his ruined mouth.

"You see, Lenko," Kevin said, "the woman you killed beat you, even if you don't know it."

Egorov looked at him oddly; then said. "She is dead."

"Exactly. She knew you were about to kill her, so she scraped different things under each of her fingernails and waited. When you got close enough she scratched you and collected a DNA sample. It is on file in a federal lab waiting to be matched with this one I just took from you."

"You do not know this," Egorov protested.

"You see, Lenko, Keith Mastin and I were never going to do a deal with you, once we realized the connection. It was all about this," Kevin said before stepping hard on Egorov's ruined knee.

Egorov tried to cry out in pain but no sound emerged. He then wretched and threw up his earlier meal. "Kaitlin died by a stream," Kevin said. "Only fitting that you will want to die by a stream, don't you think?"

Egorov said nothing as Kevin hauled him up part way by his shirt and belt and half dragged him over to the stream embankment. Kevin then pitched Egorov down onto the rocks in the stream's very shallow water. Kevin took his time walking down a section of the embankment while Egorov struggled in pain to keeps his face above the water so he could breath. Kevin then asked Egorov, "How do you think Kaitlin felt before you killed her? She knew you were about to kill her, but she kept her presence of mind. How are you holding up? Are you thinking about how you are going to turn the tables. Maybe you can grab one of those rocks and fling it at me. Maybe you'll drown yourself and make it look like I killed you. Good luck with that. I videotaped you pulling a gun on me and sent it to Mastin when I called him. All of this is self-defense, Lenko. Pity that you won't just come quietly, and that you just keep fighting."

Egorov's expression was a mask of bitterness and pain as Kevin walked through the water and used his foot to push Egorov's head under water and hold it there. Kevin counted out loud to forty, and then lifted his foot and let Egorov lift his head and gasp in air.

Kevin then leaned in close and looked into Egorov's eyes. The hubris and calm of the man he had seen before was no longer there. He saw that this was now a wounded animal trying to stay alive by painfully holding its head up to breath, a creature shaking and in shock. "I will let you live, Lenko. Only for two reasons, though. I want to visit you in prison once a year on this date to honor Kaitlin. And, Kaitlin was opposed to killing in all its forms. She would rather I let you live. Its ironic that you will live because of her compassion."

Kevin then hauled Egorov up out of the water and sat him, exhausted, beaten and in pain and shock, on one of the larger rocks near the edge of the stream. He positioned Egorov so he was straddling the rock and leaning back against the dirt embankment. Seeing the awkward way Egorov was sitting there, a thought occurred to Kevin while he was assessing Egorov's ability to hobble out to the bicycle path and how much assistance he would have to give him. "You know what Lenko. I bet you would be the kind of person who would victimize other inmates in prison. You know, after a year or two when your injuries have healed and you haven't seen women. I bet you would think nothing of raping other inmates. I don't want you to do that. So Lenko, I am considering this a public service."

Egorov was in such misery and pain that he merely looked at Kevin as he raised the metal pry-bar. The "ching" sound and blinding pain that seared through Egorov when Kevin slammed the pry-bar down hard between Egorov's legs the first time stopped Egorov's breath and made him try to wretch. Kevin held Egorov in place with his left hand while swinging the pry-bar with his right. After the seventh hard strike, Egorov just stared out into space, motionless. Kevin then stepped back. "There, that should do it. Now, let's get you into the custody of law enforcement before I get too creative in defending myself, Lenko Egorov the murderer."

Kevin then washed the pry-bar and placed it in his pocket for eventual return to his briefcase, and lifted Egorov's less injured arm to help him up the embankment.

Once back where they had been at the top of the embankment, Kevin leaned a broken Egorov against a tree. Egorov held onto the tree to avoid the pain of falling. Kevin then put the pry bar and the bag with Egorov's gun in it into his briefcase and returned to Egorov to help him out to the bicycle path. "You are going to help me bring you out, right? So I don't have to step on your knee again, right?" Kevin asked Egorov.

Egorov stared blankly and nodded in reply while holding onto the tree.

Chapter 80
(Friday 2:50 p.m.)

The relatively short walk from the edge of the stream to the edge of the bicycle path took longer than Kevin had anticipated because of Egorov's difficulty supporting his own weight. They hobbled along, then leaned on trees, then with the promise of faster access to pain medication Egorov put in more effort. They eventually left the woods and reached the edge of the trail. Egorov was wet, muddy and bruised and he had clotted blood all around his mouth and nose. Kevin released Egorov's less damaged arm and let him fall to the ground in a heap next to the paved trail. The pain shot through Egorov like electricity. He then shifted onto his back and stayed very still, not wanting to move at all or think about what he had just experienced or what his future held.

Knowing that the video he sent to Keith would have been forwarded to the federal agents on campus and that the image gave a reasonable view of the surrounding in a way that should have made his location easy to find, Kevin took a few steps in one direction trying to see if any of the agents were in sight. None were visible. Then he walked a few paces up the trail the other way and saw that two men who looked like field agents walking away from his location. Seeing this, Kevin whistled loudly and both agents immediately turned around. Recognizing Kevin waving at them and seeing another man on the ground, they broke into a run as one of the men spoke into his cell phone.

Clearing the distance in seconds, they stopped in front of Kevin, showed their badges and looked down at Egorov, who was laying as still as possible on the ground. "Is this Egorov?"

"Yes, yes it is," Kevin replied, feeling pleased to deliver Egorov into the custody of federal law enforcement.

"What happened to his face?" the other agent asked, looking closely at Egorov's face and seeing two black eyes, a wrecked nose and a bloodied mouth missing teeth.

"Well, he pulled a gun on me. I presume you saw the video I was able to capture?"

"Yes, we did," the one agent replied.

"Well it continued and got worse," Kevin continued. "I was able to get the upper hand using rocks. It was ugly, very ugly."

"Where is the weapon?" the first agent asked.

"Oh, right here," Kevin said, reaching into his leather briefcase, pulling out the weapon in the plastic bag and handing it to the closer agent. "He tried to shoot me when I tried to disarm him with a rock. I wound up breaking his wrist with the rock in the process. Luckily the shot went wide. His prints and gunshot residue should be on it. I didn't want to touch it because it may be important evidence. It looks just like the one he was holding in the videotape from Keith Mastin's house."

"How badly hurt is he?" the agent holding the bag with the gun in it asked.

"Broken wrist, probably broken knee, smashed nose and damaged teeth. He probably has a lot of other bruises. Most of them where caused by me while disarming him. I grabbed a rock and hit him repeatedly. He didn't give up easily. He is obviously bigger than me, and it was touch and go until he went over the embankment and onto the rocks in the stream."

The two agents then glanced at each other questioningly, and then looked back at Kevin. "Wow, you're lucky to be alive," one of the agents said. "It must have been quite a struggle."

"It was," Kevin replied, maintaining a serious expression.

"Interesting," one of the agents then said. "Did he happen to say anything?"

"He did. Turns out he didn't want me to leave him there in the stream unable to travel. So I asked for some information if he wanted me to help him walk out."

"Anything useful?" the other agent asked.

Kevin then took out the small tape recorder and handed it to the closer agent. "He confessed to killing Tailcrest's General Counsel, Kaitlin Clark. He mentioned some other things as well," Kevin offered matter-of-factly, watching the officers' expressions as he spoke. He noticed their look of mild shock as he described what was recorded on the tape recorder and felt mildly satisfied.

At that moment two bicyclists road down the trail, causing the men to step out of the way so the cyclists could pass. The cyclists gave the man on the ground a glance, but did not even slow down.

"Egorov landed hard on the rocks in the stream, and he may have internal injuries,' Kevin said to the agents. "He may actually need immediate medical attention."

"Were supposed to keep this low key, so I'll mark the location, carry him out and then collect evidence where the altercation happened by the stream. I'll make a call and have an agent here to walk with you back to where it happened," the agent not holding the bag with the gun said, taking out his cell phone.

"I can't right now," Kevin responded, noticing the instantaneous incredulous looks on both of the agents' faces. "I will, later. We can mark this place on the trail. It is easy to identify because of the way the trees are on both sides of the trail right here. The fight happened straight back that way at the edge of the stream. There is plenty of evidence left there, including some of his teeth. You can have an agent secure the scene without my being present. Catching Egorov was the main part of this, but there are other parts of the concerted effort that I have to take care of right now. It is important that I get right to them."

"You gave us Egorov, boxed and ready to ship. We can give you that. I'll have someone here in a few minutes to photograph everything and collect any evidence that is available. We'll need a detailed statement from you in the next twenty-four hours," the closer agent said to Kevin.

"That would be fine. I am looking forward to it," Kevin responded, before looking again over at Egorov.

"Let's go," the closer agent said to the other while dialing his phone, and they both stepped over and hoisted Egorov upright to carry him back to their car.

As the two agents carried Egorov away, the one spoke rapidly into his phone. Kevin watched them for a moment, then turned and walked quickly in the other direction, heading toward his office so he could change his cloths and make some phone calls that he was very much looking forward to.

Chapter 81

(Friday 3:00 p.m.)

Kevin had barely walked a hundred steps down the bicycle path when his cell phone rang. Looking at the number he saw that it was Karl Taylor. The prosecutor from the U.S. Department of Justice had been appraised of the situation by the field agents. Overseeing the federal law enforcement efforts involving capturing Egorov and collecting evidence of illegal export of technology was more personal to him this time because of his connection to Aaron and Kaitlin. "Taft," Kevin said into the phone as he continued to walk.

"This is Karl Taylor. I just got off the phone with our one of our field agents. Wow, you got Egorov himself, evidence of menacing and illegally carrying a weapon on campus and, did I hear my agent correctly, a taped confession to murder?"

"Yes, something like that," Kevin said.

"What happened to apprehending him as he approached the meeting place?" Taylor asked, feeling very pleased about how things had worked out.

"He changed the plan," Kevin replied. "I got lucky."

"No worries," Taylor said. "It looks like we all got lucky."

"I figure he is going to claim that I didn't read him his rights," Kevin said, "but I am a private citizen and he started talking. I just recorded it."

"It would be interesting to hear his defense attorney argue for his confession to be excluded from the trial. So, what actually happened?" Taylor asked.

"He pulled a gun on me and walked me into the woods. I turned things on him and he started talking," Kevin replied. "I'm no lawyer, but I don't see how a judge could toss out his confession. Once DNA tests confirm a match between him and the skin cells under Kaitlin's fingernail, his murder conviction should be pretty much locked down anyway."

"Murder, menacing, and illegal weapons possession on campus," Taylor said, "That should keep him locked away for a very long time. Given the nature of his crimes, I don't see deportation in his future either, not if I can help it."

Kevin smiled at the thought; then added, "Good. There is also menacing over at Keith Mastin's house. Would breaking into a person's house to menace them with a gun make the breaking in more serious?'

"Yes, it would," Taylor replied, chuckling.

"Maybe we can tack on harassment based on the photos of him outside Mastin's house too," Kevin added, "so the judge can add a few more days to his sentence and hopefully make each of the sentences run consecutively."

"Nice thought," Taylor concurred. "Even though it won't actually work that way, he will be in jail at least until the two of us are in retirement homes."

"Hey, speak for yourself," Kevin countered, feeling good about their success so far, "I don't plan on seeing the inside of one of those places ever, except maybe as a visitor."

"I hear you on that," Taylor added.

"Oh, I didn't mention it to your agents, but on the tape recording is the name of Egorov's Russian contact for receiving the technology and developing its military applications. I believe the name was Sacha Sidorov. I am not sure what you can do with that, but it will be helpful to know who he is."

"Holy shit!" Taylor said. "Aaron doesn't use the word amazing to describe people, but he has used it to describe you. I'm starting the see why. Did Egorov admit to intending to export the technology for purposes of developing its military application on the tape?"

"I think so, yes, I am pretty sure he did," Kevin replied. "It all happened very quickly, the fight and him talking and all."

"I think I see," Taylor then said. "Egorov quickly became a very cooperative individual. You are apparently persuasive."

"Hardly, he just started talking," Kevin said.

"Well, it gets better," Taylor said. "The phone calls you had President Walker make definitely generated some chatter. We collected a lot under our wiretap warrants, and it's all completely admissible in court. They are being transcribed as we speak."

Kevin had at this point reached the end of the bicycle path near the commons and was walking along the sidewalk towards his office. Students looked oddly at him because of his wet and muddy appearance, but he barely noticed them as he walked and talked on his phone. "Okay, what did you get?" Kevin asked.

"Turns out Jason Roberts from your Legal Department gave Dale Wade and Dennis Gearin information about where Kaitlin and Aaron would be vacationing, but never believed anyone would actually do anything to her. He literally thought it was a joke and figured they would find some other way of getting the contract done, like having him forge her signature and then lie about it claiming she actually did sign it without recalling."

Kevin thought about his interactions with Jason before replying. "It is surprising that he would even consider forgery. He has a lot to lose with his law license and career being in jeopardy."

"Yes. He got totally freaked out when he heard that Kaitlin had died, and more-so once he learned that she had been murdered," Taylor continued. "He took off and has been in hiding ever since. The guy is terrified. He seems like a good candidate to give a full confession and cooperate as a witness to save his own skin and maybe his career."

"That sounds more like Jason," Kevin replied. "Do you have any idea where he is?"

"No, not yet," Taylor replied, "but, like the others, he thinks the deal is basically done, or about to be, so he is flying back into town so as to minimize any attention paid to his absence. He is going to play it up as his having been upset about Kaitlin, not his being afraid because of the role he played. We will see him soon."

"Good," Kevin said as he continued to walk and the Technology Incubator came into view.

Taylor then said, "Dale Wade had some appreciation of how determined and dangerous Egorov was. In passing the information about Kaitlin and her vacation plans along to him, Wade figured Egorov would break her arms in a faked mugging or maybe ram her car in a hit and run scenario to injure her so she wouldn't be able to go to work so the contract would go through easily. From the sounds of it he really didn't want to think about what Egorov might do to her, but he knew Egorov would hurt her and gave him the information anyway. He is clearly a co-conspirator in Egorov's harming her and we got him, presuming we can find him."

"He took off too?" Kevin asked.

"Maybe. He went off the grid a few hours ago and no one seems to know where he is. He hasn't even contacted his girlfriend. Past call patterns show them talking very frequently. We'll see."

"How about my good friend, Dennis Gearin?" Kevin asked, half hoping he was involved in every aspect of the whole deal.

"From the conversation summaries it sounds like Gearin had no idea of any actual intention to hurt Kaitlin, and that he at first thought it was a legitimate accident with fortunate timing. Then from what he said on the phone he had an 'Oh shit' moment and just wanted to get the deal done and over with so no one would look too closely. He was completely in on the self-dealing, no question, but he speaks as though he had no idea about the rest of it. He may have had more knowledge and more of a participatory role then what can be confirmed from their conversations. We'll see once we have interviewed everyone."

Kevin was silent for a moment as he walked up to the front of his building and thought about what Taylor had just told him. "Anything else?" Kevin asked.

"The general impression is that, other than Dale Wade, they know very little about Lenko Egorov, other than that he was a money man who knew how to get things done. There was also no communication with the inventor and he wasn't even mentioned in any of the communications today. There is a good chance that Dr. Shen thought it was a legitimate deal and had no unusual involvement."

"Thank you. I have to take care of something now," Kevin said as he stepped into his building and headed toward his office. "Are you going to fill in Steven Walker on the details, status and any next steps?"

"Yes," Taylor replied, "we have Egorov and enough supportive information to pull the trigger on the other parts. I am calling him after I hang up with you. You took a serious risk in baiting Egorov. From the looks of things it almost got you killed. Kaitlin must have meant a lot to you."

"Yes, she did. You knew her too," Kevin said. "Would you have done any less?"

"Maybe not," Taylor replied, "but I doubt I would have ended as well as it has so far."

"Possibly, who knows?" Kevin said. "I want to thank you for your part. You put truth into the statement, 'We are from the government and we're here to help you.'"

"I try. I'll keep you posted as things progress," Taylor said.

"Thanks again," Kevin replied, hanging up and stepping into his office.

Chapter 82

(Friday 3:25 p.m.)

Kevin closed the door of his office in the Technology Incubator and twisted the blinds shut before quickly changing into an extra pair of jeans ad shirt he had stashed in his desk. Reopening the blinds, he started switching the items from his muddy jean's pockets into his fresh jeans. Before putting his wallet into his back pocket he took out the folded picture of Aaron and Kaitlin he had put in his wallet and carried with him since the day she died. Looking at it he recalled the day it had been taken about ten years earlier. The couple had been horsing around at his house and Aaron had teased her about dragging her upstairs into the guest bedroom, caveman style, and having his way with her. In response she had dared him to. Kevin had snapped the picture just after Aaron had hoisted Kaitlin over his shoulder. It captured his two friends being utterly themselves, happy with each other. "Good job, Kaitlin," Kevin said to the image of her in the photo before placing it on his desk near several other unframed pictures he kept near his computer monitor because they had special meaning to him.

He took a moment to look at the other photos and a badly chipped Tailcrest University mug that he kept as a souvenir from a previous adventure, then took out his cell phone and called Keith. "Egorov?" Keith asked without any introduction.

"Egorov is in the custody of federal law enforcement officers," Kevin replied, feeling a grin spread across his face. "It seems he thought it wise to move up the meeting time by confronting me on the bike path. I thought he might try something like that. That's why I had my phone's video feature ready."

"That video you sent should be helpful evidence," Keith added. "I forwarded it right away. I was sure you were telling me to hold tight by saying to do as we had agreed earlier when you called. I was worried as hell. How did you get him when he had a gun on you?"

"He heard a twig snap and turned to look. I just used something light and hard to break his wrist. There were a lot of rocks around."

"I think I understand," Keith said, getting the message about being discreet in what they said and understanding that Kevin had used Keith's pry-bar. "So you broke his wrist in self-defense. Did you get hurt?"

"Not really, just some bruises and scratches maybe. It was quite a struggle and he simply would not quit," Kevin said.

Keith thought for a moment about what Kevin was actually saying, then replied, "Wow, did he sustain any injuries besides the broken wrist?"

"The guy just didn't know when to quit. Seems he broke his knee pretty badly, and his nose. He even kept it up when he was down, so I had to kick him in the face. He spit half his teeth into the dirt. I didn't fully get the better of him until he went over the stream embankment and landed hard on the rocks."

Keith understood exactly what Kevin was saying and felt surprised at his own satisfaction in learning of the savage beating Egorov sustained at Kevin's hands. "Then what happened?" Keith asked.

"Well, then he seemed to become concerned that I would just leave him there. He was literally holding his head above the water and couldn't get up so he started talking. I took out my tape recorder and he gave an unprompted confession to everything, to killing Kaitlin particularly. That was something I was hoping to get and why I brought the tape recorder."

"Wow," Keith said, appreciating how important that could be in conjunction with DNA evidence. "So it's done and we can all go home?"

"Not yet," Kevin responded. "Wire taps and other evidence implicate Wade, Jason and Dennis in varying degrees. Jason is flying in and needs to be collected. Dennis is clueless but will be dealt with soon. Dale Wade is the main concern now. He seems to have disappeared. Better to sit tight until you here from Karl Taylor, just in case Dale catches on and shows up angry at your door again. Also, none of them know the deal has fallen through at this point, so better to keep you hidden."

"I agree," Keith offered, trying to imagine how enraged Dale might get.

"How are your accommodations?" Kevin asked, changing the subject.

"Karl Taylor has a lovely home," Keith replied sincerely, "and his wife is becoming fast friends with Sharon and Heather. Apparently she has had guests during her husband's adventures before and she likes company to help distract her from the stress. We're all having a pretty good time, aside from the stress of knowing you were meeting up with a killer. Heather particularly has been kind of a mess. Her hands have been shaking and you could see the worry in her face. I have never seen her this worried before."

Kevin was both warmed by the thought and concerned at her being upset. "Tell her that I am fine and that she and Chrissy have my love. I am sure she knows that already."

"I'm sure it will make her feel good to hear it," Keith responded, grinning because Heather and Sharon had walked over and could hear both sides of his and Kevin's conversation.

"I have to make some calls. Sit tight until you hear otherwise," Kevin said.

"We'll do that," Keith replied before Kevin ended the call.

Sharon and Keith didn't say anything as they both looked over at Heather. Her smile broadened and she looked both happy and relieved. She then touched Sharon's arm, hugged Keith and walked happily back into the other room with the children.

Kevin then called President Walker's office. Bobbi answered, "President's Office."

"It's Kevin. Is he around?"

KILLER DEAL: A TECHNOLOGY TRANSFER THRILLER

"Oh my God, yes," Bobbi replied. "Thank God you're okay. I'll transfer you right in."

"Steven, it went well," Kevin said when Walker answered the phone.

"So I hear. Excellent work," Walker said in reply. "I was just on a call with Karl Taylor. It seems I have a little more to do this afternoon. I'm looking forward to it. I am relieved that you are okay. Your mischief could have gotten you killed today. I heard from Karl that you defended yourself well and also got a confession. I can only imagine what that bastard went through with you in the woods."

"Oh, today's mischief was minor, nothing compared to things I've done in the past," Kevin replied obliquely. "You would have done more if you were in my place."

"I don't know," Walker replied, chuckling. "Well talk over drinks. Would that be okay?"

"Of course," Kevin answered. "One more thing. Please tell Karl to call my cell when his part with you is almost done. I want to be there to see Dennis' face as he walks out to the elevators."

"I understand completely," Walker replied. "I will have Karl call you."

"Thanks. I'll take with you more later," Kevin said.

"Most definitely," Walker replied before ending the call.

Kevin put his phone away and took a deep breath. He felt good as he leaned back in his office chair and folded his hands behind his head.

Chapter 83

(Friday 3:30 p.m.)

Dennis Gearin and Dr. Shen walked together into Walker's office suite. "We're here to meet with President Walker," Dennis said to Bobbi when she looked up at them.

Bobbi smiled politely at the men. "Yes, I am the one who called you," she said in a warm and professional manner, even though Walker had filled her in on the events of the afternoon and the purpose of the meeting. "He wants to speak with you both about the license negotiation Keith Mastin has been working on. There may have been some positive developments."

"That is very good news. Where should we wait for him?" Dennis asked.

"Oh, in the conference room right there, just down the hall," she replied. "He's finishing up a meeting now. He will join you in just a minute or two."

"Thank you," Dennis said as Dr. Shen nodded politely to her and they both turned and walked toward the conference room.

Entering the conference room Dennis became more animated and energetic. "This should be good news," he said to Dr. Shen. "I'm betting that the license is done and either signed already or on its way to be signed by Vice President Campanaro. Mastin listens to Kevin Taft and I am guessing that Taft was able to convince him that it would be good for him to approve the deal and keep his job. We'll see."

Dr. Shen listened to Dennis and noted his newfound enthusiasm as they both took seats at the conference table. "I just want the technology to be developed and to get research funding for my lab and to consult for

HematoChem. This is very good technology and it should be developed more fully through clinical studies. I don't know why Mastin was being so difficult and why he would not do as he was told to do."

"Mastin is a lawyer," Dennis replied as he leaned back in his chair. "There is a reason people think about layers the way they do. At least it looks like he has come to his senses."

"I hope so," Dr. Shen added.

The two men then waited quietly, each absorbed in their own thoughts. Dr. Shen was thinking about his graduate students and research plans and how the promised funding from the start-up company could help in his efforts. Dennis was thinking about how much money he would likely get when HematoChem was sold in a few years for about sixty million dollars because of the increased value of the technology, and how they had managed to pull it off right under the nose of Tailcrest's Administration. Dennis also felt relieved that it was almost over and pleased that everyone would move quickly on to other things and let this deal fade into memory.

While both men were still absorbed in thought, President Walker strode into the room with a tall, slim man dressed in an expensive suite. "Dennis, Dr. Shen, this is Karl Taylor. Let's get right down to business. There has been a lot of fuss about the technology you invented, Dr. Shen, and the start-up company that has been formed to commercialize it, HematoChem. I understand that Keith Mastin has been handling to license negotiation and that he has been digging in his heals and being generally difficult."

Dennis was liking the tone that Walker was using and couldn't help but chime in. "Yes, Keith has unfortunately been difficult and unprofessional in his handling of this negotiation. Granted, he is a lawyer, but sometimes he just can't see the forest through the trees. I convinced Vice President Campanaro to give him approval authority because I thought it would make things easier, but Keith let it completely go to his head and we are very close to losing a valuable deal for the University. It is going to be reflected in his annual evaluation, and frankly I would like to see him let go. I don't think he is a fit for our organization. The way he has acted here demonstrates clearly why we need someone who is more of a team player. With your approval, I would like to talk to human resources about creating a posting for his replacement, preferably an MBA, not a lawyer."

Walker nodded just slightly while he listened to Dennis, signaling general agreement with what he was saying. "I definitely think Mastin is in the wrong position," Walker said. "But that is something to deal with later. Right now I want to talk about the technology and the license to HematoChem. Dr. Shen, what has been your experience regarding the start-up and the Technology Transfer Office's handling of the negotiation?"

"Well, Dennis was handling it and it was going forward okay. He convinced me that a start-up would be better than a larger company because a larger company might put the technology on a shelf and focus on other projects, while a start-up would put its efforts toward this technology only. Mr. Wade was looking to invest in developing the technology and getting it through clinical trials. This is necessary for it to go forward and be used in humans. HematoChem is going to fund my lab and Mr. Wade asked me to consult for them to make sure everything goes well scientifically. Then Keith Mastin gets involved and it is like everything stops. I don't know why he is being so difficult. We all want to see the technology developed. We all want to make money for the University and for my lab, but Keith Mastin just says 'no.' He is being a problem. I don't know what can be done. Did he okay the agreement so the deal can be completed?"

"Thank you Dr. Shen. We'll get to that in a minute," Walker replied, while taking a picture out of a folder he had brought with him. Walker then looked over at Karl Taylor.

Taylor nodded and Walker then placed in front of the two seated men a picture of Lenko Egorov pointing a gun at Keith Mastin in his own home. While Walker and Karl watched, Dr. Shen looked at the picture in a detached and perplexed manner at the same time that Dennis' eyes widened and he froze in shock and realization.

"Dennis," Walker then said, "we are aware that you are a co-owner of HematoChem. We also know that this man in the picture, Lenko Egorov, co-owns HematoChem through his holding companies. It gets better, Dennis. This picture is of Egorov pressuring Keith Mastin to sign off on the deal that would benefit you. We also have video of him pointing a gun at Kevin Taft. There is more, Dennis, but I am sure you know the details a lot better than I do. Do you have anything to say for yourself?"

Dennis' face took on a sour expression and he just stared at the wall ahead of him. Walker then continued, "This goes far beyond unacceptable. It is utterly outrageous. You may be facing criminal charges, Dennis. You have let everyone down. As of this moment, you are fired. Do not go back to your office. Do not touch any Tailcrest computer. Do not touch your Tailcrest smartphone, other than to hand it this gentleman here. I want to say this again, Dennis, you're fired. There is a federal investigation under way, Dennis, led by Mr. Taylor here, and your actions are a central part of the investigation. When I leave, Mr. Taylor and other officers will have specific questions for you to answer. Do you understand, Dennis?"

Dennis' eyes narrowed, showing more of his bitterness about what had just transpired, but he said nothing.

"Moving on," Walker continued, "Dr. Shen, we do not know your level of involvement. There is every possibility that you have done nothing wrong, but, until we know more, you will be on paid administrative leave. We will have your colleagues step in as interim Principle Investigators for your research. Your graduate assistants can teach your classes for a while. I hope this can be resolved soon. There will be officers here to ask you questions as well. Do you understand?"

"I have done nothing wrong," Dr. Shen said in his defense. "I don't understand why I should be on leave. This is not right."

Karl replied to Dr. Shen's question. "There is an active federal investigation that involves the potential illegal export of technology developed in your lab. The steps the University is taking are precautionary. The more you cooperate with the investigation, the sooner you will get back to your lab and your research. We don't want to disturb your efforts any longer than we have to."

"I will give you whatever help you need," Dr. Shen replied.

"Thank you. We are looking forward to that," Taylor said.

"Good afternoon," Walker then said to the men seated at the table and walked out of the room as two federal agents walked in.

An hour later, Kevin Taft was standing in the lobby outside of President Walker's office suite leaning against the railing by the opening to the floor below. The same two officers who had met him at the bicycle path walked Dennis Gearin across the lobby past him. The officers recognized Kevin and nodded to him, but Kevin was mostly focused on Dennis Gearin. Dennis made eye contact with Kevin and had an expression that was a blend of bitterness, disbelief and worry that made him look drawn and older than he actually was. "See you around, Dennis," Kevin said.

Dennis did not reply, but instead looked away as he walked with the officers toward the elevator.

Chapter 84

(Friday 4:15 p.m.)

Jason Roberts took his carry-on bag out of the overhead compartment of the commercial jet and waited for the passengers in front of him to move up the aisle. He politely waited his turn and felt good about letting the women from the seats across from his go first. He felt good about coming back for a lot of reasons. As far as he knew his role in the HematoChem licensing deal had not been discovered and people believed that he had taken time off to deal with Kaitlin's death. As he made his way up the aisle he thought about how he would spend his weekend before going back into work on Monday and adjusting to how his department would operate without Kaitlin structuring it to her liking. To his thinking, people would be supportive because he was upset by the tragedy. He also felt a certain pride in himself for being brave enough to take a chance on something so risky as the HematoChem deal like Dennis had suggested he should. If HematoChem did well and was sold in two or three years, he believed he would have enough money to retire and forget about practicing law. If it didn't, no one would care and no one would know. He thought it was almost too easy.

Leaving the gait area and heading toward security to make his way toward the checked bag pickup area, Jason was feeling positive about himself and life in general. As he walked past security he got the strange sense that the airport security people were noticing him. None of them stared at him, but they all seemed to glance specifically at him. He brushed it off as him not looking like most of the other travelers, specifically because he was frequently teased about looking like a corporate attorney no matter where he went, what he was wearing or what he was doing.

While he waited by the baggage carrousel Jason stood by the women who had been seated across from him on the plane. They smiled politely at him but continued to talk among themselves. That was when Jason noticed airport security personnel station by each of the exits, just standing there, and he realized that he had not seen security positioned there any of the other times he had come through the airport. He brushed that off as well recalling how there had been a progressive increase in airport security over the years since the September Eleven attacks. But then he noticed that each of them were periodically glancing specifically at him. He started to get a nervous feeling in his stomach, but he tried to put it aside thinking that he was just nervous and being paranoid. He decided to focus instead on the lovely women around him, just appreciating how attractive some of them were. Most of the women he recognized from the plane, but several had definitely not been on the plane with him. He presumed those women had met passengers and were waiting with them, except for one. He saw that there was one woman standing all by herself who was pretty enough that he definitely would have noticed her on the plane. She had short hair and pretty features, and he tried to convince himself that he must have just missed her, but he had a growing feeling that something was wrong.

When the bags started to come out on the carousel Jason noticed that the short haired woman's bag was among the first to come out. She picked it up and then took out her cell phone and made a call. While she was talking she walked slowly and stopped in between the carousel and the exit. Jason watched this and concluded that she must be just another passenger. When Jason's bag came out he took it off the carousel and started walking toward the exit. He noticed the woman hang up her call and walk ahead of him toward the same exit he was going to be using. He couldn't help but notice her athletic figure ineffectively concealed within her business casual attire. He started to feel better as he walked past the airport security officer toward where he would get a cab. He knew his nerves were fried from the stress and he thought that a weekend at home with some expensive wine would be the best thing for him. He didn't even try to make conversation with the woman when he caught up and found himself walking along next to her.

She looked over at him and broke the silence. "Did you enjoy your trip?" she asked as she moved a little closer to him as they walked.

"Enjoyable enough," he replied. "I am looking forward to a relaxing weekend. How about you? How was yours, and what are your plans for the weekend?"

"My trip was good," she replied coyly, "and, if things work out I could see myself spending some time relaxing with you. You're very handsome. What would you say to that?"

"I would like that a lot," he replied, surprised by her assertiveness. "Maybe we can share a cab from here, or would you like to exchange numbers and meet somewhere?"

"Let's just go from here," she said, winking at him as a large man he had not noticed stepped up behind him and grabbed hold of his arm.

At that same moment an unmarked car pulled up alongside them. "What the-," was all Jason managed to say before the woman flashed her federal ID badge in Jason's face.

"You are coming with us," she said in a hard official voice, getting right up in Jason's face. "You're being questioned about your role in Kaitlin Clark's murder and the attempted illegal export of technology restricted under federal export laws. I would suggest that you cooperate fully."

Jason felt weak and nauseated, and his surrounding seemed to swirl around him. He barely heard the woman reading him is Miranda rights as the big man put him in the car and another man put his bags in the car's trunk. As the car pulled away, Jason made the decision he knew was best for him. Looking right at the woman, who was now staring at him coldly, he said, "I will cooperate fully and give you every bit of information you want, but I want a lawyer and a deal."

"I am sure that can be arranged," the female agent replied before looking away from Jason and winking at her partner.

Taking out her cell phone, the female agent dialed Karl Taylor's cell number. "We have him, there was no incident, and he wants a deal," she said without introduction.

Karl Taylor smiled as he spoke into the phone, "Excellent work. Well done. You always come through."

"I have a good team," she replied, deflecting some of the credit as the car left the airport, "but, thank you."

Chapter 85
(Friday 4:45 p.m.)

Dale Wade drove seventy five miles to a town he had been to only once, years before. He parked his car in a space at the edge of a strip mall parking lot near the town's bus station. The large man adjusted his rear view mirror and looked at his reflection. The creased lines he saw on his forehead showed the anxiety he was feeling inside. Picking his cell phone up off the seat next to him, he tried again to reach Egorov. Again there was no answer, and the phone did not ring before switching to its messaging function. He chose not to leave a message. He then tried Dennis' phone and it rang several times, but there was no answer. Again he chose not to leave a message. Dale then took stock of his situation. He thought about the flurry of calls when it seemed clear that the deal would go through and how Dennis had been so sure that he had managed to pressure Keith into okaying the deal the way they wanted. He also recalled the sick feeling he got shortly afterward thinking about how that did not fit with everything he knew about how Keith operated. He specifically recalled his conversation with Keith where his raised the idea of giving him part ownership and how Keith laughed it off. Dale's gut had told him that the way Keith brushed off the offer was the way he actually operated and that this supposed arrangement between Keith and Kevin Taft to take a payoff was as sham. Looking over at the bus station and thinking about how he could not get in touch with either Egorov or Dennis, Dale concluded that something had gone very wrong. He also thought that making himself scarce was the best approach he could take.

Turning his cell phone off and collecting the things he was bringing with him, Dale locked his Camaro and walked over to the bus station. The row of busses lined up in their oversized spaces had different destinations listed on their displays. The smell of their exhaust added to Dale's queasy feeling. Glancing back at his car, he thought about how long he had owned it and how attached he had become to it. He then chuckled, thinking that he was going to miss his car more than the girl whose apartment he had left earlier that day. He hoped that maybe things had worked out fine and that Dennis and Egorov were simply just not taking calls. He also hoped that when he called again in a few hours from the bus station in the city was travelling to as a stop-off, he would learn that the deal was done and he would be able to grab a bus back. He momentarily pictured himself driving his car back to his girlfriend's apartment later that night and walking her up to "play."

Dale then entered the bus station and got in line to buy a ticket. Standing on the worn tile floor amid people he would normally call "losers," he knew deep down that when he called later that evening from the other bus station no one would answer and he would pay cash for an additional bus ticket to a place very far away, where he and his parents had visited often as a child. As the line progressed and he got closer to the ticket counter, he thought that it would be okay to check in again in a few weeks, and that all he would have to do was catch a ride to someplace a few hundred miles from his new place and make some calls from there.

He then purchased his ticket and waited to board amid people he would normally avoid. Bothered by the smell of the bus fumes, he focused his thoughts on creating a story that would show that Egorov was actually responsible for everything that had transpired and that he had no actual responsibility at all. Confident that he could talk or charm his way out of almost anything, he knew this would be a tough one to do that with if things had actually hit the fan. Still, he knew he would give it his best shot if it came to that.

A few minutes later, sitting on the bus Dale felt strangely alone. He decided to make one more call. Dialing Keith's home number, he waited for the answering machine to pick up. He then left a simple message. "I hope we're still cool. Sorry about today," Dale said into the recording before turning off his cell phone and leaning back in his seat to make himself comfortable for what he guessed would be the first of two long bus rides.

Chapter 86
(Friday 11:15 p.m.)

Keith pulled the car into their driveway late that night and it felt like it had been days since he left. Heather and Chrissy were in the front with him. Sharon was with their two boys in the back. All three adults noticed Heather's husband sitting on the front porch waiting for them. "Wow, a rare appearance," Heather said in a sarcastic tone that really didn't suit her as her husband stood up and walked toward the car.

They all climbed out of the car; each picking up a sleeping child. It was so late that none of the children woke as they were being picked up. As they were carrying the children toward the house, another car pulled in behind them. A well-dressed man got out and walked toward them. "Keith Mastin, I am Karl Taylor. We spoke briefly on the phone," Taylor said, walking specifically up to Keith.

"Yes, of course," Keith replied, shifting his son so he could shake Taylor's hand. "Come on in. I want to thank you for your hospitality. You have a lovely home and your wife was wonderful to us. She made the day fun in spite of everything that was going on."

"You are very welcome," Taylor said, joining them as they carried the children into the house. "She loves to entertain, especially when I am in the midst of something like today. She was glad to have you all there, and you are welcome any time."

Sharon and Heather then each added their thanks as well as they all entered Keith's and Sharon's house.

"Would you like anything to drink," Sharon asked Taylor as she and Keith put their sleeping sons on either ends of the couch and stretched a blanket to partly cover each of them.

"No thank you," he replied graciously. "I will only be a minute."

Keith then asked the question he had been wondering about since the brief call where Taylor had told Keith is was okay to go home. "When we spoke on the phone you said that Dale Wade was no longer a threat. What did you mean?"

"I am sorry I did not elaborate when we spoke earlier. I only had a moment then," Taylor replied. "Dale Wade was taken into custody about a half hour before I spoke with you. He was apparently trying to go into hiding. When we took him into custody, he had most of his important documents and close to fifteen thousand dollars in cash on him. He had left his car near a bus station and caught a bus to another city. He then paid cash for another bus ticket to a city half way across the country. Our agents waited until he purchased his ticket before they picked him up so they could tell where he intended to go."

Keith thought of his friend and how horrible it must have been for him to be confronted and taken into custody. He didn't care anymore about what Dale had done at his house earlier that day, and he felt great sympathy for his friend, particularly since he knew as an attorney that Dale was in very serious trouble. "How did you catch him?" Keith asked.

"It was a combination of new school and old school field work," Taylor replied with a sense of pride in his officers. "He made several cell phone calls that allowed us to pick up his location based on the cell tower location. Then he left a message on your home answering machine. Yes we tapped that line as part of the investigation. He seemed to be apologizing to you, but our technicians could identify background sounds peculiar to a bus station. We then had our agents in that area question people at the bus station. The ticket clerk remembered the tall, handsome man and where he was going. From there we simply called ahead and had agents waiting for him. When he got off the bus, our agents followed him to see who he might be meeting or what he was doing. All he did was buy another bus ticket and wait. When he got up to board the second bus, our agents introduced themselves and took him into custody. He didn't resist at all, and from what the agents said he seemed embarrassed and wanted them to get it over with quickly."

"That sounds like Dale," Keith replied. "Is there anything else we can or should be doing?"

"Not right now. We will need detailed statements from everyone involved, especially you, but that can wait. Just take care of your family and try to decompress. Get some rest."

Taylor then nodded to the people in the group and shook Keith's hand again. "Thank you," he said, before turning and walking toward the door.

After Taylor left, Heather looked to her husband and said, "You take Chrissy home in your car. I'll follow in just a minute with mine."

"Okay," he replied simply before saying goodnight to Sharon and Keith and carrying Chrissy out.

After Heather's husband left with Chrissy, Heather looked at Sharon and Keith and said, "I am so glad it is over."

She hugged Sharon and then gave Keith a warm hug that lasted a moment longer than he thought it would. She then said, "Goodnight," and headed out to her vehicle.

"Let's get the kids to bed," Sharon said before locking the front door and picking up Thomas to carry him upstairs.

"Good idea," Keith concurred, picking up Eddy.

Once the children were in bed, Keith and Sharon made they made their way back downstairs. "You're going to check the locks even though there is nothing to worry about aren't you?" Sharon asked lightheartedly.

"Yes, yes I am," Keith replied, feeling both wound up and exhausted at the same time. "Quick glass of wine before bed?" he asked.

"Absolutely," Sharon replied.

Keith brought the two glasses of wine over and sat on the couch close to Sharon. She sipped hers while he drank half his glass straight away and rested his head on the back of the couch. "A day to remember," he said, while looking up at the ceiling and feeling the warmth of his wife next to him.

"What do you mean?" Sharon teased him. "You have a boring desk job."

Keith just looked over at her. She smiled in reply.

"You must have been really afraid when that man was here. Where exactly was he?" Sharon asked.

Keith gestured toward the sliding glass doors just a few feet from where they were sitting. "He was standing right there, holding a gun, two handed, pointing it at may face. Not something I would be inclined to experience again."

"You must have been terrified. What went through your mind?"

"I was angry that he invaded our home. I was afraid that if I pulled my pistol I had no chance. I had my hand literally on my gun and there was nothing I could do. Then in that instant I thought, 'he wants the damn contract and, if he shoots me, that won't happen, so he's not going to shoot me.'"

"You actually processed that while he was pointing a gun at you?"

"Yes," Keith replied, "then it was a negotiation like any other, and I worked in what Kevin and I had discussed."

"You were scared, huh?"

"Scared numb, yes," Keith said. "Good thing."

They then sat there in silence for several long minutes holding hands and allowing the wine to relax them. They both were startled by Keith's cell phone when it rang in quiet of the house. "I should have turned this off, sorry," Keith said.

"Take the call," Sharon responded. "God only knows what it could be now."

"Keith Mastin" Keith said, not recognizing the number of the caller.

"Keith, this is Steven Walker from the University," Walker said.

"President Walker?" Keith asked to be sure.

"It's Steven to you," Walker replied. "I am sorry for calling so late. I wanted to convey my appreciation for what you went through today. I had a long conversation with Kevin Taft about it this evening. He speaks highly of you, and I can see why. I also wanted to let you know that there is a vacancy in the Director position at the Tech Transfer Office. It's yours if you want it. Stop by my office on Monday and we'll talk about it."

"I will. Thank you," Keith responded, genuinely surprised at receiving the call.

"Enjoy your weekend," Walker then said before hanging up.

Sharon looked over at Keith. "Did I hear that right?"

"Yes, they're offering me Dennis' job," Keith replied.

Sharon laughed, "After this week, do you want it?"

Chapter 87

(Friday 11:30 p.m.)

The mood in Kevin's living room was both jovial and somber at the same time. Kevin, his wife and Aaron Konrad were seated on the long couch facing the enormous windows providing the view that was as magnificent at night as it was during the day. Walker and Bobbi were sitting close together on a loveseat positioned perpendicular to the couch but which still offered a wonderful view of the night outside. Kevin's eldest son had disappeared downstairs after mixing drinks for each of them from some of the finest liquors money could buy. Moments earlier they had all listened to Walker's part of his call with Keith. "I think I surprised him," Walker said, putting his phone back in his pocket and taking a sip of his drink.

Kevin smiled at the thought of Keith's reaction to the call. "He's a good choice for Director, and there's no question in my mind that he'll do a great job in the position," Kevin said. "I'll take him under my wing for dealing with Campanaro and some of the more difficult Deans. The rest of it he already has down."

"That's good to know," Walker replied, "because, as you know, there actually is a lot of pressure to create jobs in the region based on the technologies developed at Tailcrest. The Tech Transfer Office is key to that and we need someone in there who can walk the line between avoiding bad press because we're not doing enough and avoiding bad press because we're doing things unethically."

Kevin found amusement in how Walker presented the defensive approach to media coverage. Smiling sort of crookedly, Kevin winked at Walker, then said, "Media people are merciless, no question, but I think we can get some positive press for Tailcrest out of the Tech Transfer Office in the next few weeks, maybe a month."

Walker chuckled and looked up at the ceiling before looking over at Kevin. "Are you telling me that you're up to something that is going to end up in the newspapers soon, and that it involves the Tech Transfer Office?"

"It's just a little something I am thinking about putting together. It doesn't rise to the level of mischief, but I am sure you're going to like it," Kevin said, raising his glass to Walker and then taking a sip. "I would like to keep it a mystery for a little while longer."

"Very well," Walker agreed before leaning closer to Bobbi and saying, "Spy on him. I want to know."

The group laughed at the joke and Walker continued, speaking to both Aaron and Kevin, "But seriously, the two of you took a serious risk going after Egorov the way you did. Things could have gone horribly wrong today, but you pulled it off. Kaitlin would have been proud. I wish I could have been there to lend a hand."

"You were," Kevin countered. "Your calls made it possible, not just ensuring that Egorov would show up, but causing them to incriminate themselves in wiretapped conversations."

"That was nothing," Walker replied. "Keith Mastin had already set the stage while facing down Egorov when he had a gun pointed at his face. I want to get to know him better. I would have shit myself. Maybe we should invite him along to some of our gatherings."

Kevin smiled, "I was hoping you would suggest that. I'll make it happen."

"A toast," Walker said to the group while raising his glass.

The others raised their glasses, anticipating one of Walker's well known mini-speeches, "To the bravery and determination of Kaitlin's husband, friends and colleagues. When 'let it be' is not the answer, it takes the bravery, courage, skill and gall of those who care to bring justice and hopefully peace to those so profoundly affected by senseless wrongs."

"And," Kevin added, "to Kaitlin, whose fierce spirit, presence of mind, and shear will gave us everything we needed to learn what happened and to get the people responsible. She graced our lives for so many years, and in the moments before she was taken from us she showed us once again the wonderful essence of who she was. To Kaitlin."

There was silence for a moment as all eyes gazed toward Aaron. There were no tears in Aaron's eyes and he felt happy. He then smiled and raised his glass even higher, "To all of you. Kaitlin loved you all and she would be proud and grateful. Thank you."

They drank their toast and talked about good time they had had over the years with Kaitlin and things they hoped to do in the future. Later that evening, when Aaron was walking out to his car, he found himself humming Kaitlin's favorite tune by Trooper and quietly singing, "Raise a little hell, raise a little hell, raise a little he-ell."

Chapter 88
(Saturday 11:00 a.m.)

It was just before noon when Keith watched as a light breeze rippled the water of Green Lake. Keith slid his homemade sailing canoe across the sand to the edge of the water while Sharon, Heather and the three children watched. With all the equipment inside, and its stained wood finish, the boat looked a bit like an old fashioned rowboat. Within minutes Keith had taken out and assembled the sailboat components and the small craft had been transformed into an impressive looking small sailboat with its mast, rigging, unraised sail, rudder and ready-to-insert lee boards all in place. Keith had noticed people in the nearby swimming area watching him and his group while he set up the boat.

When the boat was all set to go, Heather walked back to the car to get the kids' life jackets. Looking after her, Keith noticed Kevin standing next to his Alfa Romeo. He had parked near their car and was just standing there, watching them and enjoying the scene. Waving to Kevin, Keith turned to Sharon and said, "Kevin's here. I texted him this morning and he texted back that he had a conflicting commitment."

Sharon looked at her husband, noticing that he seemed a little nervous about the boat launch and taking all three kids out at once. "He's taking Heather to lunch. That's his conflicting commitment. Heather told him where we would all be, and he's just picking her up here. We are going to have Chrissy for the afternoon too. I should have told you when she mentioned it. He also wants to talk to you about something."

"No worries," he replied, as the boys stood anxiously at the side of the boat, and Chrissy held onto Sharon's leg. "I just didn't expect to see him here."

A few moments later Kevin and Heather walked over with the life jackets. Kevin stepped over to Keith. "I hope you don't mind the intrusion," Kevin said, eyeing the boat.

"Hardly, I was hoping you would be here to see it," Keith replied.

Heather and Sharon set about fitting the tiny life jackets on the children as Kevin signaled for Keith to take a few steps over so they could talk more privately. "You are going to take the Director position, Right?" Kevin asked, hoping he wouldn't have to pressure Keith into accepting it.

"Yes, I am looking forward to it," Keith replied, "although Dr. Campanaro doesn't seem like the best guy to report to."

Kevin laughed at the obvious truth of Keith's statement. "I'll help you out with him," Kevin replied, grinning slyly, "I've got dirt on him. I guarantee he will treat you well."

Keith snorted a laugh. "That's good to know. Thanks."

Kevin's expression turned more serious as he looked Keith in the eye and said, "Tailcrest politics gets ugly. We'll have to watch each other's back."

Keith held his gaze and replied, "That goes without saying."

"Good," Kevin said before pretend punching Keith's shoulder. "I also want to let you know that I made a call this morning to a retired Navy doctor who served with my brother on the U.S.S. Randolph some time ago. He is interested in forming a company around Dr. Shen's nitrogen technology. He is an established expert in nitrogen narcosis and would be the Chief Scientific Officer. He has a much younger friend in mind to be the company's President and CEO. It may move pretty quickly."

Keith looked at Kevin, not sure if he was joking.

Seeing Keith's expression, Kevin said, "I'm serious. Now let's see his thing float."

"This Navy guy is solid?" Keith asked.

"As solid as they come. I guaranty it," Kevin replied.

The two men then slid the boat around, bow out, so it was mostly in the water and floating. Keith helped his two boys in, and then stepped in and sat on the stern as Heather handed Chrissy to him. Keith placed her in a foam seat next to his feet. Chrissy immediately grabbed onto his pant leg while she looked around, smiling and taking it all in. Heather felt apprehensive seeing her little girl, Keith's daughter, there in the boat. She also knew Chrissy was perfectly safe.

"It looks like we're all set," Keith said, looking around at his little group.

"One more thing before you head out," Kevin said to Keith. "If we can get Heather to watch your boys on Friday, I'd like you and Sharon to come by our house. We're having some friends over for drinks and I'd like you both to join us."

"We'd love to, if Heather's okay with it," Keith replied.

"Of course I am," Heather chimed in, knowing that Kevin had already cleared it with her while they were talking earlier.

"It's settled then," Kevin said.

With that Keith took one of the "just in case" paddles and pushed off. The boat drifted forward as Keith pulled the rope that raised the sail. The wind caught the sail and the boat pushed forward, tacking nicely on an angle. Keith then twisted around and bowed to the three people on the shore. They responded with friendly applause as the boat picked up speed, pushed along by the warm breeze.

Made in the USA
Charleston, SC
19 February 2014